C000099449

RED
COLLAR

Red Collar

Written by Andrew Mackay

Edited by Ashley Rose Miller and Aly Quinn

Cover Design & Images:
ViknCharlie & Andrew Dobell
Shutterstock: OSTILL is Franck Camhi / SFIO CRACHO / Odua Images

ISBN: 9798674671367
Copyright © 2020 Chrome Valley Books

Chapters

Chapter 1

"What a *lovely* day for a heist."

A man dressed in a business suit and a rubber rabbit mask on his head peered through the back passenger window of a silver Chevrolet.

He'd made the comment as he trained his eyes on the covered entrance to the three-story Federal Bank building.

This very moment proved to be the calm before the storm.

Rabbit slipped his wedding ring off his finger and pocketed it.

He turned to the three men in the car and lifted his wristwatch to his mouth. "Hello, hello, animals, this is Rabbit speaking. Switch your voice alternators on."

Rabbit's sleeve rolled down the hairs on his forearm as he reached under his mask and fiddled with a switch.

Now, when he spoke, his voice sounded electronic, and flew up and down in pitch. "How do I sound?"

The skinny, suited man sitting next to Rabbit fiddled with his latex dog's mask. "You sound stupid. How about me? How do I sound?"

Rabbit gripped the twelve-gauge shotgun on his lap and tapped the end on his knee. "Like a puppy with its nuts tied with electrical wire."

1

The suited man sitting in the front passenger seat adjusted the alternator under his Ram's mask. When he turned around, the two protruding horns on his latex face covering scraped across the upholstery.

"Ugh, I'm sweating up a storm in this thing and we haven't even started," Ram said, his voice sounding like that of an electronic child's. "I hate being the *bull*, my horns are catching on everything."

"Shut up," Rabbit said. "You're a Ram, okay? We've been through this."

"I wanna change back to Bull. Or Steer."

Rabbit thumped the man on the shoulder in anger. "Quit it with the goddamn *ram* thing. It's only for ten minutes. Now just shut up and get ready."

"Howard, don't hit me, man," Ram said. "I'll blow your arms off."

Rabbit tilted his head to the bizarre-looking creature with the horns and red tie. "Don't call me by my name. You're gonna get us all busted."

"Yeah," Dog added. "Remember, use our animal names."

Ram faced the windshield and reached down to his feet. His fingers slid around the straps and lifted the sports bag to his lap. "Shit. Okay, okay."

As Ram arched his back, he turned to the driver and grunted. "Remember. Lane seven."

The driver rolled his shoulders and checked his shiny, gold wristwatch, forcing his ridiculously lifelike squirrel mask to tilt forward. "Okay, we're on. You have nine minutes."

"Okay, Squirrel," Rabbit said. "Keep your nuts on."

"Let's get this done."

Rabbit lifted the wristwatch on his left arm to his rubber-covered mouth. "Comms on. Can you hear me, Squirrel?"

The feedback blew through Squirrel's wristwatch. *"Yeah, crystal clear. All comms online."*

Dog shook his head and lost his patience. "Will you two son of a bitches hurry the hell up?"

"*Feline* just fine, Doggy," Rabbit said as he exited the vehicle. "Now, let's *fetch*."

Rabbit jogged away from the car and across the road, leaving Dog and Ram to exit the back of the vehicle and catch up to him.

Each of the three men carried their sports bags as they formed a line of three and crossed the road.

The silver Chevrolet pulled away from the road and drove past them. The Squirrel behind the wheel gave the three men the thumbs up as it pushed past the federal bank building, turned right, and out of sight.

"You're right, Rabbit. It *is* a nice day for a heist," Dog said.

"Shut the hell up. Remember, no speaking unless it's to direct the assholes to shut up and do as you say," Rabbit said as they paced onto the sidewalk and made their way to the bank entrance.

Ram chose to say nothing as he pulled the zipper along his sports bag and reached inside. "Wait till they get a load of us."

The sight of a security guard came into view behind the entrance doors to the bank as the three men made their approach.

Rabbit's held his wrist to his mouth. "There's the guard. I don't recognize him. Badger, this is Rabbit. Do you read me?"

"He'll be the first to beg for his life," Dog said.

"I repeat, Badger, this is Rabbit. Do you read me?"

***

A bank employee in his thirties ducked out of sight from the private lending room and spoke into his

3

wristwatch. He ran his hand through his jet-black hair and kept an eye on the glass window.

He grabbed at his name badge on his shirt; *Mark Amos, Deputy Manager,* in an attempt to stop his hand from shaking.

"Yeah, this is Badger," Mark said into his wristwatch just as Rabbit's voice trickled out of it. *"Who's the chump at the door? I don't recognize him."*

Mark focused on the firearm strapped to the guard's belt and ran the side of his finger across his two, gold front teeth.

"Yeah, he's new. I dunno his name, but he's harmless. He started Monday. He knows nothing."

"We're twenty seconds before show time. You good to go?"

Mark licked his two front teeth, bent underneath his desk and glanced at a deflated, rubber mask poking out of a dark blue sports bag. "Yeah, I'm ready."

"Remember, when you hear us, it's guns, guns, guns. Weapons hot. Make yourself known."

Mark spread the musky mask out with his right hand to reveal a vicious-looking badger's face snarling right back at him. "Ugh. Okay, got it."

Just then, a random customer walked past the window and scared the life out of Mark. "Shit, shit, shit."

The door to the lending office pushed open. A man in his sixties walked in. Overweight, and slightly out of breath, he looked around for any sign of life. "Mark? Are you here? Where are you?"

"Shit, shit—"

"—Ah shit," the man said. "Where's Amos got to, now?"

The man frowned and slammed the door shut on his way out, leaving a thoroughly terrified Mark to squeak into his wrist from under the table. "Rabbit? Rabbit, come in?"

"Yeah, this is Rabbit. We're nearly there."

Mark reached into the sports bag and pulled out a Uzi machine gun with a 260 mm barrel. He tossed a full magazine into the gun, and locked it in place. "It's Price, he was just in the lending room. He's looking for me."

"We're at the doors. I think our new security prick's just seen us—"

"—What?"

"Get your Badger on, douche bag. We're about to come in."

Mark struggled to pull the badger's mask over his head, just as a ruckus occurred from outside the room. "Oh shit, oh shit."

***

Rabbit pushed past Dog and Ram and led the charge toward the double doors.

"I spy with my little eye…" he said as he reached into his sports bag and pulled out a shotgun. "Something beginning with…"

The security guard looked through the double doors to find a rabbit dressed in a suit and carrying a shotgun.

"…*Duck*," Dog screamed.

"Shit."

The guard flung himself to the ground before he had the chance to go for his pistol.

Rabbit fired a shot at the double doors, smashing the glass to pieces.

Blam—smash.

"Oh, shit," the guard squealed as he rolled onto his back and kicked his heels into the floor.

Rabbit turned the corner and entered the bank with his shotgun in both hands. "Get up, you fat prick."

"P-Please d-don't shoot—"

"—I said get up," Rabbit screamed as he cleared the shattered glass away with the side of his shoe. "On your feet, dickhead."

A dozen bank customers screamed for their lives and went to run for safety, but were too late. Dog fired a shot into the ceiling, pumped a new bullet into the chamber, and aimed it at anything that breathed. "Stay."

Astonished, everyone threw their hands in the air and froze on the spot, scared out of their wits.

Dog pointed at the conference room door to the right of the entrance. "Now, don't anyone get brave. Get in the conference room and shut the hell up."

He aimed his gun at a pudgy red-haired woman with red-framed glasses. "You, the fat one."

"Wh-what?"

"Open the door, and let everyone in. Do it now, or I'll put a bullet in your second—no, your *third* chin."

The girl didn't know how to react and burst into tears.

"Aww, no," Dog said. "No, no, no, you can't cry. Shit. Rabbit?"

The man in the rabbit mask was about to shoot the first of four CCTV cameras, but stopped to turn to Dog in frustration. "What the hell is it now? Can't you see I'm busy?"

"Got a problem, here, Rabbit."

"What?"

"Joanne's gone all Hallmark channel on me."

"Well shoot her, then."

The girl wiped her eyes and squinted at Dog. "Huh? How did you know my name—?"

"—Listen, lady," Dog said as he gesticulated with his gun. "I ask the questions around here, okay? Not—"

Blam.

Dog's finger slipped on the trigger and blasted Joanne in the stomach. Her body somersaulted through the air like a bloody firework, and smashed against a lending desk by the back door.

"Whoa," Dog yelped. "This gun really kicks ass."

The patrons shrieked for life and instantly dropped to their knees, hoping not to meet the same fate as Joanne.

Dog's rubbery ears seemed to wilt as he processed his accident. "I k-killed her—"

"—Never mind about that now. Get moving."

Rabbit dared to look at the mess on the far side of the line ropes and caught sight of Joanne's bleeding corpse.

He turned to Dog and screamed. "Okay. So, what are you doing now, dumb ass?"

Dog lifted his gun in haste, equally as disturbed as Rabbit. "It was an accident. I n-never meant to k-kill—"

"—Aww, shit. Now's not the time to grow a goddamn conscience."

A young woman pleaded for her life and nearly passed out. "Please, please, don't kill us."

"I've had just about enough of this."

Dog waved his shotgun around and aimed it at the conference room. "Jesus Christ, everybody get the hell up, and get in the conference room. Do it now."

One by one, the eleven remaining hostages got up from the floor as Dog took several steps back. "C'mon, c'mon, we don't have all morning."

Dog booted the door open and ushered all the hostages inside.

A large oak table sat in the middle with several chairs surrounding it. The far end of the wall offered a view to the street through its glass partitions.

Ram glanced at his wristwatch and yelled at Rabbit. "That's seven minutes."

Rabbit turned to the three teller girls behind the Plexiglass and aimed his shotgun at the skinniest of the three and approached the counter.

"You."

"Y-Yes?"

He unfastened his sports bag with one hand and tossed it over the transparent partition. "There's six registers here. Load the bag up."

"Wh-what?"

"I know it's bullet-proof glass, asshole, but that won't stop me from jumping over it and shooting you in your

7

pretty face," Rabbit squeaked in his stupid, altered voice. "Or, I could just shoot the dick off your breath?"

"N-No, please—"

"—Yeah, that's what I thought. Now, stop messing around and fill the bag."

"Shoot the dick off your breath?" Ram muttered. "What are you talking about—"

"—At times of crisis, I make jokes, okay?" Rabbit snapped, and thumped the perspex glass. "Fill the bag. Do it."

Severely rattled, he swung his gun to the other two women and threatened to shoot them.

"See that dead, fat pig my associate just executed? Over there, by the door?"

Both girls nodded as their colleague opened the first register. The haze of smoke coming from Joanne's corpse lifted into the air, serving as a stark reminder of just how violent proceedings might get.

"Wanna end up like her?"

Both girls shook their heads, intently; no, they wouldn't like to get shot.

"I figured as much," Rabbit snapped. "Now, open up the registers and fill the bag. But do *not* touch the third register. Okay? Leave the third register alone."

The first woman collected up the bills from the first register in her hands and dropped them into the sports bag. Proving to be the most experienced of the three tellers, Rabbit refocused his attention on her.

"Hey, pretty girl?"

None-too impressed, she barely made eyes at the animal as she shoved the stacks of bills into his bag. "What?"

"You know why we don't want the third register, right?"

The first woman nodded as she unlocked the second register and pulled the bills from the machine.

"Yeah. You know your stuff, evidently," she said.

"Goddamn dummy money."

"How do you know that?"

"Stop asking questions and keep filling the bag," Rabbit snapped as he turned back the other two. "You two, get away from the alarms. Stand back, or I'll blow your fingers off."

Near to tears, the girls nodded and took a step back.

Satisfied that the tellers were playing ball, Rabbit returned to the first teller as she emptied the second register into the sports bag. "What's your name?"

"Kate. Kate Durst."

"Uh-huh, *Kate Durst*," Rabbit said. "Do you like working here?"

She dropped the last few bills into the bag, picked it up, and dragged it to the fourth machine. "I did. Until today."

"Don't get funny with me, Kate."

"How did your friend know Joanne's name?"

Rabbit thought on his feet and made an excuse and rammed the end of his gun at the glass. "It's on her goddamn name badge, isn't it? Now, if you don't mind, I'll ask the questions and give the orders around here, and you can do the shutting-up-and-doing-what-I-say kind of stuff. You hear me?"

"Yeah, I guess."

Joanne's corpse slumped sideways against the wall. Her right leg had caught on the desk, resulting in a comedic final resting position.

Ram tried to ignore the sight of the disgusting and unflattering corpse as he reached the back door.

"Ugh, that's sick."

He booted the door on the back wall and made his way inside.

Whump.

Ram moved into the dimly lit corridor and scanned the area.

To his right, the lunch room.

Directly to his left, two privacy booths where the mortgage interviews were conducted, and beside that, the storage area.

"Damn it, where the *hell* is Price?"

Ram's horns seemed to prick up when he heard an echo of jubilation coming from the far end of the corridor.

"Huh?"

He lowered his shotgun and sprinted past the restrooms and entered the lunchroom.

Two men he didn't recognize chatted amongst themselves, completely oblivious to the proceedings taking place out in the banking area.

Three half eaten sandwiches and a freshly brewed coffee bubbled on the stove as the two bank workers laughed merrily.

"So, anyway," the first guy chuckled. "I was like, *Joanne,* I think you give all the *Karens* of this world a bad rap."

Ram leaned against the door frame and watched the two men continue to chat. He bounced his shotgun in his hand as loud as he could, but neither of them seemed to notice.

"Ha," the second guy said. "So what did you do?"

"Ah, I told her to go and be fat and useless somewhere else. Stupid waste of space."

Ram inhaled and yelled at the top of his lungs. "Baaa-aaa-aaa."

Startled, the two men turned around to find a ram in a business suit looking back at them. Then, they saw the shotgun in his hands.

The first man dropped the pot of coffee on the floor and raised his eyebrows in horror. "What the—?"

"—Baaa-aaa-aaa-aassholes," Ram said as he aimed his shotgun at the two men. "Hey, lookit. I got a question for *ewe*."

"Huh?"

Ram tapped his horns and giggled as his electronically altered threat bounded out from under his mask. "That's e-w-e, and not y-o-u, obviously."

The second guy put his hands in the air. "Wh-what is it? Who are y-you?"

Ram aimed down the sights on his gun and bounced between each of the two men. "I'm one pissed off, money-hungry mammal. *That's* who I am, numb nuts."

"Uh, what?"

"Where's Victor Price?" Ram asked.

"I, uh, he's here—somewhere. I dunno."

The first man swallowed hard and kept his hands above his head. "Is he n-not out front?"

"Nope."

Ram cocked the pump on his shotgun and prepared to fire, prompting the two men to soil their underwear right where they were standing.

"And him not being around when I wanna see him makes my trigger finger *real* itchy."

"He m-might be in his office?"

"His office, huh?" Ram asked, before nodding at the door over his shoulder. "That's a good idea. I like that. Let's go check his orifice together, eh?"

"Uh, o-okay," the second guy said on his way to the door. "Wait. *Orifice?*"

"And if Price isn't in his *orifice*, then I'm gonna *ram* my gun up yours and pull the trigger. Sound good?"

"Y-Yes."

"Excellent. Let's go."

The two men formed an obedient single file and marched their way past the hostile figure blocking the way.

"Hey, be careful," Ram said. "This is a new suit."

"Sorry."

Ram glanced at the young man's lapel and read his name. *Mr. A. Carlin.*

"You're new here, aren't you?"

"Y-Yes."

Ram snorted and pointed his shotgun at the door. "I'll give you *sorry*, Carlin, you sycophantic little turd. You're gonna regret the day you took this job on. Now, let's go."

***

The silver Chevrolet turned into the drive-through area and rolled to a stop a few feet in front of the seven available lanes.

The driver adjusted his Squirrel mask and lifted his wrist.

"This is Squirrel. I'm at the drive-by."

A confused Rabbit voice flew out from Squirrel's wristwatch.

"Drive-by?"

"Drive-through!" Squirrel corrected himself, quickly. "Sorry, man, it's the gun and the car, I just got a bit confused—"

"—Well stop being confused and get your bushy tail in the seventh lane. Badger will be there to meet you any second, now."

Another higher-pitched voice whirled out from the watch as Squirrel saw two cars exit the third and fourth drive-through lane and turn out of the area.

"Yeah, this is Badger, what is it?"

Rabbit's voice sped up in frustration. *"Squirrel's about to rock up to aisle seven, head for the drive-through now."*

"On it."

Satisfied, Squirrel flicked the shift into drive and stepped on the gas pedal. "Here we go."

He entered the seventh lane - the one nearest to the building itself - and stopped at the white speaker system.

The male teller behind the window spoke into his headset. Half a second later, his voice blasted out of the speaker grill.

"Good morning, sir. How can I help you today?"

Squirrel took a pause when he realized that his presence, and his voice, might perturb the man behind the counter. "Yeah, uh, can you see me?"

"Yes, sir. I can."

Concerned, the teller leaned into the window and squinted at the Squirrel behind the wheel, who turned back to him and gave him a thumbs up.

"Are you okay, sir?"

"I'm just fine," Squirrel said. "I need to make a withdrawal."

The teller shook his head and felt a wave of anxiety rush through his body. All was very much not as it seemed.

"I'm going to need you to take that, um, *thing* off your head, sir."

"What thing?" Squirrel asked.

"The mask, sir. For I.D. purposes."

"Come on," Squirrel muttered. "Where are you?"

Badger's hurried voice erupted from Squirrel's watch. *"I'm coming, I'm coming."*

Squirrel's refusal to remove his mask bought enough time to stall the teller until his associate arrived.

"Sir?" the teller asked.

"Yeah?"

"Take the mask off, and present your card, please."

Squirrel reached beside his seat and grabbed his Uzi. He knocked the end on the edge of the half-open window and grunted.

"How about this Israeli-looking gun, here? Is this proof enough for you?"

The teller's face lit up with concern when he saw the gun. "Oh, sh-shit. We're being robbed—"

He turned around and went for the alarm button under the counter, only to be greeted by a grotesquely ugly Badger smiling back at him with his permanent rubbery expression.

"Oh, shit."

"Num-num," Badger said. "I'll take it from here."

"Huh? Wh-ho are y-you—"

"—I'm a stinkin' badger, asshole," he snapped. "And this is my *bank*, now."

Whump—cratch.

Badger socked the man across the face with the butt of his Uzi, knocking him out cold. "Goddamn prick," he said, as he stepped over the unconscious man, and inserted his key into the locking mechanism on the counter.

"You took your sweet time," Squirrel said.

Badger opened up the registers and dropped his sports bag onto the counter. "Shut the hell up. I got here as quick as I could."

"Yeah, whatever, you goofy, two-gold-front-tooth protrudin' cocksucker. Load me up."

Badger slammed all the bills from the first three registers into the bag, and followed it up with a vicious boot to the mechanism under the counter.

Whump—spring.

The register opened, and coughed out a load of bills.

"Badger. Stop jerking off and fill the bag."

"Come on, come on," Badger said as he scooped the stacks of bills away from the counter. "Aww, shit. This isn't as easy as it looks."

"What took you so long to turn up, anyhow?" Squirrel asked.

"Goddamn Cherry—Uh, *Dog*, shot that fat broad. What's her name? The one with three chins?"

"Joanne Henry?"

"Yeah, her."

"Shot? As in with a gun?"

Badger dropped the cash into his sports bag and pulled on the zipper. "Yeah, as in *dead*."

"Not exactly a hard target to miss, eh?"

"Guess not."

Squirrel dropped his Uzi onto the passenger seat and pushed his hand through the open driver's window. "Come on, gimme the bag."

Badger dropped more and more handfuls of bills into the bag. "Hang on."

Frustrated, and with time truly of the essence, Squirrel peered into the side mirror felt his heart begin to palpitate.

"Please tell me someone got to the vault and that Price is playing ball?"

"Yeah. No, I don't know."

Squirrel checked his rear view mirror to see a black car turn the corner and enter the fifth, vacant drive-through lane.

"Ah, shit," Squirrel snapped as he scanned his watch. "You got a customer."

Badger was too busy stuffing the bag with money to notice. "What?"

"Come on, we only got four minutes before—"

"—I know, I know, just a bit more."

Stuff-stuff-stuff.

"Right, I'm done. Let's switch."

Badger struggled to lift his heavy sports bag in both hands, and chucked it through the service window.

Squirrel passed his own bag over to Badger, and flicked the Chevrolet into reverse gear.

"I'm round the corner, where we agreed. Please try to get to me before anyone else does."

"You got it."

Badger gave his associate the thumbs up and then pointed to the fifth lane.

"Your customer," Squirrel hollered as he drove away. "Deal with him. Or her. Or *it*."

"Shitsticks."

Vrooom.

The Chevrolet darted out of the seventh lane and turned the corner, leaving a thoroughly confused female driver demanding to be served by the suited badger behind the window on the wall.

He waved at her, slowly, knowing he'd been busted.

"Good afternoon. Welcome to Chrome Valley Federal."

She turned to the passenger seat and grimaced at her young son. "Uh, honey?"

"Yes, mommy?"

"Is that a… *badger*? At the counter window?"

The young boy giggled as he laid eyes on the mysterious-looking animal staring back at him. "Yeah, yeah, look. He has funny teeth."

The woman rolled down her window and spoke into the machine. "Um, hello?"

The badger flipped the young boy the middle finger and grabbed the microphone on the counter.

"Fuck off, lady. We're closed."

Startled, the woman clutched her chest and fumed. "What did you just say?"

"I said fuck off. We're busy."

"How *dare* you—"

Badger slammed the screen door shut and disappeared from view.

"Well, I've never, in all my life—"

"—Mommy?"

Furious, the woman thumped the steering wheel and sneered. "What?"

"What does *fuck off* mean?"

Squirrel kept a low profile behind the steering wheel.

He'd parked the Chevrolet by the building in the mostly featureless and empty back parking lot.

As he expected, a black car containing a furious woman and her child whizzed past his stationary vehicle and onto the main road.

Squirrel watched the back of the car disappear from view and lifted his left wrist to his mouth.

"Okay, looks like your girlfriend's gone, Badger-boy."

"Good. Thought I'd never get rid of that lady."

"What did you tell her, out of interest?"

"To fuck off. First time I've said that to a woman and gotten away with it."

"Nice. Very classy."

Squirrel started the engine, flicked the stick into reverse, and looked over his shoulder.

"We're all clear. I'mma back up now, and meet you at the window. Tell Rabbit and the boys we got a little under three minutes if we wanna empty the vault. Any news on Price?"

"Not yet, I don't think."

"Shit. We can't stick around, otherwise those screwballs from SecuriCore are gonna be all over us. I don't wanna be here when they arrive, man."

***

Badger lifted his arm away from his head as he pulled off his mask.

Beads of sweat rolled down his face as he spoke. "Okay, I'll tell them," he said, breathlessly. "Ugh."

Squirrel's voice drifted out of his watch. *"What?"*

"These masks, I swear to God. Whose genius idea was this?"

"Rabbit's idea, man."

"Why couldn't we just wear our fucking balaclavas from the start? Something more breathable?"

"Just shut up and make sure we're in the vault."

"Okay."

"And put your mask back on. You don't wanna be walking back in there like a shit-eating tooth fairy with Type 2 Diabetes."

"Yeah, good idea."

The sweaty mask nearly slipped out of Mark's hands as he pulled it back over his head. He tucked the loose ends under his shirt collar, grabbed his Uzi and the empty sports bag, and ran out of the drive-through area.

The corridor that led to the main banking area was long, cold, and not especially well lit. A broken water cooler that had seen better days stood opposite the one area Mark wished was being used: the safe deposit vault.

Nobody was there.

The vault door was closed, and showed no signs of life, abuse, or use.

"What the fuck? Shit, shit, shit," he said as he picked up the pace and made his way past the storage room. "What the fuck are they doing out there?"

Mark patted the side of the badger mask and raced up to the main door to the banking area.

"Don't tell me they've fucking—"

Whump.

Badger skidded on his heels and squeezed his Uzi as he clamped eyes on what was happening in the main banking area.

"Huh?"

Dog gripped a man's collar and shoved him towards Rabbit, who pointed his gun directly between the man's eyes. "Well, well, well. Look who's here."

"Victor *fucking* Price," Dog said. "Caught him hiding under one of the desks in the lending room."

Rabbit stepped towards Victor and stared him in the eyes from behind his mask. "Price?"

"Yeah."

"You're the manager, here. Right?"

Victor didn't raise his arms. Instead, he showed a ferocious disregard for the robbers and, despite their willingness to execute hostages, as evidenced by Joanne's now stinking corpse, stood his ground.

"Yes, I am. This is my bank. I'm responsible."

"You know why we're here, don't you?"

"I can take a guess."

Rabbit turned to the back door to find Badger eager to make his next move.

"Hey, Badger?"

"Yeah?"

"Take our bank-managing friend out back and open up the vault for us."

Angered by the sobs and wails from the hostages, Dog turned around and barked at them. "Shut the fuck up or I'll start shooting."

Ram ushered the three tellers from behind the counter. Kate led the way and offered a friendly hand to the other two, who had practically lost the will to live.

"Come on, girls. It'll be okay."

Ram nodded and used his shotgun to shoo them over to the conference room. "Listen to Durst, everyone. She's smart. Get in the conference room while we sort this all out."

Kate threw an evil glance at Ram on her way past. "You won't get away with this, you know."

"Shut your over painted lips up and get moving, smart-ass."

Victor grinned in Rabbit's face as Badger grabbed his shirt collar. "So, Rabbit, huh? You're the leader of this mob?"

"Say that again?"

Victor surveyed the geography of the armed men surrounding the bank.

"Look at you. Nothing but no-good cowards robbing a bank and expecting to get away with it."

Rabbit teased the trigger on his shotgun and felt a pang of violence into his chest.

"Look at *you*. Victor fucking Price. Nothing but a no-good bottom feeder in control of the state's money. You wanna talk about cowardly? How about every time the banks need a bailout, it's us, the taxpaying public, who comes to rescue your sorry ass while you sit back with your shares and options skyrocketing, huh?"

Victor scrunched his face with pure venom. "Those smart enough to be in such a position?"

"Fuck you, you scumbag," Rabbit shrieked at the top of his electronically-altered voice. "Besides, all this is insured. It doesn't affect you in the slightest, does it?"

"No?"

"Exactly," Rabbit said. "Now, be a good little boy, because that's what you are, after all, and go and unlock the vault. Help my friend Badger get what we need."

Victor grinned, his face temporarily lit up by the reflection of light coming from the tiny bit of metal hanging from the chain around his neck.

"I don't have the key."

Rabbit ripped the chain off Victor's neck and presented it to him. "Goddamn it, *there's* the vault fuckin' key."

Defeated, Victor held out his hand and let Rabbit drop it into his palm.

"B-But the code?" Victor said as Rabbit lost his temper.

"The code?"

"Yeah, it changes every—"

"—Every week," Rabbit snapped much to Ram and Dog's amusement. "And, if I'm not mistaken, this week's code is the year the Cubs won the world series."

A dagger of undiluted terror smacked across Victor's face. "How the hell did you know that?"

"The year of our Lord, two-zero-one-six, in case you'd forgotten," Rabbit said. "Now, I suggest you get to the fuckin' vault, open it, and we'll be on our merry little way back to the animal farm."

Rabbit turned the man around and kicked him up the ass.

"Oof."

"Don't worry about your colleagues, Price. We'll take care of them while you're gone. Now, move."

Badger pulled Victor away by his collar and forced him to walk past the desks. "Come on, asshole. Let's stop wasting time and load up, shall we?"

Victor snarled at the man in the badger mask as he stumbled forward and pushed the back door open. "Fuck you."

"Not if we fuck you first."

Out in the back corridor, Badger took the opportunity to thump Victor on the back as he frogmarched him to the safe deposit vault.

"Come on, stop stalling."

Victor eyed left, and right, taking note of the pocket of shadows produced by the flickering lights from the ceiling.

"Can I ask you something?"

"What? No."

"Why now? Why Wednesday, right before lunch?"

Badger didn't take any shit, and kicked the man in the small of his back as he walked.

Victor whelped and stumbled forward.

"Shut the fuck up, Price, and get to the vault, or I'll blow your fucking head clean off your shoulders."

Victor turned the corner and brushed himself down. "Just before lunch on a Wednesday? Pickup time, right on eleven thirty-five, before security comes? You guys know exactly what you're doing, don't you?"

"Damn straight we do, asshole. Now stop talking—"

"—You got it all figured out, don't you?"

"Ooooh yeah, come on down, the *Price* is most definitely fuckin' *right*," Badger screamed. "Now, stop talking and open the fucking vault."

Victor stared at the keypad on the wall and extended his index finger.

Badger unhooked his empty sports bag and clutched it in his left hand. "Fuckin' twenty-sixteen. Press it."

"Okay."

Badger felt his hands begin to shake with nerves. "Do it slow. If you fuck up and press a wrong number you'll set off the alarm."

Victor pressed his index finger to the plate, which produced a friendly, female voice from the grille.

"Fingerprint ID accepted. Welcome, Mr. Price."

"You seem to know an awful lot about this bank," Victor said as he hit the number *two* button on the pad.

"Shut up and punch the code in," Badger snapped. "Do it."

Victor hit the number two key on the pad, and then the zero, and one...

... and then went for number seven.

"Whoa," Badger said. "Do you *want* to die? I'll shoot your fingers off, scoop them up, plug your ears with them. Press *six*, you corporate scumbag."

Victor cackled like a witch and called Badger's bluff. "Ha. You dumb dildo."

"What?"

"I know it's you, *Mark*. Who put you up to it, huh? One of those useless *retards* we laid off last week?"

"What?" Badger snapped. "What are you fucking talking about? I'm not Mark."

"Yeah, right," Victor grinned. "Don't think I *don't* know what's happening, here, Amos. I always knew you were a no-good tool."

Badger jumped back and aimed his Uzi at Victor. "I'm not Mark. I don't know what you're talking about."

"I shoulda fired your sorry ass when I had the chance, and now you're ripping the joint off? Hardly managerial material, are you, you fucking prick."

Victor snarled and rammed his finger on button number seven.

Drriiiinnngg.

The wrong number triggered the internal security alarm. It exploded to life, throwing a God-almighty deafening alarm up the corridor, accompanied by spinning red wall lights.

"Fuck you, Mark," Victor shouted over the high-pitched alarms. "You think you can fuck me and my bank over? Think again, dickhead."

Badger stormed over to Victor and buried his Uzi into his temple. "Reset the alarm."

"Fuck you, Amos."

"I swear to God, you better reset the alarm, or I'll—"

"—Or you'll what, *Amos?*" Victor said.

"I'm n-not Amos."

Victor didn't buy the squeaky-sounding Badger's lie for a second. "Gonna fuck everything up, just like you've done with your career, Amos? Pfft. And they told me to not fire your ass."

Badger's hands shook with rage as he buried the barrel of his Uzi at the man's temple. "Shut up. Stop talking, and—"

"—You're not gonna shoot me, Amos, you sack of shit. Hell, you don't even know how to use that gun—"

"—Shut up, asshole," Badger shrieked at the top of his lungs. "You don't know shit about—"

Thraa-aaa—aattt-a—spattcchh.

Badger accidentally yanked on the trigger as he yelled, and released a torrent of bullets up the side of Victor's neck and head, which splattered his brains up the metal vault door.

"Oh-ohhhhh, shiiiit—"

Victor's body spun around on the spot, flinging fragments of skull and brain on Badger's mask and shirt.

Victor's corpse slumped on the floor on a smoking heap of blasted skull and brains.

"Uh, uh, uh—oh, *shitsticks.*"

Startled, Badger lowered his Uzi and considered dropping it, running around the corner, diving out of the drive-through window, and running away.

"Oh, dear."

The alarms seemed to grow even louder as an angry voice blasted out of his wristwatch.

"Badger? Badger? This is Rabbit. What's going on?"

The shaken Mark lifted his wrist to his mouth. "Uh, we got a problem."

"What, what?"

Mark removed his mask and blinked the sweat from his eyes. The vision of a thoroughly dead, and mostly decapitated, bank manager, focused into his field of vision.

"I, uh—oh, shitsticks."

He began to hyperventilate and reconsider his entire life in a split second.

"Oh my God, oh my God. What have I done?"

"What have you done? What's with the goddamn alarms? Where's Price?"

"I, uh he—"

"—Badger, talk to me. What triggered the goddamn alarm?"

"It's Price, man. He deliberately hit the wrong number on the keypad—" Mark's voice trailed to nothing as the angry Rabbit interjected.

"—Damn it, Badger. Stop stuttering like an autistic child and tell me what—"

"—Uh, Ross? I mean, uh, Rabbit?"

"Please, for the love of God, tell me you got in the vault."

"Umm, no, not exactly."

"Not exactly? What do you mean not exactly? Where's Price?"

Mark swallowed and felt his throat climb into his mouth as he returned to the thoroughly-executed corpse by his shoes.

"Aww, Jeez."

Chapter 2

HOWARD ROSS
— Monday, September 28th —

"… Aww, Jeez. What with everything that's happened, we've found ourselves in a bit of a bind, which is why we arranged to come in and speak to you."

The droll voice fell on Howard's deaf ears.

He wasn't much interested in what the man on the other side of his desk was saying. The walls in his office seemed to have closed in, what with his thoughts consumed by the sledgehammer of bad news coming his way.

"Excuse me?" the man said. "Mr. Ross? Did you hear what I said?"

Howard came to, blinked, and produced a polite smile. *Of course he was listening.*

"Yes, Mr. Kirk. Sorry, I was miles away, just there. Please, continue."

Mr. Kirk's wife pushed her spectacles up her nose and grunted as she pointed at the placard on the desk. "You *are* the Head of Lending, right?"

"I am," Howard said with a smile.

"Then you're an ambassador for the bank, and we expect a little courtesy and professionalism," she said, much to Howard's consternation. "Sorry, honey, continue."

Mr Kirk adjusted his collar and continued speaking. "Mr. Ross, the thing is, we asked for that specific amount. We're hoping we can secure the loan because…"

Mr. Kirk's voice morphed into garbled noise as Howard's eyes drifted away from the conversation and through the Lending Room window.

Victor Price tapped on his watch and cast an evil glare at Howard as he walked past the window. "Ten minutes," he mouthed.

"… When my mother suddenly fell ill, the hospital bills ruined us almost immediately," Mr. Kirk continued to little acknowledgment from Howard. "Bill after bill after bill, and we just couldn't keep up the repayments on everything else…"

Howard squinted at Price as he stopped to meet two, strange balding men in suits out on the banking floor. He leaned forward and took more interest in them than Mr. Kirk.

"I'm hoping the documents we emailed are okay, Mr. Ross? Is everything okay? Please, we could use some good news right about now."

Victor Price ushered the two men away, and out of sight, leaving a flummoxed Howard to turn his attention back to Mr. Kirk and press his hands together.

He'd heard precisely nothing, not that the sob story would change the fact that Howard had bad news for him.

"Mr. Kirk? Mrs. Kirk?"

"Yes?"

Howard abandoned his attempt to turn down the loan, and offered a contrite grin. "I'm sorry about this, but would you mind if I stop talking to you for a few minutes? I'll be right back."

"Oh," Mr. Kirk said. "But you're dealing with us right now?"

Mrs. Kirk shuffled around in her seat. "I took a whole morning off of work for this."

Howard stood up from his seat and slid around the desk, intent on getting as far as away from his lending room as possible.

"I'm very sorry, Mrs. Kirk. Please, just wait there. As I say, I'll be right back."

Howard pulled the door open and left the thoroughly unamused couple in the room to sweat whatever problems they had on their own.

The main banking area had an undeniable antagonism to it. Howard stopped still and scanned the teller counter. A cacophonous ripple of stamps, register bells, and clattering of coins battered him around the ears.

"Ugh."

This morning, the bank seemed smaller and warmer, which was unusual for this time of year.

Howard shifted left and saw the blinds in the conference room window resembled prison bars.

A couple of steps closer, and he could just about hear a muffled chatter from those who were in the conference room.

Without warning, someone tapped him on the shoulder. "Hey, Howard."

"Huh?"

Howard held his chest in fright, took a deep breath, and accosted his dark-skinned colleague. "Jesus, Lincoln. Don't sneak up on me like that."

"Sorry, man," he chuckled. "Hey, what time are you due in?"

"They said they'd call me just after lunch," Howard said. "Ten minutes, or so. And you?"

"Dunno. I think they've stacked all the brothers for later this afternoon. I think I'm in after Benjy."

Howard nodded at the conference room door. "Who are those two guys, anyway?"

"A pair of outsourced, mean-looking assholes, man. Ironside and Capone. I heard they don't take no shit from nobody."

Howard felt like vomiting and tilted his head to the ground. A lengthy strip of yellow tape crossed under his shoe, resembling a peculiar image of a tightrope bleeding out from the sides of his right sole. "This can't be happening. "

"Hey, man. It is what it is."

Just then, a man in overalls barged past the two and reached for the floor. "Sorry, gentlemen. Excuse me."

Lincoln stepped back and snorted. "Hey, man. You finally tearing all that social distancing tape up?"

The man tugged at the end of the tape and peeled it away from the floor. "Yeah, finally. No more six foot distancing nonsense. Took long enough to take down all those dumb Plexiglass guards off of all your desks."

Howard grunted and shooed the man away from his knee.

He waved Lincoln over to the door at the back of the area.

"Christ, I need some air. You coming?"

Howard stopped by the water cooler in the bowels of the bank, desperate for some refreshment. The bottle wasn't just empty, but dry to the bone, and covered with cobwebs.

Lincoln chuckled as Howard looked around the cup dispenser and found nothing but dead cockroaches.

"Ha, you really think they'll bother with that shit now they're laying motherfuckers off left, right, and center?"

Howard thumped the empty bottle and huffed. "It's inhumane. How do they expect us to work like this? We're not even back a week in this blazing heat and they haven't ordered refills? Look at the state of this damn thing."

"Dunno, man," Lincoln said. "Kinda prescient, ain't it? The state of the cooler's gonna be our careers any week now."

Howard pushed his chest out as he strode past the storage room and made for the safe deposit vault.

A man dressed in a SecuriCore uniform and face visor drifted out from round the corner and smiled at Howard. "Morning, Mr. Ross. How is everything?"

"Ah, hey Cole," Howard said. "Yeah, pretty good. I forgot it was Monday."

"Yup, I'll be back in a couple days to relieve you of your hard-earned cash."

Howard chuckled. "I'm sure you will. Have a good day."

"You too, sir."

Howard raised his eyebrows with a deft familiarity and hobbled towards the fire door.

"Hey, wait up."

Lincoln sprinted up behind him and tried to inject an air of humor into the proceedings. "You can always swing by the drive-through, you know. I got bottled water comin' outta my ass, there."

Howard pushed through the back door and reached into his pants pocket.

"As tempting as that sounds, I think I'll just inhale a bunch of carcinogens and give myself a slow death, if it's all the same to you."

The exit door pushed open and released Howard and Lincoln into the back parking lot.

Several cars, all beautifully kept and recently cleaned, baked in the intense sunlight.

Howard flicked the top of his cigarette box open and offered it to Lincoln. "Coffin nail?"

"Yeah, for what it's worth. Thanks."

Flick—flick.

Howard lit his colleague's cigarette, and then his own. He took in a lungful of smoke, held it in, and blew the thick smog out through his nostrils. "Ahh, that's better."

"See you holed up in your office with that pair of losers, man," Lincoln said.

"Oh. Yeah, the Kirks. A double-barreled pain in my ass, I don't mind admitting."

"Ain't this the second time this month they've come crawling to you looking for a favor?"

Howard closed his eyes and ground his shoulder blades against the wall. "Third, actually."

"Shit. Really? In *one* week?"

"Yup. What can I say? Quarantine ruined everyone's finances. The Kirks are smart enough, but they're terrible with their finances. Every damn time, they're in my office playing the violin, and every time I'm listening to their shit. Bane of my life, Lincoln, I swear to God. Decades of witnessing smart people being idiotic with their money and nearly ending up on the streets."

Lincoln flicked the ash away from his smoke and leaned to the right. "Amen to that," he said as he surveyed his turf.

"Hmm."

The drive-through wasn't busy, but it would only be a matter of time before the lunch hour rush would see all seven lanes filled with SUVs and mothers attempting to withdraw cash.

"Tch."

"What?"

"Drive-through is slow, even pre-lunch," Lincoln said. "The moment I turn my back on the staff, they're on their phones."

"Really?"

"Hell, yeah, Ross," he said. "Kids, man. Hey, you remember, like, five years back, when they fired the whole DT team and replaced them with college grads and dropouts?"

Howard assessed the seven lanes, along with his friend. "Uh-huh. Way to save some money."

"Yeah, and pay these chumps half of what they paid the talent they fired before them."

"What can I say, Mumford? You pay peanuts, you get monkeys," Howard said, none too concerned for Lincoln's feelings.

"Monkeys?"

"Uh, yeah."

"You calling *me* a monkey?"

"No," Howard said. "Put the race card away. *Monkeys*, idiots, hopping around with their arms swinging everywhere and flinging their own shit all over the place, is what I mean. The great unwashed. The illiterati, and the smartphones they can never look away from for more than ten minutes."

Lincoln nodded with approval, although Howard suspected he might have confused the man.

Howard continued with scorn as he watched a car exit the drive-through lane. "You're okay, right? You're a supervisor?"

"Nah, man. Ain't nobody safe, now. Not in this *new normal.*"

Howard sucked on his cigarette and thought hard about his next sentence. "That's not what I meant."

"No? What did you mean?"

"Well, you know, you're the only black member of staff here."

Lincoln flicked his half-finished cigarette at a passing car that had exited the drive-through.

"I know, I know, I'm just the good ol' token black guy. Keeping the social justice warriors and box-tickers happy. But, you know something?"

"No, what?"

"I ain't complaining, man," Lincoln chuckled. "I'll take that shit and use it to my advantage, you know?"

Howard licked his lips as he crushed his lit cigarette under his shoe. "Lincoln?"

"Yeah, man?"

"How many CCTV cameras does the drive-through have, anyhow?"

"What? Are you outta your ancient mind, old man Ross?"

"No, just—" Howard tried affably as possible. "How many? What's the surveillance like?"

"Pfft," Lincoln scoffed. "You'd have *thunk* a Federal bank would have eyes everywhere. This shit out here? Pfft. All this is barely being watched, anyhow."

"Really?"

"Yeah, man. Ain't nobody about to hold up a drive-through these days. Hell, *Burger Face* has more chance of getting robbed at the drive-through than a bank."

"Christ, I wish you hadn't said that. I could murder a *Stent Special* and fries right about now."

Lincoln pulled out a packet of mints from his shirt pocket and made for the back door. "Well, your pudgy ass could do without that fried shit. C'mon, man. Let's get back in before Price pisses his panties and has us fired."

Howard chuckled at the irony of his friend's charming little joke. "Very funny."

Five Minutes Later

Howard returned to his plush executive chair and chewed on a mint, much to the chagrin of Mr. and Mrs. Kirk, who waited patiently for his return.

"So, Mr. and Mrs. Kirk. Where were we?"

Close to exploding with anger, Mr. Kirk pointed to the gold placard with Howard's full name and job title on it. "The loan? Mr. Ross?"

"Oh, yes."

Howard wheeled himself up to his desk and prepared to scan his notes. "So, according to my loan notes on your

file from our previous phone call, it says here you're
willing to put up your horse as collateral, along with—"

"—Horse?" Mr. Kirk asked, confused. "We don't have
a horse."

"You don't?"

"No."

Howard peered at his paper and realized he'd make a
mistake.

"Oh! *House*. Sorry, not horse," he said as he scribbled
over the error with his pen. "It's not always easy to read
my own handwriting."

Mrs. Kirk sighed and clutched her handbag as she
watched Howard turn to his computer and begin typing.
"So, we'll just input the information into our little lending
calculator, here, and it seems that—"

Knock—knock.

All three sets of eyeballs in the room turned to the
door.

"Yes? Come in."

The door slid open and produced a stern-looking
Victor Price. "Sorry to interrupt."

Howard threw his boss a look of half-professionalism,
and half-concern.

"Ah, Mr. Price. I'm just dealing with Mr. and Mrs.
Kirk at the moment. Mr. and Mrs. Kirk, this is Victor
Price, our manager."

Mr. Kirk offered a smile in the vague hope that the
manager might be able to bypass the moron dealing with
his loan. "I'm pleased to meet you."

"Yes, likewise," Victor said. "I'm terribly sorry about
this, but could I borrow Mr. Ross for a a moment? It's
quite urgent."

Mr. Kirk turned away and folded his arms in a huff.
"Whatever."

"Thank you."

Victor's polite smile turned to an angry scowl as he
nodded at Howard to get off his ass and out of the room.

Victor and Howard made their way to the conference room.

"I really don't understand you sometimes, Ross. The Kirks should have been done and dusted by now. It's 1 pm. What the hell took you so long to turn their dumb asses down a second time?"

"I'm sorry," Howard said. "I got caught up."

Victor stopped by the door and sniffed around the air. "Is that cigarette smoke I can smell?"

"What?" Howard lied. "No."

"Sure smells like cigarette smoke to me."

The cold, dank nicotine reeked from Howard's shirt sleeve. Worse, when Victor scanned Howard's face, he noticed he was chewing something.

"Wow. Really? You're chewing just before you walk in?"

Gulp.

Howard's eyes teared up as the mint slid down his throat and stuck to his windpipe like a slug dying on a window pane.

"Ugh, n-nope."

"I dunno what the hell happened to you during quarantine, Ross. Did you knock your head, or something?"

"No, I just—"

"—for Christ's sake, pull yourself together, man. This is serious."

Angry, Victor moved into the conference room with a humbled and terrified Howard Ross in tow.

Whump.

Victor closed the door and made his way to a lone, plastic seat by the back window. Out in the street, Howard snatched a glance at the cars and pedestrians crisscrossing around the financial district in search of their lunchtime bagels and overpriced skinny lattes.

Victor turned the blinds shut and took his seat.

Howard approached the desk and found himself face to face with two men on the opposite side.

They seemed busy, and carrying a bucket of bad news with them.

The first man smiled as he looked up at Howard and offered his hand.

"Ah, Mr. Ross. I'm Damien Ironside. Very pleased to meet you."

Howard took the man's hand and gave it a limp shake. "Hello."

"And this is my associate, Mr. Alan Capone."

Howard couldn't help but notice that the two men were ten years younger than him. "Capone? Is that really your name?"

"Yeeeees," the man said as if he'd heard the question a million times before.

Damien and Alan might well have been brothers, what with the unamused expressions on their clean-shaved faces and shiny, bald heads.

"Please, Mr. Ross. Take a seat," Alan said.

"Okay."

Victor folded his arms with a nasty, victorious grin on his annoying face. Howard couldn't bear to look at him, and so turned to the friendlier-looking Damien Ironside and smiled.

"Uh, Mr. Ross?" Damien asked.

"Yeah, hi."

"Effectively, what we at Ironside and Capone do, is look at a corporation's workforce. Try to gauge where any streamlining may be available. If that makes sense?"

"Sort of. *Streamlining*?" Howard asked. "Sounds ominous."

"Oh, it's pretty standard procedure," Alan snapped, humorlessly. "Most streamlining these days is outsourced to professionals. Due diligence is important to a company, as I'm sure your twenty-five years experience here at Chrome Valley Federal has taught you."

Howard hadn't considered the man's pithy assessment and raced to agree. "Yes, of course."

Alan sifted through his notes and pulled out a lone sheet of paper with Howard's name on it.

Meanwhile, Damien pressed his hands together and relaxed his shoulders.

A list of familiar names slid into view on one of the papers. Among them, James Gilmour, Benjamin Cherry, Lincoln Mumford, and Mark Amos."

Howard felt his brow heat up, and the claggy remnants of mint turned to lava in the walls of his mouth.

"Now, before we get into the details, Mr. Ross, we've established who you are, and the excellent work you've done, and we believe we've put together a very generous severance package."

Howard gripped the armrests on his plastic chair and shook his head, hoping that he'd fallen asleep. "I'm sorry, say that again?"

Alan looked at Howard for the first time since the meeting began. "Severance package."

"Severance package?"

"Yes, we think you'll find it's quite generous."

"A severance package?" Howard grimaced as all his paranoid Christmases came crashing down around him at once. "No, no. There must be some mistake. What is this? What are you talking about?"

The skilled Damien smiled as if it were the best news in the world. "You have five vacation days left to take this year, so we figure the day after tomorrow, Wednesday September thirtieth, will be your last working day."

Alan slid the paper containing the severance package details across the table and up Howard's shaking right hand.

"Yes. So, as of this Thursday, the rest of your life is your own."

Howard fumbled the paper and tried to steady it as he read the details. He was shocked to find that it was, indeed, very generous.

"Okay."

The problem for Howard that he didn't want to lose his job, but everyone else in the room acted as if it was common knowledge.

An attempt to fight the inevitable would only make Howard look feeble and out of touch.

"I wasn't expecting that," he said. "B-But, can't we work something out? If it's a matter of productivity, I can assure you I'll work twice as hard."

Alan turned to Damien in amusement, and both men giggled.

"*Please*?" Howard chanced, pathetically.

The latter licked his lips and returned to the conversation at hand.

"I'm afraid not, Mr. Ross. The wheels are already in motion."

Howard felt his muscles turn to jello and chanced a glance in Victor's general direction. The man was very pleased with himself, and seemed to bask in Howard's misery.

Alan stacked his notes together, and finished the firing. "If you have any other questions, please, do not hesitate to talk to Mr. Price in the first instance. Or, of course, you can get in touch with us via our app and make a request there."

Howard stared at the floor in a daze.

"No," he muttered, regretting the day his mother chose not to have an abortion fifty-something years ago. "No. I'm *done*."

"You certainly are," Victor added.

Howard rose out of his chair like a suicidal dog with his tail between his legs, turned around, and made his way out of the conference room.

Whump.

The door closed behind him, leaving a jubilant Victor Price, and thoroughly relieved Damien and Alan, to sigh with relief.

"Well, that wasn't so bad, was it?" Price said. "Okay, I think Mr. James Gilmour is up next."

Alan sorted through his notes, intently. "James Gilmour—"

"—Yeah," Price said. "You must have seen him around here this morning. Tall? Dark hair? Bad temper?"

Confused, Damien and Alan shook their heads. "Umm, no?"

"Kind of looks like a tenth-rate Elvis impersonator crossed with a sex offender?"

"Oh, *him*?" Alan snapped and returned to his hit list. "Yes, yes, let me see. *James Gilmour*. Personal Lending & Finance Adviser?"

"That's the one," Price said. "I'll go fetch his coked-up useless ass. But be delicate with him, he has a bit of a short fuse."

Damien rubbed his hands with glee and chuckled heartily. "Well, let's cut that fuse right off, and toss the useless dynamite on the scrapheap where it belongs?"

Howard stood in front of the conference room and focused on the tiny fabric fibers that made up the scrawny, balding carpet by his feet.

He tried to ignore the inaudible, jubilant chatter muffled from within, and just stared at his shoes.

If he'd have looked up, he would have noticed his colleague from Corporate Accounts, Benjamin Cherry, staring at him with a concerned expression on his pretty, young face.

"Howard?" Ben asked.

His call-out didn't get a response. Instead, Howard Ross experienced a state of empty, mindless delirium.

Ben pushed past the line of customers for the service counter, and clicked his fingers at Howard's face.

"Earth to Ross, come in?"

All Howard could muster was a soft, desperate, "Shit."

Ben knew that what had gone down in the conference room was far from good, and the fact that he was due in later in the afternoon didn't help matters.

"Howard? What happened in there? What did they say?"

"My last day is Wednesday."

"Wednesday? What, next week? Next month?"

"Day after tomorrow, Wednesday," Howard said. "Not so much gardening leave as *eternity* leave."

"Jesus Christ, these guys don't mess around, do they?"

"Nope."

Howard moved away from the door, threw his arms out in front of his chest, and stormed back to his office.

As he stormed forward he could see Victor walking in his direction with a very pensive James Gilmour right behind him.

"Howard," Price said.

"Price," Howard said with a veneer of polite violence.

James threw Howard a glance of terror as they passed each other. "Hey."

"Hey. Is it your turn now?"

"Yeah," James said. "I'll catch you after? Go to *Bean There* and grab a coffee or six?"

"Sure."

Ben sidestepped out of James's path as he made his way to the conference room with Victor. "Howard, man, wait. Stop. Let's talk—"

"—Goddamn motherfuckers," he muttered under his breath, leaving an extremely worried Ben in his path.

"Howard, stop. *Think.*"

The customers in the bank, and the teller girls behind the counter, all watched the ravenous beast kick the door to his office open and storm inside.

Mr. and Mrs. Kirk turned to the office door, ready to launch into an angry tirade, when Howard's red-eyed anger and clenched fists made them think twice.

"Oh. Mr. Ross?" Mr. Kirk asked.

Howard grunted, near ready to punch something. "Get out."

"I *beg* your pardon?" Mrs. Kirk scowled.

Howard closed his eyes, struggling to contain his volcanic anger. "I said get the fuck out of my office before I fucking kill you."

Mr. Kirk folded his arms in defiance. "Right, that's it. This is quite ridiculous. I demand to speak to the manager—"

"—Argghhhh!"

Howard booted his computer and monitor off the desk and shrieked like a banshee as he turned around and punched the wall.

"Goddamn motherfuckers, I swear to God, I'm gonna kill some bastard—"

"—Uhh, honey?" Mrs. Kirk stammered in terror.

"Yes, dear?" came the terrified response.

"Let's get out of here."

"Good idea."

The petrified couple rose out of their seats as Howard screamed and kicked his desk with such force that it tipped over and slammed onto its side.

Whump.

Mr. Kirk exited the room. "We'll come back another time, Mr. Ross."

"Get to *fuck*."

Howard controlled his breathing when he saw everyone in the bank blink back at him from the other side of the window.

"What in the name of *ass* are you douche bags looking at?" he screamed.

When everyone turned away, Howard glanced at the underside of his desk. Several streaks of crusted, transparent fluid streaked in all directions like a crazy firework.

"Oh, shit."

The remnants of Howard's surreptitious *one-handed dealings* whenever he was alone in the office were now on full display.

Before Howard could grab the desk and turn it upright, Victor Price cleared his throat and announced himself.

"Howard?"

"Leave me alone."

He'd seen everything, including Howard's sticky, onanism souvenir splattered under the desk.

"You're sick, Howard. Don't think I've not noticed. I can understand the frustration. I get that you're angry, but jerking off under the table? Ugh. You should be put in jail."

Howard didn't have a reply.

There was nothing to be said.

"Calm your ass down and get back to work" Price said as he left the room. "I gotta calm the Kirks down, as if I don't have enough to deal with."

The Men's Room

Howard leaned against the cold, plastic tiles by the wash basins and cried his heart out like a thoroughly humiliated child.

"Awwww, *fuck.*"

Twenty-five years' worth of frustration and pain blasted down his face as he tried to catch his breath.

Beep—beep.

His buzzing cell phone quickly became the stone in the shoe of his turmoil. "Huh?"

He reached into his pocket, took it out and wiped the tears from his face.

A text message from someone named *Bunni* hovered in front of the evil-looking electronic Skull wallpaper.

"Bonnie?"

He swiped his thumb across the tempered glass, swallowed his grief to his stomach, and read the message.

> *OMG Dad!*
> *Just got a letter in the mail from WG.*
> *Too scared to open it.*
> *What do I do? Bonnie x*

Howard's nose bubbled as he chuckled at the message. He cleared his throat and typed a message back to her.

> *Just open it, Bunni.*
> *The suspense will kill you if you don't.*
> *Let me know what it says. Dad x*

Hey, Howard thought to himself, perhaps a member of the Ross family might have some good news today.

He pushed himself away from the urinal wall and flicked the screen over to his contact list. He stopped at a contact named *Miranda*.

He was about to hit the dial button with his thumb, but couldn't bring himself to go through with it. His thumb didn't want to play ball at all. "Ugh. Fuck it."

Spriiishh.

The water blasted out of the faucet on the wash basin and into Howard's shaking, reddened hands. He splashed his face with the freezing cold water, and blinked at the reflection in the mirror.

Standing before him, was a tired-looking old man with wet hair and water dripping from his face. It didn't so much resemble the face he was used to, as a slobbering St. Bernard with dangling jowls, ready to pounce and attack someone - *anyone*.

A few minutes later, Howard had calmed down to the point of being presentable to the customer-facing area of the bank.

He pushed through the staff door and was about to move to his office, when he saw what looked like an angry ram storm in his direction.

It was James Gilmour, who had just exited the conference room. His ears and nostrils seemed to shoot thick smoke into the air as he barreled towards Howard and reached for the door.

"James?" Howard asked. "How did it go? What did they say—"

"—Get the fuck out my way, Ross. I'm gonna kill some prick, I swear to God."

Howard didn't have time to stop him. If he'd have stayed in James' path, he probably would have received a punch in the face.

One of the customers in line watched on with concern. "My God. What happened to him to make him so angry?"

James brushed past Howard and held his hand out to the door.

"*Bastards!*"

He disappeared into the dark, dank bowels of the bank and kicked the door shut, leaving a thoroughly perplexed Howard to return to his office.

Chapter 3

"Bastards."

Whump.

Ram burst through the back door and into the corridor, ready to blow away anyone who stood in his path.

He kept an ear out for the conversation taking place between Rabbit and Badger on his wristwatch.

"Goddamn disease-spreadin' moron," he muttered as he reached the empty storage room.

Badger's pathetic whimpers echoed down the dirty walls, forcing Ram to take a few steps back and aim at the lock on the security unit on the wall.

Rabbit's voice waded out from the speaker on Ram's wristwatch.

"Where's Price?"

"Three... two... one..." Ram whispered, just as Badger's apologetic response drifted into his ears. *"He's dead."*

Ram yanked on the trigger and shot the lock off the security unit. The two doors flung open, crashed against the wall, and slammed back together.

Ram screamed over the alarms as he reloaded and took aim at the colorful lights on the electric box nestled inside. "Shut the hell up."

He fired another shot and blew the box apart. The mechanics inside whirred to a halt as the smoldering cavity coughed out a flurry of sparks, shutting off the alarm.

And the lights.

And any semblance of power running to the building.

"Wh-what was that noise?"

Ram kicked the doors shut and bounded down the corridor. "Badger?"

"Yeah? Is that you, Ram?"

"Yup."

"Did you knock the power out?"

"Hell yeah. Get out here, and come back into the bank with me, dickhead."

Badger walked around the corner and into Ram's path. "It wasn't my fault."

Suspicious, Ram eyeballed his associate's bloodied collar.

"What wasn't your fault?"

"The security alarm," Badger pleaded, close to passing out. "Oh, shit-shit-shit. *Shitsticks.* We're so screwed. What happened to the alarm?"

Ram bounced his shotgun in his right arm, looking quite the mercenary as he nodded at the busted electricity box. "I took care of it. We need to get out front and regroup."

Just then, Rabbit's voice blew out from both their wristwatches.

"For Christ's sake, you pair of imbeciles. Where are you?"

Ram shoved Badger down the corridor and spoke into his wristwatch. "We're coming."

Rabbit was close to losing his shit out in the banking area. Dog didn't know how to react, and didn't dare try to placate his colleague's fragile temperament.

The three teller girls, headed by Kate, kept their arms up in front of the counter.

Rabbit paced back and forth, keeping his face down at the floor. Several desks and chairs got in his way as he tried to consider their next course of action.

"Ugh, this is no good for pacing."

Dog chanced a question, all the while keeping his gun pointed at the conference room. "Rabbit?"

"What is it? Can't you see I'm trying to think, here?"

"When the vault alarm went off? The place is gonna be swarming with cops any second."

"He's right," Kate said.

"No, no," Rabbit thought aloud. "It wasn't continuous. It needs to ring for fifty seconds before the cops are alerted."

Dog breathed a sigh of relief. "Thank God. I thought we were in trouble for a second."

The back door flung open and vomited a thoroughly beat-upon and bloodied Badger, who stumbled forward and nearly tripped over Joanne's corpse.

"Whoa."

Ram followed behind and booted Badger into the banking area. "Get the fuck in there."

"Stop kicking me."

The sight of a Ram verbally abusing a Badger with his high-pitched drawl provided a bizarre sight to everyone who saw it, including Dog and Rabbit.

"Ram?"

"Yeah?"

Rabbit rolled his shoulders, snatched his shotgun with his right hand, and used it to gesticulate. "You took care of the alarm, right?"

"Sure did," he said. "Gave it a bit of the old pump-action. Beat the shit out of it like a red-headed stepchild."

"So, we're cool?"

Badger picked himself up from the floor and fumbled his Uzi with his shaking hands, causing Rabbit to launch into a tirade.

"Be careful with that. You'll blow your balls off if you're not careful."

"Sorry, Rabbit."

"I'm guessing Price isn't exactly *right*, anymore?"

"Uh, no."

"No, he is? Or, no, he isn't?"

"What?"

Rabbit shooed the Badger away and scoffed. "He's dead. So, what happened?

"I, uh, accidentally shot him."

"You accidentally shot him?"

"Uh, yes."

Kate inhaled and bit her lip, furious at the situation. A series of astonished sobs waded out from the conference room.

"How do you accidentally shoot the bank manager, you dumb ass?"

"I dunno, I just—my finger slipped, and the bullets came out and hit him in the head."

The severity of the news had hit home, and cast a dangerous and morbid shadow across the proceedings, which tested Rabbit's patience.

"Oh, fan-fuckin'-tastic. So now the power's down, we can't get in the vault, and we got *two* dead bastards to deal with? For fuck's sake."

Rabbit booted the teller counter with his heel so hard, it nearly pushed his shinbone up into his hip. "Oww."

"I'm sorry."

Rabbit stormed over to Badger and threatened to blow his mask off, and whatever lay underneath.

"If it wasn't for Ram shutting down the fucking power, we'd all be fucked, you trigger-happy moron."

"He knew it was me," Badger begged. "Price, he recognized me, and deliberately pressed the wrong number. But I didn't mean to shoot him—"

"—Yeah, right," Ram snorted and checked his wristwatch. "Rabbit?"

"What is it now you, annoying cock ring?"

"It's eleven forty-five. We were meant to be out three minutes ago, and SecuriCore are about to rock up in here any second."

Rabbit ran over to the front windows and scanned the road beyond the covered entry. "Oh, shit."

"We're meant to be halfway up the freeway with the money by now. We don't have nearly enough of what we came for."

Rabbit's eyes relaxed as the passing cars on the main road seemed to blur into one, giant image of absolute failure.

"We need to get in the vault."

"SecuriCore are turning up to take what's inside," Dog snapped. "Do we stay, or what? We should go. Fuck this, we gotta get outta here."

"Without the main score?" Badger asked. "I gotta say, I'm with Dog, you know. We got enough from the registers and the—"

"—Shut the hell up," Rabbit said. "I can't hear myself *hear myself.*"

Dog, Ram, and Badger heaved with excitement as they awaited their colleague's response.

"Ram?"

"Yeah, Rabbit?"

"How long was the alarm on for?"

"Thirty seconds, we're cool."

"Are you sure we're cool?"

"Yeah," Ram explained. "We'd have had a phone call by now, asking if everything was—"

Ring-ring.

The bright pink desk phone on the personal lending desk bounced up and down like an excited child, demanding to be answered.

Ram, Dog, Badger, and Rabbit turned, slowly, to the phone.

"Shit."

Kate clapped her hands together and jumped for joy, realizing that an abrupt end might be on the cards. Fortunately for her, nobody but her two colleagues saw her quiet merriment.

Rabbit knew the desk and the phone well. He'd spent the better part of twenty-five years working at the very desk it sat on.

Ring-ring.

"You gonna answer that?" Ram asked.

Rabbit snatched the handset and lifted it to his ear. "Hello?" he said, before realizing his voice was modulated.

"Who's this?"

Rabbit had to drop his vocal pitch down to his gut to remodulate his voice to that of someone who *didn't* sound like they were holding up the bank or about to snatch a made-up name out of thin air.

"Yes, this is Mr., uh—Jeremiah Glenden... *jin... well.* Everything's okay here at the bank, thanks for asking."

"We had a raised alarm report from your location. Chrome Valley Police wants a verification that this wasn't an accident."

"Oh, I can assure you it was. My, uh, knee knocked the button under the table. By accident."

A pause befell the phone call, forcing Rabbit to grip his collar and release some of the intense heat that had built up around his chest and neck.

"Thank you for letting us know, Mr. Glendenjinwell. Have a nice day."

"Yes, you too."

The line went dead, and Rabbit slammed the handset back onto the cradle. He turned to Badger and sneered.

"I blame *you* for this."

"Sorry."

"I blame you a lot."

Rabbit took a deep breath and surveyed the ocean of terrified hostage eyes looking back at him.

"What the fuck are you pricks looking at?"

Inconsolable, each of them turned away and looked at the walls, leaving a thoroughly annoyed Kate making evil eyes at the man in the rubber rabbit mask.

"The fuck are you looking at?"

Kate launched into sarcasm mode and stood her ground. "I'm not sure, actually. Either a bunch of idiots who don't know their elbows from their nutsacks, or a fistful of reasonably intelligent men buckling at the knees when things don't go according to plan."

Rabbit pumped his shotgun and aimed it at her face. "Say that again, bitch?"

"You're nothing but no-good, violent creatures, to a man."

Rabbit admired the woman's tenacity to the point where he decided he couldn't shoot her. He lowered the gun and defended himself and his team. "Violent?"

"Uh-huh."

"Do we look like fucking animals, to you?"

Karen eyed Rabbit, Ram, Dog, and Badger, and tried not to laugh.

"Uh, yes."

"Fuck you."

Dog stepped forward and pointed at his wristwatch. "Never mind her, man. What are we gonna do, Rabbit? SecuriCore are gonna roll up any minute."

Rabbit sighed and butted the pink phone across the desk with his palm. "Right. Now that the pigs are back in their troughs, I figure we have two options."

"Which are?" Ram asked.

"One, we get the hell out of here with what we got, which isn't nearly enough. Or, two, we stay, let SecuriCore in, let them do their thing, get in the vault, and then encourage them to hand over the fucking money, and then run."

Badger punched the air with excitement. "I'm all for option two."

Ram nodded. "I second that emotion. I'm not leaving here with chump change from some grandma's checking account."

Dog didn't look so sure. He pointed at the corpse with the red spectacles resting at a silly angle against the blood-splattered wall.

"We need to clean that up."

"Ram?" Rabbit asked. "Go clear that fat lump of useless meat away and tuck her behind the counter. Badger?"

"Yeah?"

"Where, exactly, is Price?"

"Oh, he's at the vault."

"Okay, so—"

"—*Most* of him, at any rate."

"I'm gonna regret asking this next question, but is it much of a clean-up operation?" Rabbit asked. "Because we don't wanna spook SecuriCore when they get in."

"I'll need a wet sponge, and another pair of hands."

"That bad, huh?"

Badger nodded, solemnly. "Yeah, that Uzi doesn't mess around."

Dog slammed the conference room window, which provided a terrific view of Lombardy street. Two white-and-green armored security vans loomed in the distance.

"Shit, shit, shit."

He turned around, hopped over the table, and ran into the banking area.

"They're here."

"Who?"

"The fucking tooth fairy twins," Dog snapped. "Who do you think? SecuriCore. They're pulling up outside.

Rabbit shook his head and caught a glimpse of the approaching armored vehicles. "Dog, you're on prick watch with these lunatics. Badger?"

"Yeah?"

Rabbit ran past Ram as he pulled on Joanne's legs and dragged her body away from the wall.

"You and Ram, when he's finished hiding the body, go wait at the vault, and surprise our guests. Make sure they open the vault and let you in. Are your bags empty?"

Ram wiped his hands off on Joanne's dress and made his way to the back door. "Ready to rock and roll. Badger?"

"Come on."

"Oh," Rabbit hollered after his two colleagues. "Plus, we'll need to radio in to Squirrel and Cat. Tell them we're gonna be a few minutes late."

Ram yelled over his shoulder as he pushed through the back door. "I'm on it."

Somewhat relieved, Rabbit took a moment to think, and then performed a double take of immense proportions. "Shit. Where's the fucking security guard?"

Dog's hurried voice exploded from within the conference room. "Rabbit, they're here. They've parked up. Two approaching the entrance."

"I know there's two of them. There's always two of them."

"You better hurry, man, they're carrying the deposit cases and they're nearly on us."

"Shit," Rabbit said. "Dog, close the fucking blinds. The last thing we need is for those two underpaid jobsworths seeing a bunch of terrified bank clerks and customers all huddled together."

Dog snatched the cord hanging from the ceiling and twisted it around. "On it."

The striped blinds twisted to the left, providing a brief prison-bar effect, before closing shut and cutting-off the view from the street.

"ETA forty-five seconds. Maybe less."

Rabbit stormed over to the security guard and sized him up. "You. Get over here."

Terrified, the guard raised his arms and went to beg for mercy. "Please—"

"—Aww, shut the fuck up and listen," Rabbit said and cast his eyes down to the man's name badge: *R. Richardson*. "R?"

"Uh, yes?"

"What does R stand for?"

"R-Richardson."

"Richardson Richardson?" Rabbit asked, knowing that he was probably wrong. "Isn't that a bit of a stupid name?"

"What? N-No. My first name is Richard."

"Richard Richardson, then?"

"Yes. Richard Richardson."

Rabbit examined the terrified man standing before him. "Were your parents always this creative?"

"Eh?"

Rabbit reached into Richard's holster and retrieved his gun. "Forget it, you're obviously as interesting as your fucking name."

"I'm sorry, I d-don't know what you're—"

"—So, *Richardson*," Rabbit said, ignoring the man's puzzlement. "You're new here aren't you? Never seen you before."

A quick inspection of the man's pistol was all it took to satisfy Rabbit, just as two shadows formed up the graveled entrance area.

"Yes, I started two days ago, transferred in from Chrome Valley Federal, East."

Kate whispered to her friend as the two men exchanged information. "Karen?"

The second teller whispered back. "Yeah?"

"Why did he say the guard was new here? How could he possibly have known that?"

"I dunno—"

"—Goddamn it," Rabbit snapped. "Would you two women stop speaking for two bastard seconds? I'm trying to enact a fucking heist, here."

Kate lifted her arms and acted as if she hadn't been talking to anyone, as did Karen.

"Sorry," they said in tandem.

"This isn't a negro spiritual."

"Sorry."

"Don't say you're sorry. Just stop fucking speaking."

Rabbit turned back to Richard and patted him on the back. "So you don't know the two guys at SecuriCore yet, do you Richard?"

"No, sir."

"They're about to come in. They want to relieve the vault of its contents. We would've gotten there first, only I'm working with a bunch of fucking retards. Just my luck."

"Oh."

"Yeah, it's amazing how similar it is to my *previous* job."

Richard didn't know how to react, and just squinted at his harried, big-eared oppressor, who was only to quick to continue his instructions.

"So, anyway. Richard. They're gonna ask you how your day is going. And you're going to tell them *pretty good, and you?* Okay?"

"Uh, okay."

"What is it you need to say?"

"I'm, uh, pretty good, and you?"

"Exactly," Rabbit said. "You have to phrase it exactly that way. They're looking for a verbal code from security detail that everything is fine, and you have to say it like that."

"Yes, sir."

"If you deviate or get it wrong, they'll get spooked, and I'm going to blame you if that happens. Do you understand?"

Dog and Rabbit kept a stern eye on Richard's face, and threatened to blow it off his head if he so much as looked in the wrong direction.

"Answer him, dick-face," Dog said.

"Shut up," Rabbit shouted back. "Don't make our new girlfriend nervous, otherwise he'll turn in a cable-channel performance and get us all busted."

Rabbit tilted his head and squinted, ready to blow the man's head off if he got the answer to his next question wrong.

"Right. What do you say?"

Richard felt his kneecaps turn to milkshake. "I say *pretty good, and you?*"

"Good. You're a fast learner, Richard. You'll go far. When the Siamese SecuriCore twins get in, you keep *behind* them as they make their way to the back door, and over to the vault."

"Yeah," Dog said. "The fuckers are attached at the hip, and their cases are cuffed to their hands. They're inseparable, both from their cases, and each other."

"Okay."

Rabbit adjusted Richard's collar for him. "Do you understand? Do *not* walk in front of them."

"Yes."

Rabbit tapped Richard on the back, and turned to face the back door. Both men nearly jumped in their shoes when they saw the blood-splattered wall.

"Oh, fuck—*Dog?*"

"What? They're right at the fucking door, man?"

"Cover that wall. It's got blood all over it. Quick."

Dog lowered his gun and raced over to the far wall, as Rabbit shoved Richard towards the locked bank entrance.

"Girls, get in the conference room and take a seat. Dog and I will be joining you, so leave the door open."

Richard paced, slowly, across the carpeted floor and kept a stern eye on the brightly-lit covered entrance.

He and Rabbit knew that the windows were tempered, bulletproof, and tinted. Those outside couldn't see in.

Rabbit leaned into Richard's ear. "You got a family, Richardson?"

"Uh, y-yes, I d-do."

"Their lives depend on your performance right now. If you fuck up, or it looks like you've fucked up, or I just outright *believe*, even misguidedly, that you've fucked up, then I'm going to kill everyone in this fucking building. And when I've done that, I'm gonna visit your family's home, and guess what?"

Richard's bottom lip quivered with fear.

"I'm gonna kill all of them, too. You understand me?"

"Y-Yes, s-sir."

The two SecuriCore officials reached the door with a giant case in each hand. Both men wore visors, and made sure those on the street saw the machine guns on their hips.

Rabbit and Richard slowed to a halt by the door.

"Nasty-looking bastards, aren't they?"

"Y-yes, sir."

"And it'll all be your fault if everybody dies, okay? All on your conscience. Could you live with that? Could you live with yourself, when you acted the fucking hero at the last fucking moment, and then fucked everything up. All that blood on your hands? You blue collar prick?"

"No, s-sir."

"And stop calling me sir."

"Yes, sir—uh. Yes."

"Fucking ignoramus," Rabbit muttered, and turned to see Dog move a large executive chair from the manager's office and roll it in front of the blood-stained wall.

"Done, Rabbit," Dog barked. "Get in the conference room."

"Okay, gimme a minute."

Bzzzzzz.

The first SecuriCore official hit the buzzer and waited with a fierce patience for an answer.

Rabbit smiled, counting the untold amount of wealth that was coming to him in a matter of moments from now.

"Richard?"

"Yes?"

"If they ask where everyone is, tell them we've just had a fire drill, and they're out back. Just a matter of bad timing."

"Yes, sir."

"It's show time. Break a leg. Or I'll snap both of yours off and beat you to death with them like an epileptic drummer on bath salts. Okay?"

"Okay."

Richard felt the pressure being applied to his shoulder lift away. A quick check to the side, and Rabbit had quickly and surreptitiously disappeared into the conference room.

Bzzzzz.

Richard couldn't stop his hands from shaking as he lifted the key and inserted it into the lock. He swallowed hard and collected a bead of sweat from his brow.

"Shit, shit, shit..."

Click.

The doors bolted open, and the two security guards smiled. Their SecuriCore badges provided a blinding rebound of sunlight right into Richard's retinas.

"Hi," the first guard said. "Sorry, we're a few minutes early today. Are we set?"

Richard cleared his throat and scanned the first guard's badge. *A. Cole.* He lifted his head up and produced a pithy smile at the man.

"How is everything today, my friend?" Cole asked.

"Uh, pretty good. And you?"

Cole's colleague smiled. "Heh, not too bad, thanks. May we?"

"Oh. Sure."

Richard stepped aside and allowed the two men in. From the front, they looked like a pair of terminators, ready to kill.

From the back, their sheer size forced Richard to quake in his boots as he closed the door shut.

"Very quiet in here, today?"

Cole sniffed the air as he moved past the teller counters.

"Where is everyone?"

Richard raced up to the men and pointed at the door on the back wall. "We just had a fire drill. Everyone's out back. Bad timing, I guess."

"Or *good* timing, depending on how you view it?" Cole said, before throwing a wry nod at his colleague. "Huh, Milton? What you reckon?"

"Yeah, it's a bit too quiet in here. Everyone's out back, you say?"

"Yeah, just waiting for the all-clear," Richard said, hoping they'd buy his outright lie.

Cole produced a polite smile and peered over the teller counter to find all but one of the registers had been opened. "What the hell happened, here?"

Richard began to sweat and pulled at his collar. "Oh, the alarms. Must have been a glitch. I remember them saying they had trouble with the automated registers."

Richard closed his eyes and thought about what he'd said. He decided it made little sense, which made him sweat harder.

Milton pushed forward and gripped the microphone under his visor. "Cole, I'll check the back. Stay here."

"What?" Richard gasped. "Uh, no. Why don't we get to the vault before the place gets busy?"

Cole held out his hand and prevented Richard from moving. "It's okay, this is standard operating procedure. It won't take a moment."

Richard noticed a chain running from the man's wrist all the way to the carry case handle. He'd handcuffed himself to it.

Milton moved through the door and spoke into his microphone. "This is two-five at Federal West branch, do you read me?"

"Loud and clear, two-five," came the response. *"Please report for all-clear."*

"Will do."

Cole bopped Richard on the back and smiled. "We're all good. We just need to make sure the area is secure before unloading the…"

Rabbit peered through the crack in the conference room door. He kept one of his inordinately large rubber ears out for what was being said.

"…before unloading the vault," Cole said. "Nothing to worry about."

Frustrated, Rabbit muttered. "Shit, shit, shit. This is *not* good."

Dog perched his ass on the edge of the conference table and held his shotgun against his lap. "What's up?"

"They know something. They're spooked. One of them's gone to check—" he said, before rolling up his sleeve and speaking into his wristwatch. "Shit. Badger? Ram? This is Rabbit. Listen, if you *can* hear me, keep your voices down. Our new guests think something's up, and one of them is coming to—"

Kate's colleague, a brunette woman sporting a white blouse with a green butterfly brooch pinned to it, sobbed quietly in the corner.

"Hey, hey," Kate said. "It's okay. We'll be fine once they have what they want."

Rabbit slammed his knee against the table and whispered at the two girls. "*You*. Kate?"

"What?" she snapped, angrily.

"Shut your friend up. We're not gonna shoot anyone if they play ball."

Kate didn't buy any of Rabbit's lies. "Yeah? Try telling that to Joanne, out there."

The half-dozen hostages shuffled with anxiety, pushing Rabbit further down a hole of agitation.

"Everyone shut up," Rabbit said. "We'll be out of here in three minutes, flat. After that the rest of your life is your own."

"Woof, woof," Dog added.

Unamused, Rabbit turned to Dog and threw a disapproving shake of the head his way. "Don't be funny."

"Sorry."

Worried at the lack of confirmation, Rabbit returned to his wristwatch. "Ram? Badger? Can you hear me?"

***

Ram crouched behind the water cooler in the storage area. He leaned forward for a better view of the corridor, and the storage vault door to his right.

His left horn bounced off the empty water bottle, causing him to lower his shotgun.

Bop.

"Ugh, shit. These fucking horns."

Badger looked up from behind the battered filing cabinet and readied himself to open fire with his Uzi. "What?"

"Knocked my mask."

Badger shook his head and pointed at the vault door. "Keep quiet and answer that, would you?"

"Ram? Badger? Can you hear me?"

Ram looked at his watch and swallowed. "Ugh. Yeah, Rabbit. We're at the vault. We can hear you."

"Listen, the SecuriCocks are in, but they're a bit spooked. One of them is on their way to the back room. They think everyone is out back on a fire drill."

"What?"

"Get ready, he's about to—"

Whump.

Ram jumped back and covered his wrist as the door to the back area flung open. "Shit."

Clomp.

His shotgun hit the floor by his foot, just as Badger stepped back behind the filing cabinet. "Get ready," he whispered.

Milton turned to the left to find an empty lunchroom. A bunch of tables and chairs, and a half-eaten sandwich that had seen better days greeted him from the floor.

"All good here. Checking the back parking lot and vault, then we're good to go," he said into his mouthpiece.

Satisfied that all was well, Milton turned around one-hundred-and-eighty-degrees and made his way down the corridor.

He spotted the door at the end, and the immediate turning to the left. "Checking the staircase to the underground."

"Understood, Two-Five. Please report for clearance."

"Yeah, give me two shakes of a crying baby."

Badger squeezed his eyes shut and straightened his back as Milton strode past him. "Fuck."

Ram, meanwhile, felt his trigger finger dance around the end of his hand. Milton's legs walked right past his face and off into the distance.

Ram and Badger peered forward, exchanged glances, and waved their weapons at each other. The former lifted the front of his mask up and over his head.

James Gilmour's face had perspired so heavily that his shirt collar dampened into a murky gray fusion of body odor and regret. His red tie had darkened a few shades due to the perspiration dripping from his neck.

He wiped his eyes with his shirt sleeve and mouthed "wait" at Badger, who shrugged and pointed at his Uzi.

Milton slowed down as he approached the back door, to the right of the drive-through area.

James mouthed back, shook his head, and mimed cutting his own throat. "No, no, no. Wait. *Wait.*"

Badger nodded and stepped back behind the cabinet. He slid the safety catch off on his Uzi and held his breath.

Whump.

A burst of fresh air blasted Milton's visor as he stepped into the back parking lot, leaving his shoulders and ass exposed to the corridor inside.

Nobody was around, and the parking lot was barren.

"Huh? Something's not right, here."

When he turned right, he saw the trunk of a silver Chevrolet parked by the wall.

"What the hell?"

Squirrel leaned over the steering wheel in the Chevrolet and stared into the rear view mirror. "Huh? Oh, shit."

He scrambled to grab his sleeve and pulled it up his left arm. "Fuck, fuck. Rabbit? Rabbit, this is Squirrel. What the—"

"—Squirrel, shit, I forgot you were parked there. Listen, there's—"

"—There's a motherfuckin' SecuriCore dude checking the parking lot. He's seen the car."

"Has he seen you, though?"

"No, man. I'm outta sight," Squirrel whispered. "The back rest is covering me. Shit, they better not mosey on over here or he'll see my stupid fluffy ears."

"Squirrel. Listen, stay still. He thinks there's been a fire alarm and—ugh. Damn it."

Squirrel placed his hand on the passenger seat and teased the butt of his Uzi with his index finger. "You want me to take care of a motherfucker?"

"God, no. No, stay there. Keep comms open. He'll probably walk back into the building. I dunno what he's gonna do when he finds there's nobody out back and the fire drill was just a bunch of bullshit."

Chapter 4

LINCOLN MUMFORD
— Monday, September 28th —

Howard, Ben, James, and Lincoln sat in a booth overlooking the district with a forlorn look on their faces.

The Bean There, Done That coffee shop in Chrome Valley's financial district was never busy at 4:30 pm in the afternoon.

But today wasn't any ordinary day.

The four men had been laid off by Ironside and Capone within the space of an hour, one after the other, right after lunch, and weren't too happy about it.

Tick... tick... tick.

The wall clock above the service counter snapped to 4:30 pm, just as Howard began to speak.

"Shit. We've spent our lives working for these bloodsuckers. And I'll be fucked if I go crawling to anyone begging for a job."

Lincoln licked his lips as he watched a young boy playing with his new toy gun on the adjacent table. His mother didn't try to stop him, and continued her conversation with her friend.

"Must be a birthday party," Lincoln said.

"Huh?"

"That kid, man. All that gift wrapping paper all over the table. Look."

Howard eyed the realistic-looking gun in the boy's hand as he swished it around and pretended to fire it at the ceiling.

Ben looked up from his copy of the Chrome Valley Chronicle back pages. "You okay, Howard?"

"No."

Ben chucked the paper aside. "Useless. Absolutely useless. There's nothing out there."

Howard buried his head in his hands and groaned. "And at my age? The scrapheap."

Lincoln shook his head. "Nah. I'm taking my severance check and taking my family the hell outta this godforsaken valley. Gonna set up a new business out in Devotion with a buddy of mine."

Howard glanced at the kid with the gun and felt a light bulb ping above his head as Lincoln droned on about his new plans.

"Ugh," he said. "I'd even risk twenty-five-to-life so I don't have to go back to the nine-to-five."

James fiddled with his coffee cup and raised his eyes. "You what?"

"We could rip the joint off," Howard said. "We're in, we know everything, and we're out. Take it all. Nobody moves, nobody gets hurt. We're rich in ten minutes flat."

Ben didn't seem so sure. "Did you see on the list they had? Amos' name was on it."

"Yeah, I saw that, too," Howard said. "I dunno if he knows, or not."

James was close to passing out on his chair. "Oh, who gives a fuck about Amos. This sucks."

Lincoln, on the other hand, turned to the service area and smiled at Debra, their waitress, who blew him a flirtatious kiss back as she wiped the counter down.

"*Daaaaamn*," Lincoln whispered. "That is *one* hot piece of ass right there."

"As opposed to *two* hot pieces of ass?" Ben joked.

James frowned at the lack of sexual attention. "Ugh. Debra's probably a *dude*, anyhow. All the hot chicks are these days."

"Shit. With a pair of buns like that? I don't give a shit if she is a dude, man. I'd still smash it all the way to Saturn and back."

Howard ignored the immature bounce-back between the pair, and glanced at the faces around the table.

"Are any of you in?" he asked.

Lincoln turned back to the table and pretended that he hadn't heard what Howard had suggested. "Say again?"

"I asked, are you in?"

"What? Robbing our own bank, man? Are you serious?"

"Deadly," Howard said. "And it isn't *our* bank, anyway. Hell, it never was our bank. But it *is* our turn to teach the bastards a lesson."

Lincoln examined the brown skid marks inside his coffee cup. "I dunno, Howard, man. Shit's messed up as it is. We only just got our *'fuck you'* from the bank, and now you're talking about ripping the place off?"

Ben needed persuading, but wasn't hating the idea. "Howard, I get you're angry, but we're just a bunch of white collar workers. What the hell do we know about holding up a bank?"

James groaned and folded his arms in an attempt to fight off the inexorable migraine headed his way.

"Ah, you know what? Fuck 'em. I mean, really, fuck 'em in the ass. Count me in, Howard."

The longer Lincoln thought over the opportunity, the more it made sense to him. "Yeah, yeah. I can see how we can do this."

Surprised, Howard turned to the man and tested his seriousness. "You do?"

"Uh-huh," Lincoln said. "The drive-through, man. If you're serious about this?"

Howard let out a yelp of excitement. "Of course, I'm deadly serious about—"

"—Whoa, whoa," Ben interjected, quietly, and leaned forward so nobody could eavesdrop. "You're *not* taking this seriously, are you? This is a felony we're talking about. You think you can't find employment *now*? Wait until you have a record, and see how tough it is, then. Howard, man, see sense. How many low-lives have you had trying to get a loan with a criminal record?"

"Hundreds," Howard said. "If not more."

"And they're cock-blocked before they've even sat on the chair, right?"

"They never even make it into the office."

Ben was about to launch into a tirade, and then changed tact. "I, uh—Look, I can't afford to do something like this. Brianna and me have got a baby on the way, and there's no way on Earth it's growing up without its father, man."

James grinned and tapped the table. "Oh, yeah. That hot wife of yours? I'm sure there'll be plenty of Johns lining up to take care of her when your skinny ass is behind bars."

"Hardy-fuckin'-har," Ben snapped. "Look, we're fresh outta having our asses handed to us, *and* fresh outta luck. Okay? No more bank job talk."

Lincoln decided right there and then that Howard's plan was worth considering. "Yeah, *and* fresh outta money to pay bills and feed ourselves and our kids, man. Fuck it. I'm in."

"Good man," Howard said.

The table fell silent once again, leaving Ben all on his own.

"Besides, Cherry?" Lincoln asked.

"What?"

"You gotta join in with us, now. You know too much."

"What the hell are you talking about, Mumford? Did *Ironclad and Crap-Own* smash you upside the head with their file, as well?"

"Man, fuck those two five-dollar-suited bald pricks," Lincoln snorted. "It's just that, if we do this thing, and it goes south for whatever reason, then—well, you know what I'm saying, yeah, Ben? If you ain't on the job now, you're still gonna know it was us who did it. You know *something*, and we can't have a chicken shit motherfucker who bailed out knowing our business."

James rapped the table with his knuckles and smirked. "Mumford's right, Benjy-boy. You gotta get in with this gig, now. You can't *not* do it. You can't *unhear* what you just heard, or pretend that you didn't hear it, because we *know* you heard it."

"What?"

"You can't *not* know what you now know," Howard said. "You know."

Ben wasn't sure if his soon-to-be-former bank colleagues were joking or deadly serious. "You're kidding? You can't *force* me to take part in all this."

Howard squinted at Ben and tried to talk him round.

"Cherry? That severance check is gonna run out before you even cash it. I don't care how much it is, but it's not enough. So, Brianna farts out your kid next month, and it starts screaming for food and shitting all over the place, demanding stuff. Believe me, I've been there. Before you know it, you're stacking shelves at *The Y* for less than minimum wage, cursing the day you said *no* to this gig."

Ben's mouth shimmied to the right just as he hung his head, barely able to fight back. "Shut up."

Howard continued his merciless dismantling of Ben's psyche. "And then what, Benjy? You think that pretty little broad of yours is gonna stick around in that apartment with you when you don't have a pot to piss in, or a window to throw it out? For every good-looking, single white-collar guy out there, there's a girl tired of fucking him, especially if he's about to be as broke as a bum."

"Amen. You best believe that."

Lincoln bumped his fist against Howard's hand, further sealing their bond over the proposed plan.

"Or, how about this, Benjy?" Howard continued. "You take ten or fifteen minutes out of just one morning working with friends you know pretty damn well. People you can trust. You'll walk away with *at least* six figures in your pocket. There's gotta be at least eight million in the vault on a Wednesday morning, which we'd split four ways. Set for life. Well, set for a life of someone who won't blow their slice of the score on hookers and blow, anyway."

James' ears pricked up at the inference. "What do you mean by that?"

"Nothing."

"I'm not gonna blow my take on hookers and blow, Howard. I know what you think of me, and you got it all wrong. Take that back."

"Okay, I take it back."

James leaned back and sighed. "Lousy bastard."

Howard turned from James to Ben. "So? How does a modest, comfortable life sound? As of the end of the next week."

Ben ran his hand through his hair and groaned. "Ugghhh, for *fuck's* sake."

"Listen to Howard, man," Lincoln said to Ben. "It's safe and simple—"

"—And we know the place inside-out," James finished and laughed. "*Dayum*, Howard, you're one helluva convincing asshole when you need to be. Shit, look at little Benjy's face. All red and sweaty like he's about to cave and fall in line."

Ben slammed the table in frustration and heaved. "*Okay, okay*, shut up. Just… friggin' shut the hell up for a second and let me think."

The three men smiled at Ben as he over-dramatized his dilemma and ran his hands up his face. "Okay, fuck it. Whatever. I'm in."

"Good."

"But this better be safe, and it better be quick, and I can promise you right now that if I get caught, I'm gonna sing like a coked-up canary and bring you fuckers down with me."

Howard produced a smile longer than the booth they were sitting in. "That's the spirit, Benjy. It won't come to that."

"And *quit* calling me Benjy, Howard. I'm not a goddamn dog."

***

Howard, James, Ben, and Lincoln, sprinted across Lombardy Road and down the ramp that led to the Federal Bank's underground parking lot.

Ben looked up and admired the glass-walled skyscrapers looming around him like giant, angry swords. "You know, it never fails to amaze me."

"What never fails to amaze you?"

"Just how *big* the district is. Been working here for years, and never really took the time to look around. All these buildings look like giant, shiny, silver dicks. They're so *big*."

James bopped the young man on the back and ran down the ramp. "Yeah, I bet you hear that a lot from your wife, huh?"

"Eh?" Ben asked. "That doesn't even work."

Lincoln reached his white Ford Escort and hit the button on his car key.

Biddip-bip.

"Humor ain't exactly Gilmour's strong point, Benjamin," Lincoln said. "What he doesn't have in jokes he more than makes up for when it comes to looking like Elvis."

James startled echo rumbled down the ramp after Lincoln. "What?"

"C'mon, fellas. I'll give y'all a ride home."

"Shouldn't we head back to the bank?" Ben asked.

Howard produced an evil grin, feeling freer than he'd ever done in his entire adult life. "Ha. Ah, screw the bank. What are they gonna do if we clock off early, anyhow? Fire us?"

All four men burst out laughing as they climbed into Lincoln's white Ford Escort.

"Get in, fellas."

Howard sat up front.

Ben and James fastened their seat belts in the back, and Lincoln drove up the ramp, and onto the road.

Vrooom.

The Ford Escort flew off the end of the ramp, screeching its tires as it turned into Lombardy Street. Everyone held onto something solid as the interior of the car swerved around.

Lincoln stepped on the gas and gripped the steering wheel. "Yeah, I just got this baby fixed. All souped up and ready for some action, man."

"I saw your post on *Bleater*," Ben said. "The comments you got were vicious, man."

James looked out of the passenger window as the car turned into the next road; Madhoff Avenue.

"Oh, yeah? I dunno why you guys always post your lives on that stupid *Bleater* app for the world to see. As far as I'm concerned, my life is my life, and nobody else's business."

Howard sniggered and eyed James in the rear view mirror, "Yeah, and it's *not* because you're technologically retarded, right?"

James focused on the giant, window-covered storage building in the distance. "Shut up, Ross. At my unemployable age, all my old ass needs to know is how to access PornCabin and get alcohol and blow delivered to my front door. I'm happy enough with that. Besides, I don't wanna say something on Bleater that'll get me in trouble ten years from now."

"Like what?"

"Oh, I dunno," James said. "Some bullshit about transgendered men, or whatever. Or a funny joke about Jews. You remember what happened to Anton Barber last year?"

"Yeah, Barber," Howard said. "Took unpaid leave."

"No, he didn't. Price took Barber's skinny ass aside and fired him. Apparently, he spent all night going through his *Bleats*, and found a joke about some Jew broad Barber *Bleated* eight years ago, and let him go."

Shocked, Howard looked over his shoulder to find a deadly serious look on his friend's face. "Really? Because of a *Bleat* he wrote eight years ago?"

"Yeah. The joke wasn't even all that funny."

Ben stared through the window and watched the scenery roll by. "Anton was a prick. I never liked him, anyway."

Just then, a thought entered Ben's mind which made him nudge James on the shoulder.

"Anyhow, you guys shoulda seen what happened when Mumford posted a pic of this car all fucked up."

James turned away from the view behind the window and sighed. "Okay, I'll bite. What happened?"

"Nearly had the cops roll up on my black ass, that's what," Lincoln said. "So, I was driving on the freeway talking to my wife on my cell, and I passed Exit 11A, and I lost my concentration for a minute, I drove off into the grass and crashed into a telephone pole. Fucked my hood up good."

James shook his head. "So? That's your fault for being on your cell, you daft twat."

"Whatever. So I got on *Bleater* to see if anyone could help."

Howard knew the story and how funny it was, but did his best to conceal the punchline. "Tell him what you wrote."

"Shit," Lincoln tutted. "So, I wrote *Yo, I just fucked a white fourteen year-old escort,* and, like, two minutes later, people were *re-bleating* what I wrote to everyone, and more motherfuckers saw it, and bleated me back like, *Yo, Mumford? What the fuck, gee? Not cool, bruh.*"

"Shit," Ben giggled. "That's messed up."

"So, after about five minutes, I was like *Fuck! Nah, bruh, that ain't what I meant* and I uploaded the photo of my busted-ass ride to prove to everyone I wasn't some kinda fuckin' Chimo."

Ben leaned forward with a confused look on his face. "What's a chimo?"

"Fuckin' *child molester*, man," Lincoln said. "Two words put together. The beaners use it."

"A *portmanteau*, I think you'll find," Howard offered as he stared at the road ahead. "And speaking of Exit 11A, I think you'll find it's the next turn."

"Uh-huh, Ross," Lincoln said. "Always the brains with the big words, huh? *Portman Toe?* You mean like that actress Portman? I forget her first name."

"No, it's French for a compound word made of two-"

"—*Shit*," Lincoln chuckled at his new thought. "I'd love to get my hands on *blah-blah* Portman's *camel toe*, man."

"You mean the girl from that hitman movie?" Howard asked. "She's like twelve years old."

"Nah, man. I mean *now*. Portman's gotta be at least forty fuckin' years old by now."

"You *do* know Portman's a Jew, right?" James added.

"Nah, really?"

James smirked, and turned to his left. Ben had fallen asleep during the conversation, and was making a bizarre finger salute with his index finger and thumb.

Somewhat repulsed, James faced front. "I gotta hand it to you, Mumford, my indiscriminate black friend. Your Escort story is truly messed up."

"Yeah. What I *should* have wrote was *I think I've blown the gasket on my 2007 Ford*, or something. Damn. People I know, people close to me, thought I was confessing to some mad-ass Fogle-type shit. Either that or they thought my account got hacked."

"Yeah," James said. "As much as I'd love to stick around and take part in this intellectual feast, do you think you could drop me off at the casino? All this talk of camel toes, kiddie-fiddling, and Israel is making me want to lose some money."

Lincoln eyed the man in his rear view mirror. "Sure, man."

The Place With No Name
Nightclub and Casino
— *Kaleidoscope Shopping Mall* —

Screeeech.

Lincoln slammed on the brakes and parked his car right out front of the dingy-looking nightclub.

"Yo, Gilmour. We're here."

James unfastened his seatbelt and pushed the door open. "Thanks, man. So, you'll be in touch, right?"

Before anyone could answer, Ben opened his eyes and arose from his slumber like a startled puppy and kicked the back of Howard's seat.

"Agh! Huh? Where are w-we?"

Everyone turned to the back seat.

"Wakey-wakey-Benjy-Boy. You musta fallen asleep."

Howard leaned over Lincoln's lap and spoke to James through the driver's window. "Sure will. Keep your phone on, and your ears and your eyes open."

"I'll try."

"And try *not* to blow your final check tonight on that damn roulette table, okay? Take it easy."

James offered the men a polite salute, and stepped back onto the curb. "You got it."

Ben opened his door and stepped out, much to Howard and Lincoln's surprise.

"It's okay, guys. I'll walk from here."

"Are you sure?" Lincoln asked. "It's cool, I can bring you home, you're only around the corner?"

Ben looked at the gushing stone fountain at the entrance to the Kaleidoscope Shopping Mall. "Yeah, no. I, uh, need to pick something up for Brianna. Keep her sweet for when I give her the bad news."

Lincoln nodded with approval, "Yeah, that's not a bad idea, Cherry. I like that. Do you some good. Get you some air."

"Yeah."

He looked at Ben's shoes, and then up to his socks. "Yeah, give them Space Invaders a breather, too, huh?"

"Hardy-fuckin'-har," Ben scoffed, and slammed the door shut. "I'll talk to you tomorrow."

Howard watched the young man dart across the road and narrowly avoid an oncoming bus.

"Hey!"

"Benjamin Cherry," Howard muttered as he eyed the side mirror and watch his friend walk away. "Reminds me of me at that age."

Lincoln turned on the blinker and drove onto Main Street. "What? Young, dumb and full of cum?"

"Two out of three ain't bad," Howard said. "Although, the odd one out changes from hour to hour with Cherry, these days."

"Yeah, and with that piece of ass wife of his, who can blame him? No wonder she's about to drop."

"True."

Lincoln hit the gas and grinned, settling into a breezy speed along the road.

"So. Howard. We're definitely *on*, then?"

"Yeah, I think so," Howard said. "I dunno. What do you think?"

"What?"

"We *are* serious about this idea, right?" Howard asked, suddenly feeling his nerves spring to life. "I mean, back at the coffee shop, I was mostly speaking academically."

"Academically?" Lincoln asked. "What the hell does that mean? I was talking *unacademically*, if that's even a word. Shit, Howard. You spent all that time talking up the idea, and now you're telling me, and only me, you was just kidding the whole time?"

Howard winced as he ran his right hand over his upper, left arm. "No, I just, you know—"

"—No. Howard. I *don't* know. Tell me."

"Everything just kinda happened at once, and I was angry. Just getting it all off my chest, that's all."

"Yeah, well, as impressive as your man breasts are, you talked up a good game and managed to get everyone psyched about gettin' rich."

"I know, I know."

Lincoln steadied his foot on the accelerator and chose his words very carefully.

"Lookit, I don't have your kind of education, Howard, see? I ain't some college grad with brains comin' outta my ass, for real. I ain't up on this *should-I-shouldn't-I? bullshit*, you know? I'm the kinda oh-gee who thinks of a plan—"

"—Oh-gee?"

"Original gangster, man. For real."

"Oh. *Right*."

"Yeah," Lincoln said with an invigoration usually reserved for military warfare. "And when a muthafuckin' *oh-gee* hears of a damn good plan like yours, and commits there and then, he goes through with it. You feel me?"

Remorsefully, Howard nodded and realized the damage he'd done by suggesting a heist in the first place. For him, turning back would prove to be doubly difficult, given that it was his idea.

"Yeah, Lincoln. I *feel* you."

Lincoln gouged half a coffee bean from his teeth with his index finger and spat it into the foot well.

"Shit, Ross. Don't get all shy on me now. I'm just a lowly *'yes masser'* on two bills higher than minimum wage, man. A slave to the corporation. And they got the nerve to call me a supervisor, when all I really am is a caged-up *token*, as you put it."

"I didn't mean that," Howard said. "I was making a point about something else."

"Yeah, well, that's some affirmative action bullshit government box getting checked right there to prop up some rich uncle's nephew in a job that didn't need creating. Shit. All because a dumb-ass black kid from the projects who don't know no better was willing to work twice as hard as your average white boy because he don't got a fuckin' say in the matter."

Howard grabbed the handle above the door and gripped it in his hand "Ugh. Lincoln—"

"—I just want that motherfuckin' *paper*, Howie. We know how much Federal's holding on a goddamn Wednesday morning. That *right there* is when we oughtta strike."

"You think? Wednesday morning?"

"Yeah, right before SecuriCore turns up to collect—"

Lincoln checked his face in the rear view mirror and stopped talking when he noticed an angry pair of blue police lights in the distance.

"Aww, *shit.*"

"What?"

"Fuckin' five-oh, man," Lincoln whispered. "Goddamn blue-light, blue-collar pricks. Shit, let 'em pass. Face forward. Don't make eye contact."

Howard scanned the side mirror and saw the police car slow down a few feet behind the Escort.

"But we haven't done anything wrong?"

"Nah, man, *you* ain't done nuthin' wrong."

"I've done nothing wrong?" Howard snapped, and turned to Lincoln in horror. "Why, what have you done?"

"Made the mistake of being black in a nice ride, that's what."

Howard returned to the side mirror to find the cop car had vanished, and pull up right alongside him.

"Shit."

Lincoln focused his eyes on the red stop light and gritted his teeth. "Change. *Change.*"

The two male officers spied on the Escort chatted to each other.

Lincoln kept his eyes on the traffic light and spoke without moving his lips. "They onto us?"

Howard whispered and focused on own his lap. "No. Don't look."

Just then, the traffic lights snapped to green, and the cop car bolted into the distance, leaving Lincoln and Howard to exhale with relief.

"Goddamn racist pricks," Lincoln said. "Every damn time. It's always something."

"That's terrible, man."

"The only reason they never pulled me out of the car is because you're here with me, man."

Lincoln hit the gas and gripped the steering wheel.

"I'm telling you. I need a mask when I'm driving. I dunno, like those black ones with the holes for the eyes and the mouth."

"A balaclava?"

"Yeah, one of them. Hell, even a clown mask, or one of them rubber animal ones they sell down south at Marcovicci beach, you know?"

Yes, Howard knew about the masks Lincoln referred to and, no, it didn't help him feel bad for the man he considered a decent human being.

Burger Face Drive-Through
— Chrome Valley Industrial Estate —

Lincoln sat on the hood of his car with a strawberry milkshake in his hand.

He sucked on the straw and watched Howard pace back and forth with an empty burger wrapper in his hand.

"I dunno about this, you know. Outside parties. Are you *sure* he's cool?"

Lincoln released the straw from his lips and wiped his mouth.

"Sure I'm sure. He's more connected than *InstaBate*, man. He knows a guy, who knows a guy, who knows a guy."

"He knows guys?"

"Yup, he knows all the guys. Shit, a job like this? To him it's chicken feed. You want me to hit him up? See what's good?"

Howard stopped and looked at the five towers in the horizon, and the big, orange setting sun disappearing behind them.

"And you vouch for him, right?"

"Fuckin' A right I do. He's my boy," Lincoln said. "We need someone who knows what they're doing."

Lincoln reached into his pocket and pulled out his cell phone. He knew his friend was nervous about a stranger's involvement, but he knew the stranger he had in mind would prove to be integral to the success of the plan.

"Lookit, Howard. Danny's as solid gold as Amos' two front teeth, man."

Howard chewed his lip in a mire of potential outcomes. "I was kinda thinking it'd be, you know, just us four and a couple pistols and we're in and we're out?"

Lincoln hopped off the hood of his car and hit the dial button. "Let's hear him out, okay? We ain't stealing a box of candy, here. He's gonna know shit we ain't thought about, or planned for."

Howard's knees trembled as he watched Lincoln place his cell phone to his ear and listen to the call ring out.

"Oh, wait. Before he answers, don't tell him about me. Or James, or Ben. Keep it non-committal—"

"—Heeeeey, yo!" Lincoln chirped into his phone. "Danny *motherfuckin'* Driscoll, how's life on the outside, bruh?"

Howard never ceased to be amazed at how adept Lincoln Mumford was in talking to different types of people.

At the bank, he was courteous and well-mannered. When he spoke to his friends, or to anyone in a more informal setting, his true character sprung to life like an overexcited, schizophrenic Jekyll and Hyde .

"Uh-huh," Lincoln grinned. "Yo, listen up. *Bruh*. I, uh, got this 'ting going down, you know? Like, you probably wanna piece of it. I need to fly on down and run somethin' past you."

Howard folded his arms, not because it made him more comfortable, but because they were in danger of shaking like an out-of-control food blender.

Shit, as Howard knew most youths these days would say, *just got very real.*

Lincoln had established contact with someone unknown to him, and furthermore, the person on the other end of the phone didn't exactly come across as someone of questionable standing within polite society.

A person who was much further down the criminal rabbit hole than Howard was.

"What's he saying?"

"Man, hush."

Lincoln winked at Howard and gave an enthusiastic thumbs up.

"Okay, I'll call you."

Lincoln swiped the call off, and slipped the phone into his pocket.

"Well?"

"Well what?" Lincoln asked as if he hadn't just instigated the crime of the decade.

"What did he say?"

"It's cool, man. He wants us to meet him and his contact a few blocks away."

"When?"

"Tomorrow," Lincoln said.

Howard's lungs nearly burst. "*Tomorrow*?!"

"Yeah. What, you got another heist to attend to, man?" Lincoln joked.

"No. It just seems so soon, that's all."

Lincoln couldn't believe his supposedly intelligent friend's reaction. "How the fuck long do you think it takes to plan a robbery, man?"

"I don't know."

"You think we just roll up to *Ammo Domini* by the Freeway Five and buy some guns with our shiny Chrome Valley Federal credit cards?"

"No, I—"

"—While we're there, our lame, unwashed asses ask the dude behind the counter how to use our purchases, and if he sells bala, uh, bla-carver—"

"—Balaclavas."

"Yeah, them," Lincoln spat, unhappy about the verbal correction. "And then turn up to the bank first thing the next morning, while the bank traces our transactions and busts the shit out of us?"

"No."

"Fuckin' idiot."

Howard grimaced at just how stupid his reaction must have sounded. "I'm not a dummy, Lincoln."

"Could've fooled me."

"I never thought that for a second. I know we can't just go and buy guns from *Ammo Domini.*"

"Yeah? Are you *sure* about that?"

"Yeah, no," Howard blurted, realizing there and then just how deep and complicated the rabbit hole truly was. "Ugh. I just thought—"

"—Yeah, well *stop* just thinking, okay? Fuck, it's a good job you brought me in on this, otherwise you and Cherry and Amos and Gilmour would be all over the news getting arrested before you left the damn gun store."

Howard hung his head in shame in exactly the way hardened criminals don't. "I'm sorry."

"*Fuck* sorry. You're gonna leave the *thinking,* all of the specifics, to my boy. Okay?"

"Okay."

"Damn, man, we're talking about ripping the joint off in *eight days time*, Howard. That shit takes some hardcore planning. And we hit people we know in a little over a week? I've taken leaks longer than that."

"Fine, okay. I'm sorry. I'm new to this."

"Yeah. *No shit.*"

Howard calmed himself down, but couldn't stop his arms from shaking. "Where's the meet?"

"Few miles north. Industrial Estate. Danny and Knocktoe wanna meet the team."

"The *team?*"

Lincoln made a funny face at Howard as if he was behaving like a moron. "Uh, yeah? Me, you, and Cherry, Gilmour, and Amos."

Howard gulped, afraid of the unfathomable depths of the criminal swimming pool he'd voluntarily waded into.

"Man, just eight hours ago, I was a no-good lackey with a bleak future," Lincoln said. "And now, as I sit here in this goddamn drive-through, we're about to be richer than if we worked for a hundred years straight."

Lincoln chucked his half-consumed milkshake across the parking lot. It hit the side of the *Burger Face* drive-through wall and splattered the creamy, red-and-white sludge up the brickwork.

"I decided something right now, thanks to you, Howie."

"What?"

Inspired by the thought of untold wealth, Lincoln punched the air and opened the door to his car.

"This motherfuckin' town *owes* me, Howie. The government owes me, and so does the valley. I'm owed a little slice of heaven, and I'll be a son of a bitch of a wife-beatin' bastard if I ain't gonna get myself a slice of the capitalist pie."

Chapter 5

Holed up in the conference room, the hostages watched the suited Rabbit slowly lose his big, fat latex mind, and kick one of the empty executive chairs across the room. "Ugh, I don't believe this."

"What?" Dog whispered.

"It's all going wrong."

Kate's colleagues' incessant sobbing grated around the room, forcing Rabbit to overreact in as quiet a manner as he could. "Jesus Christ, would you shut that bitch up?"

"She's scared."

Rabbit stormed over to Kate's sobbing, blonde friend and looked her in the eyes. "What's your name?"

"K-Karen," she replied, daring to point out the obvious. "You know they're onto you, r-right?"

The featureless depths of darkness in the mask's eye holes did little to allay to Karen's anxiety.

"Those security guys out there aren't stupid," she said. "You think you can just waltz in here and rip the joint off?"

"Karen, huh?"

"Y-Yes."

"I guess you're gonna color your hair blue and demand to speak to the manager, huh?"

"N-No."

Rabbit lifted the end of the shotgun to her nose. "You see this hole, here?"

Karen winced, hoping he wouldn't pull the trigger.

"It's getting bigger and bigger, ain't it? See, when we start executing hostages, I'm gonna start with *you*," he said as he pushed the end of his firearm into her chest. "I'll shoot you right about here."

The other hostages trembled with fear at the sneak preview of what might happen to them if they drew any undue attention to themselves.

"Karen, listen to me. Your petulant crying is in danger of getting us busted. So, shut the hell up, get a grip on the tears, and I *might* get a grip on *not* shooting your tits off. Understand?"

Kate hung her head down, and looked anywhere other than in their captor's direction. "You bastard."

"That's right, Durst. And don't you ever forget it."

Out in the back corridor, Ram and Badger keep utterly still as Milton pulled the exit door shut and turned around.

"This is Two-Five. The pick-up is aborted, I repeat, the pick-up is aborted. Exiting the premises now, call for CVPD assistance."

Ram scrambled to pull his mask over his face as Milton's footsteps grew louder and louder. "Shit."

Badger lifted his shoulders as if to ask, "Aww, *shitsticks*. What do we do, now?"

Thinking on his feet, Ram pumped his shotgun as hard as he could and ensured the casing of the spent round crashed to the floor. He placed his boot on the side of the water cooler and bent his knee up, ready to boot it over.

Ram's intention played out as desired.

The spent round clanged to the floor and rolled onto its side, which alerted Milton in an instant.

He went for his firearm. "Who's there?"

Boot.

The water cooler launched into the air and crashed around Milton's feet. Ram jumped out from behind it, pumped his shotgun with his right hand, and caught the grip in his left.

"Hey, fella."

Milton took a step back and held his arms out. "What the hell?!"

As if the sight of a Ram with a shotgun wasn't astonishing enough, he was joined by a well-dressed Badger pointing an Uzi in his direction.

"That's right, shithead," Badger said. "Keep your hands up."

Milton's breathing quickened and fogged up the front of his visor.

"Take your microphone in your thumb and index finger," Ram snapped. "Pull on the cord slowly, and remove it from the battery."

"Okay, okay, p-please, don't shoot."

"Shut up and do as I just said."

As the terrified man followed the order, Badger spoke into his wristwatch. "Rabbit? This is Badger. We got him."

"Got who?"

"Our snooping SecuriCock friend. He's currently doing precisely whatever we want. How's his girlfriend holding up?"

Rabbit raced up to the conference room door and peered through the window.

A thoroughly agitated Cole walked across the banking area with the intention of checking the entrance.

Alarmed, Richard turned to the conference room door with a puzzled and apologetic expression on his face.

Rabbit whispered into his wrist. "Your girlfriend's girlfriend is coming over, too—I, uh, where are you?"

"Storage area, although the water cooler might not be working too well, right now."

"I don't give a rat's ass about the water cooler. Get that *SecuriCocksucker* to de-comm himself."

"We already did. He's 'gone dark'."

"I think his girlfriend is just nosing around—oh dear," Rabbit said as he watched Cole race back to the back wall, and inspect the chair next to the door.

"What?"

"Oh dear multiplied by *fuck*."

"What is it?"

"Not good. That's what it is."

Cole slid the legs of the chair away and spotted the blood splatter up the wall. "Huh? What the hell is going on around here?"

"Badger?" Rabbit snapped in haste.

"What?"

Cole reached under his visor and turned his face away from Richard who, by now, was ready to soil himself with anxiety.

"He's about to radio in, fuck," Rabbit said. "Fuck, get back out here—no, wait. Stay where you are."

Dog jumped away from the table and, before he could inquire about the unfolding events, was surprised to see Rabbit pull the conference room door open and bolt into the teller area.

"Where are you going—?"

Rabbit pushed past Richard, pumped his shotgun, and screamed at Cole. "Hey. *You.*"

Cole turned around to face the person who'd yelled at him. He wasn't expecting to see a perverse version of Bugs Bunny threatening him with a shotgun.

"What the hell?"

"Stay right there, asshole."

Cole went for his gun. His fingers just about reached the holster and unfastened the leather, before Rabbit grabbed Richard's collar and took him as a hostage.

"No, don't do that."

Cole froze on the spot, still with his hand covering his firearm as he watched Rabbit threaten Richard with his gun.

"I'll blow this cocksucker's head off. Get your fucking hand away from the gun and put it in the air, uh, along with the other one."

"What?"

"Put *both* your hands in the air, ass head. Do it, or I'll repaint this whole place with this asshole's brains."

"Okay, okay."

Rabbit struggled to wrestle the heft of his shotgun. His right arm wasn't long enough to turn the barrel back onto his hostage's temple.

"Ugh. This isn't gonna work."

"What are you doing?" Cole asked, perplexed.

"My arm's not long enough to—ugh, fuck this."

Astonished, Cole watched as the Rabbit changed tact, and aimed his shotgun at Richard's groin.

"That's better," Rabbit huffed. "Sorry about that. Right, get your hands in the air or I'll blow this old man's droopy nuts off. Do it now."

"Okay, okay."

When Cole obliged Rabbit's instruction, the security case lifted up and hung like a two-ton vice from his wrist. He winced in pain as he struggled to keep the weight up. "Oww."

Rabbit lost his temper and stomped on the floor. "What is it now, you utter cock spoon?"

"This isn't very comfortable. My hand is hurting. Can I put my left hand down, please?"

Rabbit lost his mind and let out a blood-curdling exasperation. "Aww, for *fuck's* sake. Do I have to think of everything around here?"

Cole winced at the sheer weight pulling on his wrist.

"Oh, *okay then*, put your *left* arm down and rest the case on the chair. But keep your jerking hand up where I can see it."

Cole obeyed the order, carefully, and placed the case on the seat. "Okay, I'm doing it now."

Rabbit shoved Richard aside and pointed at the conference room. "Dog? You got a new customer. Richard, get in there with the others."

Dog ran out with his shotgun, ready to open fire. "Where? Who?"

"The goddamn security guard," Rabbit snapped. "And put that gun down, would you? This isn't a movie.

Dog lowered his gun and whined. "Sorry."

"Just take Richardson back in the room with you and make sure everyone behaves while I deal with this prick."

Rabbit and Cole exchanged glances as Dog ushered Richard over to the room. "Come on, boy. Let's go."

A thoroughly disheveled Richard traipsed past Dog and entered the conference room.

"What are we gonna do now, Rabbit?" Dog asked.

"I'm thinking. Shut up and get back in the room with the others."

"Okay, just *holler* if you need me."

Rabbit paced back and forth, waving his shotgun around, trying to envision a path to success. Cole moved his head left, then right, as he watched the scurrilous creature at work.

"I recognize you," Cole said. "I know that walk."

Rabbit stopped, making sure his pacing didn't give anything away. "What?"

Cole pointed at the lending desk. "Yeah, the walk. And that dime-store suit. You sit right over there. I see you every week."

"No. No, don't say that."

"Ha," Cole said. "Oh, that's great. It *is* you. Ross, something—?"

"—No, no, no," Rabbit snapped. "You don't know *shit.*"

Cole glanced at the desk in question just behind his right buttock. The golden placard read *Howard Ross - Head of Lending.*

"Howard Ross," Cole said. "Yeah, I knew it was Ross something."

Rabbit screamed so loud that his voice alternator squeaked like an out-of-control microphone. "Shut up. I am *not* Howard fucking Ross. I'm someone else."

Considerably amused at the robbers' predicament, Cole baited the man further. "Oh, man. That's funny. Wow, you really went to town with all these guns, too? Compensating much?"

"Shut up."

"This is great," Cole giggled. "The bankers robbing their own bank? I love it. Hey, please tell me you took care of the CCTV cameras?"

Damn, Rabbit thought to himself, he hadn't. "Shit."

Four such devices looked down at him from every corner of the area, which only added to his torment.

"And the cameras out back by the drive-through, and front?" Cole said. "You *do* know the live feed goes straight to Midwest Federal, right? You've probably got a million viewers by now."

Rabbit scanned each camera and felt them laughing back at him. Then, he remembered the power had gone down. "No, no, you don't know shit."

Cole took pity on the pathetic, floppy-eared creature standing twenty feet away from him.

"Radio silence for us, and this place is gonna be swarming with cops from all four corners of the Valley, from Devotion to Horder's Point, you're gonna have one helluva five-oh festival about two minutes from now. Better luck next time, bunny-boy."

Cole punctuated his triumph by going for his firearm.

"—No," Rabbit yelled. "Get your hand up, don't go for—"

"—Amazing, really. You've worked here for as long as I can remember, and you can't even rip your own joint off properly."

"Get your hands—uh, *hand*, up." Rabbit said. "Get it up. Don't touch your gun. I mean it."

Cole defied the demand and clutched his firearm with his right hand.

"Ah, just shut up and give yourself up, Ross. Asshole. You may be a no-good, useless banker-turned-robber who's wasted his life, but you're not about to commit first degree murder, are you? I know you white collar idiots have a reputation, but you're not *that* dumb…"

Cole's voice ground to a halt and produced a migraine-inducing echo in Rabbit's mind. His brain took a back seat and allowed his survival and preservation mode to kick in.

And kick in it did.

Before Cole was able to pull his gun out of the holster, Rabbit pulled on the trigger and blasted Cole in the chest.

Bang—spatch.

The chain attached to Cole's wrist whipped up in the air as the back of his head cracked against the wall, before dropping to the ground in a smoking, blood-splattered heap.

Whump.

The case dropped onto the corpse's lap, providing a violent denouement to Rabbit's hasty actions.

"Jesus fucking Christ, Rabbit," Dog said, utterly astonished at what his associate had just done.

"He knew me," Rabbit said. "Busted me straight away. Is it that obvious it's me?"

"Well, to *me* it is, yeah," Dog said.

"No, not you. I mean to the others?"

"Dunno."

Rabbit gripped the pump on the shotgun and ejected the spent bullet. The sound of a fresh round clanged into the chamber as he let the barrel fall into his left hand.

"Did any of the hostages hear what he said?"

"No. I don't think so. Why?"

"Because, you utter moron, if any of the staff heard it and know who I am, or who we are, then we're gonna have to execute each and every one of the bastards."

If Dog had a tail, he would have wagged it in protest. "Are you out of your fucking mind, Howard?"

Rabbit socked Dog in the face so hard that his mask nearly flew off his head.

"Have you learned nothing?" Rabbit shrieked. "Don't say my name, you fucking moron."

"I'm sorry, man."

Rabbit kicked the teller desk over and over again. "Jesus *fuck* to a man, I'm working with retards, that's what it is. Complete and utter retards."

Dog stood perfectly still as he watched his friend take out his anger on the sturdy counter. "Um, Rabbit?"

"Goddamn motherfuckers."

Rabbit kicked a nearby chair away from its desk with such force that the back leg snapped off and rolled across the floor.

He reached over to his desk and snatched the name placard from the desktop. "Goddamn fucking prick-stands."

Rabbit pocketed the shiny, rectangular slab of gold, and patted the front of his still-pristine white shirt with his left hand.

Dog swallowed and folded his arms. "Feel better?"

"Not really, no."

"You need to calm your fluffy tail down, you know."

"Don't talk to me."

"Yeah, but, we gotta—"

"—Look, why don't you be a good little doggy and just *sit*? Huh? Just stay, you cretinous little pooch, or shut the fuck up and let me think for a second."

Dog rolled his shoulders and allowed the man some space and time.

"Now, he said something about the police. Lack of communication," Rabbit said. "What time is it now?"

Dog scanned his wristwatch. "Eleven fifty-seven."

"We should have been out of here fifteen fucking minutes ago. Ugh."

Kate, Richard, Karen, and the random hostages slowly crept up to the ajar conference room door and tried to listen to what was being said.

A funny sight greeted them; a rabbit and a dog trying to think of a way out of their current predicament.

Karen squeaked in horror as she laid eyes on the dead SecuriCore man at the far end of the area. "Oh my God—"

"—Shhh," Kate said as she covered Karen's mouth. "Keep quiet."

"They killed him. Look."

Kate squinted at the pair as they chatted to each other, out of earshot. "No. No, he didn't do it on purpose. It was an accident, or he—" she said, before glancing at Howard's freshly kicked desk and missing placard.

Kate's eyes grew with shock when she realized who might be committing the robbery. "Oh, *shit*."

"What?" everyone whispered back, confused.

"Everyone, get back. Sit back down and act normal."

Karen, Richard, and the others scurried back to the table and took their seats, leaving Kate to squint at the two robbers.

She focused on the placard on Rabbit's right hand as he slipped it into his jacket pocket. "Oh, wow."

Clomp.

She pushed the door shut, and took a deep breath.

An older woman looked up from the chair. Her long, flowing blond locks draped across her shoulder as she turned to face Kate.

"Kate?"

"Yeah?"

"What's going on? You work here, right? You know something."

Kate stared at the floor and tried to process what she'd seen, or *thought* she'd seen.

"Miss?"

Kate looked at the woman. "What?"

"You *know* those guys, don't you?"

"What's your name?" Kate asked.

"Lavinia Craven," the woman said. "I was in line, and you were about to serve me next."

"Oh."

"I don't understand why we're not just running for the door and escaping?"

"No, the door's locked. You'd get shot trying to get anywhere near it, let alone unlocking it."

Richard pinched the key in his fingers and showed it to everyone. "She's right. It's locked right now. But I do have the key, of course."

A bespectacled man in his twenties sighed from the far end of the table. He pointed at the closed blinds hanging in front of the window. "There's, like, ten of us, and a handful of them. Can't we just smash the window now and run off?"

Richard dismissed the idea outright. "No, it's bulletproof. You can try to throw a chair through it, but it'd only bounce back into your face and piss them off."

Kate tried to fend off the idea that she might know the men responsible for casing the joint. "Howard Ross? No, no. It can't be."

Unfortunately for her, most everyone in the room had heard her utterance. She stared at each of them with a wry innocence. "Why are you all looking at me like that?"

"What was that you just said?" the man asked. "Something about Howard Ross?"

"No. Nothing. I didn't say—"

"—You said a name. Howard Ross."

"Look, I don't know who these guys are for sure, but I do know one thing."

"What?" everyone asked in unison.

"These guys know what they're doing," Kate said. "Well, obviously they don't really know what they're doing, but they *do* know this bank. If they are who I think they are."

"And who do you think they are?" everyone asked, quietly.

Kate shook her head, refusing to reveal the answer she had in mind. "Until the jury's in, all I can say is this…"

A series of expectant and gossip-hungry eyeballs waited for her to continue talking.

"They're experts in banking, but amateurs in bank-robbing."

A prolonged roll of stunned silence snaked round the room.

"What's that meant to mean?" Karen asked. "Who are they?"

"Yeah, stop being cryptic," the man said.

"It seems the bankers have become the robbers."

Everyone in the room gasped with horror at what she'd revealed.

"Oh, my." Lavinia said. "Really? We need to say something."

Kate hoped she was right, and then seriously regretted revealing the information that could get them all killed.

Kate raised her voice above the surreptitious chatter. "Jesus Christ, stop talking and listen to me, you fools. They've already killed three people. Granted, they did it by accident, but still, accident or not, those bullets are real, and these guys are trigger-happy idiots. You *cannot* give them *any* indication that you know who they are—"

Whump.

The door flung open and punched Kate into the wall, cutting off her sentence.

"Ooof."

Everyone turned to the door to find an angry, suited Dog with a shotgun push through. Each and every hostage smiled like an innocent cherub, awaiting instructions.

Dog surveyed the room, and found the hostage count to be on the light side.

"Where's the other one?" he asked. "The pretty one with the big tits?"

One by one, the hostages pointed to the door swinging away from the wall.

Dog turned around, yanked the door back, and discovered a wincing Kate rubbing her arm.

"What the fuck you doing there?" he asked.

Kate held her hand to her face and groaned."You hit me with the door."

Confused, Dog shook his head and offered Kate a seat. "Whatever, sit."

"Yes."

Dog perched his behind on the computer desk on the near wall and prepared to launch into a speech.

"Okay, my associate with the big, fluffy ears has asked me to tell you what's going on."

"Which one is that?" Karen asked.

"The rabbit, who do you think? Who the fuck else has big, flappy ears and two buck teeth?"

"The badger?"

Well and truly owned, Dog snapped in anger. "Fuck you. And anyway, the badger doesn't have big ears."

Karen wiped a tear from her eye and noticed the ends of Dog's pants ride up to his shins to reveal a pair of *Space Invaders* socks.

Dog hadn't noticed on account of his mask and cleared his throat.

"So, here's the pitch," he said. "We ran into a bit of a problem which we're rectifying right now. We were meant to be in and out in ten minutes when we turned up, but, unfortunately, our boss didn't play ball, so we—"

"—*Our* boss?" Kate snapped, before covering her mouth and regretting her stupid questioning tactics.

"*Your* boss I meant," Dog said, failing to realize the giveaway. "*Your boss.* A real, nasty fuckhead, so I heard. Anyway, he didn't play ball, and so we shot him in the face for being a twat."

Lavinia leaned back in her chair and sighed out loud. "Ugh, won't you just let us go——?"

Bang—Smash.

"The hell was that?" Kate asked, as the others turned to the door, wondering where the commotion had come from.

Lavinia leaned forward and pressed her fingers to her ears. "Christ, that was louder than a Pink Floyd concert. What is it?"

Bang—Smash—Bang—Smash.

Dog chuckled. "Oh, that's Rabbit. He's taking out the CCTV cameras——"

Bang—Smash.

Kate returned to her seat and rolled her eyes in acknowledgment. "Ohhh. Yeah, that makes sense now."

"Better late than never," Karen scoffed.

Dog swung his feet back and forth like an insolent child and tried to reassure the befuddled hostages. "Yeah, we were meant to shoot the cameras when we came in, but he got distracted, so he's doing it now."

The hostages nodded in a charming and polite way, realizing, once and for all, that Kate was correct; these robbers were, indeed, stupid and ill-prepared.

"And we've fucked Price's computer because it contains the footage, so at least there's no record of what went down, now."

The hostages stopped nodding, realizing that perhaps the robbers weren't so stupid, after all.

"Anyway, we won't be long. We have one of the SecuriCock guards letting us into the vault. As soon as we get what we want, we're out of here, and the rest of your life is your own."

"Yeah, you keep saying that," Kate said as she and Richard exchanged glances.

"So, yeah," Ben continued. "We had to kill one of the guards because he was being a disobedient ass-pipe. But, you know, he's dead, now. So that's all good."

Kate dared to raise her hand to ask a question. "Excuse me?"

Dog looked up and accepted her invitation. "Yes, idiot at the back?"

"Hey. Don't call me an idiot."

"Don't tell me what to do," Dog snapped. "I'm in charge here, okay, and all of you are on my leash. You understand that, you fucking packet of pricks?"

"Yes, we understand," Lavinia said, angrily.

Kate tried to win Dog's heart by expressing a sympathetic face. "Mr. Dog, listen, my colleagues and I are concerned about our deputy manager. His name is Mark Amos. He was here when you came in, but we don't know where he is now."

"Oh, yeah. Mark. What about him?"

"Well, uh, where is he? We're worried he might have been hurt."

Dog thought on his hind legs and began to enjoy his new-found control of his former colleagues. "He's okay. Well, he's a bit of a twat, if I'm honest, but whatever. We're, uh, using him as a bullet shield, just for insurance purposes. Which is a bit ironic, I guess, given his specialty is insurance products."

Kate offered a smile and lowered her arm. "Oh, okay." "Uh-huh."

"So, he's not injured? He's okay."

"Yeah, he's a dribbling imbecile, but not injured, so no different to any other day."

Kate exhaled with relief. "Okay, that's good. Thanks for letting us know."

"Hey, no sweat."

Dog swung his legs harder, excited at the power he held over his hostages who, he felt, were warming to him.

"Yeah, so when we get what we need in the vault we'll be out of here in, like, five minutes. We're expecting the police to turn up, but we'll be long gone by then."

Lavinia folded her arms and stared at the conference table. "I swear to God I'm closing my account once this is all over. I mean, really, this is outrageous."

Karen added to the litany of anger. "Yeah, Dog. You know what you're doing, don't you?"

Dog's ears pricked up at Karen's statement, just as she felt a nudge in the ribs from Kate.

"You what?"

"How did you know about Wednesdays?" Karen asked. "Just before lunch?"

"Karen, no, don't—"

"—Ah, fuck 'em," Karen said. "They roll up in here ten minutes before the contents of the vault are due to be removed."

Dog slid off the edge of the computer desk and jumped to his feet. "Say that again?"

"You're obviously professionals," Karen said, quickly backtracking on her desire to reveal what everyone knew about the situation, and who was perpetrating it.

Dog took offense and stood his ground. "You're goddamn right about that, *Karen*. We are professionals. The best of the best."

Karen snorted with disdain at the puppy dog standing before her. "Yeah. Only top breeders recommend them, huh?"

"What?"

"Nothing."

Dog tapped the conference table with his shotgun and raised his voice. "Okay, that's enough gay talk for one afternoon. Now, does anyone need the bathroom?"

Everybody put their hands in the air, suddenly very excited at the prospect of relieving themselves.

"Well, tough. I'm sure you can hold your bladders for five minutes, then you can piss as much as you like."

Just then, Dog's wristwatch crackled to life. *"Dog? This is Rabbit. Can you hear me?"*

Dog winked at the hostages, not that they could see his eyes under his mask. "Yeah, I can hear you, you buck-toothed security guard killer, you."

"We're at the vault. How are the hostages holding up?"

"Well, individually they're quite nice people, but collectively they're a pain in my fucking ass. Are you in the vault, yet?"

"Ah, no. We're at the vault. Not inside it. That's the problem."

"Why, what's up?"

***

Milton had burst into tears and sobbed hard with his arms above his head. "I'm t-telling you, I c-can't get in."

Ram kept his shotgun aimed at the man's face, as did Badger with his Uzi. Rabbit paced back and forth, angry, as he spoke into his wristwatch.

"Well, Dog, seeing as you ask. This cute piece of security guard ass says he can't open the vault. The power's down."

Rabbit stopped in his tracks and focused his pupils on two, smoldering bullet hits on the vault door's handle.

"We tried going in the hard way, but the fucking door won't budge."

"Can we try the backup generator to get the power back on?"

Rabbit rammed the butt of his palm into Milton's back, forcing him to cry harder. The unsubtle pang of terror forced Rabbit and his colleagues to smile as they came around to accepting their fate.

"Maybe," Rabbit said. "Listen, Dog, we don't know for sure, but we gotta assume the alarm tipped off the police. We can't stick around. And we've given our girlfriend, here, sixty seconds to think of a way to get in the vault."

"Okay. Well, I hope he can come up with a solution to our problem, then."

"Yeah, me too," Rabbit said. "Because in precisely fifty-five seconds time, one of two things will happen."

He shuffled up behind Milton and spoke directly into the man's right ear.

"One, a miracle happens and he finds a way to get in the vault, gives us what's inside, and we leave, and he gets to go back home to his family. Or, two—"

"—We blow his fucking brains out all over this bitch," Ram screamed with a curious, perverted delight.

"P-Please, n-no," Milton squirmed. "L-Look, I swear, if the power is off, there's no w-way we can get in. I d-don't stand a chance."

"Power?"

Ram looked at Badger, who in turn threw Rabbit a wry eye, and then back to Ram.

Dog's voice spoiled the quiet revelation.

"Uh, hello? Are you still there, or have you all decided to become monks and take a vow of silence?"

"Ram?" Rabbit asked.

"Did I mention the backup generator, or did I just imagine it?"

Ram forced a mocking spit of acknowledgment with his best Elvis impersonation. "Uh-huh-huh?"

"Yeah, listen, do you think *The King* could find the time to go and switch the backup generator on?"

Excited, Ram squeaked through his alternator. "Sure, Priscilla. Keep them legs warm for me, honey."

"Will do, sweetie."

"Thank y'very much."

"Aww, Christ. Is he doing his fucking Elvis' thing again?"

"Yeah," Rabbit said into his arm. "The heat must be getting to him. Dog, just keep our guests entertained for a few minutes. We're throwing the power back on, and praying Mrs. *SecuriCocksucker* can get us in. Ain't that right, *Girlfriend?*"

Rabbit budged Milton's back with the butt of the shotgun. "Well, answer me?"

"Yes, yes," Milton yelped.

"Yeah, I think he gets the picture," Rabbit said. "Ram?"

"Uh-huh?"

"The back up generator. Power, please."

Ram saluted and shifted off down the corridor. "Elvis has left the building."

Rabbit, Badger, and even Milton, face-palmed themselves with regret that they'd ever met the guy.

Further up the corridor, Ram held his shotgun like a guitar and danced forward on both feet, singing to his own, high-pitched rendition of Elvis' *A Little less Conversation.*

"Dum-de-dum, da-da-da, da-dum."

He reached the white electronics box on the wall by the storage room and inspected the burnt, busted doors he'd shot open minutes ago.

His left sleeve rolled up as he grabbed the lever to the generator next to the electrical box. "And now, for my next trick."

Whump—clump.

The handle flung down, and he pushed it right back up into the *on* position.

A small humming sound pushed through, forcing a bank of lights to blast on.

The mechanism inside whirred to life.

"Uh-huh-huh, we have the technology," Ram said in his best Elvis impression, before speaking into his wrist. "Well, well, well, whaddya know? We have power."

"Good," Rabbit said. *"Get back over to the vault, and bring your bag with you."*

"Understood."

"And try not to lose it all on your way here, you degenerate gambler, you."

Ram rubbed his hands together, tucked his shotgun under his arm, and sprinted away from the cabinet. "That's not funny."

"I know."

"I don't have any cash on me to lose. Not yet, anyway."

"All that's about to change, Ram. Get your bony ass back to the vault."

***

Out in the back parking lot, Squirrel had taken it upon himself to plant Badger's sports bag and inspect the contents.

The bag was heavier than he'd expected.

"Jeez, this is heavy. What's in here, a bunch of bricks?"

The silver Chevrolet rocked from side to side as he pulled the zipper open and dipped his hand inside.

"What the fuck?"

A few bills lined the seams inside, but most of the take from the drive-through had been bagged up in cellophane.

"Coins?" Squirrel muttered in astonishment. "Where's the fuckin' paper—"

He stopped speaking when he saw a flurry of blue lights bounce off the surface of the Chrome Valley Federal Bank placard hanging on the wall.

Squirrel dropped the bag back onto the passenger seat and leaned over the steering wheel. He held his breath as he listened out for the sirens, but before they arrived, a giant helicopter blew past a tree behind the wall.

Whudda-whudda-whudda.

"Oh, fuck."

Squirrel turned on the Chevrolet's ignition and flicked the shift into reverse. "Shit, shit, shit."

Screeech.

The two front tires swung across the concrete as he spun the steering wheel to the left and roared into his wrist.

"Rabbit, Rabbit? This is Squirrel. Shit. Can you hear me?"

"Yeah, this is Rabbit," came the response. *"This better be good, Squirrel. What do you want? We're about to get in the vault—"*

"—No, this is very fuckin' far from good, Rabbit," Squirrel snapped and slammed on the accelarator. "Motherfuckin' five-oh are rollin' up on us. Man, we're fucked. They got a chopper and shit."

"Shit."

"Yeah, the place is about to turn blue as all hell, man."

"What are you gonna do? You're a sitting duck out there."

Squirrel turned the wheel and headed for the parking lot entrance at the side of the building.

"A sitting squirrel, man. Fuck this, I'mma use the underground parking lot. I'll wait there for your asses."

The car bolted the wrong way down the seventh drive-through lane and spun its wheels as it turned the corner around the bank.

"Good idea. Anywhere but the drive-through. Once we've gotten into the vault, we'll meet you in the underground parking lot by the stairwell."

Squirrel focused on the ramp that led down into the bowels of the bank. "I didn't wanna do this, but we got no choice. You got three minutes tops till the place is swarming with blue bacon, man."

Rabbit's voice sped up through Squirrel's watch. *"Radio into Cat. Tell him we're massively late, but that we're nearly ready."*

"On it."

The Chevrolet's hood crashed against the lip of the ramp as it slipped down into the basement, and out of sight…

***

Rabbit lowered his left wrist and stormed over to the terrified Milton, who struggled to reach for the key hanging around his neck.

Ram and Badger stepped aside and allowed Rabbit to accost the man. "He's all yours."

"Right, I've had just about enough of this bullshit," Rabbit screamed. "Open the vault. Now."

"Is the p-power back on?"

"Duh, you stuttering prick. *Yes*, it's back on, unlike your head on your shoulders if you don't open this goddamn thing right the fuck *now*."

Rabbit, Ram, and Badger watched the man enter the four-digit number on the keypad.

"C'mon, c'mon, c'mon," Rabbit sneered with venom, all the while keeping an eye out for any sign of action coming from either end of the corridor.

Just then, Milton spotted a pair of legs sticking out from the storage room. "Is that Victor Price?"

"Uh-huh," Ram said. "Tall fucker wouldn't completely fit in there. And as for his head, well, probably best you don't see it."

Rabbit lowered his head and exhaled. "Ugh. Look, stop stalling and just open the damn vault."

Beep-swish.

The door to the vault slid open.

Milton didn't know what to do next, but half-expected to be asked to open the iron cage barricading access to the shelves of boxes and money inside.

"Good, we're in," Badger said.

Rabbit shoved Milton forward and tore the key from his neck.

"Open the cage."

The terrified man's shaking hand inserted the key into the lock. Each of the four interior walls began to rumble like a rabid washing machine on full power.

Ram looked up, ready to fire at the ceiling. "The fuck is that?"

"Listen," Rabbit whispered. "I don't wanna freak anybody out, okay, but I just talked to Squirrel."

"What he say?"

"The cops are already here."

Badger lost his footing upon hearing the news and yelped. "What? The cops?"

"Yeah."

Ram threw his arms out in frustration. "And we're stuck down here in a vault full of money? Shit."

Furious, Rabbit pulled Milton away from the open gate. "Step aside, lover boy."

Ram and Badger unstrapped their sports bags from their back. Rabbit had already beaten them to it, and chucked his own bag at Badger.

"Fill up my bag, too. High denominations only, left wall. Bearer bonds on the right."

"Hell yeah," Badger said.

"Whatever you do, do *not* come back out into the bank. The place is gonna be swarming with cop-shaped flies around this piece of shit bank, so stay the fuck away from any windows. Get to the staircase door and radio me when you're there, and we'll meet Squirrel in the basement."

Badger raced into the vault, and smashed the boxes lining the right-hand wall inside the vault with the butt of his Uzi. "It's payday."

"Ram?"

"Yeah, Rabbit?"

"You got sixty seconds, no more," Rabbit said. "The longer we wait to leave, the more cop trouble we got."

Ram bolted inside the vault and approached the wall on the left. He raised his shotgun and went to blow the larger of three huge safes. "Sure. Stand back."

"I'm gonna join Dog out front, and make sure the cops can't see shit, or do shit, or know shit. Anything, basically, that involves shit."

"Yeah," Ram said. "As little shit as possible."

"Exactly."

Rabbit thumped Milton on the back a little too hard.

"Oww."

"And don't take any shit from this little shit, either. I'm thinking he might be useful for when we get outta here."

"Shit, yeah," Ram spat. "Don't worry, he won't give us any shit."

"Good. Fifty seconds, and we're gone. Good luck."

Rabbit nodded, swiftly, and ran off in the opposite direction.

He ran past the storage room, turned the corner, and headed for the door to the main banking area.

A thunderous bang echoed up the walls, which inspired Rabbit to slow his sprint to a gentle jog.

"Thank Christ, it's almost over."

Chapter 6

DANNY DRISCOLL &
"KNOCKTOE" JOE DEVITO
— 10 pm, Tuesday, September 29th —

Unit #237 at Chrome Valley Industrial Estate was one of the bigger warehouses on the lot. The interior was as dull as it was expansive and featureless; the ideal dwelling for what was about to go down.

Howard, Ben, Mark, and James looked seriously out of place in the featureless cocoon located in the bowels of Chrome Valley's Industrial Estate, and even stranger in their casual clothes.

Lincoln leaned against the wall with his arms folded, wondering how the meet might go down.

Howard finally mustered the courage to speak. "We've been here ten minutes. Where are they?"

Lincoln acknowledged his four friends' anxiety, and did his best to allay their fears. "Gettin' ready, Howard, relax."

Nervous, Mark fiddled with a plastic grocery bag with *Marcovicci Beach Attire* scrawled across it in large, sun-drenched text. "I don't like this at all. I don't know if I wanna—"

"—Mark, man, this is non-committal, okay? It's all good. Let's just hear them out."

If it weren't for Lincoln's performance of serenity, each of the four men would have run for the hills by now.

The sprawling, rectangular waist-high table in the middle of the room resembled a tomb of regret and failure. The red tarpaulin sheet covering whatever lay beneath it only added to the already volatile atmosphere.

Despite the September warmth, the evening had grown much colder, almost to the point where James thought he could see his own breath drift up past his eyes. "Yeah, it'll be fine. They divulge stuff we need to know. We're all in this together. All with the same goal."

Howard shuffled in his seat and was about to say something, when the service door at the far end of the warehouse opened up.

Lincoln kicked himself away from the wall and clapped his hands together with excitement.

"Well, well, well, if it ain't Danny motherfuckin' Driscoll before my very eyes."

Lincoln was a skinny guy, but compared to Danny Driscoll, he might have been accused of being obese. Much like his friend, Danny was a black gentleman, and his sagging shirt and pants barely concealed his malnourished body.

Danny paced forward with his right hand up, and beamed with delight as Lincoln approached him.

"Lincoln *mutha-rapin'* Mumford," he chirped with delight. "My man."

The two men hugged each other for the first time in years. Lincoln stepped back and checked his friend out.

"Shit. What did they feed your ass up in Horder's Point Penitentiary, anyhow? Bread and water, judging by your skinny ass."

"Ah, fuck that. Yo. I was gonna ask you how shit's goin' down at the bank, but I guess y'all already kinda gave it away now that we got the meet on."

Danny turned to the four nervous-looking men.

"These your boys, yeah?"

Lincoln moved into Danny's ear and whispered. "They ain't on the level, man, see, 'cuz? Gotta play it a little straight with them, or they'll get spooked."

"Fuck, bruh," Danny said. "For eight mil, I'll go all motherfuckin' Royal Highness on 'em. Check it."

Ben leaned over to Howard as they watched the two masterminds continue their conversation. "Howard?"

"Yeah?"

"You noticed how Lincoln changes his behavior when he's talking to us, and customers, and when he's talking to his friends?"

"Yes, I *have* noticed. Just let him do his thing."

Lincoln held his hand out at Danny and stepped towards his colleagues. "Okay, guys. This is my boy, Danny."

"S'up," Danny said with a cheeky grin.

Howard stood up and introduced himself. "Hi, I'm Howard. Lincoln's associate."

Danny offered his fist for Howard to bump. "Oh, yeah? Mumford mentioned you, man. You're the brains behind this operation, yeah?"

Howard didn't know what to do with the fist, and so took it in his right hand and shook it. "Yes, I guess so. Lincoln mentioned you could help us."

Danny watched in horror as the white man shook his fist, and decided to laugh it off. He nodded at Ben, Mark, and James. "This your crew, yeah?"

"Oh, uh, yes. This is my *crew*."

Mark felt queasy and turned away, leaving Ben and James to wave at back at him.

It took Danny all of half a second to assess the men sitting before him. "Well, shit. Check this out. A regular bunch of hardcore fuckin' bank robbers, huh?"

"Oh, no, we're not bank robbers," Ben said. "We work at the bank. We're just, uh, you know, gonna go in there and clean them out."

Mark finally spoke up, simply to see if his vocal cords were still working. "It's very much a no-rough-stuff-type-deal."

Danny tutted and giggled. "Is that so, Mr. Buscemi?"

"Yeah, it is."

"Y'all ain't got no idea what that meant, do you?" Danny said. "Please tell me you've seen at least *one* heist movie in your life, else your white asses - *all your white asses* - are in for a helluva motherfuckin' shock an' kickin'."

"What?" Ben asked.

Danny elbowed Lincoln and nodded at Ben. "Yo, Mumford?"

"Yeah?"

"Who's this craggy-ass lookin' cracker? The one with the puppy dog eyes and stupid video game socks?"

"That's Ben Cherry," Lincoln said. "Trustworthy as all hell, and with change to spare, man. He's good."

Satisfied with Lincoln's answer, Danny clapped his hands together and prepared for war.

"Okay, so here's what's up. Right about now, my partner, Knocktoe Joe, is gonna come out and show you what's good. He's taken enough time to figure out the best way to pull off this motherfucker with what y'all fed to him via my boy Mumford, and how much this little white collar gig is gonna cost. So, y'all are gonna listen and don't give him no shit."

Howard understood most of what had been said, and felt somewhat reassured.

James leaned back in his chair and cracked his knuckles. "Okay, I'm *down* with that. But can I ask something?"

"As long as it's to do with the job," Danny said. "Sure, ask."

"Who are you?"

Danny took offense to the statement, just as Lincoln winced with embarrassment. "James, man, be nice."

"I am nice," James said. "I just wanna know who your buddy is."

"You wanna know who I *is*?" Danny asked. "Man, who the fuck are you?"

"Me?"

"Yeah, you."

James stood up and rolled his shoulders, ready for a verbal standoff.

"I'm James Gilmour. Soon-to-be-former staff member of the personal lending team at Chrome Valley Federal."

Danny snorted at the man's torn jeans and Elvis Presley t-shirt. "Yeah, *King*, you look it."

"So, I ask again, not in a weird way, or whatever, but who are you?"

Danny sneered at the man and scratched his chin. "Who am I? Hmm," he pretended to think aloud. "I'm your motherfuckin' guardian angel, man. Your hookup to the thing that's gonna make your ass rich if you listen to me and do what I tell ya."

"Okay, cool, that's all I wanted to know," James said.

"Pfft. Yeah, Elvis *bitch*. That's *what* I am," Danny quipped, and then lowered his voice to a venomous grunt. "But *who* I am? Now, that right there is a different fuckin' story."

James, Ben, and especially Mark, bit their lips and tried to fight the nerves away.

Danny glanced at Lincoln, who knew exactly what was coming their way from the man with the plan.

"My name is Danny Driscoll. You ever heard of the Driscolls?"

No, none of the men had heard that name, and shook their heads.

"Yeah, figures. And you know why y'ain't heard that name?"

No, none of the men knew why, either.

"That's because y'all don't waltz on the same dance floor as the mother-fuck-in' *devil*, you know? Driscoll, bitches, you remember that name. Six outta my eight brothers are dead, leavin' my black ass alive to fend for my name, and the west side of this shit-tin valley. And over here? On the west side? West side's a place y'all have no business bein' in, until now, when y'all want a charming genius like me to wipe your great unwashed assholes after you finished shittin' your grand ideas all over my patch."

James' ears pricked up, and chanced a question. "Do you know the Eighteenth Gate Rollers?"

"Man, *fuck* Eighteenth Gate," Danny said. "I *shit* Eighteenth Gate. Nuttin' but a bunch of dread-locked swingin' cocksuckers. Driscoll's where it's at, *King*. We got the tools."

James took some comfort in the strange man's attitude. "Good, good."

Mark ran his hands through his hair and sighed. Danny caught him doing it, and took it as license to continue speaking.

"Horder's Point pen, north of the valley, was my home till two weeks ago. They gave me four years. Most of what Knocktoe put together for this new work is from that fuckin' job I got busted on. And you know who I trust to see this shit through on a job like this?"

Howard, Ben, Mark, and James listened for the answer with an acute intensity.

Danny thumped Lincoln on the shoulder.

"My boy, right here. Motherfucker Mumford. Y'all wanna see about *Angels With Dirty Faces*, and two brothers going two different ways, one way good, one bad. Well, Mumford's the angel, and I'm the brother with the dirty face and the Tommy Gun."

Lincoln and Danny bumped fists without even looking. A solid partnership, as evidenced by the bond in their eyes.

"*This* motherfucker sent me my packages and rolled up each and every week, Fridays, six pm, to visit me on the inside, and no fuckin' around. The only brother who gave a shit about me. He's my boy, and I trust *both* his bony buttocks with my life. See, I see y'all lookin' at me like what the fuck? Why the fuck is he sayin' all this? The question y'all need to ask yourselves, and I need to ask myself about you, is can we say the same for each other?"

For the first time since devising the idea to rob his place of work, Howard realized he hadn't considered the issue of trust.

Until now, he didn't need to.

He knew *most* of the guys involved, and two of them were sitting down.

"You can trust me, and us," Howard chanced.

"Is that so, Howard Ross?"

"Yes, of course," he said. "Listen, we're not hardened criminals."

"You. *Don't*. Say."

"I do say," Howard said. "Our rap sheet is all financial, but as far as criminality goes, none of us has had so much as a parking ticket."

"I have," Ben said.

"Shut up," Howard snapped, and looked Danny in his deep, dark-brown eyes. "Mr. Driscoll?"

"Danny."

"Danny," Howard continued, stony-faced. "We're not criminals, and we don't intend to be."

"Oh, you *ain't*, is you?"

"No. We, is—uh, we're... *ain't?*" Howard said, struggling to spar with his new partner-in-crime's vernacular. "Look, I'm kinda hoping we can keep it that way. All we want is to exploit a ten-minute window and get rich with the absolute minimum of fuss. Nobody gets hurt, and everybody in this room, and those claiming on the insurance, get rich in the process. That's it. James said so himself, we don't want any rough stuff."

Danny warmed to the man who had so eloquently explained his position.

"Howard?"

"Yeah?"

"I'mma tell you something. I'mma tell all-a-y'all something which I think you wanna hear, before we take this shit further, you know? Past the point of no return."

Eager to please, Howard was all ears. "Yes, yes, please do."

"It's about a week till this gig goes down, right?"

"We're thinking next Wednesday. Yes."

"And, uh, I'm sure you and your boys, here, have spent most of the past few hours runnin' through shit in your heads, like, how you *think* you're gonna feel when you point a gun at some unlucky motherfucker who was in the wrong place at the wrong time? Or, how y'all are concealing your identity from them bitches you work with so they don't suddenly figure out who you are, and become witnesses you gotta execute, right?"

James nodded, somewhat perturbed by the idea that Danny had been through all this before, and had a psychological advantage. "Yeah, I have."

"Good, man," Danny said. "I'm sure all y'all have, but talk to me about *this*. Have y'all thought *ahead*? How y'all are gonna behave after shit goes down and you got your paper?"

Mark bit his lip and considered leaving the group altogether. "I have. I think about it all the time."

"Oh, yeah, you with the gold teeth," Danny chuckled. "Yeah, Mumford mentioned you. You the deputy manager, the one who ain't been fired, yet, right? You're gonna be our mole inside the motherfucker when the day of reckonin' comes?"

"My name is Mark. And, yes, and I don't mind admitting that it makes me very nervous."

"Shit, Mark. You got the luckiest fuckin' duty on this work outta everyone. As far as motherfuckers are concerned, you're a hostage. No-damn-body need know what the fuck your involvement was. Shit, I *wish* I had that action on my previous jobs."

"I guess," Mark said. "I've considered what you said, though. I know I'm on the Federal's shit-list and going to get canned, but for the days I need to work, and be around those who we robbed, well, it's gonna be difficult. It's a pretense I'll have to keep up."

"And *not* fuck up, too," Danny said. "Listen to your boy Mark, here, guys. He's got a smart head surrounding them twenty-four karat skunk's teeth."

Danny stepped back and walked up to the metal table. He gripped the end of the red sheet and waved the four men over.

Ben grew fascinated by the man as he walked over to stand beside Howard. James and Mark reached the table with a keen eye trained on the tarpaulin.

Danny teased the red cover and grinned. "Before I show you this thing, I wanna know sumthin' else. Who here's thought about how you'll react when shit goes wrong, and y'all asses *get catched?*"

Mark coughed, almost to his own surprise. "Catched?"

"Uh-huh," Danny said. "As in, *police-fuckin'-got-you-and-now-you're-lookin'-at-twenty-five-to-life-in-a-Federal-pound-me-in-the-asshole-with-a-bread-knife-prison* kinda *catched*, motherfucker."

None of the men, including Lincoln Mumford, had entertained the notion of being collared by the cops.

Danny could almost hear the sound of bowels shifting around the room. He tightened his grip on the red cover and displayed his ultra-serious face.

"Y'all think about that, okay? You *ponder*. Think real hard about if you can survive in a prison designed to bullet-fuck your virgin assholes till they look like chewed bubblegum. Nobody hurt? Think about at least ten years for armed robbery. Then, if the bodies start pilin' up because you accidentally shot some broad who got all up in your face and gave you some shit. Chrome Valley, man, they still got the death penalty."

The fear of God seeped into each of the men's being. Danny was talking sense, and they knew it.

"For real, the corrupt old fellas running the show in the valley ain't too slow about putting a white boy in the chair because he fucked over a Federal fuckin' bank, man. Fuck, you think scumbags who fuck children get off easy with lame-ass sentences? Wait till you see how fuckin' fast they *execute brave* bitches who try to fuck the rich white boys out of their soft-earned millions, man. You rob a Korean store at gunpoint? You get a year. You rob a corporation, or a Federal joint? You get twenty-five life sentences."

"That's messed up," Ben said.

"Fuck yeah it is, but we mess 'em up, and we don't get fuckin' catched."

And with that final parting shot of wisdom, Danny yanked the sheet away from the table.

Whup.

Howard, Ben, Mark, and James' jaws would have dropped to the floor if what they had seen wasn't so damn serious in nature.

"Jesus Christ," Ben said. "Are these real?"

"Uh-huh. Real as a heart attack, man."

An impressive array of weapons lay on the table.

Three Remington 870 twelve-gauge pump-action shotguns.

Three Uzi 260 mm sub machine guns, each with 100-round extended magazines.

Five Glock 17s, and dozens boxes of yellow Winchester PDX1 .233 bullets

Five extra-strong waterproof *ProState* sports bags, each containing a black cotton balaclava.

Lincoln already knew what was under the sheet, and displayed little in the way of surprise. "Danny, man?"

"Yeah?"

"I get the feeling this ain't all you got."

Danny watched Howard lean into the shotgun closest to him on the table.

"Damn right this ain't all we got," Danny said. "We got guns comin' outta our asses all over the place, but— Yo, Ross?"

Howard looked up and moved his hand back from the shotgun. "Yeah?"

"Don't touch my shit, man. *Fuck*."

"Sorry."

"You'll touch the wrong part and end up blowing your nuts off, man. Leave it the fuck alone."

"I'm sorry."

"You *look* at the pieces, man, but you don't touch. Not till we green-light this gig and discuss what's up, you hear me? You fuckin' corporate pussy?"

Danny took real offense to the fact that four men he barely knew, and who knew absolutely nothing about crime, even dared to try and touch his merchandise.

"Shit, Mumford, are you seriously tellin' me a federal bank *hired* these four assholes?"

"Yeah, I know right?"

"And *I* can't even go straight no more because of my history, but these assholes can? Shit. They probably couldn't even count to eleven with two hands and their zipper undone, man."

Whump.

The back door slammed open and produced a steady *tap-tap-tapping* sound from within.

"And with any luck," came the weak, but stern voice from within the shadows behind the door, "They won't have to do that."

Everyone turned to the shadowy depths lurking behind the door and held their breath.

"Yo, Knocktoe, babe, we're out here."

"I know that, sweetheart."

Howard peered at the door with an intense anxiety.

He expected a behemoth of a man to walk out and introduce himself. Instead, a scrawny-looking man, around five feet in height, appeared and made his way to the table.

Knocktoe Joe DeVito wasn't what anyone would describe as intimidating, much to the surprise of those who had yet to meet him.

His checkered, buttoned shirt blanketed his pudgy belly, and the days of a bountiful head of hair were well behind him.

Joe's right foot seemed bigger than his left, and went some way to address the reason for his waddling gait which, in turn, explained why he was using a beautiful chrome-plated stick to aid his journey to the table.

The ungainly man barely made eye contact with the five strangers as he traversed the cold, bumpy floor.

"So, you must be the intellectuals?" Joe asked.

Ben leaned into Howard's ear. "He looks like a fucked-up Yoda."

Howard sniggered and thought of a fitting response. "Rob the bank, you will."

Both men snickered like children, which caught Joe's attention almost immediately. "What did you say?"

"Oh, nothing."

Joe slapped the end of his cane on the metal table, which produced an almighty *clang*.

"You think this is the time for jokes, huh? You sorry bunch of bankers?"

Howard cleared the giggling away from his throat. "No. I'm sorry."

"What's your name?"

"Howard. Howard Ross."

Joe scrunched his face, having misunderstood the man's reaffirmation. "Howard *Howard* Ross?"

"No, just Howard Ross."

The man with the cane dismissed Howard outright and continued with his speech. "I'm Knocktoe Joe

DeVito. I'm not one for small talk, or getting to know people I'm never gonna see again after working with them, so you'll forgive my aging old posterior if we skip the dick comparisons and just get down to the business at hand."

Mark nodded and leaned against the table. "I'm good with that."

Joe pushed his spectacles up the bridge of his nose and pulled out a folded sheet from under his arm.

"I don't care what you're good with, just pay attention."

The grubby-looking man's next move raised more questions than it answered; he walked up to Danny, squeezed his butt, and kissed him on the neck.

Somewhat taken aback, Mark rubbed his ear in embarrassment, and decided against making a comment.

"Okay," Joe said. "Before we get down to the specifics, I want to get some stuff out in the open so we don't have to talk about it."

Howard folded his arms and put on his best professional face.

"One. Yes, Danny and I *are* partners. In both senses of the word. We're business partners, and have been for many years. He's one of the best drivers in the valley for a job like this, and he's fully qualified for all licenses, including the Mack truck we'll be using."

"Okay," Ben said.

"Shut up," Joe snapped, as he returned to his train of thought and explained himself matter-of-factly.

"Two. Danny and I *are* partners in the biblical sense, as well. We have been since we became business partners. I dunno, in my view, there's not much of a difference between business and pleasure, and so we felt we'd mix the two. I don't give a shit what you think about this information, other than to say that it comes as a shock to most people who hear about it, and neither Danny nor I actually give a single, solitary *fuck* about what other people think, although, somewhat ironically, we do *fuck* each other on a semi-regular basis, which is more than can be said for most married, hetero-normative couples."

James became fascinated with Knocktoe Joe, and his beyond-autistic way of speaking; that, and the man's reluctance to look anyone other than Danny in the face.

"Hey, man, all good with me," James said.

"Shut up, I'm speaking."

"Sorry."

James winked at Danny. "He's quite a catch," he whispered, concealing his immediate contempt for the man with the cane.

"I know," Danny said. "Sorry, Joe, babe. Keep talking."

"And finally, three. Because I don't want to have to explain this again, and because it's irrelevant to the task at hand, the issue of my nickname, *Knocktoe*, which, as I'm sure you've already gleaned by now, is in reference to my right foot."

"Oh, uh, no," Howard chanced politely as he could. "We hadn't noticed."

Joe finally looked up at the man who'd spoken. "Don't patronize me, Howard *Howard* Ross," he said, and then turned to Danny. "Which one is he?"

"Howard Ross, babe.

"I know that, pumpkin cheeks. What I mean is, what did he do at the bank?"

"Ah, he was Head of Lending. He's kinda the one in charge of these dudes."

Joe didn't much like the answer, and shook his head. "*He's* in charge?"

"Yes, in a manner of speaking, anyway," Howard said. "I am. This whole thing was my idea."

"Whatever," Joe continued. "When I was in prison, a bunch of guys held me down and smashed my big toe with a ball-peen hammer. Knocked it out of joint and into the next toe, and into the next, like a bunch of dominoes, like that fat chick did to that wheelchair-bound cripple writer in *Misery*."

Ben's eyebrows raised when he figured out which movie Joe had referred to. "Ah, yeah, Kathy Bates."

"Shut up," Joe snapped and addressed everyone around the table. "Have any of you seen that movie?"

Everyone but Mark nodded, indicating that they had, indeed, seen it.

"And have any of you ever had that done to your feet?"

Everyone shook their head, politely, "no."

"Well, it *really* fucking hurt, and the damage was irreparable. So, now you know what happens when you chat shit to the bad guys and expect to get away with it."

All four men accepted the information and got on with their lives.

"Danny and I live together in our apartment, and we don't like people poking their noses in our affairs, not that we have affairs, obviously, because we're loyal to each other. Which brings me, quite neatly, really, to the plan I've devised."

Joe unfurled the huge sheet of paper and wafted it out over the length of the metal table. It rested atop the weapons, not that Joe seemed to care.

"This is the blueprint of the Chrome Valley Federal Bank in the financial district where you work."

He used his stick to point to the north end of the diagram.

"Covered entrance here, one external CCTV camera with a view of approximately thirty degrees, which includes most of the sidewalk on Lombardy, and the corner of Madhoff Ave."

He moved the cane to the mid-section. "This, what we'll refer to as the main banking area, contains eight desks in two quadrants, with two wide paths giving access to the three offices that line the north wall, one lending, one manager, one conference."

James and Mark couldn't help but marvel at the knowledge Knocktoe was revealing. Their eyes followed the end of the cane to the other end of the map.

"The teller counter, six registers, one of which is a dummy that contains the dye packets and marked bills. Someone here must know which of the six it is?"

Ben waved his hand, eagerly. "It's the third one on Week A, and the fifth on Week B."

"Interesting," Joe said. "You're on a bi-weekly rotation. Which week is this week?"

"Week B, sir," Ben said.

Joe nodded, and felt a bond develop with Ben who, to the others, came across as a bit *on the spectrum* anyway, and so thought nothing more of it.

"So next week is Week A," Joe said as he moved the cane to the other end of the map. "Third register is hot, leave it alone. Here, we have the back room area, with the typical areas. Lunch room, power hub, safe deposit vault, the stairs to the underground parking lot, and the drive-through area that serves seven lanes."

"Yeah," Lincoln said. "That's my area."

"Your area?"

"Yeah. There's a two-hour window where we have one teller on hand between ten and twelve in the morning."

"Just before the lunch hour rush, then?"

"Exactly."

Joe scratched his head and thought for a while. To the others, it seemed as if he was buffering.

Ben leaned back to Howard and whispered. "Hey, I just realized something."

"What?"

"If Knocktoe and Danny get married, then Danny's name would be *Danny DeVito*. Like the actor."

Howard huffed. "Ben?"

"Yeah?"

"Shut up."

Joe slammed his cane and shook his head. "Okay. Someone here went to buy the masks. Who was it?"

Mark stepped forward and produced the Marcovicci Beach bag. "Yes, that was me."

"Good. Take them out."

"Okay."

Mark tipped the bag upside down and shook the contents on top of the map.

All the men around the table smirked when they saw the rubbery latex masks roll around to a stop.

A rabbit, dog, bull, squirrel, and badger stared up at the ceiling lights, all with black, featureless holes in place of eyes.

Knocktoe pointed at them and turned away. "Okay, each of you choose one. I don't give a shit who gets which mask. Just hurry up and choose. We can't do this next bit without knowing who's who."

Ben went for the Ram's mask. "Well, hell, I'll have this one."

"No, I want the bull," James said.

Lincoln pointed at the squirrel mask. "I'll take this for *deez nuts*, man."

Howard held his arms out and waved. "Whoa, whoa, hold on. *Stop.*"

Ben and James gripped the ends of the ram mask and nearly pulled it apart. "What?"

"Put the goat mask down, or whatever it is. Put it down."

Ben protested, "But, I chose it first—"

Slam.

Knocktoe slapped his cane on the table and got angry. "I don't know if you remember what I said not sixty seconds ago? I said I don't give a flying *fuck* who gets what. Howard, you decide who gets which mask, and hurry up about it."

"Right."

131

Howard scanned the masks on the table and looked at the men.

He took the dog mask and flung it at Ben. "Right, you're the dog."

"What? Why?"

"Because your name's *Benjy*, okay?" Howard said. "Now, be a good little doggy—"

"—*Bitch*, more like," James scoffed.

"—Shut up, Gilmour," Howard snapped, unhappy at the interruption. "Cherry, be a good little doggy and be the dog. Period"

"The *dog period*?" Ben asked. "That's disgusting."

"Just shut the hell up and take the mask."

Next up, the ominous-looking gray bull mask. Howard grabbed by the right horn and tossed it at James. "You can be the sheep."

James caught the unwieldy mask and analyzed the horns. "Nah, this isn't a sheep. Or a goat. It's a bull."

Ben squinted at the mask in James' hands. "Nah, that's a steer. Maybe a longhorn?"

James opened the mask out and sniffed around the rim. "I'm not gonna be a steer. Rhymes with queer."

Howard took charge once he saw Knocktoe and Danny were unhappy with James' assessment.

"Okay, *enough*," Howard barked. "I don't care if it's a bull, or a longhorn, or a steer, or a goddamn milkshake with two twelve-inch dicks poking out the top," he fumed. "It's a fucking ram. Okay?"

James returned to the mask and chuckled. "Not a bull?"

Howard shook his head insistently. "Nope."

"Because the horns are—"

"—Shut up," Howard snapped. "With the amount of bullshit that usually comes out of your mouth, *bull* would be fitting. But it's not a bull. Some other guy on some other bank job is a bull, nut you. You're the ram."

Danny and Joe chuckled quietly, and threw Howard a knowing wink. A wave of relief set in now that the leader of the pack had clearly won the adulation of the two experienced criminals in the room.

"I'm good with that," James huffed. "The horns are cool, despite it being the wrong animal."

"Doesn't matter if you're good with it, James. Just shut up and accept it."

Howard pick up the next mask; a brown badger with black spots patched around the face. "Here," he said to Mark. "Catch."

"I'm the badger?" Mark asked as he fumbled the soft latex mask in his hands. "Why not the squirrel?"

"Because you've got two, fucked-up gold teeth, you buck-toothed bronco. So, you're the badger."

Lincoln snatched the squirrel mask and beamed at its adorable face. "So, that makes me the nut-eater, then? Good. Big, bushy tail, and cute. That's the one I wanted, anyhow."

All Howard was left with was the rabbit's mask, which made him grin with glee. "Quite fitting, really. Bunny. It's my daughter's nickname."

"Bunny?" Ben asked. "Not a rabbit?"

Howard slipped the latex mask over his head and patted down the flapping ears.

"You're right. I'd better not have you guys shouting out my daughter's nickname for everyone to hear. I'm the rabbit."

Joe folded his arms and cleared his throat. "Okay, are we quite finished now?"

Howard removed his mask and placed it on the tabletop. "Yes, I think so."

Joe lifted his head at the floppy ears on Howard's mask. "I think you'll find this is a rabbit. A bunny looks softer, it has finer hair, and not all coarse like it is on that mask."

"Is it?"

"Yes, it's a fucking rabbit," Joe said. "Plus, only a fucking moron would want his associates screaming his daughter's nickname at him in the bank."

"Oh. I hadn't thought of that."

"Yeah, you're quite good when it comes to *not* thinking," Joe said with his right fist clenched. "You're the rabbit, okay? If you wanna discuss further I'll happily take you aside and shoot you in the face?"

Howard balked at the idea and played it cool, despite wanting to shit in his pants. "No, no, I'm good. I'm the rabbit."

Ben turned around with his dog mask on his head, and when he spoke, it came out muffled. "What about Danny? Doesn't he get a mask?"

"No," Joe said. "He does not."

"Why?"

Joe slapped the canine mask clean off the man's head with his cane. "Because he's driving the Mack truck, you imbecile."

"Oww, hey."

"Danny's call sign is *Cat*. He doesn't need a mask."

Ben massaged his head and complained. "But why do we all have to wear masks, and Danny doesn't?"

"Oh, *right genius*. Yeah, how's that going to look?" Joe fumed. "Young Daniel Driscoll sitting in a Mack truck by the side of the freeway with a cat mask on his head, and his hands all looking blacker than Wesley Snipes, meowing at every police car that passes by?"

Ben collected the sweaty dog mask from the floor and patted it down. "*Fine.* Shit, I'm sorry I asked."

Joe went to strike him again. "My friend, you will be *sorry* if you ever question my methods again. See this cane?"

Ben flinched. "Y-Yeah, I see it. Please don't hit me again."

"I got a furnace out back. I could make the end of this stick white hot, and shove the cold end up your ass so the rest of us can laugh at you burning your hands trying to pull it out."

Mark covered his involuntary smirk with his hand. "Jesus Christ, I think I'm falling in love."

Joe moved his cane away and scowled at Ben. "Who is this guy, anyway?"

"That's Benjamin Cherry," Howard said. "Corporate Accounts."

"A corporate accountant, huh?" Joe snapped. "He looks like he should be in diapers and sucking on a cock-shaped pacifier. How old are you, anyway, *Benjamin*?"

"Old enough," Ben said.

"You know what they say about corporate accountants, don't you?"

"No. What?"

"That they're two-thirds accountant, one *half* incompetent."

Howard, James, and Mark chuckled quietly to themselves, further embarrassed to be associated with the man on the receiving end of a joke he didn't get.

"What?" Ben asked. "I don't get it."

"Yeah, that's what's concerning me," Joe spat. "So, now we know which filthy animal you filthy animals all are, we can move these pieces around and assign duties."

Slap.

The end of the cane hit the drive-through. "Simple enough, Squirrel?"

"Yeah?" Lincoln said.

"You're the getaway. We're gonna modify a Chevy for you. But while you're there, you can assist the clear-out of the cash in the drive-through. Use the seventh lane, the one closest to the window. Switch bags so the recipient can go to the vault with a fresh bag to fill it with."

"Okay, cool," Lincoln said. "So I wait at the drive-through, after?"

Joe moved his cane to the crossed-out void square at the bottom of the diagram. "Back parking lot. You won't be there long, and the back door to the drive-through is everyone's way out and into the modified Chevy for the escape."

Joe looked at the mask in Mark's hand. "You. *Badger*. The one with the gold teeth."

"My name's Mark."

"Is it really?" Joe spat. "What's your shoe size?"

"Umm, nine?"

"Right, that's *two* things I don't give a shit about, now. Listen to me, Badger."

"Okay?"

Joe moved his cane to the left of the map. "Once the others make themselves known, you hit up the drive-through, that is unless the animals out front need your help. I can't think why they would need your verminous little behind for anything other than a bullet shield, but if they don't need you, your primary concerns are the drive-through, and the vault. Three minutes tops."

"Okay."

Joe nodded at Ben. "*You*, the big mouthed, droopy-faced accountant type of bitch?"

"You talking to me?"

"Oh, fuck me, we got Robert De Niro in *Taxi Driver* joining in. Yes, you, you unwashed, scummy little cock-bell. Listen to me."

"Okay."

"You're on lookout, like a good doggy should be," Joe explained. "Guard your territory, and keep an eye out for the mailman. Spray your little puppy seed around the hostages and make sure they know who owns them."

"Uh, okay?"

"In this case, the mailman is anyone in authority. Security guards, police officers, off-duty hard men coming in to complain about their mortgage application being turned down, that kind of bullshit."

"Okay."

"Anyone with a gun or the power of arrest, is what I mean."

"Yeah, I get it."

Joe glanced at Ben, suspiciously. "You're good with people, right?"

"Well," Ben said. "They didn't make me Director of Corporate Accounts for nothing."

And they didn't fire your twelve year old ass for nothing, either, did they?"

"No, but—"

"—Right, enough of this gay talk," Joe said. "Put your affable character to use in case you have to use this, uh—" he said as he tried to read his writing on the map, "—conference room. Wow, that's kinda small, actually. Even the manager's office is bigger."

"Yeah, we've been saying that for ages," James said. "Fuckin' prick."

Joe shot the man a look of evil. "Who, me?"

"What?"

"The fuckin' prick? Were you talking about *me*?"

"Oh, God, no," James said. "No, I meant Victor Price. Our manager."

Joe put two-and-two together and, fortunately for James, arrived at four.

"*Phew.* I thought for a second I was gonna have to shoot you in the face. Good job I checked, eh?"

James felt a distinct quaking erupt in his boots. "Uh, Yeah? I guess?"

Joe stood up straight and bent his elbows back. "Ah, that reminds me. When you're giving orders to the customers in the bank, and your fellow ex-employees, you must be specific with your instructions, okay?"

Joe scanned the room to find an ocean of confused faces.

"For example, when you bust in there like retards on bath salts with your stupid animal masks on and your guns waving, if you want the customers and employees to put their hands up, then you *need* to say it exactly like that. Be specific. Or, another example, if you want them to hole up in the conference room, because they know the place, actually use the locations."

Maybe Joe had spoken too fast? Confused, he lost his temper, reached under the map, grabbed one of the Winchester shotguns, and slid the pump forward and back.

Tcha-Shtick.

"Get on the fuckin' ground, motherfuckers," he screamed. "On the floor, or I'll blow your fuckin' heads off."

Howard, Mark, Ben, and James dropped to the floor in an instant and squealed for dear life.

Without a trace of emotion, Joe slid the gun back under the map, and finished his explanation.

"Something along those lines. Just make sure it's specific. Specificity is *the thing*."

Four very terrified heads slowly slid out from behind the table, and assessed whether or not it was safe to stand up again.

Danny and Lincoln fist-bumped each other and offered the men a cheeky grin.

"Jesus Christ, the guy's insane," James muttered.

Joe looked at the table to find four of the six men had suddenly left the meeting. "Eh? Where did they all go?"

"Umm, babe? I think they're under the table," Danny said, and then hollered to the others. "It's okay, guys. Y'all can stand up, now. I think there's been a misunderstanding."

Baffled, Joe pursued his line of questioning. "Why would they be under the table?"

"Because you told them to, babe."

"No, no, no, *that* was an example. It was an example of me threatening to shoot them. I wasn't going to actually *shoot* them."

Joe returned to the table and nearly had a heart attack when he saw everyone had reappeared. "Oh, shit. Don't sneak up on me like that. I have a bad heart."

Howard looked at the map. "Joe?"

"Yeah, hi."

"That just leaves me and James. The rabbit and the ram."

Joe sniffed and returned to the map. "Squirrel parks the Chevy by the fire hydrant on Lombardy, which is just out of view of the external camera."

James watched on with interest. "Okay."

"Rabbit, Ram, and Dog exit the vehicle there and enter the bank just after eleven-thirty when the second guard is taking his, or her, lunch hour. I presume it's a *he*."

"It is," Lincoln said.

"When you're in, Dog's on customer watch, Rabbit's the face of the operation and makes the announcement, and Ram's on field duty."

James scanned the ram mask, quizzically. "Field duty?"

"Yeah, you're on-hand to communicate between the customer-facing side of the bank, and all the good stuff out back."

"Okay."

"Now, Rabbit?"

"Yeah?" Howard asked.

"The three of you will have the Winchester shotguns, but you *need* to show everyone inside you mean business. So when you announce yourselves, and it's up to you how you get their attention, you fire a shot in the ceiling. Shit them up, show them you're serious."

The child in Howard loved the proposition of being tasked with the opening line, just like he'd seen in the movies. "Okay, cool. I can do that."

"We'll see about that," Joe said. "Obviously don't shoot right *above* your head, or you'll get showered with plaster, and that's the last thing you need clogging up your mask, what with the building being sixty years old, at least, and probably full of asbestos."

"No, okay. I won't do that."

"Yeah, and don't come running to me when you develop lung cancer in forty years' time because of something I told you to do, because if you *do* do that, then guess what'll happen?"

"What?"

"I'll shoot you in the face," Joe snapped, and then turned to Danny. "Sweetheart?"

"Uh-huh?"

"Go get the voice alternators."

"Okay, babe."

He ran off towards the back door, and left Joe to address the team. "Are you all following me so far?"

Everyone nodded, expecting more details to follow. But they didn't.

"Any questions?" Joe asked, without room for a response. "No? Good. So, you have a nine-minute window, pre-lunch hour rush. Eleven-thirty, you exit the car, you enter the building, Dog keeps the little doggies in the conference kennel, while Rabbit shoots out the CCTV and destroys the footage on the computer."

The end of the cane screeched across the paper to the north end of the diagram, just in time for Danny to return with a heavy grocery bag.

"Ram and Rabbit empty the registers while Squirrel and Badger alleviate the drive-through of its soft-earned bills. And then the vault, all five *ProState* sports bags filled, one each. You unmask and switch to the balaclavas, and exit via the parking lot and into the Chevy. Squirrel takes you back here to the rendezvous point, via the Mack truck."

Happy with his plan, Joe stepped aside and rubbed his palms together.

"Pretty damn good, wouldn't you say?"

"Uh-huh," Howard said. "Seems easy enough to me."

"Nobody needs to get hurt here, gentlemen. What you lack in experience, you more than make up for with knowledge of the bank and everybody inside."

Danny reached the desk, lifted the bag and tapped the handle. "Babe, you want we should do these now?"

"Yeah, the voice alternators. Do it now."

The bag flipped upside down, and puked out six headsets and six wristwatches.

"What are these?" Mark asked.

"Well, the animal masks will disguise your gold teeth and any identifying features, but the one thing they *won't* disguise is your voice. Take a look, and hook them up to your left ear, and the watches on your left wrist."

Howard, Mark, Ben, James, and Lincoln each took a headset and slung it over their left ear.

"These don't come cheap gentlemen, and they're going to suck having to wear them under your masks, but it's only for a few minutes."

One by one, each of the five men took the corresponding watch, and strapped it to their left wrist.

"Hit the slider on the watch," Joe instructed. "You'll feel the earpiece and mouthpiece vibrate, which means you're comms-ready with each other."

Howard pinched the microphone. "Hello, hello? Can you hear me—"

Bwweeeoooww.

A thunderclap of intense feedback blasted from Howard's device and delivered a sharp dagger of tinnitus into everyone's brain via their ear holes.

"Yaaooow—*fuck*," James shrieked. "Shut it off."

Joe plugged his ear holes with his fingers. "Shit, stop speaking."

"Sorry."

"Each headset is fitted with a speaker, which modifies your voice, and connects to your watch. Turn the volume down on the mic and try again."

Ben kept his wrist away from his mouth and spoke into the microphone. "Woof, woof, this is Dog."

His voice blew out from the headset at several pitches higher than normal, and at varying speeds.

"Shit, man, I sound like the girl in The Exorcist crossed with a chipmunk."

"Exactly," Joe said. "Would you rather sound like yourself when you're ordering hostages to shut the fuck up? Hostages who, without your mask and alternator, would know who you were instantly?"

"No."

"No, I figured," Joe smiled, happy with his success so far. "Sweetheart, tell them about the mods."

Danny held up his cell phone sideways for all to see. An image of a silver Chevrolet with several arrows pointing at various parts of the vehicle glared across the screen.

"So, if you're all cool with this, I'mma modify the Chevy we have and tuned, upgrade the engine and transmission, fit bulletproof tires on, and temper and tint the windows. We don't need the car shittin' out on us when we're tryna get away."

"Cargo space?" Ben asked.

"Car no do that," Danny joked. "Car go road. Car not spaceship."

Joe laughed for the first time tonight. "Good one, sweetie."

Ben grimaced amongst the surreptitious giggling from his friends. "Hardy-fuckin'-har."

"No, straight up," Danny said. "Cargo's cool, plenty big enough for everything we're taking."

James scoffed at the idea. "The guns, the mods, all the equipment. Sounds expensive. How much is all this gonna cost?"

"It is," Danny said. "With the Mack rental, and this warehouse, all in all, we're looking at about fifteen thousand bucks in the red before we've even started."

Everyone balked at the idea and began to entertain their inevitable second thoughts.

"But the score is a little over eight million," Joe said. "So, I think we can afford to speculate to accumulate. Once your severance checks clear, it'll fund everything we need for the task at hand next Wednesday."

Despite James' unfailing scorn for the man, he knew he was right. The score was too good to turn down. "As much as I hate to say it, he's right."

"You're goddamn right I'm right, Mr. Presley."

Danny grew tired of the naivety in the room and thumped the table.

"Look, man. We ain't about to take chances, okay? We can go the cheap route, y'all. But if you wanna do that, you can count my sweet ass out. We do this shit properly, or we don't. Eight grand, fellas, and this vehicle leaves nothing to chance."

It took a while for Howard to act as ambassador for the group, none of whom would dare to be the one to walk away and ruin the plan.

Howard nodded, and saw sense in the idea. "Eight grand? Okay. That's fine."

"You bet your white ass it's fine," Danny fumed, and then pointed at the grid of roads at the end of the map. "I'm in the Mack truck waiting for you one mile south of Exit 11A."

Ben moved up to the table and asked a question, forgetting his alternator was still active. "The underpass?" he asked in a ridiculously high-pitched squeak.

"Man, take that thing off your head. This is serious."

Ben caught his headset in his hands as clumsily as he could muster. "Sorry."

"The underpass is insurance. When you leave the bank, every fuckin' cop from here to Horder's Point is gonna be looking for an unmarked silver Chevy. The valley's full of cameras and they'll trace its every movement. So, that's where I come in."

He pointed to the grass verge on the map, next to the freeway.

"I'll be stationed here in the truck, waitin' for y'all to call me. I drive up, enter the underpass, and you drive up the ramp, and I swallow you whole. All outta sight. As far as anyone watchin' is concerned, a Chevy went into the underpass, and never came back out."

"Like a regular Houdini act?" Mark said. "Clever. I like it."

"Now see you my black ass, now you don't," Danny chuckled. "Vanish into thin air, and we return right back here to the rendezvous for the count."

Joe stared each man in the eyes, which was a first for him since the meet began. He'd saved his seriousness to punctuate the question everyone would have to answer.

"That's it," he said. "So. Are you in?"

Convinced of the plan, Howard nodded. "Well, what good are we when we fail to take the opportunities presented to us? I'm in."

Danny nodded at James. "How about you, Elvis?"

"What Howard said. Yeah, I'm in."

Lincoln fist-bumped Danny. "Shit, you know I'm in."

That just left Ben and Mark, the latter of whom was still very much undecided. Joe's mood soured enough for him to change tact. "You're the deputy manager?"

"I am."

"You're already in the bank and at work," Joe said. "The safest role in this whole thing. I guess the question you have to ask yourself is this. Knowing what's coming your way, can you afford *not* to be in?"

Ben kept a careful watch for Mark's response. "C'mon man, if you're in, I'm in."

Danny moved in for the kill. "Plus, Mark, You know what's about to go down. And if you're in the bank, and you're not on board, then you're one of them. You're a hostage. A cheap-ass, gold-toothed hostage, with a front row seat of watching all your former colleagues and friends getting rich right before your eyes."

Mark had heard enough and snapped. "Fuck it. I'm in."

"Good for you," Joe said. "And you, Benjy-boy?"

Ben said nothing and hoped a quick nod of the head would suffice. "Uh-huh."

"No, no use nodding like a little epileptic infant in an electrified crib," Joe said. "I need to hear you say the words."

"Say it, Cherry," Howard spat. "Say the words."

"Okay, fine, *I'm in*."

And with that, the heist was on.

A damp, congratulatory haze lifted in the air, along with everyone's spirits.

Joe slapped the end of his cane onto his right palm. "Okay, that's settled. Danny and I take a ten percent cut, each, of the final score, including the bearer bonds. The cash is split five ways, which you'll take in your bags and stash someplace safe. I'll get Jimmy the Fence to take care of the bonds, and wire the cash to your accounts a few days after. You're all a *wunch of bankers*, so I assume you have secure accounts?"

"Yeah, we do," James said.

Joe giggled at the use of his new, offensive collective noun. "Ha. *Wunch of bankers*. I quite like that."

"Yeah, babe, it's cool," Danny said.

"I think I might use that phrase more often in future."

Knocktoe turned around and made his way to the door on the back wall. "This Saturday, gentlemen. Firearm training at Three Springs Common."

Howard hollered after him. "Joe?"

"Yes, Howard?"

"Firearm training?"

"Yes, firearm training," Joe said. "Like young Daniel said, if you're going in brute force, then you'll need a refresher at the very least. How to take down a bank without accidentally blowing your nuts off."

The idea was one nobody had considered.

A grin plastered across Howard's face when he decided, there and then, that Knocktoe Joe truly was their wise, guardian angel.

Chapter 7

An angry, wailing siren bounced around the dashboard as the Chrome Valley Federal Bank zoomed into view behind the windshield.

"Okay, slow down. Slow down. Take it easy."

"Yes, Lieutenant."

Lieutenant Fox gripped the passenger door handle as his driver pulled the unmarked Crown Vic over to the side of the road.

The decades hadn't been too kind to Lt. Fox. The bags under his eyes ruined what otherwise would have been a grizzled and world-weary complexion, complete with a brilliant ruff of jet black hair.

"Tape off the intersection, end of Lombardy Street and Madhoff."

"Understood."

A torrent of speeding police vehicles screeched to a halt all around Lt. Fox. As soon as the tires locked, the doors flung out and produced dozens of armed police officers.

Each of them used their vehicles for semi-cover as they aimed the vehicles at the building.

Fox reached into his holster and produced his police-issue MP5 Carbine firearm. He grabbed his megaphone and stepped out of the Ford.

"Nobody move till I've spoken to these guys," he hollered, forgetting that he could have used the megaphone in his hand.

A rotund man by the name of Detective Cohen raced up to Fox, who immediately sized him up. "The bank?"

"Yeah," Cohen said.

"Area secured?"

Cohen pointed to a handful of officers erecting a Police Barricade. "As we speak."

"How long have our friends been in the bank?"

"Twenty minutes, maybe longer."

"Any demands been made?"

"No."

Cohen produced his Android tablet and showed Fox footage of three suited animals walking towards the building.

"Okay, camera five caught three individuals at exactly 11:34 walking up Lombardy and up to the bank's entrance, just over there."

Fox squinted at the image and pointed at the Chevrolet in the bottom part of the screen. "This their car?"

"Yeah."

Fox surveyed the landscape of police vehicles and armed officers, all of whom readied themselves for action.

"I wanna know about the Chevy, and I want all the surveillance footage from every building sent to CVPD via the FTP server."

"It'll take a while, I think."

"No," Fox said. "It'll take five minutes. Every building here, five blocks in each direction, they're all hooked up. I want a full report on the Chevy's whereabouts prior to arrival, and where it is now. It must be somewhere."

Cohen scrubbed the timer on the video footage to the right. The Chevrolet fast-forwarded off the left-hand side of the screen. "We think it went to the drive-through."

"You *think,* or you know?"

"We think," Cohen explained. "By the angle it moved off at."

Fox sidestepped over to the nearest police vehicle, a white Jeep Cherokee, and switched on his megaphone. "Stop thinking, Detective, and start *knowing*."

"Yes, Lieutenant."

"When you update me, it'd better be factual, and not some bullshit conjecture."

"Understood."

"If the Chevy entered the drive-through, then the cameras at the back of the bank will have picked it up. These guys have run into trouble. They clearly didn't plan to stick around for the party to start out here, and I'm willing to bet a candy bar to a Chimo that their ride ain't about to leave without 'em. Find it. Find it *now*."

"Yes, sir."

"And get me a direct line to the bank," Fox hollered. "Let 'em know we wanna talk."

Detective Cohen acknowledged the assessment and ran over to a telecommunications van.

Fox ran his fingers through his jet black hair and spoke to the sergeant standing to his left, who aimed his pistol at the bank entrance double door.

"Any sign of movement?"

"No, sir."

Fox knocked the side of the megaphone and raised his voice. "This is the Chrome Valley Police Department. We know you're in there. Place your guns on the floor, and exit the building with your hands behind your heads."

***

Rabbit pushed through back the door and entered the main banking area. Though he couldn't quite see the street through the windows, he knew they were full of itchy-fingered police.

Before he made his way to the conference room, he stopped in his tracks and carefully removed his mask.

Howard's sweating face had been cocooned underneath the rubber for half an hour at this point, and the temporary lack of power and air conditioner had produced an ungodly amount of perspiration on his face, neck, and on the voice modulator hanging over his right ear.

"Ugh, what the fuck am I doing?" he whispered, quietly lamenting his predicament.

It was just his luck that his eyes landed on his former desk.

His right hand felt along his jacket pocket and rubbed against the sturdy metal name placard inside.

"I swear to God I'm going fucking insane."

He walked over to his desk and sat into his chair. Taking a proud position at the end of the tabletop was a brand new, ultra-shiny name placeholder, engraved on a rectangular gold slab. *Mr. A. Carlin: Head of Personal Borrowing.*

"Huh?"

Head of Personal *Borrowing*, Howard thought to himself. "Is that all it took? A stupid name change?"

From Head of Lending to Head of Personal Borrowing. Not so much as a lay-off as a fuck-off, in Howard's view.

"Spineless douche bags."

Howard stretched out the worn ends of the Rabbit mask and slipped the sweaty mask back over his head. "Ugh, this sucks."

A soon as he made his way to the conference room, the pink telephone on the adjacent banking table began to ring.

Rabbit froze solid and considered firing a shot into the cackling piece of plastic. The call might have been coming from someone important, he decided, and went to pick it up.

"Hello?"

"Who's this?"

"Who's this?"

"This is Lieutenant Fox of the Chrome Valley Police Department—"

"—Shit."

Rabbit slammed the phone down without thinking. He regretted it immediately after and, without sparing a thought for his actions, ran towards the conference room door. "Dog? Dog! They're here—"

Ring-ring.

Rabbit jumped in his shoes and nearly opened fire on his desk. The pink phone bounced along the desktop as it rang.

Dog pushed the door open, stepped into the main banking area, and hollered at Rabbit. "What the hell are you doing, now?"

"Look."

Ring-ring.

"So? It's a phone."

Rabbit shook his head and approached the phone once again. "No, it's the police. Some Lieutenant guy."

"How do you know?"

"I just talked to him."

"The cops know we're here?"

"*Know* we're here?" Rabbit yelped, close to losing his tail with worry. "There's a million of 'em outside having a fucking barbecue!"

Dog dived into the conference room, slid across the lengthy table, and jumped to the floor. He pulled the blinds away from the window and nearly puked when he saw scores of police with their weapons drawn behind the glass.

Hundreds of armed police, some in uniform, others in combat gear, marked and unmarked vehicles, and scores of pedestrians all lined the streets curious to witness the event.

Two ferocious-looking helicopters circled the scene, vying for death.

Dog's limbs turned to jelly as he struggled to shut the blinds on the windows. "Yeah, y-you're right. They're here."

"Told you."

"I don't see any barbecue, though?"

Rabbit couldn't figure out if Dog was joking or not, and decided to let it go. He turned from the banking area to a sea of stunned expressions from the hostages. "How many of them are out there?"

"Oh, you know, one or two—"

"—Good," Rabbit said. "We can take care of one or two of them—"

"—Hundred. Yeah, one or two hundred."

"What?"

Dog pushed past Karen and jumped through the opened door. "Rabbit, man, the whole fucking valley and their mother is out there. And they're all carrying."

The pink telephone continued to ring… and ring and ring…

Dog pointed his shotgun at the pink, plastic nuisance on the desk. "You gonna answer that?"

"No point, Ram and Badger are nearly done," Rabbit said. "We're meeting them at the stairs. There's no way on God's green Earth that this is turning into a siege, or some dumb-ass HBO crime drama."

"No. Good."

Rabbit turned around, picked up the handset, and slammed it back down onto the cradle. "Christ, at least it's stopped ringing, now," he said as he lifted his left wrist to his mouth.

"Amen," Dog said. "The stairs?"

"Yeah, hold on. Ram? Badger? Do you read me?"

"Yeah. We're just about done."

"Ram? Is that you?"

"Yeah, this is Ram. Give us a few minutes. We're nearly in the last safe, and the bearer bonds. The big money."

"I told you sixty seconds five fucking minutes ago," Rabbit said. "We got company outside, and I—"

Ring-ring.

The pink telephone jumped around again, demanding to be answered.

Rabbit thumped the table and grabbed the handset. "Shit."

"What are you doing?" Dog asked, surprised.

"Telling them to fuck off," Rabbit snapped as he spoke into the phone. "Right. What the fuck do you want, *now*?"

"This is Lieutenant Fox of the Chrome Valley—"

"—of the Chrome Fucking Valley Police Department, yeah, I remember when you told me the last time. Why do you keep calling, can't you see we're busy?"

"Actually, no. That's the problem. We can't see anything."

Howard knew the man was talking sense, and couldn't help but agree. "Well, yeah, that's kinda the point, isn't it?"

"Yeah, listen. This doesn't have to drag on and on, you know. We just want to know everyone in the building is safe. That's our main priority. At least give me that much."

"Of course everyone is safe."

Dog glanced at the dried-up blood splat on the wall and whimpered, quietly.

"Look, Lieutenant, we're nearly done, here. This isn't a hostage type of situation, or anything."

"It isn't?"

"No, not exactly. We overran a little bit, but we're all good, now," Rabbit said as he examined his wristwatch. "Listen, why don't I give you a quick call to let you know we're all good? Say, in a couple minutes from now?"

"Well, we're a bit short on time, really."

"Why? Do you have another bank robbery to go to?" Howard snapped.

"No, it's just that—"

Confused, Fox held the handset to his ear, with Detective Cohen listening in at the side.

"—Just that we'd like to get one of the hostages," Fox said. "Just so we know we can trust you. An act of good faith, if you like."

The giant surveillance truck loomed behind them with a bank of officials working on computer terminals in the back.

Howard's assured high-pitched whine drifted out from the speakers in the truck, and into Fox's ear.

"No, we're not here long enough. Just wait, it'll all be done with, soon."

Fox couldn't quite believe what he was hearing from the bank robber. "Well, that's kinda disappointing, uh—" he said as he shrugged his shoulders at Cohen, and then glanced at the printout of a furry creature dressed in a suit. "Actually, can I ask, are you the bunny?"

"The bunny?"

"Yeah," Fox explained as he leaned into the still image of the three animals in Cohen's hand. "We kinda, sorta, know you guys are wearing masks. The one in front has big, floppy ears and buck teeth?"

Detective Cohen pushed his tablet in front of Fox's face. A still CCTV image of a Rabbit, Dog, and Ram looked back at him.

"Ohhh, no. No, I'm a Rabbit. You can call me Rabbit."

"Rabbit?" Fox repeated. "Okay. *Rabbit*. And your friends, the Puppy and Goat. Are they there with you?"

"Goat?"

"Yeah, one of them is a goat?" Fox said. "Two big horns on his head. A bit taller than you?"

"You fucking idiot, that's not a goat. A goat doesn't have horns."

"Doesn't it?"

"Of course it fucking doesn't. It's a ram. Why do you think it's called a ram? It uses its horns to ram morons like you up the ass."

Fox threw Cohen a puzzled expression, and then turned to the snipers setting up for a shot atop the surrounding buildings. "Well, gee, sorry about that, Rabbit. We thought he was a goat. I didn't mean any offense."

"Whatever, no offense taken."

Fox winked at one of the snipers and pointed at the bank's entrance. "Listen, Rabbit, what's taken you so long, huh? Why didn't you leave before we got here? I'm just trying to understand."

"None of your business."

Fox suppressed his desire to burst out laughing at the silly-sounding, high-pitch voice. "And why do you sound like a drunk twelve-year-old girl?"

"It's a voice changer thing. For disguise. Asshole."

"Well, despite the change in voice, you seem like a decent, educated man. If nobody's hurt, and things are basically all good, why not walk away, huh? No damage done. We'll pretend this never happened?"

Fox mimed a sarcastic cross-my-heart-and-swear-to-die sign across his chest to an amused Cohen.

"Fox?"

"Yeah, Rabbit?"

A small pause drifted through the phone, which only served to underscore just how *wrong* Fox had gotten his foe.

"Do you think I'm fucking stupid?"

"Whoa, hold on, no, no, no. No, of course I don't think you're stupid, Rabbit."

"You and I both know we're not walking away from this thing without consequences. I can see you. I can see each and every one of you…"

Rabbit spoke on the pink telephone as he pulled the blinds away from the window in the manager's office.

"I can see each and every one of you, and the crowd that's gathered on the street. All those bored, listless

157

citizens wanting to catch a piece of the action to add color to their tawdry, boring lives."

To Howard, Lieutenant Fox resembled more a tiny, black ant in the distance amongst all the vehicles and quizzical civilians.

Dog peered over Rabbit's shoulder as Fox turned around in an attempt to see which window his opposite number was looking through.

"Come on, Rabbit. It's not that bad."

Rabbit pulled the blind shut and turned to Dog as he talked. "It's a Federal bank, Lieutenant Fox. Federal property. A Federal offense. We're not talking jail time, here, we're talking multiple take-turns-to-destroy-my-bowels-gang-bang prison time if we don't get away squeaky clean."

Rabbit didn't have the best view of the street, but he could at least see nervousness building up underneath the Dog's mask.

"So, if I were you, Fox, I'd have your men put their guns away and back the fuck up—"

"—But, but—"

"—Before we start executing the hostages."

"Rabbit?"

"Yeah?"

Lt. Fox fell silent before delivering a hasty change in his manner.

"I am going to catch you. Might not be today, or next week, but it's going to happen. When you least expect it, I'll be right there behind you, ready to grab your fluffy little tail and wrap it round your neck."

"Oh, really?"

"Yeah. Really. I just wanted you to know that."

Howard pretended to shudder and spat into the phone. "Ooh, I'm really scared."

"Yeah, you better be."

"Yeah. Fuckety-bye."

Rabbit slammed the phone back on its cradle and marched out of the manager's office.

Confused, Dog chased after him. "Howard, man?"

Rabbit turned around and smacked Dog's shoulders over and over again in anger. "Shut the fuck up. Shut the fuck up, and stop calling me by my name, you fucking imbecile."

Dog flinched and protested. "Hey."

"*Benjamin fucking Cherry*," Rabbit squeaked in frustration. "There. How do *you* like having your fucking real name being said out loud, you malformed, deranged, idiotic cock juggler? Shit."

"Jeez, man, calm the fuck down," Dog said. "Seriously, you're gonna make a mistake if we—"

"—What the hell are you talking about, you jumped-up little turd? This *whole* damn thing is one giant mistake."

Rabbit kicked the table, and recoiled from the pain caused to his shin. "Ah, fuck my life."

"Rabbit, man—"

"—Shut up," Rabbit screamed and grabbed his shotgun in both hands. "Oh, fuck this I'll show 'em. I'll show those white-collar son of a bitches who's *boss* around here."

Rabbit kicked the conference room door open to find Karen and Kate peering through the blinds and marveling at the commotion on the main road.

He fired a shot into the ceiling, startling everyone in the room into a state of terror.

"Get away from the goddamn window, girls."

Kate held her beating chest and backed away from the window. "Okay, okay. Don't shoot."

Dog walked to the conference room door and kept his gun trained on the entrance.

Rabbit watched the terrified hostages lose their minds. He clutched the pump on his shotgun and chambered a fresh round.

"Right, listen up you gaggle of insanely irritating fuck-nuggets. Here's the thing. I am *monumentally* fucking angry, like, to an almost psychopathic degree, so don't, you know, get all clever and shit and test me, okay?"

Everyone nodded, obediently.

"Okay, good. If you move, I'll blow your fucking nipples off. Now, I'm looking for a piece of shit named Carlin. First name, A. Is there a useless, waste of oxygen-sucking piece of shit in here named Carlin? Where are you?"

Everyone remained perfectly still.

The man with spectacles remained a little too still for comfort and stood out like a sore thumb.

It caught Rabbit's attention in an instant.

"You?"

The man nodded so hard his head almost fell off his shoulders. "Y-Yes."

"So, you're the douche bag Ram found hiding in the lunchroom?"

"I w-wasn't hiding."

"Don't answer me back, you prick. You shoulda escaped out the back while you had the chance."

"Y-Yes."

"What does the A stand for, anyhow?" Rabbit asked, before thinking of a way to antagonize the young man. "No, let me guess. Asshole? It stands for Asshole, right? You look like an asshole, asshole."

Close to tears, the young man shook his head and cleared his throat. "No. My n-name is Aaron."

"You're new here, aren't you? *Asshole?*"

"Y-Yes."

"Okay, *asshole*. Get up and come over here. We're gonna play a little game called *I'm a Piece of Shit and I Don't Give a Shit Whose Job I Fucking Steal.*"

Aaron slowly rose to his feet with his hands in the air and stepped behind the row of chairs in his path. "Sorry, excuse me. Sorry."

Moments later, Aaron came face-to-face with the expectant Rabbit, who sized him up and snorted. "How the fuck old are you, anyway, *Asshole*?"

"Twenty-two next week, sir."

Shocked, Rabbit demanded some confirmation that his hearing was okay. "Twenty-two?"

"Y-Yes."

"*Fuck*. I've got jerk-off cum socks older than you. Now, out."

Rabbit socked Aaron in the back with his shotgun and booted him out of the room.

Dog scanned the street through the front doors and hollered at Rabbit as he walked out of the room.

"Jesus H Christmas, there must be, like, a hundred of them out there—whoa, hang on. Who's this guy?"

Rabbit pushed Aaron forward a few steps and waved his gun around. "This is Asshole Carlin. Head of Ass-Fondling, or whatever the fuck they're calling it this week."

"Asshole Carlin?"

"Uh-huh," Rabbit said. "For some reason they insist on calling him Aaron, according to his name thing."

"Aaron?" Dog asked.

"Y-Yes, sir—"

"—Shut up," Dog snapped. "Ohh, yeah, yeah. I heard the guy before you got laid off, right?"

Aaron nodded, thinking he was developing a knowing friendship with his oppressors. "Yeah, they changed the job title so they could hire me, and get rid of the other guy. I heard he was useless."

Rabbit stepped forward and got in Aaron's face.

"That useless guy you replaced had a family. He was older and more experienced than you. He was a good man. Very loyal, so I heard. But that probably doesn't mean much to a goddamn Millennial home-wrecker like you, eh, *Asshole*?"

"That's not what I heard."

Rabbit stared the man in the eyes, hoping to catch him out and give him a reason to kill. "Oh no?"

"No," Aaron said. "Apparently, he was a real lazy dick. Price called him a waste of space asshole behind his back and whenever he spoke about him."

Rabbit's ears slumped at the news. "Really?"

"Yeah. And, I heard he jerked off under his desk."

Rabbit threatened to knock the man out. "Shut the fuck up. Those were *not* cum stains."

"P-Please don't hit me," Aaron flinched and yelped. "I'm only t-telling you what Mr. Price said."

"Yeah," Rabbit growled "And look what happened to *him.*"

"Happens all the time," Dog said. "I heard they lay people off and just change the job title, add a few more desk duties, just so they can replace them with new, cheaper blood."

"Yeah, those willing to take an ass-pounding as a salary," Rabbit said as he lifted his head and eyeballed his associate. "Dog. Mask, please."

"You what, now?"

"Gimme your fucking mask," Rabbit said, before returning to Aaron. "So, the guy you replaced was useless, huh? Some useless piece of shit, eh?"

"Yeah."

Rabbit held the man's shoulder and sighed. "Well, *Aaron*, I hear he speaks very highly of you, my friend."

Dog removed his sweaty mask and blinked three times. "Whoa. It's mighty hot in there."

Aaron protested and looked away, fearful for his life. "What? No, I don't want to see your face. Please, don't."

Rabbit wrestled the soaking wet Dog mask from Ben's clutches and pushed it into Aaron's chest.

"Put it on."

He shoved the mask into Aaron's chest and palmed his shoulder.

"Don't make me ask again, Asshole Carlin. Put it on."

"Okay, okay."

As the youngster pulled the flaps over his head, Rabbit opened the chamber on his shotgun and pushed the bullets out, one by one.

"Uh, Rabbit?"

"What?"

"What are you doing?"

The angry, floppy-eared robber stared at the Dog face crawling down Aaron's head.

"Shut up."

He pushed his empty shotgun into Aaron's hands. "Here, take it."

Aaron's muffled voice waded from the holes in the Dog mask mouth. "Wh-what are you d-doing?"

"You're gonna give the cops out there a message. Come with me."

Rabbit pushed Aaron forward and held out his free hand. "Ben, give me your gun."

"What? Don't say my name?"

"Aww, shut the fuck up and give me your gun, you flea-ridden dumb ass."

Push.

Aaron, now wearing the dog mask, stumbled forwards and crashed against the double doors with the shotgun in both hands. "P-Please, d-don't—they're gonna shoot me."

"Shut up."

Rabbit booted the door open and dragged Aaron to the door. "Now, be a good doggy, and run across the road. Point the gun at the guy dressed in black by the van. I hear he's a real prick."

"N-No, please."

"If you don't do it, I'll go back in the room and execute everyone in there. And then we'll leave. And it'll all be your fault because you didn't do as instructed. Your choice, *Fido*."

"Okay, p-please, d-don't shoot anyone. I'll d-do it."

Rabbit stepped aside and allowed the man through the doors and into the covered entrance.

"Okay, boy. *Fetch*."

Rabbit stepped back and pulled the doors shut, leaving a thoroughly shaken Aaron to take two steps forward and into view of every officer aiming their assault rifles at the building…

Chapter 8

MARK AMOS
— Wednesday, September 30th —

It had been a weird morning for Mark Amos, Deputy Manager at Chrome Valley Federal.

If anything, it was atypical of his usual Monday morning.

The 8 am team meeting had been canceled, and because there was no meeting, there were no coffees and pastries lining the stomachs of the main employees, which meant most of them were already in a bad mood.

It was the reason Mark had a *Bean There, Done That* takeout coffee in his hand as he perched on the teller counter and greeted the customers in line.

The first among them was a woman by the name of Lavinia Craven, who always found Mark's presence a sight for sore eyes.

She threw a cheeky wink at him as she clutched her handbag. "Ooo. Hello, Mr. Amos."

"Good morning, Mrs. Craven," Mark said. "How are you?"

"Oh, I'm fine. It's Monday morning, which means this old bag of bones collects her social security and lives to see another week."

"Ha."

Lavinia noticed something peculiar about Mark's behavior, this morning. It could have been something to do with the cell phone he was looking at, safely ensconced in the right hand of one of the prettier female tellers; Karen Compston.

Or, it might have been the fact that Mark occasionally glanced at the conference room with a degree of concern on his face. Ironside and Capone were dealing with Howard.

Lavinia broke Mark out of his inattention and pointed at the phone in Karen's hand. "What is that you're watching, Mr. Amos?"

"Oh this? Ha. Here, look."

Kate turned the landscape image around and showed Lavinia a two-minute video of a boy playing on a piano.

Lavinia adjusted her spectacles and focused on the footage. "Who's this fella?"

"My son, Charlie," Karen explained. "He's just turned eight, and he just loves his piano."

"Aww, ain't he a cutie?"

Karen made the mistake of looking up at the teller counter. Kate Durst hollered at her as she served a customer.

"Karen, back to work, please."

"Yeah, you better go," Mark said. "You don't wanna piss Durst off, right?"

"Right."

"Ooh, the language around here," Lavinia tutted. "Piss this, and piss that. You can't move around here for the pissing language from some of the staff members."

Mark rubbed the woman's shoulder with affection. "Well, when it comes to urination, we *aim* to please."

"Ooh, you cheeky devil."

The pair enjoyed the moment, when a large woman with red spectacles accosted Karen behind the counter.

"Where have you been, Compston? Can't you see we've got customers waiting?"

Karen pocketed her phone and rolled up her sleeves. "I was on my break, Joanne. What do you want from me?"

"A bit of professionalism and common courtesy, if that's not too much to ask. Now, get serving that line on till four."

The fastidious Joanne pushed her glasses up the bridge of her nose and threw a smile to her next customer. "Yes, ma'am, how can I help you?"

Just then, Mark turned to the conference room door and saw Howard trundle out with an EZ-Flex box in his arms, his metaphorical tail between his legs.

"Oh dear."

Lavinia squinted, and looked at Mark. "What?"

"Over there," Mark said. "Poor Mr. Ross. Don't tell anyone, but today is his last day."

"Oh, that's a shame. I kind of liked him."

"Yeah, he was laid off on Monday."

Howard clenched his fists and stormed over to his office with murder in his eyes. Ben chased after him in a vain attempt to calm him down.

"Eh, he doesn't look too happy, does he?" Lavinia said.

"Not as such, no."

Mark moved away from the woman and dared to approach Howard on his way out of the building. "Hey."

"Hey," Howard muttered, feeling sorry for himself. "Any news on your lay-off, yet?"

Mark's mood soured in a heartbeat. "Next round is week after next, so I guess that's when I get my marching orders."

"Walk with me."

Howard moved off and scanned the four CCTV cameras dotted around the banking area.

"Listen, Knocktoe's received the money. We're still on for Saturday, right?"

Mark checked the security guard in the corner of his right eye. "Yes, of course," he said, as he turned to James at his desk, who rolled forward and ducked underneath it.

"Ugh, I wish he wasn't so blatant about using at work."

"Never mind that, I'll have a word with him," Howard said. "I'll see you on Saturday. Don't be late."

How to Take Down a Bank
Without Accidentally Blowing Your Nuts off
Three Springs Common
— *Saturday, October 3rd* —

Knocktoe Joe hobbled through the grass with his cane, and approached the makeshift wooden table.

"Okay, you bunch of filthy animals, listen up."

Mark took center stage amongst his associates, and marveled at the vast array of weaponry on the table; the same collection they'd seen at the first meet four days ago:

Five pump-action shotguns.

Five Glock 17s.

Three Uzi sub machine guns, two with attached silencers…

… and an inordinate amount of ammunition stacked in boxes, right next to a plastic *Ammo Domini* carrier bag.

Howard, James, Ben, and Lincoln waited for the initiation to begin.

"Variety is the spice of life," Joe said. "It's also the life of spies, of course, but that doesn't apply here, because you're not spies. You're robbers. Albeit for a measly ten minutes, but that's the way it goes."

Everyone watched Joe grab the grip of the first shotgun and point it at the muddied ground.

"Okay, here we have Remington eight-seventy. Twelve-gauge pump-action. Rabbit, Dog, and Ram, you'll have these."

Mark folded his arms and squinted at the man. "Why them?"

"Because they're out in the front with the lowlifes," Joe said. "These are for show, and they have a helluva kick.

You, Badger, and our little black squirrel get the Uzis. They're smaller, much like the back of the bank, and easier to carry."

Joe pointed to the Glock 17s. "One each, as a back up. You probably won't need them. But it's better to have them and not need them, than—"

"—Than to *not* have them and need them?" Howard finished.

"Oh," Joe snapped, angered by the interruption. "So you're the one using the brain cell, today, huh?"

"What?"

Joe lifted the shotgun and offered it to Howard. "Seeing as you're such an expert. You used one of these before?"

"Yeah," Howard said. "My father had a ranch up at Horder's Point. We used to go shooting on the weekends."

He chucked the gun into Howard's hands.

"This isn't a straightforward shooting weekend, now, Howard Ross. Load up. Show us what you got."

"Okay."

Careful to avoid confusing the others, and annoying Joe, he unlocked the pump and inspected the empty magazine.

Ben and Lincoln stepped closer and watched.

"Now, see how Howard loads it? The chamber is clear. You always perform a safety check before handling. Use the lever to push down, unlock the pump, and you can manipulate it."

Howard loaded a snap cap bullet into the chamber, and slid the pump along the barrel.

Joe continued to explain what was happening. "Push the round into the loading gate, up, and across.

Slot.

"When it clears the elevator, you're good to go. It feeds into the chamber, and you're ready to fire."

"Ready," Howard said, just in time for Joe to stand aside and reveal a target several feet away.

Joe pointed at a wooden target stump with a blown-up printout of Victor Price's photo ID stuck to it. "Who's idea was that?"

"Mine," Mark said. "Rather fitting, I think."

Howard took aim at the target. "Ready."

"Sights down, and tease the trigger—"

Blam.

The picture of Victor Price's head exploded into a shower of wood fragments, tearing the paper in two.

"Helluva recoil," Howard said.

He turned around to see Mark, Lincoln, Ben, and James ducking with their fingers in their ears.

"Okay, you fairies can get up, now," Joe said to the men. "I'm splitting you into pairs. Howard, you're with Mark. Teach our spotty little youth how to shoot. As for the rest of you? You're with me."

***

Bang—blam—blam.

The sound of random shots from the distance rang out through the trees as Howard passed his shotgun to Mark. "While Joe's not looking. Wanna try?"

"Sure."

"It's ready to fire, so don't point it at anyone you like."

Mark lifted it up and aimed down the sight. Another target with Victor Price's head focused into view.

"*Bastard.*"

"Uh-huh."

Mark went for the trigger, and accidentally pulled it.

Blam.

He missed the target completely, and the recoil was so forceful that the shotgun jumped out of his hand.

"Agh!"

The bullet hit a tree, causing the leaves to ping into the air, just as the gun hit the mud.

"Hey, be careful, numb nuts. It's not a toy."

"I'm sorry."

Howard picked the gun off the floor and wiped the dirt on his jeans. "Nearly blew your balls off there, you idiot."

"I think I'll stick with the Uzi."

A cool gust of wind calmed Mark's sweating pores for the briefest of moments, right before he patted his own buttocks through his pants.

"It's so hot today. For October?"

"Yeah, I'm sweating like a pig, too," Howard said.

"I feel as if Shrek and my buttocks are arguing about whose swamp it is."

Howard produced a childlike snort of amusement, and let his friend rant.

"I just *knew* Price was up to something," Mark said. "I just knew, you know?"

"Yeah, I know," Howard said. "What can I say? I told you it was true."

Mark kept an eye out for Joe, who busied himself with Ben trying to use the shotgun.

Mark snorted and bounced the Uzi in his hand. "The way Price was behaving around me since we've been back after months of working from home. Even during those *Vroom* conference calls he had us in management take during quarantine. I knew he was plotting something. Talking to the shills further up the ladder. Bad-mouthing me behind my back. All the good time."

"I'm not surprised in the slightest."

"I mean, after all, he did it to you, and Cherry, and Mumford, and Gilmour, as well. So why not me, too? The asshole never liked me, and believe me, Howie, the feeling is fucking mutual. You definitely saw my name on their hit list, right?"

Howard held his breath as he aimed at the next target. "Firing."

Mark held his fingers his ear. "Do it."

Blam—spatch.

"Gotcha, you fucker," Howard said as he lowered the gun and ejected the spent ammunition from the gun. "Hell, the papers they had? Full of names, including yours, and all the boys who got their asses machine-fucked. They were talking shit about you while I was in the room, too."

"They were?"

"Yeah," Howard lied, hoping Mark would cross over to his way of thinking. "Calling you all sorts of names, like, you know, *Teeth Curtains, Goldfingerer*, and *Golden-Brown Eye*, the *asshole* from the James Bond movies."

"Bastards."

"And *Bumraker*."

"Double bastards."

Howard thought aloud and corrected himself. "Although, I think they switched the '*k*' for a '*p*' on that last one. I don't really remember, to be honest. The fact they said it means they obviously know that your wife caught you sucking a dick. Pfft. *Bumraper*, my ass."

"Fucking *triple* bastards."

"I know right?" Howard offered. "I love that movie. Totally ruined it, now. I'm never gonna be able to sing that Shirley Bassey theme tune without thinking of your bony, hairy ass."

Mark stomped on the floor like an angry little child and released the safety catch on his Uzi. "Dude, that's not funny."

Now fully enraged, Mark aimed the Uzi at the trees and teased the trigger. "You know, those bastards should—Wah!"

Thraa-aa-tat-a-taaaat.

Mark's hand jumped up, carried by the weight of the gunfire. The rope of a hundred bullets burst up the tree and flew out of control

"Agh."

He dropped the gun on the ground, and hoped it would stop firing.

"Jesus Christ, Amos. Be careful with those triggers, they're sensitive."

"Okay, okay."

Howard scooped the gun off the ground, flicked the safety back on, and handed it back to Mark. "You're gonna end up shooting some poor bastard in the face by mistake if you're not careful."

"I know, I know."

Mark placed the gun on the table and wiped his hands together. "Guns aren't my thing, really."

"You don't say."

Mark scoffed and realized just how useless he was being. "I can't hold up a bank."

"You won't have to," Howard said. "You leave that part to us. You're on vault duty. You just have to hold up Price and get him to open the vault."

Mark grinned at the next target a few feet away. "Yeah, we'll show 'em who's boss."

Howard pumped his shotgun and took aim once again. "We can *stick* it to 'em, you know? Show 'em who they're messing with, and make sure we never get shit on or have to work ever again."

Just then, the sound of a super engine rumbled through the trees, forcing Mark and Howard to inspect what was causing the noise.

A shiny, silver Chevy rolled to a stop, and produced an elated Danny Driscoll from the driver's side.

"Okay, now *that* is what's up."

Danny clapped his hands together and walked over to Joe in the distance. The two embraced and admired the car.

"I guess that's our severance checks put to good use, then," Howard said.

"Look at the way those two lover boys behave," Mark said. "How do we know we can even trust them?"

"I trust Lincoln. So, that's good enough for me."

Mark watched on as Danny and Knocktoe talked,

quietly, by the car. "I dunno, you know. Something seems fishy about them."

Chapter 9

Aaron Carlin took a deep breath through the sweaty Dog mask and scanned the cop-lined street behind the bank's entrance doors.

"Oh, shit. What am I g-gonna do?"

Ben and Rabbit watched from the other side of the double doors. When Aaron turned his doggy face to them, Rabbit aimed his shotgun right back at him and indicated for him to move out.

Aaron took a deep breath. "Shit."

He stepped through the door and entered the covered entrance with his gun in both hands. "Don't shoot."

"Freeze," came a voice from behind the first police vehicle.

What felt like ten thousand assault rifles all pointed in Aaron's direction.

Lt. Fox spotted him and raised his megaphone. "You. Get on the ground. Now."

"Please, don't shoot. I didn't do anything."

Detective Cohen squinted at the bizarre sight of a suited dog carrying a shotgun. "That's him."

"Hold your fire, they're giving themselves up."

Aaron screamed at the top of his lungs. "Don't shoot."

Rabbit marched through the personal banking area and went for the pink phone. Ben stopped in his tracks and paused to look at the hostages all watching the stand-off through the blinds in the conference room.

"Ah, damn it, Ross. Why did you do this?"

Ben ducked out of view and reached into his sports bag, just as Kate turned to look at him. He whipped out a balaclava from the depths of the bag and pulled it over his face.

"Ahh, that's better. At least the cotton is soaking up the sweat."

Rabbit checked over his shoulder to see that Ben's was faceless. He grabbed the pink handset and lifted it to his giant, floppy rabbit ear.

"Are you there, Lieutenant? I know you're there. You're always on the other end of the line."

Fox's voice flew out of the ear piece in haste. *"Rabbit?"*

"Uh-huh," he said. "What you're about to see is an example of just how fucking serious we are, asshole."

"Listen, uh, Rabbit. I don't know why you have one of yours out here, but something ain't right."

"I want you to pass on a message to the Dog with the shotgun."

Rabbit moved forward and peered through the window in the manager's office. He saw Fox with the telecommunication phone in his right hand, and his MP5 in his left.

"What's that?"

"Tell him if he doesn't do as we agreed, that every single woman in the room is gonna die."

Rabbit blinked three times, and watched as Lt. Fox lowered the megaphone and hollered at the man in the dog mask. "Hey, you. Dog."

Just then, the back door to the bank flew open. Ram and Badger pushed through with Milton in tow. The latter grabbed the man's collar and flung him against Howard's old desk.

"Stay there."

"Okay."

Milton's face sported black and blue bruises, and several cuts above his right eye. Rabbit chuckled at the grief his associates had given him.

Escape was imminent.

Fox spoke into the phone. *"What do you want me to say, Rabbit?"*

"Tell Fido over there he has five seconds to do what we want, or else the hostages die," he said, before turning to Ben, Ram, and Badger. "Get ready. When you hear the gunshots, we're outta here. Back staircase."

Badger kept the back door open with his foot. "Okay, ready when you are."

Fox cleared his throat and ignored Detective Cohen's asinine look of confusion. "What's he saying?"

"He wants me to pass a message to his associate, over there. The Dog."

"The Dog?"

Fox lifted the megaphone to his lips. "Hey. Dog?"

Aaron turned his head to the left and looked at the man who had spoken. "Don't shoot."

"I got a message from Rabbit. He says you're to do the *thing* you agreed, or else he'll kill the hostages."

"Oh, shit."

"And believe me, we don't want *any* hostages hurt. So, you know, do what you gotta do and let's get this thing over with."

Dog's voice trembled. "He said that?"

"No, not that last bit," lt. Fox explained. "That last bit was me speaking, not, uh, Rabbit."

"Ugh."

"Does he want you to surrender?" Fox asked. "Get on your knees. Let us take it from here."

Aaron slid his index finger around the trigger and bolted across the road. "It isn't me. It's not my fault."

Aaron swung the shotgun around and, before he could pull on the trigger, one of the armed officers screamed and opened fire.

"Gun!"

Blam-blam-blam.

Fox, Cohen, and the armed officers opened fire on Aaron as he fired back and raced towards the other side of the road.

A whirlwind of bullets exploded up Aaron's legs, which pushed him to his knees. A second round blasted from the assault rifles.

Bam-bam-spatch.

Aaron's chest burst open, along with his abdomen and neck. Bits of rubber pinged away from his head, as the gunfire chewed through his mask, skull, and body in a haze of blood and gunfire.

Fox yelled into the megaphone. "Hold your fire."

"Ngggg."

Aaron stumbled onto his right knee and tried to make it to the road. A stray, lone bullet clipped the end of his shotgun, catapulting it from his hands and through a nearby storefront window.

Finally, Aaron breathed his last, and crashed to the ground, face-first in a pool of his own blood.

Rabbit punched the air in excitement as he held the phone to his ear. "Oh, yeah. Nice work Lieutenant."

Fox's agitated voice burst through the phone. *"You asshole. You'd willingly give up one of your own like that?"*

"Close, but no cigar. Why don't you go check on him and see just how badly you fucked up?"

"What?"

"That ain't no bank robber, asshole."

"What are you talking ab—"

"—See ya."

Slam.

Rabbit dropped the phone onto the desk and raced over to the conference room. He pointed at Milton and screamed at Ram.

"Okay, staircase. Take *Girlfriend* with you. She's gonna be our little bullet shield if it all goes south."

Milton lifted his arms in protest. "No, p-please—"

"—Shut up, bitch," Ram said. "You're coming with us. Can't wait to wear you as protection."

Badger bolted through the door and waved Ram and Ben over. "Let's go."

Rabbit arrived at the conference room and stared at the concerned hostages still reeling from the event that had gone down outside.

"You bastard," Kate screamed. "You killed him."

"Ah, he deserved it, anyway."

Kate, Karen, Richard, Lavinia, and the others all stared at the energized rabbit, wondering what he was about to do next.

He pulled his shotgun to his chest and threatened to open fire. "Did you see what happened to Carlin? The fucking authorities murdered him."

"That was *your* fault," Kate said.

Unimpressed, Rabbit pointed his gun at the woman's face. "No, it wasn't my fault. It's the fault of the trigger-happy police force. Protect and serve, my ass. More like shoot first and ask questions later. Now, sit down and shut up."

Kate had little choice but to oblige her oppressor. She sat into the executive chair and folded her arms. "What?"

"Any minute now those motherfuckers in blue are gonna bust in here. Try to incapacitate us. What are you gonna tell them about us when they talk to you?"

"N-Nothing, sir," Richard said.

"*Abso-fuckin'-tactly*, my friend."

Rabbit clutched the grip on his shotgun and slung his sports bag over his back.

"Kate Durst. Karen Compston. Richard Richardson. I know each and every one of you, and I know where you all live. If you say anything when they ask you anything, then I'm afraid *anything* can, and will, happen to your families."

To underscore his point, he nodded at one of the women and raised his voice.

"Karen Compston?"

"Yes?"

"You have a little boy named Charlie, don't you? Now, stand up."

Karen rose to her feet, moved across the room and approached the rabbit. "Y-Yes?"

"That annoying little bastard you just won't shut the fuck up about turned eight, if I remember correctly. On September thirtieth, right?"

"Y-Yes? Oh, please, d-don't do anything—"

"—Aw, shut the hell up and listen. I won't fuck you over if you don't fuck me over, got it?"

"Okay."

Rabbit grabbed her arm and marched her out of the room.

Ben booted a chair over to Rabbit. It rolled on its casters, and the seat turned around for her to sit into.

"Young Charlie is a bit of a genius on the piano, so I hear? A bit of a prodigy?"

A roll of thunderous horror rolled across her face when she heard what he'd said. "How did you know that?"

Rabbit pushed her into the chair and let Ben shut the conference room door.

"Turn Karen around."

Ben pushed her into the chair and wiped his sweaty hand on his balaclava. "Keep looking at me."

Little did Karen know that Howard had taken off his rabbit mask, and replaced it with his own balaclava. She felt the moist, rubbery end of the rabbit mask stretch down her face.

"Wha—?"

Pull.

Howard reached into his case and pulled out a plastic zip tie. He set about tying Karen's wrists together, and then moved on to her ankles.

"You wanna know how I know about your kid?" Howard asked.

All she did was exhale and fight off an impending hyperventilating fit.

"I know everything about you, Karen Compston. Where you live, who you love, and where they all are. Now, no arguing, and no asking to speak to the manager, okay, *Karen*?"

Boot.

Howard booted the back of Karen's chair. She squealed like a child as the casters rolled along the carpet and slowed to a halt near the entrance doors.

"Let's hope they don't make the same mistake with Karen as they did with Aaron. Eh?"

"Karen and Aaron," Ben chuckled. "That rhymes!"

"Dog?"

"Uh-huh?"

"Shut up."

Now wearing balaclavas, Howard and Ben raced in the opposite direction and headed for the back door.

"Ram, Badger, the staircase. Now."

***

The vault's shelves had been cleared by Ram and Badger, who stuffed wedges of rolled-up bills into their sports bags.

Empty boxes and crates lined, all upturned in the hasty raid.

"Ram, Badger, the staircase. Now."

Badger checked his wristwatch as he tipped the last of the security cages into his bag. "Yeah, we're coming. We're nearly—"

"—I don't give a shit, get to the stairs now. Do it," came the angry response from Howard. *"We're here already. Bring our new girlfriend with you."*

Badger turned to Ram and saw that he wasn't wearing his mask. Instead, he sported a jet black balaclava with a SecuriCore visor on top.

"What are you doing?" Badger asked.

James strapped his sports bag over his back and snatched his shotgun from the shelf. "What do you mean what am I doing?"

James had put the Ram mask on Milton's head, and took the SecuriCore visor for himself.

"Oh, shit. What did you do that for?"

James grabbed the left horn on the Ram's mask and lifted Milton to his feet. "Come on, loverboy. We gotta truck to catch."

"Hey!" Badger snapped.

"What?"

"Why did you put your mask on him?"

Ram shoved Milton out of the vault with the end of his gun.

"Because, dickhead, when we're out, if the cops wanna shoot at us, they're gonna aim for the animals, aren't they?"

"Animals dressed in SecuriCore threads? Ugh, you're a moron."

"Hey, the mask sticks out more than the clothes. It's a bigger target, anyhow. It'll confuse the bastards at the very least."

Badger raced after James as he and Milton paced down the corridor and made for the staircase door.

"Shit."

"Take that stupid skunk mask off," James said.

"My fucking pleasure."

Badger struggled to pull the rubber away from his damp skin. It eventually came off, and took a few strands of his hair with it.

Mark's face looked as if someone had thrown a bucket of water over it.

"Damn it, this bag is fucking heavy," he said as he slammed the badger's mask on the broken water cooler and pulled his balaclava over his head.

"You got the big bills," James said. "I got most of the bonds, so between us we're covered."

Milton struggled to breathe inside the Ram's mask as he walked in front of James.

"The fuck's wrong with you?"

"I c-can't breath in here."

"Yeah, now you know how we felt," James said. "Keep moving—"

"—*Ram? Badger? I don't know where you are, but get to the fucking stairs. Now.*"

James lifted his wristwatch to his face. "Actually, we're not coming."

"*What? Why not?*"

James kicked Milton up the ass and sent him stumbling around the corner, and into Howard's arms.

"Because we're already here, you buck-toothed bandit."

"Don't sneak up on us like that. I nearly shot you in your stupid fucking face."

James slapped Milton's new mask and grinned. "Ooh, plus, we brought Girlfriend along with us."

Ben hit the keypad on the wall by the door to the stairs - 7070. "About fucking time. They're about to blow the roof off this place."

Whump.

The door unbolted and pushed open, letting Ben onto the first step on the staircase. He stopped, turned around, and raised his eyebrows at Howard, who took the opportunity to threaten the Ram-faced Milton.

"Ugh. Are you two gonna kiss?" Ben asked, to the amusement of Mark and James.

Howard sized up the Ram and saw a pair of very frightened eyes lurking underneath the eye slits in the rubber. "Listen to me, *girlfriend*."

The Ram nodded, slowly, close to tears.

"You're coming with us. And if the cops start firing, guess who we're gonna use as a bullet shield?"

It proved to be a very unusual sight for all concerned; a man in a balaclava threatening an horned animal.

"Aww, no, Girlfriend. You can't cry. This is a heist, not a kindergarten class. Now, move."

Ben hopped down the stairs, leaving Mark and James to escort Milton shortly behind him. Howard made a final call to his wristwatch.

"Okay, Squirrel. We're twenty seconds away. Start the engine."

***

The underground parking lot had filled with smog from the silver Chevrolet's overactive tailpipe.

"Understood, Rabbit. This is Squirrel, ready to rock and roll."

Squirrel gripped the steering wheel and revved the engine as he kept an eye on the ramp at the far end of the area.

Beep-beep-beep.

A large police van backed up in front of the barrier to the parking lot, and acted as a blockade.

"What the fuck?" Squirrel muttered, as he saw the side and back doors fling open. Dozens of black shoes and combat pants jumped out and raced around the tires.

"Shit. There must be dozens of 'em," Squirrel snapped as he flicked his wrist into the air. "Shit, shit, Rabbit? This is Squirrel. Do you read me? Rabbit, do you read me?"

No response came from his watch.

"Shit. Rabbit, if you can hear me, do not come downstairs. I repeat, *do not* come downstairs. Can you hear me?"

As the men and women in combat pants and shoes pushed down the ramp, it became increasingly clear to Squirrel that a gunfight might break out between them and the police.

Flak jackets, combat visors, and extremely heavy artillery was being deployed.

"Okay—Squi—Went—econds—Ay."

The static rumbled through Squirrel's wristwatch, indicating that the connection wasn't as strong as it could be in the stairwell.

"No, no, Rabbit. You're breaking up. Get back. Go back up. Don't come down here, they're everywhere—"

Whump.

The door to the parking lot slammed open and punched the wall. When Squirrel looked over his shoulder, he saw four men - three in balaclavas, and one with a Ram's mask - running towards them.

"Start the goddamn car," Ben screamed as he raced over to the Chevy with Howard right behind him.

Squirrel flicked the stick shift into reverse and slammed on the gas, with the intention of barricading them from the ramp.

"No, Ben, Howard—get back."

"What? Shit, Squirrel, open the fucking doors—"

"—Open fire," came a vicious, guttural command from the ramp. "Open fire."

Then, everything dove into slow motion.

Howard reached the car and faced the ramp to find a dozen armed officers shooting at them.

Blam-blam-blam.

Howard screamed at the others. "Shit, get down."

"Fuck."

Six bullet holes tore along the side of the Chevrolet. Squirrel grabbed his Uzi, released the safety catch, and hung his left arm out of the window.

"Take this, you fucking bastards."

Thraaa-aaa-tat-a-tat.

A torrent of Uzi bullets sprayed up the ramp, many of which hit the first two officers in their thighs and chest.

They stumbled to the floor and continued firing back at the robbers.

"Fuck's sake, get in the fuckin' car," Squirrel screamed at his associates.

Thinking on his feet, Mark grabbed Milton's arm, twisted it behind his back, and used him as a bullet shield. "See? I told you you'd come in handy."

"No, p-please, I'm g-gonna die—"

"—Shut up, they ain't gonna shoot an innocent civilian."

"Yeah, b-but they might shoot a g-goat."

Mark extended his right arm over Milton's shoulder and fired his Uzi at the cops as he sidestepped with Milton to the waiting Chevy. "Eat lead, you cocksuckers."

Thraaaa-aaa-tataaa-aat.

Mark blasted two officers in the head. The carbon-tipped helmets blew apart, and vomited clumps of blood in all directions, most of which splattered up the nearby concrete pillar.

James dived into the back seat and pumped his shotgun. "They're just like that fucking virus that got us all quarantined, man. They're every-fucking-where."

Squirrel emptied his Uzi's magazine at the ramp, and finished off the officers he'd hit in the knees seconds earlier.

"Reloading. Cover me."

James pumped his shotgun and shot through the open back passenger window.

"Fuckin' die, you blue-assed pricks.

Blam—blam—blaaam.

Three more bullets fired by James produced three direct hits, and blew a tire on the police van blocking the exit ramp on the road.

Psssshhhh.

190

James pumped his shotgun and took aim at the oncoming horde of armed officers, who all fired back. "Gah!"

A bullet clipped a few strands of James' hair as he ducked for cover behind the door. "Shit, shit, shit."

Ben climbed into the back of the car and opened fire with his Uzi. "Fucking die, already."

Thrraa-aaa—aaatt.

The body count rocketed up a few notches as the bullets took out three more officers in an instant.

"Yeah, yeah, yeah," Ben screamed at the top of his adrenalin-fueled lungs. "Get some of that."

"Never mind that," Howard said, as he took cover behind the hood of the Chevrolet. "Hit the gas."

"What? Are you crazy, man?"

Howard fired one shot, then another, blowing the back tires of the police van.

"Hit the fucking gas."

Whump—screeeeeech.

Howard pulled the front passenger door open and launched inside, with his feet hanging out of the vehicle.

James reached out the back of the car and grabbed Mark's hand. "C'mon, we're going."

"What about Girlfriend?"

Both men looked as Milton staggered around the car park in a daze with his fingers in his ears.

"Ah, fuck her. Let's go."

Howard clutched the hand grip on his shotgun, took aim at the remaining armed officers, and yelled over the echoing, cacophonous gunfire.

"Come here you nasty, little cocksuckers. Daddy's got a little something for ya."

Blam-blam—smaaaash.

The side windows on the police van shattered and rained fragments of sharp glass around the wounded police officers.

He turned the gun to the windshield and yanked on the trigger.

Bang—smash.

The windshield shattered and produced a delicate spider's web of a crack in all directions. Squirrel didn't have time to complain, and punched the pieces of glass out, some of which bounced onto the hood and onto the dashboard.

"Ugh, I can't see, now," Lincoln yelped from inside his Squirrel mask.

"I had to break the glass, whaddya want?"

"What the hell for, man?"

"To get a clear shot," Howard said as he pumped his shotgun and aimed it through the windowless dash. "Now keep your nuts in your mouth, you dumb rodent, and step your furry little foot on it."

Blam—blam.

Two more armed officers stumbled back, shredded to death from the hail of Howard's gunfire.

Mark hung out of the back window and emptied his Uzi up the ramp. "Jesus Christ, step on it, Lincoln."

"If I do, then we're gonna have to smash right through that piece of shit cop van, you know."

"Do it."

Vrooom.

James elbowed the back-left passenger window and opened fire with his shotgun, hitting an officer in the head. The bullet blasted him between the eyes, which obliterated his skull and chucked up a mound of congealed blood up the inside of his visor.

"Gotcha, ya filthy fuckin' *pig.*"

James chuckled as he reloaded his gun.

"Heh, that was a helluva fuckin' head shot. Just like in Grand Theft Auto."

"This isn't a goddamn video game, Gilmour," Ben snapped. "This is serious."

"Yeah, unlike your stupid fuckin' socks."

Ben slotted a fresh magazine into his gun and considered shooting James in the face. "Shut up."

"Ah, relax your buttocks, Benjy-boy. I could get used to this. All this power at our hands? Fuck, I feel *great.*"

"Get back in, we're pushing through."

Mark moved back into the car and placed his left hand on the driver's seat for balance. "Hell yeah, let's fuck these blue collar bastards up."

"I'll give you ten grand outta my cut of the take for each prick you mow down," James said. "Do it."

Inspired by the potential monetary gain, Squirrel chuckled and hit the gas. "Now that's an offer I can't refuse."

"Hit it."

Vroom-vroooom.

Sparks flew out from the Chevy's hood as the return fire chewed through the chassis and bounced off the bulletproof tires.

"Hold tight," Lincoln screamed as the Chevy rocketed up the ramp.

Much to the occupants' surprise, the car bolted backwards, and headed for the discombobulated Milton, who staggered around in his ram mask in an attempt to figure out where he was.

Screeeech.

"There, there's one over there," one of the armed officers yelled at the Ram. "Open fire."

Blam-blam-blam.

Milton's abdomen exploded all the way up to his neck as six bullets tore into his body, just in time for Squirrel to yank on the handbrake and mow his bullet-riddled body down with the hood.

Crunch.

Milton's shredded body catapulted off the hood as it swung round and delivered his battered corpse into the flurry of approaching officers like a bloodied ten pin bowling ball.

Slam.

Squirrel hit the gas and bolted towards the ramp. "Hold on to your cash, fellas. This is gonna be a bumpy ride."

The officers lowered their guns when they saw the silver Chevrolet scream towards them.

"Shit, shit, shit, hold your fire!" the first among them said. "Back up, back up—"

Splatt.

The blood-splattered Chevrolet hood drove into the armed officer's waist, slammed the back of his head against the ground, and crunched over his body.

Badum-bump.

"Here we go," Squirrel screamed as he gripped the steering wheel and drove the car up the ramp.

Both sides of the vehicle lit up, ablaze with police fire, and barreled through three more men on its way up the car.

"Step on it," Howard yelled. "Do it."

"I am, I am. Stay low."

Everyone ducked and held onto to their seats as the Chevrolet bolted up the ramp.

All five men yelled for dear life. "Oh, shiiiiii—"

Vrooom—Whoooosh.

The Chevy catapulted off the end of the ramp, launched into the air…

… and crashed into the side of the police van like a flying battering ram.

Crunch.

Howard pressed his hands on the dashboard and yelped. "Whaaaa—"

Ker-raaaaam.

The force of the impact pushed Howard out of his seat and through the gaping hole where the windshield used to be.

The Chevrolet spun around and around, having rebounded off the collision with the police van. The two left tires lifted up and slammed back down to the road.

Whump.

Ben leaned forward and saw Howard rolling across the road. "Ah, shit. Ross!"

Squirrel pulled off his mask and flung it over his shoulder.

Mark caught it in his hands and dumped it into the foot well. "Mumford? What are you doing?"

Lincoln hit the gas and spun the wheel, performing a dust-ridden donut on the road.

Screeeeeech.

"I can't see a fuckin' thing in that thing," he said, before slamming the Chevy into reverse. "Howard—Oh, shit."

Howard staggered to his feet and limped towards the car with his sports bag still strapped to his back. If he turned around, he would have seen the armed officers behind their parked vehicles, all firing at him.

James yelled from the back seat and. "Howard, behind you."

He booted the back passenger door open and jumped onto the road with his shotgun aimed at the officers behind his limping friend.

"Behind you. Get down."

Dazed, Howard turned around and instinctively fired at the police. "What—? Ah, fuck."

Blam-blam.

James opened fire on the police, pumped his shotgun, and continued to fire.

Mark, Ben, and Lincoln watched on as Howard lost his footing and stumbled back.

"We need some help over here," James yelled. "Howard's fucked, man. Someone help him while I shoot these pricks."

Mark wasted no time.

He climbed out of the car with his sports bag on his back, and emptied a full, extended magazine at the officers, hitting three of them in the chest.

"Got 'em. C'mon, Howard, get in the car."

James had no choice but to push forward and reach for Howard. "Grab my hand, man. We gotta get outta here."

"Fuck 'em," Howard spluttered. "Eat lead, you fucking pricks."

Both of them fired at the police as they moved back to the car. The haze of return gunfire missed both men, but only just.

Lt. Fox had seen enough. Five men in balaclavas one hundred feet away, by a silver Chevrolet, and a dozen wounded and killed officers compelled him to drop his megaphone and fire at them with his MP5.

"Keep firing. Don't let them get away."

He ran forward and aimed at Howard, who took a few steps back.

"Freeze!"

Instead of complying, Howard, James, and Mark fired back, forcing Fox to take cover behind the freshly-smashed police van.

Ben bopped Lincoln on the shoulder from the back seat. "Jesus fucking Christ, what are they doing?"

"I dunno, man, but these motherfuckers are enjoying their weapons a little too much, you get me?"

Lt. Fox kept his cover behind the police van, and waved his hand at the officers to take cover.

"Can *some* bastard please take these bastards out?"

Breathless, Fox closed his eyes, took a deep breath, and peered around the back of the van. He pulled on the trigger and fired at the Chevrolet.

The bullets bounced off the Chevy's tires, leaving the remainder to chew through the hood of the car. "Fuck, fuck, *fuck*."

The police pushed forward, with many of them taking cover behind their parked vehicles.

Fox looked up to see one of his helicopters whiz past the bank's roof and hover over the shoot-out taking place on the road.

"Goddamnit, take the fuckers out," Fox roared, as he released his empty magazine, and slotted a fresh one into his gun.

He jumped out and fired at Howard, before sliding behind the police van once again.

Twelve officers pushed past Fox, continually firing their guns. Fox lowered his gun and caught the attention of the closest officer to him.

"Hey."

"Yes, sir?"

"Take out the fucking car," Fox said.

"Yes, sir—"

Bam-spatch.

The officer's forehead bust apart, vomiting a chunky, red mist into the air.

Fox gasped as he watched his colleague fall down, dead. "Whoa, shit."

He slid out from behind the van and opened fire on the car once again, spraying bullets from the hood, across the road, over to Howard and James.

Fox reloaded and pressed his back to the van. He tilted his head up to the sniper on the building and performed a cut-throat sign with his fingers. "Fucking take them out."

James dragged Howard back by his sports bag and gripped the passenger door with his free hand.

Ben shifted his buttocks into the middle seat in the back of the Chevy and kicked both doors open. "Get the fuck in the car—"

Balm-spritch.

A stray bullet from an MP5 clipped Howard on the side of his upper-left arm. His suit split apart, and chucked a rope of blood up James' suit.

"Yaaaooowww... *fuck.*"

Howard squealed in pain and pulled on his trigger. The bullet blasted the closest of the twelve officers in the kneecap, forcing the man to somersault on the spot and crash head-first to the road. His visor split apart upon impact, and killed him in an instant.

"My arm," Howard shrieked. "Agh, f-fuck—"

"—Get in the car," Lincoln said. "C'mon, we can't hold these pricks off for much longer—"

Spitch-spitch.

The fabric on Lincoln's seat burst apart and produced a mound of fluffy white stuffing.

A sniper's bullet had hit it, and narrowly missed Lincoln's chest. Two inches to the left, and it would have punctured his lung.

"Oh, fuck me."

He stepped on the gas pedal and drove the car backwards.

Howard pulled him into the passenger seat, and as the car rolled back with James jumping into the car. "Yeah, g-get in. Ugh."

Mark remained on the road, and continued to spray bullets at the approaching police officers.

"Fuck you. Get the fuck back."

The fierce and unrelenting bullet storm rocketed towards them, and hit the hood of the car, forcing a flurry of orange sparks into the air.

Thraaa-taaaaa—click-click-click.

Mark was out of bullets, having killed two more armed officers. He released the empty magazine to the ground and went for a fresh one, when Lincoln and James yelled at him from ten feet away within the car.

"Mark, sniper. Run."

"Wha—?"

As Mark pulled out a fresh magazine, he made the mistake of turning back to the car.

"Noooo—"

Schpit—spatch.

A sniper's bullet caught Mark in the back of the head, blowing the front of his face open like a budding flower.

"W-Wait f-for me-eeeee—" Mark said as he fell to his knees with the top half of his head missing.

The backs of each of his legs burst open on the next round of bullets, pushing his two feet forward, snapping the knee bones.

"Oh, shit. Mark," Lincoln screamed as he fired back at the police with his Uzi. "You bastards."

The last three bullets from a heavy artillery firearm finished Mark off, and burst the sports bag

It exploded under his neck and flung thousands of bloodied bills into the air like overactive confetti.

"No! Our money!" James said. "Fuck, we need to—"

"—Y-You're not s-seriously suggesting we go b-back out there t-to g-get it, are you?" Howard whined as he clutched his wounded arm.

"No, I—" James said, as he felt the anger rifle up through his throat. "Fuck. *Fuck.*"

Lincoln slammed the gas, and performed a screeching donut with the Chevy's back tires.

"Fuck this, we're outta here," he said. "And don't worry about Amos, man, he was still one of 'em when we started this shit."

"One of what?"

"A fucking *banker*. So, fuck him. Ain't our fault."

Howard considered what Lincoln had said, and decided he no longer knew the man. Or any of his associates.

"Nothing but a bunch of bloodthirsty fucking killers."

"Let he who is without sin cast the first stone, Howard fucking Ross. This ain't no time or place for a hypocritical pot to accuse the kettle of being black. Now, hold onto something, we're outta here."

Lincoln flung the stick shift into drive and hit the gas.

The Chevrolet screeched around the corner, and entered Madhoff Avenue, leaving scores of police corpses, and a thoroughly dead Milton and Mark, in their wake.

Lincoln squinted as the rush of wind blasted through the windowless windshield and up his balaclava.

James leaned out of the passenger window and tilted his head up at the sky. Two police helicopters followed at speed directly above them.

"I bet they weren't expecting *that*. We got choppers on us, by the way."

"Yeah, I can see that," Lincoln said.

"What are we gonna do?"

Lincoln moved his wristwatch to his lips and stepped on the gas pedal. "Cat? Cat, come in. This is Squirrel. Do you read me?"

A brief pause of silence set the fear of God into Lincoln and his two remaining accomplices.

"Why isn't he answering?" James asked, and then to Howard with concern. "Hey, Ross. How you holding up?"

"I've b-been shot, how do you think I feel?"

"I dunno why he's not answering," Lincoln screamed. "Cat, come in? This is Squirrel. Answer me, you no-good feline fuck head."

Vroooom.

Howard groaned in pain and dropped his shotgun on his lap. He gripped his left arm with his right hand and shrieked. "Fuck, I'm bleeding. I'll be okay. I'll be okay."

James leaned over the back of Howard's seat and glanced at the wound. "Looks okay to me. It most probably just nicked the skin."

Howard turned to him with an *are you joking?* look on his face. "Yeah, right. It's more than a flesh wound. Stings like a bitch."

"We'll get a bandage on it. You'll be fine, just keep pressure on it."

Lincoln slammed the steering wheel and checked the rear view mirror as he radioed into his watch. "I ain't asking a motherfucker again, man. Cat, are you reading me?"

Lincoln squinted at the mirror and saw unmarked Dodge Chargers slide into view and give chase.

"Ah, shit. Just what we need, now. More fucking cops."

Howard's left arm shook as he tried to raise his wristwatch to his face and speak. "Yargh," he grunted and screamed as he grabbed his left wrist with his right hand and forced it up.

Lincoln kept his eyes on the rear view mirror and turned the vehicle onto the next road. "Shit man, they're gainin' on us. Ben?"

"Yeah?"

"Smash the back window, and keep an eye on these pricks—"

"—Yaarrggghhh," Howard screamed at the top of his lungs into his watch. "Answer us, you stupid cat *twat*."

Ben giggled and pumped his shotgun. The spent ammunition flew out of the chamber and bopped Howard on the back of his head.

"Ow, *fuck*. Stop that—"

"—Sorry. Just reloading."

"Well, reload *carefuller*."

Just then, a tired-sounding voice erupted through all four wristwatches.

"Hey, Rabbit? Is that you? This is Cat."

Howard spluttered and rammed the back of his head against the headrest in pain. "J-James, just take care of those-m-motherfuckers, ugh—"

"—I repeat, this is Cat standing by. Where the fuck have you animal motherfuckers been? I been waiting ages for your asses out here."

Howard squeezed his eyes shut and wailed once again, due to the pain from his wound.

"Ngggggggg—agggghhh, you little prick, I swear I'm gonna bundle you in a b-bag and toss you in the river."

"What, man? What I do? You're the ones who are late."

"Listen man," Lincoln said. "Howard's taken a bullet. We're about three minutes from Exit 11A on the freeway, and we're bringing half the fuckin' CVPD with us. Get the spikes ready."

"Okay."

"I'll radio you when you're in our sights. Keep it slow," Lincoln said. "Shit, I hope we make the fucking transfer."

"Just f-fucking *drive*," Howard said.

Ben climbed to his knees on the back seat and twisted his body around. He placed the barrel of his gun on the backrest and took aim at the three Dodge Chargers racing behind them.

"Come here my little pretties."

He focused on the sight at the end of the barrel, and tilted the gun down to the left tire on the leftmost vehicle.

"I spy with my little eye…"

The tires on the first Dodge Charger pulled into Ben's sight and remained steady.

"… Something beginning with…"

Blam—spatch.

"… Tee."

The bullet burst the tire, forcing the Dodge Charger to swivel left and right, before swerving around one-hundred-and-eighty-degrees and tumbling across the road, injuring everyone inside.

Ben punched the air and pumped his shotgun. "Got 'em!"

"Woohoo!" Lincoln screamed. "Have some of that, you dirty fucking pig."

"God, I love this fucking gun as much as James loves his suede shoes, I swear," Ben said. "At first, you know, I wasn't sure about using guns, but—damn, man, I feel like I'm ten feet tall right now."

Ben planted his lips on the barrel and immediately shrieked when the intense heat burned his mouth.

"Agh, fuck. Ptchoo."

Lincoln chuckled as he drove the Chevrolet onto the slip road and joined the freeway. "Yeah, don't kiss the weaponry, Ben. And *definitely* don't try fucking the barrel tonight when you get home."

"*If* w-we g-get home at all," Howard spluttered. "This isn't over, y-yet."

"Hey, Ross, quit it with the pessimism, okay? We'll get there. I own the road, man."

Howard screamed in pain and frustration. "Quit it with the pessimism? I've been f-fucking shot, here."

Howard's words echoed in Ben's ears as he watched the Dodge Chargers fall in line with the traffic. "That's right, dickheads. I see you. You hang back now, you hear?

***

Lt. Fox placed his MP5 into his holster and approached the bank's entrance.

"Okay, ramblers. What's the story, here?"

Detective Cohen walked out of the building and waved his hands. "All clear. They've gone."

"The smoke grenade worked, then?"

"Unnecessary, really, but we couldn't take any chances. We got two dead behind the counter, and one out back by the vault. Three poor souls, all executed."

Both men walked through the door, leaving Fox to scan the teller counter.

"Tell me about the weapons. Preferably before the feds get here and snatch this case outta my beautiful hands."

Cohen placed his hands on his considerably large hips and sighed. "PDX1 point two-three-three used on the girl behind the counter, same with the SecuriCore guy. Bank manager, a guy named Price, caught a succession of twelve bullets from an Uzi."

"Who the hell shoots someone in the face with a fuckin' *Uzi?*"

"Some nervous chump who's never used a gun before?"

"Damn skippy," Fox said. "I want all records checked on firearms acquired over the past week, and go get some bluey two-shoes to hassle all known dealers while you're at it."

Fox stepped forward with a beady eye on all four visible CCTV cameras, three of which were still coughing up smoke.

"This must've just happened. They're still hot."

"Uh-huh," Cohen said.

"That means the recordings are still safe and backed up. Where do these cameras send their footage to?"

"Ah, the main computer in the manager's room. And it's fucked."

"Ask Midwest Federal HQ where the automatic backups are sent, and threaten them with a warrant. Now, talk to me about hostages."

"Right," Cohen said. "Nine hostages, all shaken, obviously, but not injured. We've taken them to the ambulance for a once-over."

"Okay. Okay."

Before Fox could fully assess the damage, he saw a young woman sitting on a stool with a silver blanket wrapped around her shoulders.

A female officer sat with her, and tried to calm her down.

Curious, Fox whispered to Cohen and kept his eyes on the woman. "Who's this?"

"Her name's Compston. She's one of the teller girls, here."

"Go and check the fucker we gunned down outside. Hopefully we won't need the dental records."

"We're already on it."

"I'll meet you out there."

Cohen smiled as he made his way out of the building, leaving Fox to put on a sympathetic face as he approached the sobbing woman.

"Ah. Uh, Miss Compston?"

She tried to take a sip of water from a paper cup, and noticed him walk up to her.

"*Mrs.* Compston, officer."

"How are you?" he asked.

"I've had better days."

Fox nodded at the female officer to move off and leave them alone. She duly obliged and moved away, allowing Fox to sit next to the woman.

"What's your first name?"

"Karen. Karen Compston."

He reached into his pocket and produced his badge. "Lieutenant Vincent Fox, CVPD."

"I figured."

"Yeah, I know. I know what it's like to go through something like this. The torment, the shock, the anger. I can assure you it passes, though—"

"—Please, Lieutenant. Please tell me you caught them."

"Ah. No, not exactly. Well, we got *one* of them. He's currently outside turning the concrete red. We're checking him out right now, but, uh, Karen?"

She offered no acknowledgment, and instead looked down at her shoes.

"We're gonna need to talk to you about what happened. We're talking to all the others as well."

"I don't care, I just want those bastards caught and brought to justice. They threatened me. They threatened my family."

Fox deliberately held his line of questioning and offered her a smile of contrition. "Karen?"

"What?"

"Do you know anything about these guys? Who might have done this? You know, anything that might help us catch the felons responsible for all this?"

"Oh, I dunno. It's all such a blur right now. I'm just glad it's over."

"Did you catch anything we could identify? Anything they said, or did? Anything physical? Anything that, you know, stands out in your memory?"

"Well," she said. "One of them was wearing Space Invaders socks."

"Space Invaders?"

"Yes," she sighed and cleared her throat. "Benjamin Cherry used to wear socks with Space Invaders on them."

"Who's Benjamin Cherry?"

"Oh," she whimpered. "I'm sorry. Ben Cherry. Director of Corporate Accounts. He used to work here. Until last week."

Fox's ears pricked up as his investigative mind went into overdrive. "Until last week?"

"No. He got laid off."

"Interesting."

"And we never found out what happened to Mark. One moment he was here with us, and the next, he was gone."

Karen burst into tears at the thought of what might have happened to him.

Fox rubbed her shoulder and tried to calm her down. "Hey, hey, Karen. It's okay. I'm sure he'll turn up. Was he not here when it was all over?"

"No."

"I mean, he's not hard to miss. He has two gold teeth."

Fox didn't know what to say. Before he could muster up some pithy words of kindness, Karen shifted away from him and spoke once again.

"Look, Lieutenant Fox, I'm sure there's more, but that's enough to be getting on with right now, I think. I'm sorry. I just need to get out of here."

Karen rose out of her chair to Fox's surprise. "Oh?"

"I want to see Kate and my girls. I think they'll need me. They're probably upset."

"Upset, yes."

"Take me to them. We can talk later."

Karen suddenly had the upper hand in the situation, and Fox wasn't about to stop her search for her colleagues.

He followed her out into the street where a massive clean-up operation was in full force.

Two paramedics and a police officer caught up to Karen and led her away from the carnage.

Detritus from the building and burning vehicles littered the road, and attracted a swathe of onlookers behind the yellow tape.

The whole place resembled a bloodied, deadly battlefield - quite the removal from a usually vibrant and futuristic-looking financial sector.

"Goddamn it, you bastards," Fox muttered as he took in the apocalyptic sight. "Look what you've done. I hope it was worth it."

A voice came from over behind Fox's shoulder. "Ah, Lieutenant?"

He turned around to see an out-of-breath Cohen running up to him. "Oh, you again? What you got?"

"An update on our bank robbing friend."

Fox took a cautious step towards Mark's upturned, bullet-strewn corpse. The forensics officer kneeling beside him held a rigid blanket over the dead body and prepared to reveal what lay underneath.

"Let me see him," Fox said.

"You sure you want to, right now?"

"Nah, I can wait till tomorrow," Fox snapped, sarcastically, before getting serious. "No, dickhead. Show me now."

"Okay. Don't say you weren't warned."

Cohen knew to turn away well before the forensic officer revealed Mark's head, or what was left of it.

"My... *God.*"

Fox nearly puked and held his wrist over his mouth. "Oh, holy fucking Mary Mother of God's shit-biscuits-in-a-barrel-of-piss. That's, uh—uh, that's *not* good, is it?"

The forensics officer turned back to Mark's corpse and swatted the circling flies away with his hand. "No, I'd say it was pretty far from good, in my expert opinion. As you can see, most of his skull was—"

"—Can I look, now?" Cohen asked, still with his head turned.

"You can cover that back up, now," Fox said, mostly relieved that his instruction was being followed in an instant.

Three more paramedics surrounded the scene, and set about lifting the corpse onto the stretcher.

"Yes, as you saw, most of the skull was missing. Once we're back at the lab, we can start to piece together, literally, who this guy was."

"I feel like throwing up," Fox said. "Okay, I've seen enough."

Cohen shook his head and pointed at another group of paramedics carrying a stretcher with a man wearing a Dog mask on it. "You should've seen this guy, too. Some fresh-outta-college grad named Carlin. Just his luck. He only started work here two days ago."

"Yeah, well. They'll get what's coming to 'em, that I can tell you."

Fox would have said more, but his attention was caught by two, tiny nuggets of gold glinting in the sunlight.

He stepped over to get a better view of what the two things actually were. They'd been inserted into an official evidence bag, along with a label with text written on it - *Exhibit 506.1 / Central Incisor Left / Central Incisor Right.*

"Teeth?" Fox muttered, finally connecting the dots in his mind when he saw most of the pearly whites scattered around the corpse's shoulders. "Hey, Cohen?"

"Yeah?"

"Two front teeth. Made of gold?"

Cohen turned to Fox, confused. "That's right. So what?"

Fox nodded Mark's recovered corpse. "Did they come outta this fella's head?"

Cohen pointed to the litter of pearly whites scattered around the corpse. "They sure did. Along with all the normal white ones."

With a renewed confidence and a bright, shining metaphorical bulb appearing above his head like an overzealous halo, Fox tapped Cohen on the shoulder.

"Have the team dig up all the security cameras, and the footage from outside the building. I wanna know who these murderous assholes are. I want a positive I.D. on both our Ram-headed SecuriCorpse in the underground parking lot, *and* our gold-toothed corpse before sundown. I wouldn't bet the farm just yet, but we could be dealing with an inside job."

"An inside job?"

"Fuck me, there's an echo out here," Fox snapped. "Yes, *an inside job.* Now, just get me what I asked for."

Chapter 10

JAMES GILMOUR
— Wednesday, September 30th —

James experienced thousands of mornings at the bank, and each and every one of them paled in comparison to this morning's.

The usual annoyances, from customer complaints, to the incessant vacuuming from the cleaners just before the doors opened, finally got to James as he sat at his desk and tapped his shiny, golden name placard on the desk like a ticking time bomb.

"Chrome Valley Federal, how may I direct your call?"

"Ugh," James thought to himself, "that goddamn woman's voice. I'm gonna get up, walk over there, and tear her voice box right outta her throat."

He couldn't bring himself to look at the woman's pudgy body and double chin as she put on her professional voice, which meant elevating her tone several octaves.

"Chrome Valley Federal, how may I direct your call?"

James' eyes drifted to the EZ-Flex box sitting on his desk. He'd already emptied the stationery from his drawers, including the very expensive hole punch he'd won at a recent prize-draw, and tossed them into the box.

Most of his Elvis memorabilia was in there, too, although carefully tucked into the corners and covered with bubble wrap for safe-keeping. Among his prized possession was the coffee mug he got from Las Vegas last year. It made him smile whenever he saw it. The words

World's Greatest Dad were wrapped around the curvature on the fine bone china. *Dad* had been crossed out, and had *King* scrawled in over it in thick, red permanent ink.

"Chrome Valley Federal, how may I direct your call?"

There were a few people milling around at 10 am this morning. The usual customers, the usual staff members, punctuated with an infrequent appearance from an invigorated Victor Price, who seemed to relish the new refit at the bank.

"Chrome Valley Federal, how may I direct your call?"

It was in the way the bastard smiled with his eyes at James whenever he walked past. It was an award-winning performance of sycophancy and faux-sympathy, and the mere sight of the man made James' blood boil.

Irritated by the woman's voice, he turned his attention to his lap. He gripped his house key in his fingers and stared at the mound of white powder lining the grooves of the metal.

"Chrome Valley Federal, how may I direct your call?"

"Ugh," James muttered as he lowered his head under the table and brought the end of the key to his nose. "I wish I could direct your fat, useless ass in the ground."

Sniff.

His nose twitched as the white powder lifted off the key, having been vacuumed up his right nostril and right into his brain like a heavyweight punch to the cranium.

"Whug."

James rubbed his knuckle under his nose and released the key onto his desk. Suddenly, the original colors in the bank - varying shades of white and beige - bubbled to life and swirl around the wall like a spoon stirring oatmeal.

The bank's ambiance hanging around his ears raised in volume as the powder tore through his brain, and mercifully lowered Joanne's voice as she answered yet another call a few feet away from his desk.

"Rich Capitalist Rip-Off Merchants, how may I suck up to you?" Joanne said.

Or, at least, that's what James *thought* she said.

He shrugged it off and burst out laughing as he rose out of his chair with a spring in his step, and tossed his mouse and keyboard into the EZ-Flex box.

James' freshly-acquired jubilant attitude caught the attention of the customers and staff members.

"Uh-huh-huh," he said as he danced around the box with his voice raised. "*Thankyouverymuch.*"

Irritated by James' ridiculous dalliance, Joanne covered her phone and threw him a look of disdain. "Excuse me. Mr. Gilmour?"

"Uh-huh-huh?"

"Would you *please* keep the noise down? I'm on the phone."

James mimed playing air guitar and pointed to her. "Would you *please* keep your weight under control? I'm thinking about having lunch."

Shocked and offended, Joanne's eyes almost popped out of her skull. "How rude! I must say, never, in all my life, have I *ever*—"

"—Gone on a diet?"

"No!" she protested. "I've never been told—"

"—That you're a fat and ugly pigeon?"

Joanne fumed and tried to calm herself down.

"James, I know this is your last day, but what's gotten into you?"

He pulled his ID card off his neck, picked up his EZ-Flex box, and booted the table in a coke-fueled haze of fury.

"Oh, I dunno? A sudden sense of self-worth, perhaps? Oh, no, wait. No, I tell you what's gotten into me."

Everyone within earshot clapped their eyes on James, and waited for the punchline.

"What's gotten *into* me is opportunity. A way out of my humdrum, dull fucking existence. An opportunity to have something other than '*Yeah, he was an okay kinda-of-a-guy*' written on my tombstone. You know?"

No, everyone watching *didn't* know what James was talking about, not that it mattered to the man, who barged past as many customers as he could with his box in his hands.

Howard stepped out of his office and immediately saw James addressing everyone in the bank. "Mr. Gilmour?"

"Hey, Howard. Are you all packed and ready to get the fuck outta this piece of shit, risk-averse, communist-lovin' assembly line of hell, or what?"

Gasp!

Most of the longer words James had used flew over everyone's heads, but it sounded like a very mean thing to have said.

Satisfied that everyone was suitably shocked, he winked at Howard and nodded at the back door.

"C'mon, Ross. Let's get the hell outta here and blow our severance checks on hookers and fine dining."

Howard didn't want to join the giant, coked-up F-U James had launched into, and smiled at the customers. "Umm. Sorry about this, everyone, Mr. Gilmour has had a bit of a tough morning."

One of the customers folded her arms in anger. "What's going on around here, anyway? Why all the foul language."

"I'll tell you, why, Ma'am," James said, preparing to launch head-first into a diatribe of magnificent proportions.

"Oh dear." Howard turned away and held his palm to his face as James made good on his threat to air his parting thoughts.

"This *fine* banking establishment we find ourselves standing in, and entrusting our hard-earned savings to, has decided, in its infinite ass-pounding wisdom, to fire the majority of its loyal, long-standing employees it was lucky to have working for them in the first place."

The loud chatter caught the attention of Victor Price, who made his way into the main banking area from the back door.

"Mr. Gilmour?"

"Ah, everyone, I'd like you to meet Mr. Victor Price. Ten years younger than me, and at least ten rungs higher up the ladder, to boot."

"Mr. Gilmour," Victor said, carefully. "Return to your desk. Stop making a fool of yourself."

All sets of eyeballs turned to James for a response.

"Aww, you've already done *that* for me. Making a fool out of me, you dumb, trust-fund cock-smoker."

Some of the customers giggled, and the others held their breath in shock at the sheer tenacity on display.

Mark, Ben, and Lincoln, made the mistake of walking in through the entrance, blissfully unaware of what was taking place.

"Gilmour?"

"Ah, hey guys," James said, loudly. "I was just telling everyone here how much of a prick our boss is. It's okay, though, you haven't missed much. I've only just started."

"Oh," Ben said.

James used his red tie to wipe the scraggy white powder remnants off his nose. "Yeah, Cherry. Hey, guys, have you all cleared your offices and ready to get outta here?"

"Umm, yeah?"

"Good."

James walked the length of the teller counter with his box in his arms and made for the back door. Victor Price sidestepped to the left and blocked his path.

"Gilmour? I want a word with you."

"Get out of my way, ass-face."

"No."

James stopped two feet in front of him, rolled his head, and screamed in the man's face. "I said *move*."

Stunned at the insubordination, Victor slid aside and let the man through.

"Christ, I *hate* you, Victor Price. I hope someone shoots you in the face."

James booted the back door open and walked through, with a deeply concerned Howard chasing after him.

"Ah, shit. James, wait."

Lincoln chuckled at what had just happened. "Damn, Gilmour's lost his mind."

"That's not all he's lost," Ben said, suddenly realizing how much of a monster his colleague had become.

James stumbled down the staircase that led to the underground parking lot, and paused to catch his breath. "Ugh, I feel like shit."

Howard's voice echoed down the walls a few steps behind his shoulder. "James!"

"Ugh, not *him* again."

James exhaled, and continued his stumbling descent with his box in his arms, and made for the parking lot door.

Howard double-timed it down the steps and chased after him. "Goddamnit, Gilmour. Wait."

Whump.

The door to the underground parking lot swung out, having been kicked open by James, who made his way past the parked cars and headed for the ramp.

"Gilmour, stop. Wait. Let's talk."

"Nothing left to talk about."

James let out a raspy sigh of exasperation, stopped walking, and turned around.

"James, *please.*"

"What do you want, Ross? Can't you see I'm trying to quit with dignity?"

"Yeah, I saw that little hissy fit you had back up at the bank in front of everyone. *Real classy.*"

The two men faced-off in the middle of the shadowy, vehicular concrete jungle.

Every time one of them spoke, their voices bounced off the walls, and drifted up the ramp and into the clean, fresh air out on the road.

"Talk about burning bridges, James," he said. "What the hell do you think you're doing?"

"I'm leaving. Like I was asked to. You might do the same."

"You're creating a goddamn scene in front of everyone," Howard snapped. "You're gonna get us busted. You *do* remember what we're doing, don't you?"

"Yeah, I can't think about anything else. Revenge, my friend."

"James?"

"What is it now, you irritating little homo?"

Howard's face turned to stone as he examined the bloodshot whites of his friend's eyes.

"Have you been using?"

James had endured more than enough BS for one morning. He sighed, turned around, and walked over to the trunk of Jeep parked by the ramp.

"Just a little breakfast hit. See me through till the end of the day."

"You'll be lucky to see the end of the *day* with the amount of blow you vacuum up your nose. You gotta quit that shit and get sober before next Wednesday."

"Nah."

Howard raced after him and tapped him on the shoulder.

"Look, James. I dunno what you think you're playing at, but you *need* to keep that coked-up mouth of yours shut."

"I know, I know."

"James, this is *serious*," Howard snapped, and looked around for anyone that might be snooping in on their conversation. "You have to keep quiet before *and* after the job. Until the end of recorded time, or when you finally keel over and die, whichever is the sooner."

The trunk of the jeep sprang up and offered James the chance to drop his EZ-Flex into it, right next to a bunch of grocery bags and empty bottles of *Rollneck Kojak*.

James placed the box inside, right next to a pair of bolt cutters, and slammed the trunk back down.

"Right, that's taken care of. Now, what were you saying?"

"I'm saying, no—*insisting*, that you shut the hell up, or you're gonna get us all in trouble."

"Actions speak louder than words, ain't that right? Howard Ross?

Howard nodded, but failed to make the connection between what his friend had said, and the topic at hand. "Uh, yeah? So?"

James tapped his nose in a knowing manner and winked at his friend. "Actions, my friend."

"What the hell's that meant to mean?"

James grinned and backed up to the driver's door on the Jeep and waved the car keys in his right hand.

"I did as Knocktoe said. We all did. Actions, Howard. All but five grand of my severance check is with him, now, ready to do this thing. I've fulfilled my end of the bargain."

Howard's eyebrows bent up in horror, scared that all was going to be revealed. "Shhhh. For Christ's sake, you madman. Don't say—"

"—Oh, oh, oh," James sniffed, and lost his temper. "I'm *not* mad. Do I look mad to you, Ross? Huh? Is this the behavior of a fucking mad man? Go on, tell me. I'm all ears."

Howard began to regret the day he told James about his idea, and doubly regretted letting him in on the action.

"And *you* wanna talk about actions, right?" James said. "Have you told Miranda, yet?"

"About what?"

"About not being in gainful employment as of next week?"

"No," Howard said. "And with what we've got planned, I'm hoping I won't have to."

"You wanna talk about being classy, you fucking hypocrite?" James said. "Not telling your wife you've been kicked to the curb by the commies who've kept you in cheap wine and microwave meals the past two-and-a-half decades? How can you delude yourself."

Howard knew James had a point, but the point had veered seriously off-track, and needed rectifying.

"At the rate you're going, James, it looks like I won't have to tell her at all. Wanna know why?"

"No, but I'm sure you're gonna tell me."

"Because everyone from the valley to Devotion is gonna know about what we're up to next week. *That's why.* You and your big fucking mouth. Jesus Christ."

James Gilmour had been rumbled. Forward, it was a case of placating the madman and silently praying that he'd start to play ball.

"Are you finished?" James asked. "Got it off your chest? Feeling better, now?"

"James, look—uh, we're just all a bit on edge right now, okay? We got a big few days coming up before next week. Let's be sensible for a little while like regular guys. I think we just need to relax and, you know—" Howard said, before failing to find a way to finish his sentence without sounding like a dumb ass trying to patronize the coked-stuffed demon standing before him.

James pulled the driver's door open and wiped his runny nose off on his tie once again.

"It ain't me, Howard. It's you. You're the one with the problem, okay?"

"What do you mean?"

"I've done what's been asked of me, okay?" James fumed. "I've been doing just that all my life. My wife doesn't want kids? I don't want kids. My wife wants a divorce so she can fuck her gym instructor and elope to the Bahamas? I grant her a divorce so she can fuck her gym instructor and elope to the Bahamas."

Howard knew that the more James reached into his subconscious and dug up old old, hateful memories, the angrier it would make him. "Listen, James—"

"—Price, or whoever, needs the account audit done by Friday with two fucking hours notice? I *get* the job done in an hour and a half, with half an hour spare and room for milk. My goddamn boss *hires* a pair of balding, commie bastards on the outside to fuck my life and career after months of furlough because he doesn't have the balls to do it himself? I sit there, Howard, like a chump and spread my ass cheeks for 'em. You know? I *sit* there and take it like a fucking man, and I don't even complain about having not been bought dinner beforehand. You understand what I'm saying?"

Howard couldn't argue back at all. These, and many more reasons, were exactly the springboard required to hop aboard the heist idea in the first place.

"Yeah, James. I understand."

"Well not anymore, damn it. This is *my* life, and from now on, I get to say what happens in it."

Howard sucked his tongue with reverence for James' newfound outlook on life. "Yeah. I hear you."

"So, when Knocktoe whatever-his-fucking-name-is asks me, and you, and Cherry, and Mumford, *and Mark motherfucking Amos*, to wire ninety percent of their severance pay to fund this goddamn proposed corporate takeover of ours, then I do as I'm fucking told. Okay?"

Howard bit his lip and turned to the ramp with as much dignity as he could. "Yeah, I know. We all did."

"Hey, dime-store suit boy," James spat at the top of his lungs. "Don't look at the street, asshole. Look at *me* when I'm talking to you. Do me that courtesy, at least."

Howard returned his eyes to the furious monster sweating in his shirt.

"I don't trust that knock-toed, autistic-looking mound of blubber, man. I was put in this position. Him, and that black Danny guy, who's to say those pair of faggots ain't gonna just gun us down when we get back to the rendezvous with the cash? Huh?"

"They won't, James. Lincoln vouched for Danny. You saw how they behaved, they're practically kids around each other."

Howard kept a keen eye on James' face as he spoke. "I don't like that Joe guy, you know. Something isn't right. The way he turned on a dime and threatened us with that gun."

The corner of James' mouth rocked with concern. His bottom lip opened half an inch as he recalled the event, just enough to reveal his quaking tongue.

"I dunno about him, he's weird," he continued. "I don't want anything to do with him when this is all done. And I know Lincoln vouches for them, but, hell, how can we even trust Lincoln, either?"

Confused, Howard didn't dare broach the subject of race, in case he came across as a right wing nut job. "What are you saying, James?"

"You *know* what I'm saying, Howard."

James stopped short of vocalizing the fact that Lincoln and Danny, and by association, Knocktoe, might be out to screw them over, and it had little to do with the color of their skin.

"Ugh, forget it. I don't mean to throw shade on Lincoln, man. I just hope we're not getting used only to go on to get fucked by a couple of gay madmen I barely know, that's all."

"Yeah," Howard said. "The thought had crossed my mind, too, but that's just paranoia messing with your mind, James. Knocktoe and Danny are solid. They're friends of Lincoln's."

"And that's good enough for you, is it?"

"Actually, yes. It is. He vouched for them."

James huffed and clenched his fist. "He vouched for Danny. Not the cripple."

"It's paranoia, James," Howard said. "All in your head. So, you best just get that paranoid shit out of your drugged-up brain before it figures out how to control your mouth and ruins the whole plan. You know?"

James felt around his face and gave serious consideration to Howard's remarks. Eventually, he relaxed and produced a smile.

"You were right about one thing, though, Howie.

"Oh, yeah?"

"Yeah. *Relaxing.* Taking a break? That's exactly what I'm about to do now."

James climbed into his car, pulled the door shut, and started the engine.

"Where are you going?"

The window wound down as James shoved the gear into reverse. "Gonna go to the casino and lose some money. Get drunk. Maybe get a steak and a beer and get laid. You know, Howard? All the *sensible* stuff regular, good ol' white-collar boys do."

The car rolled back, and out from the disabled parking spot James had left his Jeep in.

"Don't do anything stupid," Howard said.

"Elvis, my friend, for the penultimate time, with next Wednesday being the last, has *left the motherfucking building.*"

The two front tires on the Jeep screeched around and kicked dust into Howard's face.

Seconds later, it bolted up the ramp at speed and joined the main road, leaving a worried and dirty-shirted Howard to traipse back to the bank, cursing the day he'd ever suggested robbing their place of work.

The Place With No Name
Chrome Valley's Premiere Nightclub & Casino
—1978 Main Street—

Glug-glug-glug.

James clutched the edge of the roulette table and downed his *Rollneck Kojak* beer down in one, sloppy go.

Buuuurrp-pp.

"Ahhh, *yeah*. That hit the spot," he said and slammed the empty bottle onto the ledge in time to the white ball circling around the roulette wheel.

He leaned over the table and tried to focus on the ball's trajectory, and where it might land. "Ah, c'mon, you little beauty."

By now, an impressive crowd had formed to watch the result. Among them were men in suits, younger guys in slacks and casual wear, and a string of beautiful women, all hoping to score big.

James glanced at his stack of chips on the felt-covered grid of numbers. A five-chip-high stack of one thousand bucks belonged to him on a red square with the number eleven obfuscated under the plastic pieces.

"Come on," James roared.

Clomp.

The dealer, a pretty woman with bushy black hair, announced the result. "Twenty-seven, black."

Two of the men cheered and collected their winnings, leaving James reeling with disappointment.

"Awww, shit."

He looked at his stash of plastic discs, and pushed three more chips onto red-eleven.

"Place your bets, gentlemen," the dealer said.

James hadn't taken in the ambiance of the nightclub. It was busy on this warm, Wednesday evening, when the neighboring nightclub had their DJ session night.

"Okay, ladies and gentlemen," the DJ said, as he placed the needle onto the next vinyl disc. *"Here's a golden oldie for all you gamblers out there."*

James swigged his next bottle of beer and instantly recognized the opening bars of the music track blaring through the speakers."

"Hell, yeah."

"This is the King himself, with A Little Less Conversation."

James used the edge of the roulette table to prop himself up. He'd downed at least ten bottles of beer, and refocused his mind on the game at hand. "Woohoo."

Just then, he felt a soft hand on his shoulder. He turned to see who it was, and focused on the well-manicured fingers and their gold-painted nails.

"Huh?"

"Okay, all bets are off gentlemen," the dealer said.

James grinned and winked at the woman. "They certainly are *now*."

"Standby."

The ball thundered and bounced around the spinning roulette wheel.

It was the most beautiful woman he'd ever seen. Her shiny, white teeth reminded him of a piano, minus the black keys. Her refined cheekbones complemented her beautiful, voluptuous lips, cute bridged nose, and sparkling, green eyes.

"Oh, hello?" James said.

The woman's sultry, husky tone melted James' heart in an instant. "Hey, honey. You're on a roll tonight, huh?"

James checked her up and down and gulped. "God, I hope so."

She pressed her not-inconsiderable cleavage against his upper arm for a clearer view of his stack of chips. "Mmm, big spender, huh?"

"Uh, yeah."

She shifted her head to the right and planted a lipstick-laden kiss on his neck. "My kinda guy."

James felt his crotch spring to life and tried to play it cool. He slid his right hand around her ass and gave it a squeeze, almost without realizing he'd done it.

"What's your name, honey?" she asked, enjoying the physical contact.

"James," he said. "What's yours?"

"Maria, honey. But you can call me *mommy*, if you want to."

Clunk-clunk-clop.

James' luck all rolled together at once.

The ball dropped into a slot on the wheel, right before the dealer announced the result.

"Red, eleven."

"Woohoooooo!"

Maria and James punched the air in exhilaration, to the amusement and congratulation of the others around the roulette table.

"Thirty-motherfuckin'-five-to-*one*," James said. "Oh, hell, *yes*."

He went to collect his winnings, and bent over the table. The further he leaned, the tighter something tugged on his manhood, having slipped in through his zipper.

"And speaking of *mother* fucking."

"Umm?"

He glanced at Maria and saw a fey, mucky smile formed across her face. She bit her lip and tightened her grip on him.

"Uh, Maria?"

"Yeah, honey?"

"Your hand is in my pants?"

She grinned as she *pulled* him up to her. "You just won over a hundred grand, honey. Tonight's your lucky night, and mommy's *real hungry* to get to know little James."

Slack-jawed with shock, he collected his chips and decided to take her up on her offer. He grabbed her arm, and walked her away from the table.

If he had turned back to the table, he would have noticed a tall, black gentleman with dreadlocks and dark shades watching him walk away.

The man approached the table, took an interest in the next roulette game taking place, and spoke into his cell phone.

"Yeah, the little prick's here, man. Just won big. Meet me out back."

Whump.

Maria and James burst through the men's room door, hands all over each other, and stumbled against the urinals, kissing, slurping, and exercising their tongues on each other.

"Mmm."

Maria grabbed his face, moved her lips away from his, and stared into his eyes. "You wanna put your dick in mommy's mouth, honey?"

He didn't need asking *once*, let alone twice. Breathless, James grabbed for his belt and shoved her across the urine-soaked floor. "Quick, in the stall."

She wiped her lip and licked the side of her finger. "Uh-huh."

James elbowed the first stall door open and yanked his pants down to his ankles. Maria walked in as coquettishly as she could muster, accentuating her hips as one foot glided in front of the other, and ran her tongue across her teeth.

Maria crouched before him with her knees wide open. "Get that bad boy out, baby. Mommy's thirsty."

James' heart jumped up and down inside his chest like an expectant child as he *revealed* himself. "Uh-huh, mmmm, yup, good idea. This okay?"

She gasped at the size of James' appendage. "Oh, wow. That's—"

Whump—Smash.

The stall door blasted open, smacked Maria in the side of the face, and knocked her out cold.

James looked up, covered his genitals, and screamed. "What the—?"

"—*Motherfucker*," the angry man with dreadlocks at the door said. "Gilmour."

"O-Oxide?"

"Where's the fuckin' broad who came in here wit you?"

"Wh-what?"

"The broad from the roulette wheel you dragged in here and was about to suck yo tiny-ass dick?"

James pointed to the unconscious Maria slumped against the wall. "Uh, there?"

The man moved in and peered into the corner of the stall and saw the evidence for himself.

"Shit, Gilmour. You know that's one of them white-ass trans-whatever broads, don'tcha?"

"Huh?"

The man's tongue ran across his lips. Daggered through the middle of the muscle was a shiny, chrome-plated spear. "Shit, Gilmour, that's a motherfuckin' *dude*, right there. You was about you dick sucked by a fuckin' *man*, man."

The gender identity of the woman was the very last of James' concerns. "Please, Oxide. Not here, m-man. I swear, I got your—"

"—Bitch, step your tiny dick out here and speak a goddamn motherfucker, proper."

Oxide backed out of the stall and held his arms out at three of his henchmen, who all stared at James' hands covering his groin.

Very slowly and carefully, James bent over and went for his belt.

"No, Gilmour. Drop that shit, and step out."

Utterly humiliated, James had no choice but to waddle like a penguin out of the stall, and into the men's room.

As he did, the chips bounced out of his pants pocket and rolled across the dank, murky puddles either side of his feet.

"Pick 'em up, boys," Oxide said, never once tearing his eyes away from the bewildered James, who continued to cover his genitals.

"Oxide, please? Allow me my modesty."

"Man, fuck your modesty, Gilmour," Oxide said. "Boys, this motherfucker owes me *beaucoup* bills."

"Oxide, p-please, I just won b-big, okay? Just out there? The broad you knocked out back there can back me up."

"Tch, that bitch couldn't back up a homo's boner with that skinny ass."

The three men gathered up the piss-laden chips from the floor and handed them to Oxide.

"Go man the door. Make sure a motherfucker don't get in."

The first of the three men bolted over to the men's room door and stood in front of it with the small of his back pressing against the handle.

Oxide turned to James and slipped his shades down to get a brighter view of him. "How much y'all lame-ass win at the wheel, Gilmour?"

"A hundred grand. I got more chips."

Oxide couldn't refuse such a huge payout for what, so far, had been a little over five minutes of work. He slipped James' chips into his pocket and sized the half-naked loser up and down once again.

"Gilmour?"

"Yeah?"

"You been ignoring my ass for a long while now, you know? Got so bad I had to tail your ass, and ride up in your shit on a personal level, just to get my message across."

"What message?"

"Don't act the white-ass dumb fuck with an Eighteenth Gate Oh-Gee, motherfucker. We represent, we take your bets, and when shit don't pay out too good like you thought it would, you ghost on me with my product, too, and your crazy white ass thinks it can get away with that shit? Man, you crazier than I thought."

Oxide lifted the flap of his jacket aside with his wrist and made sure James could see his Glock 17.

The three men surrounding James did the same, and threatened to go for their guns as soon as Oxide gave the order.

"No, no—Oxide, please," James begged. "Listen, something big is comin' up. I'll have the rest next week, I swear."

"You owe me five-hundred gees, you bankin' motherfucker. Now, how I'mma take that? In cash? Or outta your bony buttocks?"

Oxide ran his index finger and thumb down each side of his chin and felt a spike of pity for the half dressed man covering his thighs.

"Okay, seeing as you gave us a hundred gees down payment, I'mma allow your tiny dick till Wednesday to pay the balance."

James breathed a sigh of relief. "Thanks, man. I appreciate it."

"I'mma fillet both your buttocks, ram an old mp3 player in the asshole, and gift them to my momma as a pair of *Beatz* headphones if you don't got my fuckin' paper by Wednesday night when I'mma come knocking at you door. And you *best* be home when me and my boys come-a-motherfuckin'-knockin'."

"Y-Yes. Yes, I will. Thank you."

Oxide tutted, shook his head, and made for the men's room door. "Pull your damn pants back up, asshole."

James crouched down and raced to do as instructed. "Thanks."

Oxide reached the door and grabbed the handle, ready to exit the room. "Don't thank me, Gilmour. My boys here are gonna remind you of what happens if you fuck me over *two times*."

The three men crowded around James, vying for blood.

"Oxide, no—"

"—Don't touch the face, boys. Just the body," Oxide said, before throwing a demonic smile at James. "Wednesday, motherfucker."

The door closed behind him, just in time for the first of his men to sock James in the stomach.

He doubled over and puked on the floor, as the second man grabbed his collar, wrenched him upright and kneed him in the groin.

As James suffered his relentless beating, Maria awoke in the stall, and screamed blue murder. "Agh! Where am I?"

"Bitch, get outta here. This ain't got *shit* to do with you."

The first man grabbed a fistful of Maria's hair and went to lift her to her feet.

Riiipp.

Her bangs tore off the front of her head, and her entire wig came free in the man's hands.

"What the fuck?"

Maria staggered to her feet, slipped across the yellow puddles, and ran screaming with her hands covering her bald scalp.

"Help, help."

James wished for such an easy escape, but it wasn't to be.

The three men resumed their merciless, violent punishment and proceeded to knock the wind out of James Gilmour.

Chapter 11

One Mile South of Exit 11A

The bright blue Mack truck sat on the grass verge by the slip road.

Danny Driscoll had grown tired waiting for his associates to arrive. He glanced at the dashboard and attempted to read the time as he puffed on his weed-stuffed cigarette.

"Whoa," he spluttered, coughing out a lungful of air. "Damn, man, where are they?"

The digital clock focused into view as he wafted the smoke away from his face. It was 12:45, and he remembered little of the past forty-five minutes.

His wristwatch sprang to life and produced a sarcastic whelp.

"Meow, meow. Cat can you hear me?"

Danny coughed up a mound of phlegm and spat it out of the window. "Yeah, Squirrel. This is Cat, man. Is that you?"

"Cat? Is that you?"

"In space no one can hear you purr, motherfucker."

"Cat, listen, we're nearly behind you. Get ready to move. You should see us about half a mile behind you. We, uh, got a few coattail-hangers on us, man."

Danny peered into the side mirror as he rolled the eighteen-wheeler away from its resting position. "Cool, cool, and don't worry about them motherfuckers. Once we're in the underpass, they ain't gonna find shit."

"That is reassuring, Cat. Remind me to give you a saucer of milk when we reach the rendezvous."

"Meow, motherfucker."

A swathe of oncoming cars bolted past the Mack truck as Danny hit the gas and joined the freeway.

The silver Chevrolet bolted into the fast lane, less than half a mile behind the truck,

Lincoln kept his wrist to his mouth as he steered the car with one hand. "And remember, Cat?"

"Uh-huh?"

"Drop the ramp once you're under the flyover, and not before. We got choppers on us."

"I ain't a stupid motherfucker, man. I got this. Just ride up my ass."

"Not the first time a guy's said that to me."

"Man, shut the hell up and get your beautiful, black ass in the motherfuckin' fast lane."

Ben booted the back of the driver's seat in a fit of frustration. "Lincoln, man. Speed up, they're gaining on us."

"I know, I know," came the response. "Don't worry, they're not gonna smash into us with a freeway full of civilians, are they?"

"No, but—"

Ben and James turned around in their seats and prepared to open fire on the traffic behind them. They spotted two unmarked Dodge Chargers about three cars behind them, along with two helicopters giving chase in the skies above.

"Shit," James said. "Lincoln, I dunno what you're doing with that foot of yours, but make sure it's planted on the fucking ground. These choppers have a clear shot once we're on our own."

Lincoln shouted over his shoulder as he weaved in and out of the slower vehicles in front. "Jesus H. Shit,

Gilmour? Does the King of Rock 'n' Roll wanna drive, instead?"

"No," Ben quipped. "Those fucking police cars are stepping up, and they're getting closer."

Howard groaned and thumped the inner door in agony. "Would you assholes quit your whining and make sure we get to the truck, please? Is that too much to ask?"

Quick-thinking, he bit the end of his shirt sleeve and tore away a ribbon of cloth. "Ugh."

The strip of torn shirt peeled away from the sleeve and hung from his mouth.

Lincoln couldn't help but watch Howard stretch out the piece of fabric between his fingers. "Howard? What are you doing?"

"Shut up and drive."

Swerve.

A civilian car blared its horn as Lincoln spun the steering wheel to the left and forced their vehicle into the fast lane.

Howard's head slapped against the window as the car veered to the left. "Oww. Drive nicely."

"You want us to make the truck, or not?"

"Yes I do, you cretin, but I want my balls intact when we get there."

Furious, Howard tied the torn piece of cotton around his upper, left arm, and applied pressure to his bleeding wound. "Ugh, fuck me backwards. What a shitty day this is turning out to be."

The first police helicopter rocketed through the air a safe distance behind the silver Chevrolet.

The pilot lowered the aircraft and banked to the left, all the while trailing the tail-end of the speeding Chevy.

"This is Metal Bird One to Metal Bird Two. Come in Metal Bird Two?"

The pilot's headset sprang to life. *"This is Metal Bird Two. We are receiving you, over."*

"Ground units, ground units. The mark is headed for the Horder's Point Underpass, three clicks north."

"Understood, Metal Bird One," came the response.

The pilot looked to his left to see the adjacent helicopter bank right and fly into the distance. *"We'll catch them on the other side."*

Lincoln wiped his brow as he drove at a steady 80 mph in the fast lane. "Okay, we're about twenty seconds away. The underpass is just up ahead."

He pointed to the back-end of the bright blue mack truck.

"There's Danny," he said, before speaking into his wristwatch. "Cat, we're right behind you. Wait for it. Wait for it."

Danny's voice returned from the device on Lincoln's wrist. *"Cool. All hands on ramp. Going dark now. Steady ninety, no more, no less."*

"Gotcha."

A fierce blanket of darkness rolled over the front of the blue eighteen-wheeler Mack truck as Danny drove it into the underpass.

"Okay, you filthy animals, you got thirty seconds before we're out of the underpass and the chopper sees you rollin' in. So do it before."

Danny stepped on the gas, sped up to 90 mph, and yanked on the lever by his right knee.

"Dropping ramp now."

Whirrrr—slam.

The back doors on the Mack truck opened up, and produced a giant, silver tongue of a ramp, which slammed to the ground.

Scores of thick, orange sparks burst continuously at the end of the metal ramp it scraped at speed across the road.

"Go, go, go—"

"—Here we come," Lincoln said, as he applied pressure to the gas pedal. "Hold tight, everyone."

The silver Chevy bolted forward and entered the underpass. Howard looked up as he snatched his shotgun and sports bag from the foot well, and pointed at the large truck up ahead.

"There's Danny, there's the ramp."

Ben kept an eye on the cars behind the vehicle, and saw one of the Dodge Chargers peel out from the middle lane, and into theirs. "Fucking assholes are right on us. Shit, there's the other one."

He lifted his Uzi up and flicked the safety catch off. "Want me to shoot 'em?"

Lincoln focused on the ramp up ahead. "No, Cherry. Don't shoot anything. The choppers can't see shit. Wait till we're in the truck."

Ben snorted with disappointment. "Ah, shit."

James gripped the back door handle and held his breath. "Cherry, face forward. Hold onto something."

"Okay, okay."

Ben dropped the Uzi between his legs and held the back of Lincoln's seat.

"Okay, here we go."

Vroooooom.

The two front tires on the Chevrolet rolled onto the trailing Mack truck ramp. Lincoln dug his heel onto the gas pedal, as everyone in the car flung back into their seats by the tilt and force.

"Go, go, go," Howard said. "Get *in.*"

"Come on—"

Whump—craaaam.

The Chevrolet bolted up the ramp, and daggered hood-first into the back of the Mack truck.

Lincoln punched the air with excitement, forcing James and Ben to do the same.

"Fuck, yes. We're in, motherfuckers."

Howard snorted and chirped, "Good. Cat, close the doors—"

"—No, wait," Ben said. "The spikes."

James nodded and opened his side door. "Yeah, c'mon. Let's take 'em out."

Now safely ensconced in the back of the Mack truck, Ben booted the Chevy door open and jumped onto the metal ground.

The interior of the Mack truck rumbled back and forth at speed as Ben and James grabbed a coiled-up bunch of wires, each with several chrome-plated bolts weaved into them.

"Come on, come on."

Lincoln stepped out of the Chevy and thumped the back wall of the Mack truck as he spoke into his wrist. "Cat, we're in."

"Yeah, man. I see you. I'mma close the ramp now, so stand back."

Lincoln watched Ben and James carry the rolled-up bunch of spikes to the back end of the truck.

"No, wait."

"The fuck y'all talkin' about?"

"Dog and Ram are giving our prissy little coattail-riders a parting gift."

"I'd rather he gave them a parting shot in the fuckin' head."

"No, Cat. You dummy," Lincoln huffed. "The road spikes.

"Ohhh. The spikes. Yeah, cool. Burst their fuckin' tires out. Do it."

"Uh-huh."

Ben and James struggled to carry the bunch of wires over to the end of the truck.

"Okay, now," James said, as he and Ben unfurled the length of carbon sheet up the ramp.

Clang—spang—clang.

The chrome-plated spikes clanged, one by one, as they rolled out on the sheet.

Ben focused on the two Dodge Chargers daring to join the ramp. They sped up and the tires clipped the ends, denting the ramp against the floor.

"Now."

Whump.

Ben and James whipped the spiked strip into the air. It clanged against the ground, streaking from one end of the lane to the other, with the viciously sharp chrome-plated spikes facing the upwards.

"You're about to go *bust*, motherfucker," James screamed.

Whooosh—spitch—spitch—burst.

The first Dodge Charger's wheels exploded as its rubber tires punctured over the spikes, sending it hurtling around like an out-of-control Waltzer.

Zip—Crash.

The front end of the first vehicle punched the hood of the car behind, forcing it to catapult into the air and crash into the windshield of the second Dodge Charger.

"Whoa," Ben said. "Those spikes really kick ass—"

Vroom—vroom—crash—smash—smash.

The next four civilian cars hit the spikes, forcing all four tires to burst and plow trunk-first into the sides of more oncoming vehicles in the other lanes.

Dozens of cars screeched, catapulted, and collided into each other, leaving a fiery mess of vehicular carnage in the truck's wake.

James clapped his hands together and moonwalked with excitement up the back of the truck.

"Now *that's* what I call a pile-up."

Howard yelled into his wrist. "Most of those were innocent people, you dickhead. Close the fucking ramp."

Danny's voice billowed out from everyone's wristwatches.

"I heard that, Rabbit. Closing the ramp, now. So calm your white ass down and get back from the doors."

Whiirrrrrr—shunt.

The ramp lifted up and back into the ceiling frame of the Mack truck.

Shortly after that, the doors slammed shut, sealing Howard, Lincoln, James, and Ben in the bowels of the moving vehicle.

"Good job, my bruddas."

After a brief pause, each of the men looked to each other in utter silence.

"Exiting the underpass now. ETA to the rendezvous is fifteen minutes. Smoke if you got 'em."

The silence didn't last long.

A mighty explosion of sheer, undiluted congratulation was due.

"Fuck, yes," Howard screamed. "You goddamn motherfuckers. We pulled it off."

Lincoln, James, and Ben roared with delight. "Yeah!"

Metal Bird Two flew through the sky and hovered at the far end of the underpass. "That's a negative on the Chevrolet. I do not have a positive I.D."

"Metal Bird Two, this is One," came the response from the other helicopter. *"That's a negative on the silver Chevrolet."*

"Executing a drop now, we will search the underpass."

"Understood, Metal Bird One. We will keep eyes on the mark."

Far below the two helicopters, a blue Mack truck bolted out from the underpass and headed north on the freeway with the missing silver Chevrolet, and heist perpetrators, safely tucked away inside…

Chapter 12

BENJAMIN CHERRY
— Monday, September 28th —

"Nice socks, Mr. Cherry."

"Thanks."

"You got the pajamas to go with them?"

Ben had forgotten that he'd crossed his legs shortly after sitting down for what turned out to be his exit interview.

The end of his right pant leg rode up his shin and exposed his daft *Space Invaders* socks.

Both Damien Ironside and Alan Capone found it difficult to look at anything else from their side of the desk, let alone concentrate on the task at hand.

"Oh, these?" Ben said. "Yeah, they were a gift from my wife. She has a strange sense of humor."

Alan perused his notes at the desk and smirked at the text. "Ah, yes, your wife. I was a big fan of hers back in the day."

Ben knew exactly what the man was talking about, and was well within his rights to make a complaint if the conversation went any farther.

"Really."

Damien winked at Victor, who kept out of Ben's field of vision on the executive chair by the window.

"Oh, yeah," Alan said. "I really enjoyed her work. Does she still dabble in adult movies?"

Ben sneered, determination to bring the subject to a crashing halt. "No, She doesn't."

Damien sniggered. "Yes, she's found herself a man to take care of her, now, hasn't she? Mr. Cherry?"

"Look, I don't know what's going on, here, but can we get back to why I'm here, please?"

Alan shrugged his shoulders and returned to his notes. "Sure, Benjamin Cherry. Director of Corporate Accounts. You have several guys working underneath you—"

"—Much like his wife had at one point, it seems," Damien said with a grin, very much to Ben's consternation.

"Fifteen people working out of six branches. You must be a very busy bee, Mr. Cherry?"

"Yeah, I—"

"—Although," Alan interrupted. "According to the last audit, a number of irregularities were found. That was back in March when quarantine came into effect, only to be left unattended for five months, and now with a situation that throws a spotlight on the entire accounting team in a very troubling way?"

Ben knew about the irregularities Alan referred to, and had rehearsed, in his mind at least, a reason for why they remained *irregular*.

"Yeah, uh, we were under very strict instructions to *not* work from home while we were on furlough. Mr. Price had the accounts passed higher up the chain, and they took care of it."

Damien raised his eyebrows, "Interesting. Tell me, Mr. Cherry, what did you do the whole time you were on furlough on full pay?"

"Not much," Ben said, suspicious of the line of questions being thrown his way. "Why, what did you do?"

"Me? I continued to work. Chartered jets around the country, visiting with people. Sometimes with a mask, and sometimes without. Always kept a six-foot distance and adhered to social distancing. I ask again, what did you do?"

"Watched *MovieFlix* and ate *Cheetah Stix*, mostly. My wife is eight months pregnant, now, so most of my time was spent—"

"—Pregnant?" Alan said, surprised. "Well, there's a surprise."

The atmosphere in the room threatened to grab Ben's neck and throttle him to death. He hadn't felt such an antagonist aura since the day he told his mother he was marrying his wife.

"Congratulations, Mr. Cherry," Damien said.

Alan seemed impressed and cast a knowing wink. "Yes, and *well done*."

Before Ben's temper could liaise with his brain, his mouth opened. "What do you mean by that?"

"What do I mean by what?" Alan asked.

"Well done? You said *well done*, and I wanna know what you meant when you said that."

Alan felt around his collar and cleared his throat. "Well, I'm not saying your wife gets around, per se, but—"

"—But what?"

"Well, if her videos on *PornCabin* are anything to go by, her sperm count is higher than mine."

Ben jumped out of his seat and clenched his fist. "Say that again, you balding, fat *fuck*."

"Mr. Cherry. Can you sit back down, please?"

Ben heaved with fury and approached the desk, ready to strike the man in his face. "You don't know *shit* about me, or my wife, or my life."

Alan pointed to the columns of names on his hit list. "On the contrary, I know everything, Mr. Cherry. And your colleagues."

"We know everything, Mr. Cherry," Damien added. "Including your last day of work, which, as it happens, is the day after tomorrow."

"What?"

"Chrome Valley Federal is incredibly indebted to your service over the years," Alan said. "And we wish you all the best."

"You're letting me go?"

"Yes."

All four walls seem to grind to life and spin around. The floor beneath Ben's *Space Invaders* socks shimmied like a miniature Earthquake, and tilted towards the door.

Utterly deflated, Ben hung his head and made for the door.

"Thank you, Mr. Cherry," Damien said. "Could you send Mr. Mumford in on your way out, please?"

Ben grabbed the door handle and considered tearing it off, and clubbing himself to death.

"Oh," Alan hollered. "And say hello to your wife for me."

"Not a chance."

"Give her one from me," Alan joked.

Ben snapped the door handle off in his hand, turned around, and launched himself at the desk.

"Goddamn motherfuckers!"

Ben socked Alan across the face and broke his nose, before threatening Damien with more of the same.

"No, d-don't hit me—"

"—You ruined my life," Ben yelled as he daggered the sharp end of the handle into the man's mouth, and pushed through the back of his neck.

A geyser of blood splattered up the wall behind his chair, as Ben climbed off the table and eyed the terrified Victor Price.

"B-Ben?"

"*You.*"

"No, get back. What are you d-doing?"

Ben reached into his jacket pocket and pulled out a Glock 17 firearm. He slid the safety catch off, aimed the weapon at Victor's forehead, and teased the trigger with his finger.

"This is all your fault, asshole."

"No, Ben," Victor screamed as Ben yanked on the trigger. "No—"

"—Bastard."

Blam—schpatt.

***

"Agh!"

Ben opened his eyes and kicked the back of Howard's seat. "Huh? Where are w-we?"

He found himself breathless in the back of Lincoln's Ford Escort, having jumped straight out of his bizarre nightmare.

"Wakey-wakey, Benji-boy. You musta fallen asleep" Lincoln giggled as he pulled the car up outside *The Place With No Name*.

Ben turned to his left and saw a thoroughly hassled James next to him, and about to exit the car.

Howard leaned over Lincoln's lap and spoke to James through the driver's window. "Keep your phone on, and your ears and your eyes open."

"I'll try."

Ben squinted at the building behind James. It was a place he knew reasonably well; A nightclub and casino called *The Place With No Name*.

"And try *not* to blow your final check tonight on that damn roulette table, okay? Take it easy."

James saluted the men and made his way to the nightclub. "You got it."

Ben wiped his eyes, and felt a strong desire to get out of the car for some fresh air.

"It's okay, guys. I'll walk from here."

"Are you sure?" Lincoln asked. "It's cool, I can bring you home, you're only around the corner?"

Ben looked out of the window and focused on the stone fountains at the entrance to the Kaleidoscope.

"Yeah, no. I, uh, need to pick something up for Brianna. Keep her sweet for when I give her the bad news."

"Yeah, that's not a bad idea, Cherry," Lincoln said. "I like that. Walking home, get some air."

Ben stepped out of the car and went to push the door shut. "Yeah."

"Yeah, give them *Space Invaders* socks a breather, too, huh?"

"Hardy-fuckin'-har," Ben scoffed. "I'll talk to you tomorrow."

The late afternoon air was a welcome feeling for Ben as he crossed the road.

"Ahh, that feels good—"

Blaaarree.

A bus screamed past with its horn blaring, narrowly avoiding Ben, who managed to jump back just in the nick of time. A half-second earlier, and he'd have ended up as roadkill all over the sidewalk.

"Goddamn asshole," the driver screamed out of the window as it raced into the distance.

Ben fought off the shock, and flipped the bus a vicious middle finger. "Yeah? Eat this. *Prick.*"

Still reeling from the shock, Ben made his way to the Kaleidoscope Shopping Mall entrance and tried to avoid eye contact with the scurrilous teenagers playing in the water.

He pushed past the crowds of shoppers, and could feel something growling in his direction. When he lifted his head to investigate the source of the bizarre sound, he discovered it belonged to an angry-looking St. Bernard.

Woof—Woof.

Ben clutched his chest in fright. "Jeez."

He followed the leash that ran from the St. Bernard's gold collar, and all the way up to its owner; a young, blonde teenager dressed in a Chrome Junction Academy uniform.

"Hey, Mister. Don't worry about him. He doesn't bite."

"Thank God for that."

Ben relaxed, and tried to pat the St. Bernard's head. "Hey, good boy—"

Growl.

The schoolgirl's friend, a boyish-looking brunette named Lizzie, cackled like a witch at the man attempting to stroke the dog's head. "Hey, Vicky, man. I don't think Benjy likes this guy, you know."

"Huh?" Ben asked. "How did you know my name?"

Vicky snorted at him. "Eh? What are you talking about?"

"My name's Ben," Ben said.

Vicky rolled her eyes and yanked on the leash. "Ohhh, no shit? That's my dog's name, too. Benjy."

A comforting blanket of familiarity smothered both girls, and Ben, as he went to pet the dog a second time.

"Here, boy—"

Woof—Growl.

Ben jumped back and covered his hand. "Ah, maybe he doesn't wanna be touched."

"I don't think he likes you, mister," Vicky said.

Today was proving to be one of Ben's least favorite of the year, as he abandoned his pathetic attempt to show anyone any sign of kindness and made for the entrance to the mall.

Little did Benjamin Cherry know, however, that his day would be turning into a series of calamities and paranoia, all culminating in having to deliver bad news to his wife.

He knew as much, and the firearm sticking out of the mall entrance's security guard's holster did little to quell Ben's anxiety.

"Good afternoon, sir."

"Hello."

The security guard held the ten-foot door open for Ben as he walked in.

And there was the damn gun on the guard's hip, getting bigger and bigger the closer he got to the man.

Ben couldn't tear his eyes away from it, as he walked through the door and, for the briefest of moments, entertained the weirdest notion he'd ever had.

What if he snatched the gun from the guard's holster and held everyone hostage?

What would happen if he did that? Would other guards come rushing around him from the southern perimeter?

What if one of them was hiding in the restrooms down the corridor, right by the child's elephant ride and vending machine?

What would he do with the hostages, and what might his demands be?

And, of course, which of the many hundreds of stores in the mall would he want to rob?

Today, daydreaming was Ben's business, and business, as they always seem to say these days, was pretty damn good.

"Nah," Ben laughed away the idea and walked past the guard, before stopping and remembering to ask where he was going. "Oh, excuse me?"

"Yes, sir?"

"Can you tell me where *The Brand* clothing store is?"

"Certainly, sir," the guard said. "Top of the escalator, upper level, and make a right."

"Thanks."

"*The Brand*, huh? Nice. Expensive threads, man."

Ben knew all-too well just how damned expensive *The Brand* was, and didn't appreciate the reminder.

"Yeah. Tell me something I don't know."

THE BRAND
Unit 44 - Upper Level
— Kaleidoscope Shopping Mall —

Biddip-beep-bip-bip.

Ben stared at the female assistant's blouse as she rang up the bill for a red sequined *Signature Collection* dress.

The light from the ceiling bounced across the text groove on her name badge; *Lizzie Holmes.*

"Nice name," Ben muttered a little too loud.

Lizzie grinned and slid the card machine across the counter. "Thank you."

Ben had little else to say as he reached into his pocket and retrieved his wallet.

"Okay. So, that comes to five hundred and eighty-five exactly. Will you be paying by cash or card?"

Ben wiggled his wrist and displayed his Chrome Valley Federal Express card.

"Card, please."

"Ooo. CV Federal, huh?" she said with an approving grin. "Not often we see those, especially around here."

She took the card and swiped it through the machine.

"So, you're in banking, huh?"

"Me?"

"Mmm."

"Oh, no. Well, yeah. Kinda."

"Kinda?" Lizzie chuckled. "You're not a bank robber are you?"

"No," Ben spat, thinking he'd been rumbled. "Why?"

"Only kidding, only kidding—"

Bzzzz.

Lizzie examined the card and scrunched her face. "Oh. Card declined."

"What? That's impossible. Try again."

She licked the side of her thumb and rubbed it against the gold smart chip.

"Yeah, if these things get dirty, it can play havoc with the card reader. Let's try again."

"Thank you."

Ben's mouth turned to stone with fear.

Embarrassing as the first declination was, the prospect of a second would bury him, particularly now that Lizzie knew he worked at the bank.

Bzzzz.

"Card declined again."

Ben took the card from her hand and considered slashing his wrists with it. "It can't be?"

"Well, you work for the bank, don't you? Do you want to give them a call? It's not all that uncommon for the bank to halt card transactions—"

"—I fucking *know* how a bank works, don't I?"

The man's violent snap caught the sudden, puzzled attention of the customers in the store.

Lizzie stood back and held out her hands in disapproval. "Don't take that attitude with me, sir. I'm just trying to help."

Ben calmed himself down and pulled out his phone.

"Look, I'm sorry. Okay? I'm just a bit on edge. Forgive me."

"That's quite all right, sir."

Ben tapped the bag containing the dress and put his phone to his ear. "Can you give a few minutes, please?"

Lizzie slid the bag from the counter and placed it under the desk. "Of course. I'll look after this for you until you return."

Ben sprinted away from the counter with his cell phone pressed to his ear, praying that the person he was calling would answer.

"C'mon, pick up. Aww, please, man, just answer the fuckin'—"

"—Cherry? What do you want?"

"Howard, man, it's me," Ben hushed, suddenly realizing he was now keeping out of sight in the lingerie department.

Shelves and shelves of panties, brassieres, and mannequins modeling various undergarments, all swooped down around him as if they were listening-in on his phone call.

"Listen, man, I can't talk long. I need you to do me a favor?"

"Lincoln and I just pulling into Burger Face. What's up?"

"Ugh. Look, I wouldn't ask otherwise, but I'm in a bit of a bind. Fuckin' Price, man, I swear."

"What?"

"Federal's cut off my card, and I can't pay for shit. It's been declined twice, and I really need to buy this thing for Brianna, otherwise my life won't be worth living if I go home without it. Can you spot me? Till our Ironside checks clear, and I'll square up with you, then."

"How much is it?"

Ben winced hard, and bit his knuckle; an unusual praying technique he'd developed when he got caught stealing from the candy store as a child. "Uh, five hundred and eighty-five—"

"—What?!"

"Shhh."

Ben lowered his head behind the rows of *Teeter Tots* cotton underwear. "Please, Howard. I wouldn't ask otherwise," he whispered.

"Ugh, five hundred? I've barely got that much in my account as it is."

"Okay, forget it."

"Okay, Ben. I'll do it. But tell me something."

"Sure."

"Just how fucked are you?"

"Money-wise?" Ben whispered back.

"Any-wise."

"Biblically-speaking, Brianna and I are just fine," Ben said. "But money-wise? We're well and truly in the red. Doubly screwed now that I don't have an income."

"Shit. Have you told Brianna, yet?"

"About what?"

"About the fucking layoff, whaddya think?"

Ben kept his voice down as he spied on the other customers in the store.

"Of course I haven't told her, man, I've barely had time to get hit by a bus, attacked by a dog, and buy an overpriced dress, let alone *think* about how I'm gonna break the news to her."

"Okay, okay. I'll buy the damn dress. Shit. Put the violin away, and put me on to the girl behind the desk. I'll get my card out. But you better pay me back."

Ben exhaled and felt like kissing the man through the phone. "Thanks, man."

"Or we can use that five hundred to put toward what Knocktoe needs."

"Sure, put it on my tab," Ben said. "You're a lifesaver, Howard. Remind me to take a bullet for you when you need me to."

"Hey, any time. But only because it's you, Cherry. I wouldn't do this for just anybody."

One Hour Later

The door to Ben's apartment opened out with the key still in the lock.

The Brand bag swung in, followed by a pair of pantsuit legs.

"BeeBee? It's me. I'm home early."

Ben shut the door and kicked the dirt from his shoe onto the floor mat.

The floorboards from the bedroom shuffled around, indicating that someone was home.

"Good."

Ben saw his opportunity to hide *The Brand* bag behind the sofa. He placed it behind the left seat, rubbed his hands, and took a deep breath.

"You're home early."

"Huh?"

Ben turned to the petite brunette woman with the baby bump. She clutched a stack of papers in her right hand and chucked them to the floor.

"What are those?" Ben asked.

A pang of upset ruptured through her throat when she spoke. "The foreclosure documents came through. I've just been on the phone to mom."

"What did she say?"

"She said we should put our stuff in storage for a week till she can get her place cleared up. Store-N-Go have a sale, so we can dismantle the sofa and bed, and a few other bits and pieces. Store them there until mom's ready for us."

Brianna wiped a tear from her eye and sat on the right-hand seat on the sofa.

"Our bills haven't been paid for months," she said. "The mortgage holiday saved us most of the summer, but the water, gas, electrical, hell, even the service charge, they never got paid."

Ben felt like hell warmed up, knowing full-well what was coming next. "Hey, it's okay."

"Some guy came knocking earlier, but I hid in the bedroom and pretended no one was in."

The news gnawed at Ben's heart, producing a wave of helplessness that he couldn't shake off.

"Did he leave?"

"Eventually, yeah," Brianna said. "I thought he was gonna kick the door down. I was so scared."

"Don't worry, it'll be okay."

"It's pretty goddamn far from okay, Benjy," she said. "You know Linda, the old woman down the hall?"

"Yeah?"

"I got talking to her. They cut off her electricity, and her husband's in the hospital."

Ben perched his ass on the edge of the sofa and took his wife's hands in his. "Listen, BeeBee, I got something to tell you."

"Ugh," she said. "Please, let it be *some* good news for once."

"Well, one piece of bad news, and a piece of good news."

Brianna released his hand and placed her right hand on her baby bump. "Give me the bad news."

"They laid me off today."

"What?"

"Fuckin' Victor Price, man, I just knew it was coming. They're laying everyone off. Howard, Lincoln, James, and a couple of boys out in the backroom."

Brianna found the devastating news almost comical in nature. Instead of bursting into tears, as Ben imagined she might do, she burst out laughing and slapped the sofa.

He smiled for a moment, thinking he'd gotten away with delivering his message of doom.

"Oh-ho, those goddamn, motherfucking cocksuckers," Brianna shrieked with unbridled poison in her voice. "They've got some fucking nerve. Fuck, I feel as if I wanna go down there and kick their nuts up into their throats."

"No, Brianna—"

"—These stinkin' rich pussy holes think they can screw-over the genuinely talented workers who run their crappy shit show? People like you? The ones who do all the heavy lifting? Good people like you, and they haven't given any goddamn consideration to the families they're affecting?"

Ben aided his wife with her vicious temper. It was one of the things he loved about her, after all.

"Exactly. Thank you."

"I bet they had the money to outsource the firings, right?"

"Right."

"I might've guessed," Brianna spat. "Goddamn assholes. God, what a bunch of homos, you know? Spineless, gutless, lily-livered ass hairs like Price always avoiding the chop when it comes to restructuring. I'm telling you, Benjy, the minute your chair goes cold, they're gonna change the remit and the job title, and hire someone else. Probably someone younger than you, to take your place."

Ben nodded in complete agreement, and marveled at how his wife was stealing all the lines he'd planned to use on her.

"It's ironic, you know. Some people take it up the ass as a career," she said.

"I know."

"You *do* know. And then there's you, Mr. Ex-Banker, getting fucked in the ass every day until they don't wanna do it anymore. They pull out, wipe their dick off on the curtain, make their excuse, and order you a taxi home."

Ben frowned at his wife's analogy, and changed the subject.

"Yeah. Look, that was the bad news. I've actually got a meeting with a couple guys tomorrow night about a new job. Pretty well paid, actually."

The news came as a shock to the woman. "You do?"

"Yeah. Actually, they're kinda interviewing me and Howard and a few others for it. It's still industry-related, sort of. But if this all goes to plan, we could be set for a while."

Brianna wasn't stupid.

She knew in this day and age that career opportunities never arose out of the blue so soon after getting fired. The taciturn, micro expressions plastered all over Ben's face suggested he knew as much, too.

To Brianna, money was money, and she didn't exactly possess the resume to challenge any unorthodoxy and morality when it came to earning a fast buck.

"Well, I guess that's something," she said. "It'd better not be a get-rich-quick kind of scheme. You know what I'm talking about, right?"

"Right. No, it isn't."

Brianna accepted the answer, and let it lie, leaving Ben to introduce his final magic trick of exceptional brilliance. She watched him struggling to reach over the sofa's backrest and pick up a medium-sized paper bag.

"Ta-Daa!"

"What's this?"

Ben passed it to her. "It's for you. A kind of, uh, *thing* to show you how much I love you."

Suspicious, Brianna peered inside and gasped. "Oh. Ben. You shouldn't have."

"You like it?"

She pulled the dress out of the bag, lifted it in the air, and marveled at the spectacle. "Oh, I *love* it."

"Good."

She folded it neatly over her arm, and placed it back in the bag without a trace of emotion.

A look of confusion folded across Ben's face. "BeeBee? What are you doing?"

Insistent, she passed the bag back to him. "Bring it back to the store."

"What?"

"We can't afford this, Benjy," she said. "So, bring it back, and get a refund."

"B-But—"

"—Not buts. As nice as it is, and as lovely a thought as it was, I don't need some dumb, expensive dress from some tax-dodging company to know that you love me."

She held her belly as she stood to her feet, and pecked the bewildered Ben on his forehead, and stared into his young, brown, puppy dog eyes.

"As long as I have you, then I'm happy. And I don't care *where* that is. In our own home, or at my mother's. Hell, even out on the street in a cardboard box. I don't give a shit."

Ben produced a whimper of a smile and felt like crying. "I love you so goddamn much, Bee."

"I love you too," she said. "I'm gonna go take a shower."

Chapter 13

The Rendezvous
—Unit 237: Chrome Valley (West) Industrial Estate—

The Mack truck sat by the side wall of the vast warehouse with its back doors wide open and ramp fully extended to the ground.

Ben stepped out of his suit pants and into a pair of well-worn jeans.

"Ahh, that feels good. If I never wear a goddamn business suit ever again it'll be too soon."

He chucked his suit into the garbage bag at the end of the truck, which contained two rubber masks, and a heap of wristwatches and voice alternators.

"Bon voyage."

Howard had already changed into his slacks and sweatshirt, and slipped his wedding ring back onto his finger. "Feels good to be outta that suit. Now, and forever."

"Amen to that," Lincoln said as he stuffed his suit and tie into a garbage bag. "Never wearing that damn noose around my neck ever again, man."

A huge, rectangular table took place in the middle of the warehouse. Six counting machines whirred and flapped, sifting through the bills that had been loaded into them.

Danny watched each device sift through the paper, and tapped his finger on the calculator. "Nearly there, y'all. Get ready."

Four empty sports bags lined the rectangular table in the middle of the room. Lincoln kept an eye on the four foot-high stacks of bills lining the edge of the table.

"Count it again," James snapped. "Make damn sure, this time."

His anger, largely ignored for the time being by Lincoln and Howard, was directed at Danny, who fed the next stack of bills into the counters.

"This can't be right, man. You must have fucked up the count the last time."

"Shit. I *am* counting them," Danny said. "There's a lot here to count, so just shut up and wait."

Ben perched his ass on the Chevy trunk sitting inside the Mack truck, and cracked open a tin of *Rollneck Kojak* beer.

"James?"

"Don't fuckin' talk to me, okay?"

"You need to learn to control your anger, you know."

Howard slammed the table and turned his back to the counting machines. He ducked his head in fury, and folded his arms.

"Would you two girls stop shouting and think, okay. Just think. There must have been a mistake with the count—"

"—Fucking Mark Amos, I swear," James snapped. "That's what the problem was. Stupid prick getting himself shot by the pigs. That gold-toothed fucking nincom-fucking-poop cleared out the big bucks. It was all in his bag, and all that paper is floating around the financial district like a bunch of drugged-up insects."

Lincoln didn't have the words to express his disappointment. He felt it best to stare at the papers folding out at speed through the machine and pray for the best.

"Come on, come on."

Danny loaded the next stack into the machine and kept quiet, concentrating on the count from the first five machines. He scribbled a series of numbers from each one into his notepad. "This is the last stack, man. Let's see what's up."

Howard closed his eyes and enjoyed a brief moment of respite. It had been an afternoon of chaos and many, many errors. The simple, comforting sound of victory felt distinctly Pyrrhic, at best.

His gunshot wound on his left arm had stopped bleeding but remained tender. It hurt like thunder whenever something so much as looked at it.

Then, he opened his eyes, and saw a pair of legs in jeans, and a shiny cane tapping across the floor.

"Oh," Howard snorted. "Joe? You're here?"

Knocktoe Joe was present, hobbling towards him with a shit-eating grin on his face.

"Yeah, I am. I figure this place is safe enough now you're out of the firing line. You weren't followed here, were you?"

"No. We took care of that."

"Good.

"Hey, Joe," Ben hollered from within the truck.

"Good afternoon, Mr. Cherry," Joe said. "You looking forward to a wealth of untold riches and an early retirement?"

"Yup."

James snorted with disgust and thumped the table so hard that the machines bounced an inch away from each other.

"Hey," Danny shouted. "Be careful. You want the count to be accurate, don't you?"

"I want it to be *at least ten times as much as the last count*, you mouthy prick."

Danny extended his middle finger at the angry man. "Tch. Motherfucker's got some balls tryna blame *me*, asshole. This ain't my fault."

Joe slammed his chrome-plated cane on the table and raised his right hand. "Right, shut the hell up and listen carefully to me."

Lincoln looked up, and joined Howard, Ben, and James as they sneered at the man who'd demanded their attention.

Joe cleared his throat and offered them a smile for a job well done.

"You, each of you, did well, today. We got what we came for, and we're all back in one piece."

"All but one," Howard said.

"All but one," Joe repeated, softly. "Yes, but if anyone was gonna take a hit, then I'm glad it was the gold-toothed asshat who was already on the corporate dark side. Nevertheless, I hear Amos did his best, an unfortunate casualty on this, our wage against corporate greed."

"Amen to that," Ben said.

"It's a shame," Joe continued. "But it is the way of things in this game, as I'm sure you're all learning."

Ben held up his beer and went to sip it. "To Mark Amos. A good man."

The others bowed their heads solemnly, and joined in the tribute.

"To Mark Amos. A good man."

Joe held up his cell phone for everyone to see. "And congratulations are in order, too. You've made history, gentlemen."

Howard stepped out of Joe's path as he moved towards the table. "Here, take a look."

Joe pressed the play button...

A young woman in a silver suit spoke into her microphone with the clean-up of the financial district mayhem playing out behind her.

"—When the Chrome Valley Federal Bank was raided by masked gunmen just before noon today, leaving a devastating trail of death and destruction in their wake," she said with an excited grin plastered on her smug face. "Five dead, including the manager of the bank, and scores, if not hundreds, of civilians, including at least ten hostages, are injured as a result of what is believed to be Chrome Valley's biggest, most deadliest robbery in its entire history."

Howard felt his heart stop beating as he watched the closeups of dead bodies being carted out of the building.

"I feel sick," he said. "I can't watch this."

Lincoln agreed and ran his fingers across his brow. "It wasn't our fault. It wasn't. If they'd have done as we instructed, they'd be alive. What were we supposed to do?"

"Yeah," Ben added. "It was either them or us."

Howard sighed at the thought of the money being counted behind him. "I dunno, I just—I thought, you know, *fuck 'em*. It's all insured. The money being gone. It's all insured. Nobody would lose anything."

Ben smirked to himself. "Yeah, except their lives, huh, Ross?"

"Fuck you."

The reporter posed in front of the smoking vehicular carnage and shoved her microphone into the face of a young woman named Kate.

"I talked to one of the hostages, Miss Kate Durst, who had this to say."

Kate spoke to the camera, slowly, as if in a daze. "They just came in, shot one of my colleagues, and had us empty the registers. They knew what they were doing. They killed two of my colleagues in cold blood. I hope they rot in hell."

James scrunched his face. "Shut the hell up, Durst. She better say nothing to the pigs, or I'll have to visit her home and shut her the fuck up."

The reporter nodded politely as she pulled her microphone back to her mouth and addressed the camera. "Thank you, Kate. Well, as you can see, the clean-up operation here is going to take a while yet. A valley reeling from the shock of its biggest ever heist, which leaves just one question. Who are these robbers dressed in suits and animal masks, and where are they now?"

Howard stared at the woman's shit-eating grin as she signed off the report.

"For SNN Sense Nation News, live from Chrome Valley's financial district, I'm Dana Doubleday—"

"—Shut that shit off," Howard snapped. "I don't wanna see her smug face, anymore. Goddamn media bloodsucker. Shut it off."

Joe lowered the phone and slipped it into his pocket. "You got it."

Howard shoved the man out of his path and paced around the large table. "No, I don't *got* it. I got nothing, okay? Sure, we may have a little bit of money, but, ugh, a large chunk of my fucking *soul* was chipped away about an hour ago, and I'm not too happy about it. *That's* what I got."

"It was your idea," Joe said. "You came to me for help, and you got it."

Howard chucked his half-empty beer across the floor. It smashed against the closed door and puked out the contents across the concrete ground.

"Goddamn it, Joe, you tooled us up. I did *not* want a bunch of dead assholes, back there. You don't know what you're talking about. We were meant to be in and out with the money. No damage done. For fuck's sake."

Lincoln felt the urge to interject, all without looking at Howard and starting a fight. "Howard, man. None of us meant what happened, okay? You knew shit could go down, man, yeah? It's a risk we all knew we were taking. Now, lookit, I'm cool with that shit, okay? My conscience is clear."

James arched his back and exhaled. "Ah, shit. This is fucked up."

Whiiirr—Clunk.

The sudden halt of the money counters, and the resultant silence, fell across everyone's ears like a slap in the face.

The machines had finished counting.

The sound of Danny scribbling on his notepad was the only in the room, followed by the clearing of a throat.

Danny Driscoll had the results in his hands, and judging by his seemingly hasty look of bewilderment, the news was *not* good.

"Okay, fellas. The results are in."

Nobody wanted to be the first to say anything, and waited as patiently as possible for Danny to say something - anything - to break the silence.

James threw his arms up in the air. "Well?"

Danny looked up and licked his lips. "What?"

"What's the fucking score, asshole?"

"Tch. Don't call me a fuckin asshole, asshole."

Everyone's ears pricked up, expecting the worst, as they watched Danny point at the first machine.

"Back your white ass up and pay attention, Gilmour. Okay, so, the take from the registers. Comes in at fifteen thousand and sixty-five."

James bit his lip and clenched his fists. "For *fuck's* sake."

"And the drive-through?" Lincoln dared to ask, apprehensively. "Most of that shit wasn't the kind of money that folds."

"Yeah," Danny said. "Drive-through take was five thousand, and a few pennies. A grand in paper, and the rest in change. Chump fuckin' change."

Lincoln pushed himself away from the table and sucked his teeth. "Shit, man."

"Yeah, so fifteen plus five is twenty."

Danny moved to the next two counters and referred to his notepad.

"I'm sure y'all won't be surprised to learn that most of the bills came from the vault. Thank God you got in there, otherwise this particular score would have been as embarrassing as a motherfucker."

Ben climbed out of the back of the truck and walked over to Howard at the table. "Go on."

Danny looked up from his hand and spoke to the men directly. "Final takes on paper from the vault comes to two-hundred—"

"—Ugh," James said upon hearing a six-figure amount. "No, no, no—"

"—And sixty five thousand."

Exasperated, James thumped the side of the truck. "Fuck, fuck, *fuck*."

Howard ignored his friend's expletive and stared back at Danny. "And the bonds?"

"The bonds clocked in at three-hundred-and-eighty thousand. After they go through Jimmy the fence, it'll probably grind down to around three-fifty. And that right there, gentlemen, is the final score."

"What's the total?"

A wave of depression and regret filled the warehouse air. A suffocating sensation for Howard, and Ben, who weren't able to look one another in the face.

Lincoln sucked on the side of his thumb, and felt like bursting into tears.

Danny and Joe exchanged glances, compartmentalizing their disappointment from the others and their own relatively little involvement in the proceedings.

"So," Danny chanced as he totaled the figures on his calculator. "That's a grand total of six hundred and sixty-six thousand, and sixty-five bucks. Take off mine and Joe's ten percent each and that leaves five hundred and ninety thousand, or thereabouts. With Amos out of the picture-"

"—And most of the score," James snapped. "Fuck's sake."

"That leaves five-hundred and ninety, divided by four, for a take-home of one hundred and forty-seven grand. Each."

Joe shrugged. "Not a bad morning's work, huh fellas?"

James clenched his fist and shouted at the man. "Are you fucking *kidding* me?"

Everyone turned to James and feared the worst.

"No, hey, it's better than your dumb severance pay—"

"—This is bullshit."

James punched the money counters with the side of his arms and shrieked with fury.

"Fuckin' less than one-fifty? Each?! Goddamn it. Where are the big bills? Fuckin' twenties and fifties? Where are the hundreds? There was meant to be tons of fucking cash there on a Wednesday. There was meant to be *eight mil* in that fuckin' vault. Eight fuckin' mil."

Howard kept his cool and watched the man slowly lose his shit. "We know what happened, half of it's flying around the road back at the bank."

"And who's great idea was it to have fucking *Amos* clear the vault with me?" James snapped. "That guy couldn't empty a condom machine without getting his dick caught in the slot, the useless fuckin' prick."

Howard's call for James to stop speaking echoed around the room. "Hey."

"What?"

"It wasn't Amos' fault, okay? If it weren't for Lincoln having to move the car to the underground, Mark might be here with us right now."

"Yeah, and reducing all our slices of the take by another fifth. Fuck Amos."

Howard's eyes filled with pure, concentrated venom at the man. "You're really starting to piss me off now, Gilmour. We all made mistakes, and we should be thanking our lucky stars that all but one of us made it back here in one piece."

James ran his hands through his hair and growled at the top of his lungs. "Eight fuckin' mil, man. There was meant to be eight million, here. *Minimum*."

Howard folded his arms and fought the desire to punch James in the face. "I'm sorry you're disappointed."

"Disappointed? Ugh, this is turning out to be a *really shitty day*, you know."

He ran over to the truck and punched an almighty dent into its side, and didn't stop, releasing all the anger through his arm as he battered the vehicle and showed no sign of slowing down.

"For *fuck's* sake."

"Stop doing that," Howard snapped. "That truck is rented."

James waved the pain from his fist around and took a deep breath.

"Are you finished?" Howard asked.

James spat to the floor and caught his breath. "With less than one-fifty each? Don't talk to me about *finished*, Howard, we've barely even *started*."

"That may be so, but we need to split the score five ways, bag it up, and get out of here. Lay low for a while till the media circus and police run out of leads, or get bored, whichever is the sooner."

The monster named James Gilmour stared Howard in the eyes with a fierce brutality.

"Maybe we should have put someone else in charge, huh? And not some washed-up, laid off has-been who couldn't organize a bum rape at a gay bar."

"You wanna take a pop at me?" Howard asked. "Because if you do, now's the time."

James backed off as a flood despair set into his bones. "No, Howard. I'm sorry, man, look—I'm just a little disappointed, that's all."

"We're *all* disappointed, but it is what it is."

Ben offered a word of consolation. "It's not even one hundred and fifty each, either. It doesn't include all the money we needed to rent the truck, or the Chevy, or the guns. We're all down a few grand each before we've even bagged up the cash."

"Cherry's popped himself a good point, there," Lincoln said. "This *ain't* a good outcome at all. It's pretty fuckin' far from good, you know. But it's a hell of a lot better than a kick up the ass. Six figures? Each? Shit. That's more than we usually make in two years back at Federal, and that's good enough for my sweet ass to take care of business for a while."

"That's exactly the right attitude, Lincoln," Howard said. "We've done perfectly fine."

James shook his head and refused to buy into everyone's attempt to justify how good they had it.

Ben nodded at Howard. "Yeah, and besides, we're all still breathing and stuff. Could've been worse. *A lot* worse."

James crouched to his knees and caught his breath. "Fuck this."

Joe had heard enough. He tapped his cane on the floor and approached the table.

"Okay, guys, that's enough cock-waving. Let's get all this bagged up. Each of you take an equal slice in your bags, and keep them someplace safe."

Ben, Lincoln, and Howard grabbed their sports bag. James remained crouched down and watched them all remove their stacks of money from the table.

"Don't tell a soul where you're stashing your cash, by the way," Joe said. "That'll just lead to trouble. Leave the bonds with me. I'll push them to Jimmy the Fence. Should take a couple days, and I'll wire your slice to your accounts."

Danny and Lincoln set about removing the bills from the counters. The latter slid his empty sports bag across the table and pulled the flaps out.

"Remember, make sure your alibis are straight," Joe said. "You say shit to the police if they show up at your door. If they cuff you and take you to the precinct, you say shit and keep saying *shit* in as few words as possible till you use your one phone call to call me, and I send a lawyer down. If the pigs say all they want is a *quick chat*, tell them to fuck off back to the sty they came from. If they keep hassling you, tell them to arrest you, which they won't, but if they do, say shit until I get a legal eagle down there to prevent you from getting shit on by those shitheads. Okay?"

Danny chuckled and threw Howard's sports bag into his chest.

"Yeah, I understand. "We say shit."

"Yes. Although don't actually say the word *shit*. I mean, say *nothing*. Shit being a colloquial term, here. You keep your mouths sealed tighter than a nun's crack during lent."

Ben picked up his sports bag full of takings, and passed another bag to James.

"Thanks."

"You're welcome," Ben said. "Don't spend it all at once."

Joe snapped and raised his voice. "No!"

"What?"

"That's not a joke. All of you. None of you are to spend a fucking *dime*, okay? Not for a few days at least, until I give you the all-clear. You've ripped off a goddamn Federal bank, here, not some Mom-and-Pop candy store. The cops are gonna be buzzing around like flies for at least a week, so you gotta make sure you're not the turd they wanna land on and start poking around."

The men looked at Joe as if he was some kind of Grand Master of crime.

"I mean it, you don't even buy so much as a goddamn box of *Jizz Flakes* with your slices of the score. I dunno where you're stashing it, and I don't wanna know."

Ben squinted at the others and gripped his own bag in his hand as tightly as he could.

"Keep your bags safe until further notice," Joe said, catching Ben's smirk out of the corner of his eye. "Go and watch PornCabin, or hang out with your family, or whatever the fuck it is you fresh-faced, bushy-tailed, recently-out-of-work red collar fellas do, till I call you, and not before."

"Joe?" Ben asked, confused.

"Yes, Benjamin?"

"*Red collar?*"

"Yeah, *red* collar. Blue for laborers, white for middle-class office dwellers, and *red* for anyone sick enough in the head to accumulate vast sums of wealth using aggressive tax avoidance, or just outright murder, because after all they're both the same thing, right? They both kill the poor with equal efficiency."

"Right, right," Ben said, chewing over the new term he'd learned. "Red Collar, huh?"

"At the end of the day, from bricklayers to CEOs and every prick in between, it's all just simple capitalism at work."

Ben considered the response and frowned when he failed to understand it. "I guess."

"Good. Now, if you'll all excuse me, gentlemen, Danny and I have a bag full of heist apparatus to incinerate, and an expensively modified Chevy to drive off the edge of a cliff after Gilmour drops us back at our apartment."

The man nodded, quietly, having lost the will to argue or debate any further.

"Oh," Joe said. "And switch your cell phones off, all of you. The last thing we need is for anybody who might be snooping to know what we're doing."

Joe waved his cane at James, who eventually saw sense and wiped his eyes.

"Yeah, c'mon," James said. "I'll give you and Danny a ride home."

Chapter 14

Howard drove his Saab 101 up the Main Street and took in the sights of the storefronts. At a casual 40 mph, the slow speed was at odds with the day he'd had so far.

He looked at the digital clock on the dashboard. It was nearly 4 pm, although it felt much later.

Exhausted, Howard recounted the events of the morning, and the distant echoes of anguish from the hostages rifled through his ears.

His wandering mind moved away from the pain caused by his gunshot wound. Half an inch to the left, and he'd have lost his arm. If anything, he felt completely removed from his own actions now that he was on his own.

Howard's portion of the take from the bank, such as it was, nestled comfortably in the *ProState* sports bag sitting on the passenger seat.

Quite to his surprise, he felt a smile creep across his face. Right at this very moment, he was escorting more cash than he'd ever had in his lifetime, with the intention of stashing it at the one place he thought safest.

Howard's Father's House
—440 Thackeray Road—

A leafy suburb in the valley's east side boasting homes with enormous front yards and white picket fences.

Thackeray Road was only a few blocks from Howard's home on Sears Road, but extended into middle class territory.

Howard had spent his childhood here with his mother and father, and was always happy to visit whenever he could. He had brought a little gift with him, and smiled at the thought of his father receiving it.

Knock-knock-knock.

Howard removed his fist from the bright white door and took a step back, knowing his father might need the extra space.

The door opened inward, and a frail, old man peered through the crack. "Who is it?"

"It's me, Dad."

The man's face lit up like a Christmas tree. "Howard!"

"Uh-huh. Can I come in?"

***

Howard scanned the hallway as he carried the sports bag over his shoulder. At first, the pictures on the wall seemed in place. Portraits of his late mother smiled back at him, and, despite the walls feeling a lot smaller than usual, the child inside him beamed with glee.

"I like what you've done with the place, Dad. Nice, fresh lick of paint, huh?"

His father coughed as he hobbled behind him. "Oh, yes. Your mother would never have gone for this color. You remember Cyril Myra, don't you? From next door?"

"Yes, how is he?"

"He's good. Anyway, he came over and helped me."

The walls had been painted a pleasing shade of red, which Howard found difficult to ignore. As his father relayed the story of his friend offering a helping hand, his voice seemed to drift into a dull, prolonged drawl.

Howard felt like he was gliding towards the front room, with the red on the walls turning darker, and producing wails from screaming hostages in his mind.

He shook the fatigue from his head as he entered the front room, and mentally blocked the onslaught of regret. A pang of anger beat away at his chest as he clenched his fists.

"So, yeah, it took a few days, but we got it done in the end," his father said as he took a seat on the couch. "How have you been, Howie?"

"Oh, I'm good."

"How's the banking world, these days?"

"Lucrative," Howard said as he took a seat on the chair opposite his father.

He set the sports bag on the floor and reached into his pocket.

"Oh, here. I got you something—"

His father watched as he pulled out a thin stack of bills.

"Here, take it."

"Oh, no, son. That's not necessary—"

"—*Take it*, Dad."

His father was never one for turning down a golden opportunity. Obliging Howard had always been a mainstay during the boy's youth, and this turn of events was no different. Surprised, his father took the stack and flicked his thumb through the bills.

"Are you sure?"

"Yeah," Howard said. "Severance check came through, and I wanted to give you something."

"Bless your heart, son."

Howard nodded and wiped his nose on his left sleeve. He winced as quietly as possible when the wound pushed a dagger of pain down his arm.

"Are you okay, Howie?"

"Yeah, Dad."

His father saw the sports bag and raised his eyebrows. "What's this? Are you back in on the tennis courts again?"

"No, Dad. Listen, I need you to do something for me. Can I keep this here with you for a day or two? Just till I come back for it. A few days, or so."

"Oh."

"It's nothing bad. But you need to promise me you won't go peeking inside. I've put a lock on it, but if we can keep it upstairs? Maybe under your bed, or something?"

"Of course. Is it a gift for Miranda?"

Howard grinned at the remark. His father had drawn up the perfect excuse on his behalf. "Yeah. It's a birthday gift, Dad. *For Miranda.*"

His father winked at him and pulled the bag across the carpet. "Don't worry. Your secret is safe with me."

"How do you mean?"

His father protested, innocently. "The gift. I won't tell her."

Paranoia set in with Howard now that the day's adrenaline had all but subsided. "Oh. Yeah, good one."

The pair didn't have much else to say to each other now that Howard had indicated his intention for visiting.

"Have you told Miranda, yet?"

"Told her?"

"About those crooks at the bank laying you off?"

Howard shook his head, and ran his knuckle under his left eye. "No, Dad. Not yet."

"When are you going to tell her?"

A very good question, Howard thought, and grew angry at the fact that his father was so perceptive. He'd given way more thought to proceedings than Howard could have.

"I don't know. I don't know what to say."

"It's been more than a week now," his father said. "How can you tell me, but not your own wife? Or your daughter?"

"I dunno. It somehow feels as if it hasn't happened, you know?"

"If it was me and your mother, I'd have told her straight away."

"Yeah, but mom wasn't an evil witch who delighted in you screwing up every minute of the day, was she?"

"Well, no. But Miranda isn't stupid, son. She's going to find out sooner or later. And she's not nearly the evil witch you think she is. It's only because she cares about you, you know."

Howard collected a teardrop from his eye and cleared his throat, braving his answer. "Uh, I dunno, Dad. I know Miranda's good, but, it's just, you know, things were fine the way they were. I kinda just wanna go back to how it was before, you know?"

"I know, Howie."

His father smiled at the young boy, despite his size and age; ever the child in the eyes of the father.

"You're a good kid, Howard. Hell, you're *my* kid, so that goes without saying, and you've always done the right thing, no matter the cost."

"Have I?"

"There's no doubt about it. You didn't turn out too shabby. Got yourself qualified, and a stable career, made a name for yourself in an excellent sector and industry. You have a loving and understanding wife, and a beautiful kid. That's not easy, you know."

Howard nodded, but lost the ability to speak.

"Howie, I'm a big believer in fate," his father explained. "I never really told you this, but whenever your mom and I faced the odds, we stared at them face-on, and we always had faith. You want to know about fate? Fate is a good thing, and it happens to good people—"

Howard stood up from the chair and rolled his shoulders, covering the upset from his face the entire time.

"I better be going, Dad."

His father looked up, offended. "Oh. Okay."

279

Howard coughed into his hand, and held it there to disguise his quivering mouth. "I never told you I'm sorry, but I'm telling you I'm sorry now, okay?"

"Aww."

His father wasn't stupid. Far from it. He knew his son was crying, but was man enough to let the boy erect his defense.

"Here, gimme a hug. You big fairy."

Howard wasted no time, and wrapped his arms around his father, and pulled him tight. "I'm sorry, Dad. I'm sorry."

"Don't you dare apologize to me, Howie. You've nothing to be sorry for. If anything, apologize to Miranda for not telling her what you've been through."

"Yeah," Howard sniffed.

He revealed his tear-strewn face and laughed through his constricted throat. "If something happens to me. I'm just thinking aloud, here, really. But, if something does happen to me, can you make sure the girls are looked after?"

"You know I will. I just hope they won't mind hearing from me," his father said, before looking at his son's left hand. "Huh? Where's your wedding ring?"

"Oh. I must have left it at home."

Curious, the old man cast a suspicious eye at his son's face. "You're not cheating on her, are you? That's not what this is all about?"

"No, Dad. Never. *Never.*"

"Well, that's good. In my book, cheaters are worse than criminals and killers."

The revelation grated at Howard's heart.

He exhaled with a huge lump of sorrow, and backed away from his father. "I gotta go," he said, and pointed at the sports bag. "Keep it under the bed in the spare room. I'll call you tomorrow, okay?"

"Okay."

Howard sobbed silently as he turned around and made his way to the front door, leaving a perplexed father behind him.

Swarms of ominous, gray clouds had formed over the skies at Thackeray Road by the time Howard reached his car.

He slipped his hand into his pocket, pulled out his cell phone, and switched it on.

As he waited for the screen to load, he noticed a Jeep parked at the far end of the road, right in front of the graffiti on the brick wall: *Capitalism Sucks.*

"Huh?"

The more he stared at it the more, the lone, darkened figure behind the wheel stared back. Howard couldn't quite make out who it was.

Bzzz—bzzz.

His cell phone jumped in his palm as the messages came flooding in.

Several missed calls from his wife, and it was only 5 pm. A text message from *Bunni* bounced up and down behind the tempered glass.

> *Dad! OMG! Got some great news.*
> *Text me back. C x*

Howard smiled at the message, and unlocked the screen. He thumbed through the various emails he'd received, and then glanced at the road up ahead.

The Jeep had moved away in the time he'd spent looking at his screen.

"Weird people."

As he moved over to his car, he discovered a missed call from "Knocktoe." According to the phone's history, the attempt to call came in at 4:35 pm, but there was no follow up message.

Howard slid into his car and held the phone to his ear. It rang, and rang, and rang.

Finally, someone answered. *"Hello?"*

Careful to avoid revealing too much, Howard spoke softly, "Hey, Knocktoe, it's, uh *Rabbit*. I got a missed call from you. I gotta ask, is everything—"

"—Haha, gotcha! No, this is my voice mail. Please leave your request after the beep, and maybe I'll get back to you if I deem you worthy of my time."

Boop.

Howard dropped the phone into his left hand and swiped the call dead. "Goddamn knock-toed Asshole."

He started the engine, spun the steering wheel to the left, and pulled away from the side of the road.

Howard's House
—70 Sears Road—

A mere ten-minute journey through Chrome Valley's residential streets, and Howard was home.

He parked his Saab 101 on the driveway, and entered his house.

A million thoughts whirled around his mind as he stepped through his front door.

"Hello? Anyone home?"

No response.

Good, he thought. He had the place to himself, at least for now.

Chief among his thoughts was his daughter's text message. If it was good news, then surely it would be better to wait to speak to her in person.

For now, the upstairs bathroom beckoned.

Howard sat on the edge of the bathtub and placed his shirt over the shower rail.

"Ugh."

He lifted his left arm and peeled the gauze away from his right index finger and thumb. The bullet wound had at least stopped bleeding, which was something to celebrate.

The cut in his arm elevated beyond a mere scratch, however, and burrowed deep into the flesh.

He dropped the gauze into the wash basin and pressed around the pudgy swelling that had formed around the injury.

Yellow puss bled from the pressure, and the skin around the cavity had turned black.

"Owww—fug," he muttered, knowing full-well that he couldn't visit the hospital anytime soon. He looked at his lap and stared at his cell phone, giving thought to whether or not Knocktoe Joe had called to offer some advice. Perhaps he knew of a doctor who wouldn't ask questions when he fixed his arm?

"Nah," Howard said to himself as he stood up and opened the medicine cabinet. "He'd have called back, by now."

Schrriiip.

Howard tore another length of bandage from a packet of dressings, and wrapped it around his wound. When the cabinet slammed shut, the mirror offered Howard a reflection of his tired face.

His eyes were bloodshot, presumably, he thought, due to the fatigue he'd sustained during the day. He looked like shit, and felt even worse.

The bags under his eyes hung lower than they usually did, and the dressing over the wound had turned a murky shade of red.

He spat the remnants of the gauze into the basin and leaned forward to inspect his face.

Wrinkles everywhere, including parts of his face he thought were unaffected.

Just above the brow.

Down the left side of his face.

Various red blotches formed across his brow and temple where the latex on the rabbit mask had clung to the skin.

Howard needed a shower, not least to wash the nastiness of the day from his body, but the thought of willingly putting himself into an even more compromising position at this point in time sent a chill down his spine.

Howard was sprawled out on the sofa five minutes later. His 65" TV played quietly as he relaxed into the cushions, resting his right arm against the armrest.

He tapped his phone on his leg in time to the theme tune playing on the TV screen, accompanied by a five-pronged star fish strutting its stuff along a theater stage.

'It's six o'clock, and you know what that means? Yes, it's time for every boy and girl's favorite space explorer without a skeleton. It's…'

"Hello boys and girls," the cartoon character said with its gruff, electronically modulated voice. "My name is Star Jelly!"

Suddenly, Star Jelly's limbs went limp, and the character fell onto the stage to howls of cartoonish laughter.

"Oh dear, Star Jelly," the narrator said. "You have no bones, so you can't walk."

A chirpy, musical jingle played out just as Howard's eyelids grew heavier, and heavier…

***

Lock—Whump.

The cacophonous sound of the front door slamming against the wall woke Howard up in a state of terror.

"What the hell was *that?*"

The noise had come from the lower landing, right by the front door.

"What the—?"

Slam.

A thunderous sound of hurried footsteps cracked along the linoleum floor behind the door to the front room, causing Howard to jump to his feet.

"Dad? Dad, are you in?" came a familiar voice from the staircase.

"Bonnie?"

Rumble-rumble-rumble.

Howard wiped the gunk from his eyes as he approached the landing and looked up the stairs. "Bonnie?"

His daughter had run up the stairs in search of him. "Dad?"

He was relieved to see the bottom of a pair of skin-tight jeans hit the top step, and make their way down the stairs.

Quite by accident, he turned to the TV. A news report played out and showed videotape of bodies being stretchered out of a bank.

"Oh, shit—"

"—Dad?"

The ticker tape at the bottom of the screen read: *Chrome Valley Federal Bank raided. At least five dead.*

He grabbed the remote control from the coffee table and fumbled at speed for the *off* button and winced as his left arm did most of the work. "Oww. Shit, shit, shit—"

Bonnie slid into the room just as the TV screen shut off. "Hey, Dad."

Howard did too good a job of putting on a brave and innocent act. Filled with relief, he dropped the remote control to the sofa and held out his arms for a hug. "Hey, *Bunni.*"

Bonnie smirked and turned her head to the side with suspicion. "Are you on drugs?"

"What?"

"Why are you acting weird?"

"Uh," Howard thought aloud for a moment as he battled the pain in his left arm. "Can't I get a hug?"

"Uh, sure."

Puzzled, Bonnie stepped up to him and gently pressed the side of her face against his, making his outstretched arms resemble a stilted and perverse scarecrow.

Fortunately, his sweater covered the damage done to his left arm, and now that the TV wasn't ratting the day's events out to his daughter, all was well.

"There, Dad. Happy now?"

"Well, I hope that wasn't too much trouble for you, Bunni."

"Nah, you're all right," she giggled. "I texted you earlier, but you never messaged me back."

"Sorry. I did see it, but I was busy today."

Bonnie threaded her fingers together, turned her hands out, and squeaked with excitement. "I got into Waddling Gate College. They accepted my grades."

Howard's eyebrows nearly lifted right over his skull in half surprise, half delight. "You did?"

"Yeah," she beamed. "I took your advice and opened the letter. I got brave. Dad, I'm so psyched."

Howard beamed with pride. "Oh, Bunni, that's brilliant. Well done."

"Yeah, it sure beats getting stuck at Chrome Junction College. That Academy is shithole."

"Language, Bunni."

"Sorry."

Howard threw her a knowing wink. "But, you're right, though. Chrome Junction is a shit hole, for sure."

Bonnie giggled at her father's cool sense of humor. "Yeah, Michael Amos, that useless creep who keeps checking me out, will probably end up there."

"Yeah," Howard thought aloud. "Hey, did you tell your mom?"

"No, I haven't seen her. She's out at Nanna's today, at the care home. I'm gonna tell her later tonight."

Before Howard could ask any more questions, Bonnie darted out of the front room and raced up the stairs. "Dad, I gotta get changed. Chris is picking me up in ten minutes. We're going to the movies."

Relieved, Howard trundled into the landing and hollered up the stairs. "What? Who's Chris?"

"Just this guy I'm seeing."

A series of heavy thuds bounced across the ceiling where her bedroom was located.

"Bunni?"

Bonnie's hurried voice blew out from her room. "Yeah?"

Howard checked his watch. "It's seven-thirty. Did mom say when she'd be back?"

Before Bonnie could answer, the lock on the front door rattled and startled the breath out of Howard's lungs.

"Huh?"

Paranoia sunk into Howard's chest as the handle spun around on the spot in front of a shadow folding across the frosted door window. It seemed to move in ultra-slow motion, as the darkened, featureless figure expanded across the glass.

"Oh, G-God."

Howard gripped the stair rail and considered running up the steps, into the master bedroom, and jumping out of the window.

"Oh, sh-shit—"

Clunk.

The door opened and introduced the shapely silhouette, which stepped into the landing and shut the door behind it.

"Miranda?"

"Yeah, hi."

Howard exhaled with relief when he laid eyes on his wife. Miranda lifted the two grocery bags in her right hand and huffed.

"Why are you standing there?" she asked. "You look like you've seen a ghost."

"Oh, uh, I don't know?"

"Well, get away from there, and help me in the kitchen."

Howard ran his right hand over his head and stepped off the bottom step, lamenting the day he was born.

Stomp-stomp-stomp.

The sound cascading of footsteps erupting behind him resembled shotgun blasts. Howard turned around once again and saw Bonnie bounding down the stairs at speed.

She looked like an angel with her skirt and blouse, and slid her hands down the rail as she raced down the stairs two steps at a time.

"Please d-don't shoot me. *Please,*" she begged.

Confused, Howard focused his eyes on the angel descending the steps. "What?"

"I said move, Dad. I'm kinda in a hurry."

Howard stepped out of her path and offered her a chance to reach the door. "I swear to God I'm going out of my mind."

"Okay, I'll see ya later, Dad. Love you," she said as she pulled the door open. "Bye mom."

"Okay, Bunni," Miranda hollered from the kitchen. "Be careful, tonight."

"I will."

Without acknowledging his actions, Howard grabbed Bonnie's arm and pulled her back. "Bunni."

"What, Dad? You're hurting me."

He released her arm and stared her in the eyes. "I dunno who this guy you're seeing is, but you make sure he doesn't try anything weird, okay?"

"Dad, please. I have *some* dignity."

"I know, but still. Call me if things get outta hand, and I'll be right there. Okay?"

Bonnie offered him a polite smile. "I will."

"Okay, go on. Go and have fun."

Bonnie pecked him on the cheek and yanked on the door. "Love you."

"Love you, too."

Whump.

The door slammed shut in Howard's face, seeming to swallow his daughter out of his life once and for all.

A shuffling noise came from the kitchen, not that Howard could see that far from the foot of the stairs. Miranda began unpacking the grocery bags, leaving her husband feeling apprehensive about joining her.

Howard gripped the wooden handrail on the stairs and felt the warmth seep into the skin in his palm. It provided him with a stark contrast to the cold, metal rails of the staircase leading to the underground car park.

Heavy gunshot sounds rang across his brain as the visions of dead officers and panicked civilians etched across his eyes.

"Ugh."

Howard hung his head and considered confessing everything to his wife. It'd only be a matter of time before someone he knew would hear of what went down.

It was, after all, just a matter of time before somebody, probably his wife, would notice the injury he'd sustained on his left arm.

Clunk.

It sounded as if something had hit the floor in the kitchen. "Ah, shit."

The accident in the kitchen brought Howard out of his temporary daydream and hurtling back to reality. He sprinted across the lower landing and arrived at the kitchen door.

Miranda had dropped a bottle of ketchup, and the contents had splattered across the otherwise pristine white linoleum floor.

"Are you just gonna stand there and watch, or are you gonna help me?" she snapped.

"Oh. Sure."

In his attempt to fend off her agitated mood, Howard raced forward and scooped the bizarre blood splatter with the side of his hand and flung it into the sink.

Miranda placed her hands on her hips and scowled at him. "I've had a terrible day, you know. So much BS."

Howard tore a length of paper towels from the holder on the counter and winced as he wiped his hand.

"I'm sorry to hear that."

"I wake up this morning with a splitting headache, and find you've left the house two hours earlier than usual," she complained. "Then, Bunni wakes up, and comes downstairs looking like a cow—"

"—Yeah, I saw."

"I get to the retirement home ten minutes before they open, just as it starts raining, only to find out they've moved mom to a different room without her belongings."

Howard collected the half-empty ketchup bottle from the floor and set it beside the sink. Miranda expected some sympathy from her husband, but never received it, which angered her even more.

"You're quiet, tonight," she snapped. "That's unlike you."

"Uh, no. I'm just a bit tired."

She turned to the refrigerator and pulled the door open. "How was work?"

Howard swallowed and dumped the bloodied paper towel in the pedal bin. "Yeah. Fine."

"I tried calling you earlier to see if you could come see me at the home, but you never answered."

"Yeah, I, uh, had a conference all afternoon. Right through lunch."

Miranda pulled out a packet of chicken from the freezer and inspected the expiry date. "This is all we have.

I didn't get time to drop by *The Y* on the way back, and *Patel's Furnace* is closed for the day. Ugh."

Howard focused on the wrinkly, white skin on the chicken. "Yeah, I don't mind."

Miranda pushed the refrigerator door shut, turned around, and brushed past Howard's left arm on her way to the dining table.

"Agh, shit."

Miranda turned to him, quizzically. "What the hell's wrong with you, tonight?"

"Nothing, nothing. Took a bit of a knock on my funny bone earlier."

Miranda sized up her husband as he doubled-over and winced.

"You want me to take a look? It might have bruised."

"No, no, no, it's fine. I, uh—"

"—I dunno what you're up to, Howie, but I don't like it. You're aloof, and you're acting all weird."

She was right, and Howard knew it. He arched his back and took a deep breath, preparing to launch into a thorough display of absolute normalcy.

"Did Bunni tell you?" he asked.

"No, what?"

"She got accepted at Waddling Gate College."

"She did?" Miranda asked with a quick smile. "No, she never told me. Well, I haven't seen her since this morning."

"Yeah, better than having to go to Chrome Junction Academy, at any rate."

Miranda took a seat at the dining table, all the while keeping her eyes trained on her husband's face.

"Damn straight. Here, come sit with me."

"Okay."

Howard's buttocks slammed onto the oak bench at the table. He relaxed every muscle in his arm, and tried for a smile.

"You know, you have that look on your face," Miranda said. "Like you want to tell me something."

"What do you mean?"

"I dunno. The past week or so, you've been acting strange. Don't think I've not noticed."

"Oh? Strange?"

"Yeah, you seem… *happier.* More confident. You're not smoking again, are you?"

Howard pulled his cell phone out of his jacket and placed it on the table. The screen remained a distant, murky black. Nobody had called, much to his paranoia.

"God, no. I'm not back on the smokes—" Howard said as he dared to unlock the screen on his phone.

Miranda snorted. "Can't we have a conversation without you looking at your damn phone every five minutes, Howard Ross?"

"Sorry."

"What's gotten into you? You're all on-edge. Oh, wait, don't tell me. That asshole Victor Price is giving you shit again, right?"

"Not anymore," Howard muttered, happily, as he glanced at his phone.

"Having trouble adjusting to work again, after all those months at home during quarantine?"

"No."

Howard tried to shoo her questions out of his mind, and the impending urge to confide in her once and for all. "Look, Miranda, there's something I need to tell you."

"At last."

"Yeah, look—"

"—Yeah," she said. "Just skip the opening sales pitch and get right to the point. I'm not one of your financial victims, here."

"Fine."

Howard considered how best to approach the subject. He could come right out with it and embrace the brevity, or lead her in slowly for the sucker punch.

"It's, uh, funny you should mention Price, actually."

She stared at him quizzically. "Yeeess?"

"Yeah, because last week, Monday, he called me into his office and—"

Thud-thud-thud.

Howard and Miranda turned to the lower landing in fright.

"What the hell was that?" Miranda asked.

"The front door—"

Thud-thud-thud-thud-thud.

"Christ, they're keen, aren't they?" she said.

Howard jumped off the bench and held his left arm with his right hand.

"Shh. Stay here. It might be a Jehovah's Witness or something. Stay outta sight, I'll go check."

Thud-thud-thud.

Howard's spine turned to mush as he moved across the landing and approached the door. He didn't know who the castrated banshee knocking at the door was, but he could tell by the darkened shape behind the glass that it was a man.

And the man appeared to be erratic.

Howard muttered in an attempt to elicit a chuckle to dispel the fear soaking into his muscles. "Jehovah's Witness? Shit."

The silhouette shouted over his knocks on the door. "Howard, man. Open up. Please, open the fuck up."

Howard grabbed the door handle, yanked it down, and pulled it back.

"Holy shit," he said. "James?"

The man covered his face with both hands as he pushed into Howard's home. Each had blood pouring down over the webbings between his fingers and his sideburns.

Terrified, he uncovered his face to reveal two bruises on his face, and a nasty cut over his right eye.

"Yeah, it's m-me," James squealed in pain. "Oh, shit. Oh, shit."

"Jesus, James? What happened?"

Howard closed the door and tried to get a better look at his friend. "Calm down," he hushed. "My wife is in the kitchen—"

"—They took my fuckin' money," James cried.

"—Whoa, whoa, hold up," Howard said as the fear of God set in. He batted James' arm away and held him by the shoulders.

"James, stop. Listen to me. Think. Tell me. What happened?"

"I was at home, and—"

"—Goddamnit, tell me."

James burst into a fit of fury and tears as he recounted what had happened. "I dunno, man, I was at home, falling asleep. They kicked my front door in, man, and took my bag."

"Who did?"

"I dunno, some guy. I tried to fight back, but he whacked me over the head with some metal stick and knocked me out cold. Took my fuckin' bag."

Howard scanned James' face to see just how delirious he was. "What did he look like?"

"Dunno. It all happened so fast."

"And he took your bag?"

"Yeah, yeah—"

"—When did this happen?"

"About ten minutes ago," James cried and scooped a blob of blood from his head. "I came-to, like, five minutes after that and my front door was wide open. I didn't know what to do, and I didn't wanna use my cell, and you were the first person I thought of."

"Yeah, yeah," Howard whispered. "You did the right thing."

Howard didn't know what to ask, what to say, or what to do next. He looked over his shoulder and glanced at the kitchen.

"Shit, James, you can't stay here. Quick, it's okay. Come with me."

Howard grabbed James' arm and pulled him to the front door. "Did you drive here?"

"Yeah."

"Okay, wait outside by your car. I'll—oh, wait."

He stopped talking to reach into his pocket and pull out some tissues.

"Wipe your face, and wait by your car. Call Knocktoe and Ben, see if they know anything."

"Okay, okay."

"Good. Gimme a second."

James' breathing slowed when he raised his eyes at the far end of the landing. "Oh, f-fuck."

"What?"

Howard pulled the door open, and looked at the kitchen - to find Miranda had seen everything. She folded her arms and rested against the door frame.

"James?"

"Miranda," he said, politely, with his face and hands covered in blood.

"What the hell happened to your face?"

"I, uh—"

"—No, James," Howard said. "Go wait outside. Go."

With great obedience, James slid through the door as Howard closed it behind him. He didn't have much in his explanation arsenal that would satisfy his wife, and decided to keep it that way.

"Are you gonna tell me what the hell is going on?" Miranda asked.

Hassled by her inquiry, Howard ran his fingers through his hair and felt like screaming. "Miranda, not now. Okay?"

"Not now? Gilmour turns up looking like roadkill? Go wait by the car? Tell me what's going on, or I'm gonna raise hell."

"Miranda, listen—"

"—And what the hell is a *Knocktoe*, anyhow?"

"Miranda," Howard snapped as he turned to the door, and then back to her, in a carousel of terrified confusion. "Not now, Miranda, okay? You need to trust me, I—Oh, Jeez. For *fuck's sake*."

Miranda remained utterly still, and utterly in control of the situation. "You better start telling me things right now, Howard Ross."

She'd barely finished her sentence when Howard let out an ear-piercing wail of death, and stormed over to her with his right fist clench. "Goddamn it."

Miranda flinched as he went to strike her. "No!"

He grabbed her shirt collar and pulled her head as he prepared to punch her. "Listen to me, you fucking bitch. Listen."

Miranda's tears couldn't mask her undiluted terror as she stared into the man she thought she knew. "No, p-please, Howie—"

"—You don't know *shit* about me, you understand? Do you understand?"

"Yes, y-yes—"

"—Now, pack some bags and get out of here. It isn't safe. Go to your mother's, and call Bonnie and tell her she can't come back here. You understand?"

Howard digested his wife's torment and released his grip on her shoulder, suddenly shocked at his own behavior.

"Wh-why?" she cried. "What's h-happening—"

Howard shoved her against the wall, knowing time was of the essence. He gripped the top of his shirt and tore the buttons away, revealing the bandaged gunshot wound on his arm. "Damn it, I don't have time for this. Look. *Look. You s*ee that?"

"Y-Yes?"

He pushed the cotton covering up and introduced the blackened, red wound. "I got *shot* today."

Miranda's eyes bulged out of their sockets, terrorizing her further. "Wh-what?""

"Wanna know more about it? Why don't you check out the fucking news? It's everywhere."

The staggering news perplexed Miranda into pure, stunned silence. "I, I—"

"—You—you," he mocked. "I gotta get out of here, and so do you. So stop stammering like a retard, pack a bag, and get the fuck out of the valley. James and I need to go fix whatever the hell is going on."

Miranda nodded and wiped her eyes, taking her husband's command extremely seriously. "Okay. Okay, I trust you."

"No, don't trust me, just do as I say. And *don't* call me. I'll call you from a pay phone. Our cell phones might be tapped."

Howard walked backwards, never tearing his eyes from hers.

"Go on, get packing. I'll call you later. Keep your phone on."

Howard's adrenaline reintroduced itself to his body, forcing him to button his shirt up and push through the front door, leaving his thoroughly discombobulated better half in tears.

Chapter 15

Howard muttered to himself as he ran down the path in his front yard and glanced at James.

"For fuck's sake, this cannot be happening."

His injured, bloodied friend paced around his Jeep, waiting for someone to answer his cell phone.

"James? What's happening? You got through to anyone, yet?"

James lowered his phone and shook his head. "Knocktoe isn't answering, and I can't get through to Cherry."

"Useless fucking pricks."

Howard stopped by the vehicle and took a moment to breathe. Both ends of the street were remarkably calm, as ever. It was as if nothing was wrong.

"He's not picking up," James said. "What do we do now?"

Howard raced over to James' Jeep and opened the passenger door. "You did the right thing not calling me. Nobody's gonna answer their phones. Get in and drive. We need to go check on Ben. Make sure he's okay."

James got into the car and pulled the door shut as he sat into the driver's seat.

The key slid into the ignition, and James started the engine. "Where does Cherry live?"

"A few blocks over," Howard said. "At least nobody is answering their phone as instructed. That's some good news, at least."

"Are they not answering their phone because they're playing ball, or because they've been robbed, too?"

"That's what we're gonna find out."

James pulled out from the side of the road and hit the gas. "Where did you stash your bag?"

Howard pulled his cell phone out from his jacket pocket and thumbed through the call history.

"Don't ask me that. Have you learned nothing from that hit on the head?"

He rifled through the contacts list, and then hit a green button.

James looked at Howard's hand. "Who are you calling?"

"Danny. If Ben and Knocktoe aren't answering, maybe Danny will."

"I doubt it," James said. "Danny and Knocktoe live together."

Boop-boop-boop.

The call rang out and cut off, leaving Howard fuming. "Shit."

"No answer?"

"*No.*"

James turned out of Sears Road, and onto the next road. He glanced at the shuttered convenience store named *Patel's Furnace* and half-chuckled. "It's so quiet around here tonight."

Howard turned away from James' bloodied brow to his own grubby hands. A patch of dried blood had caught the butt of his palm when he'd removed the bandage.

"Ugh. I got your blood on my fingers. You have any wipes in here?"

"Yeah, in the glove box."

Howard lifted the catch out and opened the box. A bunch of tissues, mints, stationery, and note pads nearly tumbled out and onto his lap.

"Jeez, James. Your ride is filthy."

"Yeah, but not as filthy as Ben's wife, eh?"

"True."

After a thorough and deep rummage, Howard found an old packet of baby wipes. He tore a strip from the plastic lid and wiped the blood from his hand. "Ugh, this is gross."

James focused on the road and pressed his foot on the gas. "Speaking of filthy, what did you say to your wife?"

"You don't wanna know."

"Yeah, I do. I'm kinda curious."

"Well, you barreling into my home like a bull on steroids with blood all over your face didn't help—"

Howard's lips stopped moving when he spotted something buried behind the tissues deep within the glove box. "Huh?"

"What?"

Howard reached in and grabbed the glistening object; a Glock 17. "What the fuck, Gilmour? What's this doing in your car?"

"Dunno," he shrugged. "I kinda wanted to keep it, just in case any mad shit went down."

Howard snapped. "Are you crazy? If you get pulled over you'll get *four years* for this. At least."

"Howie, if we get connected to what went down at the bank, we're looking at lethal injection. We'd be lucky to make twenty-five-to-life."

Howard lifted the gun and resisted the urge to blow his friend's brains all over the windshield. "And you thought *this* would help?"

"Fuck, Howie, I *wish* I'd taken the damn thing into the house with me. Maybe then I'd still have my money. And don't get all prissy-panties, social justice warrior on me now, okay? I'm planning on keeping that piece on me till the bonds are wired to my checking account, and I'm halfway to Barbados."

"Is that so?"

"It *is* so, Mr. Fuckin' Ross," James snapped. "We went to all that trouble learning how to use them over the weekend, so, I figure I'll keep it and defend myself and my money, or use it on the bastards who took my money. When I find them."

"*If* you find them," Howard said. "You'll probably blow your nuts off trying."

"The rate things are going, we'd have been better off keeping our stash *at* the fucking bank," James said. "Irony of ironies."

Howard checked the side mirrors on the Jeep as he dropped the Glock 17 back into the glove box and rammed it shut with his knee. "You're a goddamn idiot, you know that?"

"A soon-to-be-*rich* goddamn idiot, I think you mean?"

Howard closed his eyes and exasperated. "Rich or not, you're still an idiot. Keep an eye out, Ben's place is just up ahead.

Ben's Apartment
—*#1215 Karl Marx Drive*—

James rolled his Jeep to a stop, just outside the bright red gates that secured the two-story apartment block behind it.

"Okay, Ben's at twelve-fifteen," Howard said. "Dunno how we're gonna get past the gates."

James thumped the glove box and took out his Glock 17. "Some good ol' manual love might help."

"No, you are *not* shooting the lock off the gate, you stupid animal."

"I wasn't gonna. If we run into the prick who snatched my paper, I wanna make sure he runs into one of my bullets first."

Howard felt very uneasy around the firearm, and so turned away and exited the car, "Ugh. What's *another* dead body, anyhow?"

The pair approached the free-standing buzzer in front of the iron fence. Steeped with suspicion, James kept his hand inside his jacket pocket, ready to pull out his gun on anyone he deemed worthy of being shot.

But there was nobody around to threaten, or shoot.

Howard typed a four-digit code on the keypad and thumped his friend on the back. "Take your hand out of there, Gilmour. You look weird."

James pointed to a green dumpster by the gate. It had been pushed over, and sported muddy sneaker tracks over the side.

"I'm not taking any chances. Hey, we could just jump the gate. Look."

"Why would we do that—?"

Bzzzz.

The intercom flashed and produced a deafening scream, followed by an irritated female voice.

"Hello?"

"Oh, hey, it's Howard. Howard Ross. Is Ben there?"

"Howard?"

"Yeah. Is Ben there?"

A brief pause heightened Howard's anxiety. "Brianna? Is that you?"

"Yeah. Hold on."

Bzzz.

The gate unbolted and drifted away from the gates, allowing Howard through. He waved James after him, both entered the apartment complex.

Three small children kicked an empty bottle of *Rollneck Kojak* beer around the mini playground and laughed amongst themselves. Once the two men entered the premises, the children stopped and gave them the stink-eye.

"What are you doing here?" one of them asked.

Howard shooed them away. "Mind your own business."

The smaller of the three kids, a young, ginger girl with a ponytail, pointed at James. "I know you, mister."

James retaliated and flipped her the middle finger. "Yeah? Remember *this*."

"Go away," the girl squeaked. "You dirty, old bastard."

The girl and her two friends ran around the corner of the building, and headed for the parking garage building opposite the complex.

Howard sighed as he made his way to the apartment building. "Pfft. Kids these days."

James nodded with relief. "I know, right? I shoulda just shot all three of those little fuck trophies and saved the taxpayer some money in food stamps."

Howard ignored the callous remark and lowered his voice. "Listen, James. I don't wanna spook Ben and Brianna, okay? Just wait out here, and keep watch. Keep an eye out on your phone."

"Why?"

"Lincoln might call, or turn up. He might know something," Howard said. "If I don't come back down in ten minutes for any reason, then come up and check on me."

James grinned. "Paranoid much?"

"No, just a precaution. If I don't come back down in ten minutes, come straight up. Okay?"

James squinted at the parking garage with an intensity usually reserved for ninjas. "Okay."

"Okay, good."

***

Howard took his time ascending the cold, barren staircase. Dozens of tiny, bullet-shaped capsules pervaded the stone steps, indicating a drug user's haven.

"Ugh, Prizm," Howard muttered. "Goddamn valley."

A hazy recollection of a similar event he'd undertaken only a few, short hours ago put the fear of God up his spine.

Eventually, he reached door #1215 and wished he'd borrowed James' Glock 17.

Knock-knock-knock.

Howard faced the peephole in the door and held his breath just as it opened inward. A young brunette woman dressed in a black shirt and panties peeled into view. Her shirt featured a large, multicolored skull, which bulged out at the jawline, the result of a huge baby bump pushing it out.

"Hey, Brianna."

"Howard," she said, none too impressed with the imposition.

"You're looking good."

"Thanks."

Howard knew the woman was unhappy with him, and launched into affable mode. "How long is it, now?"

She ran her palm over the skull's jaw on her shirt, instinctively protecting her unborn child. "About a month. What are you doing here, Howard?"

"I need to see Ben. It's nothing to worry about. Is he in?"

"Yeah, in the front room."

"Can I come in?"

Brianna stepped aside and offered Howard into her home.

A quiet sound from a television shook the walls of the corridor as Howard carefully made his way to the front room with Brianna in tow.

"I guess you've heard the news, right?"

"No, why?" Howard lied.

"The bank was robbed today. It's all over the news."

Howard stopped walking to emphasize his ignorance of the day's events. "Was it?"

"Don't act dumb with me, Howard," she said. "I'm not stupid. Are you seriously telling me nobody got in touch with you to tell you, and you're finding this out from me?"

Howard protested a little too much, hoping Brianna wouldn't quiz him too hard. "No, honest. I didn't know."

She sneered at him. "Aren't you going to ask what happened?"

"Oh. What happened?"

"There were at least five of them," she explained. "They said on the news that one of them was the deputy manager. Mark Amos."

"Really? Mark got shot?"

"Yeah, he and Ben knew each other. Turns out he was in on the whole thing."

Howard's ears burned at the news, and tugged at his throat. "They know that already?"

"Yeah. It's just as well you guys were laid off last week, right? Otherwise you would've got caught up in all this."

"Yeah," Howard thought aloud. "I guess."

"My Ben would have been there, too, and he could've gotten himself killed."

Unable to look the woman in the eyes, Howard turned around and entered the front room.

As expected, footage from the news report played silently on the television. Mark Amos' mugshot plastered at the top-right corner of the screen, along with footage of the mass clean-up on the road.

Ben lay sprawled on the sofa on the opposite wall, next to five empty bottles of *Rollneck Kojak*, and a half-finished joint.

The stench of weed hung in the air, despite the draft coming through the open window.

"He's not been acting right since losing his job," Brianna said. "Ever since Benjy came back home today, he's been acting weird. Yesterday, he was—"

"—Brianna, listen," Howard said. "Can you give me a few minutes with Ben?"

Her bottom lip quivered. "What's going on?"

"It's nothing to worry about, but I really need to speak to Ben. Go and make us a cup of coffee, or something. Don't worry, it's all good."

Brianna didn't buy a single word of Howard's reassurance, but felt the urge to leave the room anyway.

"Fine."

Howard offered her a smile as she exited the front room, leaving him to glance at his former colleague snoring on the sofa.

He looked down the man's bare legs and winced at his stupid *Space Invaders* socks. "Ah, to be their age again."

Ben licked his lips and murmured as he slept.

"Woof," Howard snapped.

"Agh!"

Ben came-to up in a stupor, sat up straight, and groaned. "Uggghhh, my head."

"Wake wakey, Cherry Popsicle."

Ben wiped his eyes and, before he could reach for his half-smoked joint, suddenly noticed a rabbit with a man's body looming over him. "Oh, shit—"

"—No, Ben. It's me. Howard."

Ben rubbed his eyes again, and when his fingers moved out of his field of vision, the stupid rabbit head had vanished.

"Ross?"

Howard sat on the single chair by the television set, leaned forward, and planted his elbows on his knees. "Yeah."

"What the hell are you doing here?"

"Listen," he said as he watched Ben go for his cigarette lighter. "I don't want to alarm you, but something's happened. I just wanna make sure you're okay."

Click-click.

Ben clicked his lighter, inhaled a lungful of weed and blew it out of his nostrils. "I'm okay. Why wouldn't I be?"

"Good."

Ben nodded at the muted image of Lt. Fox being interviewed on the television. Five blacked-out mugshots with question marks appeared on screen, which relieved both men.

"We're in the clear, right?" Ben asked.

"Yeah, but that's not the problem. Someone fucked Gilmour over. Took his cash. Nobody's answering their phone—"

"—Yeah, we're not meant to, right? I've switched mine off."

"I know," Howard said. "Nobody's been here, right? Except me? Nobody snooping around?"

"No."

Howard leaned back and stared Ben in his spluttering face. "Good stuff?"

Ben finished his spliff and crushed the end in the ashtray. "Yeah, it's okay. Danny hooked me up with this Peruvian stuff over the weekend. It's good shit. Strong, but good."

"Aren't you gonna ask how James is?"

Ben eyed Howard with suspicion, and found he got the same treatment back.

"Okay, sure. What happened to James?"

"They broke into his house and beat the shit out of him and took his money."

Surprised, Ben coughed out the last intake of weed and retched into his fist. "What?"

Howard nodded, and considered grabbing the man by his shoulders and knocking him out. "Yeah."

"He kept his cash in his own house?" Ben spluttered. "What kinda idiot does that?"

"The same kinda idiot who keeps their money at Chrome Valley Federal, probably? He didn't even have a chance to change clothes and go stash it someplace safe."

"A fool and his money are soon parted, right?" Ben snapped, relishing the opportunity to take a dig at James' character. "He's had at least five hours to stash it someplace safe. Gilmour's an idiot. A crazy, out-of-his-head idiot."

"Ben?"

"Yeah?"

"Is your money safe?"

"What do you mean?"

Howard looked around the damp on the ceiling, and ignored the family pictures on the walls. "I mean, it's safe, right? Please don't tell me you're keeping it here in your apartment with your pregnant wife."

"Of course not," Ben said. "I'm not a dumb-ass like Gilmour."

Howard wafted the weed smoke away from his face. "Where is it?"

"It's safe. Don't worry—" Ben said, just as his unearned confidence morphed into a pile driver of concern. "Ah, shit. *No, no, no.*"

Ben jumped to his feet and brushed the front of his underwear with the back of his hand.

"What are you doing?"

"I know what you're saying, Howard. I'm not taking any chances. Screw that. I'm gonna go ."

"What? Is it *here?*"

"No, in the garage. Out back."

Ben stumbled by the coffee table as he made his way out of the front room, and past Brianna who had caught much of the conversation between the two men by the door.

Howard offered her a smile, but she wasn't in the mood to return it.

"Nothing to worry about, huh?" she asked Howard.

"That's right, Brianna. Nothing to worry about. Ben and I need to head out for a few minutes."

***

James held his cell phone to his ear as he kept a watch on the parking garage. "C'mon, answer. Answer."

Just then, he saw Howard and Ben exit the apartment building and make their way across the grass.

Howard glanced in James' direction as Ben pushed forward and entered the parking garage. A stern nod was all it took for James to acknowledge that he needed to keep back and out of sight.

The closer Ben got to his lock-up, the more tense his muscles became. "Shit, shit. Please be there. Please be there," his voice echoed.

Howard kept a look-out as Ben reached the door to his lock-up, and found that the handle had been busted clean off.

"Aww, noooo."

Howard shooed James away as Ben pulled the garage door open and switched on the light. He dashed over to the safe in the corner of the dwelling and wiped away the cobwebs.

"Shit. No, no, no."

The door on the safe was wide open.

Somebody had broken in and emptied it.

When Ben peeked inside, he found nothing but the Glock 17 he'd left in there with his sports bag, the latter of which was nowhere to be found.

"Shit," he screamed.

Ben snatched the Glock 17 from out of the safe, stood up, and kicked the door so hard that it rebounded and swung back out.

"Motherfuckers," he fumed. "Goddamn fuckin' thieving *bastards*."

Howard raced inside and clutched his chest. "What?"

Ben wailed like a banshee, kicked the bicycle against the wall, and paced back and forth with the gun in his hand. "It's gone. It's fucking gone. They fucking took my bag, man."

"Oh, shit."

Howard didn't know where to turn, or what to do. He expected to find James at the door when he looked up, but found a young, ginger-haired girl with a ponytail staring back at him with a concerned expression on her face.

"What the fuck are you looking at?"

The girl saw Ben release the safety catch on his gun and ran away screaming.

"Right," Ben fumed. "They took my money, but they left my gun. They obviously thought I was never gonna notice. They're gonna regret that when I put a hole in the back of their head, I swear to God."

Howard tried to calm him down, just as James made his presence known. "Ben, calm down—"

"—It's *you*, isn't it?"

Ben pointed his Glock 17 at Howard, who immediately raised his arms in the air and pleaded his innocence.

"What? Of course it isn't me."

"Where is my fucking bag?" Ben shrieked. "Answer me, Ross?"

Howard sputtered, hoping his friend wouldn't execute him. "Ben, think. If it was me who robbed you, why would I come back here to tell you about it?"

"To make yourself look like a fucking victim?" Ben snapped.

Click.

The sound of a firearm hammer snapping into place echoed up the walls. Ben looked over Howard's shoulder and saw James pointing his Glock 17 right back at him. "Put the gun down, Benjy."

"What the *fuck* is he doing here?" Ben screamed.

"Don't make me ask again. Put the gun down."

Howard winced at the two men ready to turn the garage into a cavalcade of bullets and corpses.

Ben squealed and threatened to shoot Howard in the face. "Some bastard better tell me where my money is or I'll turn this place into a goddamn morgue."

"We wanna know, too," James said, calmly. "Now, stop aiming that gun at Howard. Put it down."

Howard tried to fight off his impending coronary and added to James' sentiment. "Ben, it's not me, and it isn't James."

"We're gonna get nowhere standing around like this pointing our dicks at each other, Cherry," James said. "Now, for the final time of asking, put your gun away or I'm gonna shoot you in the tongue and disappoint your wife on your behalf."

Ben couldn't bring himself to lower his defenses, which angered James all the more.

"Put the gun down."

Ben eventually saw sense and took a deep breath. He lowered his gun and slipped it into his jacket pocket.

"Okay."

Howard breathed a sigh of relief and dropped his arms. "James, put yours away, too."

"Good decision, Cherry."

"Sorry, Howard," Ben said. "I'm just a bit fucking pissed, that's all."

"I know. We all are. Now, *think*. If it wasn't us, then who does that leave?"

Ben punched his hands together and raced past Howard and James with a red mist of vengeance on his eyes.

"Lincoln Mumford. Right? Am I right? That no-good, two-faced, snarky fuckin' black bastard."

"Hey," Howard snapped. "We don't know that for sure. For all we know Lincoln might be missing his slice of the score, as well."

Ben scoffed and produced a half-chuckle of pure mirth. "*Never* trust a black guy. I fucking knew it."

"Ben!"

"What?"

"Quit that bullshit," Howard snapped. "Now, we know it isn't any of us."

Ben hung his head in shame and paced around the tiny garage in a pathetic attempt to quell his desire for blood. "Ugh, this is no good for pacing."

Howard ignored Ben's pathetic complaint and turned to James. "Hey."

"Yeah?"

Howard nodded at the cell phone in James' hand. "Did you try calling Mumford? Or Driscoll?"

"Yeah, they aren't picking up."

Howard barged past Ben and made his way out of the garage.

"Shit, as if being seen by that ginger kid wasn't enough. That's it, there's only one thing left for us to do."

James ran after Howard and grabbed his left arm. "Oww, my hole."

He released his grip on his friend's arm, remembering that he'd been shot. "Sorry."

"You fucking idiot," Howard shrieked. "Shit, be careful."

"I'm sorry, Howard."

"That fucking *hurt*."

James sighed. "Look, we're not going to Lincoln's place, Howard. No way."

Ben's interest in visiting Lincoln finally surfaced. "No, Howard's right. We need to pay Mumford a visit and make sure his black ass isn't dead and still has his money. He'd better not have ours, or else he's one *dead* motherfucker. Come on."

James followed behind the two men as they exited the garage and slipped his gun inside his inner jacket pocket.

Chapter 16

Howard shouted into his phone from the front passenger seat of James' Jeep.

"Come on, you stupid piece of shit, answer your phone."

Ben stared out of the back passenger window at the buildings whizzing from left to right.

"James, man. Don't drive too fast. The last thing we need is to get pulled over by the cops, you know."

"It's okay, I'm doing a steady seventy."

Ben turned to Howard up front. "Is Lincoln picking up?"

"Yeah, I just spoke to him a few seconds ago."

Surprised, Ben's face lit up. "Really?"

Howard looked over his shoulder and scowled at the man who'd asked the dumbest question he'd ever heard.

"No, not really, you moron. Did you hear me having a conversation since we got in the car? Mumford's not picking up. It's just ringing out like the dull, idiotic thoughts in your head."

Howard's phone slipped from his hand when he faced forward. It fell between his sneakers, and directly amongst the detritus that had collected in the foot well.

"Ugh, your car is disgusting, Gilmour."

"Yeah, I haven't had a chance to get it cleaned, yet."

Howard shoveled a bunch of empty *Rollneck Kojak* beer bottles, cigarette packs, receipts, parking stubs, and candy wrappers aside with the side of his hand. "Ugh, what is all this shit, anyway?"

He scrunched a few of the receipts in his hand and read them. "*Store-N-Go*? *Patel's Furnace*?"

"Yeah, that last one was for the beer."

Howard squinted at what looked like a five-year-old ticket stub. "Elvis tribute band at *The Place with No Name*?"

"Yeah, that dude was pretty fucking good, actually. Practically as good as the real thing."

Howard flicked it back into the foot well, and read another receipt. "Is your car any indication of the state of your brain?"

"What do you mean?"

"All messy and all over the place?"

"Yeah," James giggled. "Just like us being great with other people's money, eh? But we can't get our own affairs in order?"

"Pfft. Why don't you throw all this stuff away?"

"The valley doesn't have any trash cans on the street anymore," James said. "You could bundle all that shit up and trash them for me? Make yourself useful for once."

Howard slipped some of them in his pocket and straightened his back. Lost in a world of his own, he bounced his cell phone on his right knee.

James snorted. "You've gone quiet all of a sudden, Ross? The mess ain't that bad, is it?"

Howard stared through the passenger window and focused on the five towers looming in the horizon.

"Howard, that's the Freeway Five," Ben said. "Seventh floor, Lincoln said. Danny and Knocktoe's apartment."

No response came from the front passenger seat.

"That's right, Benjy," James said. "Though, it seems Howard has taken a vow of silence like the little nun he is."

"Ha."

Howard blinked and exited his daydream. "Gilmour?"

"Yeah?"

"What did you do after we left the rendezvous? Did you go straight back home?"

"Yeah," James said. "Why do you ask?"

"I ask because keeping your slice of the score at your own home was a really fucking stupid thing to do—"

"—Eh? What are you trying to say?"

"Well, I'm saying this, James. So far, nobody has been that dumb, neither me or Ben, to keep our stash *inside* of our own homes."

James slammed the horn with the butt of his palm in anger. "Fuck you, Howard. You think I don't know that? All I needed to do was get home, get changed, maybe jerk off for ten minutes to relieve some stress, and then go stash my cash."

"Yeah, long enough to get jumped and relieved of your hard-earned cash."

"I fell asleep, you dumb motherfucker," James yelped. "Jesus, Howard. It's been a tough day, all right? I took a seat and chilled out for a few minutes, and the next thing I know it's dark outside, and I'm getting the shit kicked out of me."

"All right, fine. But where *were* you gonna hide it? Under the stairs?"

"No," James snapped. "Someplace safe, where no fucker could find it. Somewhere only I can get to. And I sure as shit ain't telling no-goddamn-body where that is. Ain't that right? We keep our fucking mouths shut about details like that?"

"Yeah, it's a little late for that now, especially for you."

"You think I haven't thought about that?" James spat. "I'm glad it was me who got fucked-over first, because if it had been you, or Benjy-boy in the back, that they got to first, then they'd have probably killed you. It was only me fighting them off that stopped me from getting murdered."

Howard shook his head with disbelief and rolled the kinks out of his neck. "Yeah," he said with a pinch of quiet disappointment.

The red digital clock on the dashboard read 8:35 pm. It produced a distinct red glow from the digits which brought about visions of the haze of red mist that had erupted during the day.

Howard tried to keep his concrete-heavy eyelids open as he concentrated on the road. "Make a left at the next turn."

Lincoln's Pad
—#1861 Proudhon Blvd—

The Jeep rolled along the curbside and slowed to a complete stop. Howard unfastened his seatbelt and suddenly felt naked as he patted his jacket pockets.

"I'm beginning to wish I'd kept my sidearm, now."

James reached into his pocket. "You wanna take mine?"

Howard evaluated the front of Lincoln's house. A pang of relief set in when he saw the light in both the front and bedroom window.

"No. Lincoln's cool."

James sneered at Howard. "Oh, yeah? And how do you know that?"

"If he and his family are in, I doubt he's the one who's fucked us over. And if he *is* the one who did it, do you really think he'd be back at home with his feet up in front of the TV?"

Ben leaned forward and eyed the front door to the house. "You're right. He might not *be* home, though. Might just be his family inside."

"Keep an eye on the front door. I'll have him come out and we can speak. If he did it, then we kick his fucking head in. If he hasn't been relieved of his cash, then it's probably just a matter of time before someone comes for it."

Ben gripped the back of Howard's seat and pulled himself forward. "We got your back, buddy. Just bring him out here."

Howard kicked the car door open and prepared to exit. "In any event, we'll definitely have to pay Danny and Knocktoe a visit at home."

Ben swallowed hard and watched as Howard stepped out of the vehicle and made his way up Lincoln's front yard path.

Ben turned to James with a stilted look of concern. "Hey."

"Yeah?"

"Who do you think fucked us over?"

"What?"

"Who do *you* think took our money?"

James shrugged and glanced into the rear view mirror just in time to catch a pair of headlights roll across the reflective surface.

"I got my suspicions," James said, before turning around and throwing a nasty glance at Ben. "We *are* gonna find out, aren't we?"

Afraid, Ben stammered as he answered. "Y-Yeah. Definitely—"

"—Because, *Benjamin*," James interrupted. "It's like you said. If the soon-to-be-dead asshole who did this is capable of ripping you and me off, then he's capable of acting the victim in all this."

"What are you trying to say?"

"I'm saying nothing. Just keeping my wits about me, that's all."

Ben looked away from the monster in the driver's seat and watched Howard step up to the front door of Lincoln's house.

"I guess we'll find out."

Driiii-iiing.

Howard lifted his finger away from the doorbell and took a step back. A quick check on the Jeep made him feel more secure as the door opened.

He turned back to find Lincoln dressed in a purple robe, fresh out of the shower.

"Hey."

Lincoln leaned forward and tied the fuzzy belt across his waist in an attempt to secure his modesty.

He spotted the Jeep immediately, and then scanned the street. "Shit, Howard? What are you doing here? Aren't we meant to be laying low—"

"—Yeah, we are," Howard whispered. "Listen, I couldn't call you, so that's why I'm here. something bad has gone down."

Lincoln's pupils dilated as soon as Howard finished his sentence. "Shit. What? The cops?"

"God, no. Nothing like that. Something much worse."

"Something *worse* than the cops being onto us?"

"Yeah, look, I'm with James and Ben, and we—"

"—Lincoln?"

A hurried voice flew down the staircase behind the man in the robe. The tips of his ears pricked up, and sent him spinning around on the spot. "Yeah, babe?"

The voice had an air of displeasure about it. "Who's at the door at this hour?"

"Oh, it's nothing. I'll be back in a minute."

Lincoln tilted his head to the front yard and waved Howard away from the porch. "Quick, out here."

"Okay," Howard said.

Lincoln stepped onto his well-kept lawn with his bare feet and sidestepped by the front window.

"Man, this better be good. I got my girl and my kids inside waiting for me, you know?"

Howard grabbed the man's shoulder. "Someone's fucking us."

"Fucking us?"

"James turns up at my place. Someone broke in, beat the shit outta him, and took his stash."

Howard scanned the man's face for any sign of untruth. Lincoln seemed genuinely surprised, and at a loss for words.

"You're fucking with me? Tell me you're fucking with me."

"I am not fucking with you. Whoever did this knows what they're doing, and they know who was involved. And we aren't exactly gonna go crying to the cops and complain about it, are we?"

"Fuck no."

"Whoever's done this *knows*, Lincoln, I'm telling you right here and now."

Lincoln eyed the Jeep and saw James in the front seat. Ben waved through the window in the back and offered a polite smile.

Confused, Lincoln half-waved back. "What about Benjy?"

Howard ran his tongue across his dry bottom lip. "He hid his stash in his garage. They broke in and stole it."

Lincoln averted his eyes from the car to Howard's concerned face. "And you, Howard? Is your stash okay?"

"No, I'm cool. Don't worry about me. Nobody will ever find my slice."

"They're gonna get to you, ain't they?" Lincoln asked. "What about Miranda and Bonnie—"

"—No, no, it's all good. I've sent them to my —uh, no," Howard said, deciding to reveal nothing more. "Look, they're cool. My stash is safe, and there's nobody home, so if I'm next it doesn't matter."

"It doesn't?"

"No. Look, we don't have time for this. Where did you stash your bag?"

Lincoln tutted. "It's safe."

"Are you *sure* about that?"

Lincoln had heard enough, and made his way back to the front door.

"Shit. I dunno what this white-man bullshit is, but I'm cool. Ain't nobody about to roll up at my place and give me any shit. I'll put a bullet in their fuckin' head, for real."

"Lincoln, *please*. I'm only asking you where you stashed your bag because we need to know if it's still there."

Back in the Jeep, Ben had become utterly absorbed in Howard and Lincoln's physical behavior.

"I reckon they're about to smack ten shades of shit out of each other. Lincoln looks *pissed*, man. I think he just told Howard to fuck off. Yeah, he's *definitely* told him to fuck off."

James hadn't heard much of Ben's assessment. Instead, he focused on the rear view mirror and took an interest in the Ford Crown Victoria parked further up the street.

"Huh?"

"Aren't you watching? Look at the way they're chatting to each other. Lincoln doesn't look too happy. You think Howard's accusing him of something?"

James took more of an interest in the surreptitious light show taking place behind the car. "Hey, Benjy, look behind you. You see those headlights?"

"What?"

"Behind you. Look."

Ben placed his hand on the seat and used it to turn his body around. Sure enough, two headlights spread across the back window, threatening to blind him.

"Uh, yeah. So what?"

"Dunno, man. I got a gut feeling we're being tailed."

"Yeah, well, as substantial as your guts are, I think you're being paranoid," Ben said. "No, wait. Look. They're moving to the other side of the street."

"An unmarked Ford Crown Victoria?" James said. "No. No, I don't like this—"

"—This is bullshit."

Ben averted his eyes to Lincoln's house to find the two men had disappeared.

"Where are they? Did they go inside?"

James watched the headlights drift over to their side of the road and pull up three cars behind them. "I dunno, I wasn't looking."

"Shit. Where did they go?"

James grabbed his cell phone from the dashboard and unlocked it in a hurry. "Okay, fuck this. We're not sitting here like a couple of gay ducks waiting to get fucked, and especially not when you and me are carrying."

Ben felt his jacket pocket and realized that he was carrying his Glock 17. "Who are you calling?"

James turned the key in the ignition, started the engine, and waited for Howard to answer. "If it's one of Lincoln's goons coming to pay us a visit, or the fucking cops, I don't wanna be here."

A bead of sweat formed on Ben's brow as he returned to the back window. "Shit."

"You wanna talk about who did this? I'm thinking it's that gay, little autistic shit with the cane."

"Knocktoe?" Ben asked. "He can barely move without that third leg of his."

James flicked the gear into drive, ready to pull out from the side of the road. "Doesn't stop him from getting Danny onto us, though. Or hiring a couple of heavies to carry out his dirty work."

A lone street lamp illuminated the fake, green turf in Lincoln's back yard. Two elongated, man-shaped shadows stretched across the grass from the back door and streaked up to the back alley gate.

"You better be wrong about this, Howard, I swear."

"It's just a precaution. We need to know."

Lincoln dipped his hand in his right robe pocket and pulled out his Glock 17. The light from the street lamp pinged off the metallic surface as he bounced the weight in his palm. "Glad I kept this."

"Huh? You kept the gun in your house? Are you mad?"

"Why, didn't you keep yours?"

"No."

"Why not? Dumb ass, you might need it. You definitely need it now."

Lincoln booted the gate open with his foot and turned into the gravel-scattered alleyway.

"Shit, Lincoln, if the cops raid you and they find that piece you'll get four years."

"They ain't gonna find it hidden in the bathroom cistern, are they? You never watched *The Godfather*?"

"This isn't some wacky movie or book, you know," Howard said. "This is serious."

Lincoln grinned and gripped the gun in his hand. "So's my gun. If some motherfucker wants to rob a motherfucker, then I'mma shoot a motherfucker, you know what I'm saying?"

Meow.

The two men looked down at the brick wall. A mangy orange tabby cat snaked in and out of the first three dumpsters as she trundled along the ground.

Meow.

Lincoln kicked the cat aside. "Get outta here, Jelly. Goddamn pest."

Hissss.

"Fuck off, there's a good girl."

The cat meowed and bolted away, leaving the two men to inspect the third dumpster.

"Goddamn cat. The Andersons, next door, that boy lets his annoying fuzzball shit all over my lawn when she's not keeping us awake at night howlin' at the goddamn moon."

"Yeah, whatever. Hurry up and check your stuff."

Lincoln pinched the lock on the dumpster and, as he reached for his key, noticed the lock had been cut clean off. "*Shit*, man."

"What?"

"I don't believe this."

"What, what?"

Lincoln tore the busted lock away from the dumpster. "Fuckin' bolt cutters, man. A clean cut. Look at it?"

He presented Howard with the clean snap on the metal lock.

"Shit."

"You know somethin', Howard? I had a feeling you might come knocking."

"Oh yeah? Why's that?"

"Dunno. Just had a feeling. I mean, I know Mark got his bony, white buttocks shot the fuck up, but everything else went mostly to plan. Too good to be true. And now you're telling me someone in the know is thieving from the motherfuckin' *thieves*? It's almost as if the whole damn game wrote itself."

Bzzzz.

Lincoln cast his eyes down to Howard's groin. "Is that a vibrator you've stuffed in your pants, Ross?"

"No, no, it's my phone—"

"—Shit," Lincoln scoffed as he punched the lid of the dumpster up and into the wall. "Crazy white boy."

"The lock?" Howard asked. "Was it broken?"

"Yeah."

Howard answered the call as he watched Lincoln hoist himself up to the edge of the dumpster. "James? This better be good."

"Yeah, Howard, it's me. Listen, we need to move. I think we've been followed."

"Followed?"

Lincoln threw Howard a menacing look when he heard what he'd said.

"Followed?" he mouthed.

Howard shook his head and signaled the cut-throat sign, and waved that everything was okay. "James?"

"Yeah."

"Can you see who's following you? Like, who's behind the wheel? What kinda vehicle are they in?"

"It's a Crown Victoria. Can't see the driver, it's too dark. But we're not sticking around to find out. How's Mumford? Is he cool?"

Howard turned back to find Lincoln rummaging around in the dumpster like a ravenous hobo.

"Yeah, he's cool. I think. He's just checking where he stashed his—"

"—Aww, shit," Lincoln screamed. "No, no, no, man. Goddamn, motherfuckin', son of a bitch-ass, cocksucking motherfuckers."

Howard's eyes grew in their sockets as he took a step back. "Uh, I think we have an answer already."

"What's that noise?"

"That," Howard explained, dryly. "Is the sound of a black man finding out that he's just been relieved of his money."

Lincoln hopped out of the dumpster with several items of garbage stuck to his legs - and no sports bag with his money inside it.

"Where the fuck is it? I swear to *Christ,* I'mma execute some prick," Lincoln wailed as he slid to his knees and checked underneath the dumpster.

"Okay, I'm guessing now Lincoln's fucked, that he's gonna wanna know who's got his money?"

"Yeah, I'd say that's a pretty safe bet, but let me check," Howard said, and then hollered at Lincoln. "Hey, Lincoln? You wanna help us find out who stole our money?"

"You bet your goddamn, punk-ass, throat-strangulatin', cocksucking, red-collar white *asses* I wanna know who took my motherfuckin' paper, man. *Fuck.*"

Howard nodded, knowingly, "Yup, James. That's a *yes* from Lincoln."

"Right, that narrows it down, now we know Lincoln's cool. Me and Benji are gonna go visit Danny and Knocktoe."

"You're going to Freeway Five?" Howard asked. "That's bad territory. You got your pieces with you?"

"Yeah, both of us got our guns."

"Good. Is that car still following you?"

"No. I think we lost 'em. I'll call you when we're at Knocktoe and Danny's."

Lincoln slammed the dumpster shut and chucked the now-useless key into the trees. "Fuckin' pricks."

"Hey, Howard?"

"Yeah, James?"

"Are you staying at Lincoln's? What are you doing? You wanna get a taxi and meet us at Freeway Five?"

Howard watched Lincoln eviscerate the side of the dumpster with his hands. He reached into his robe pocket and pulled out his Glock 17.

"Umm," Howard hushed. "I dunno if I wanna stay—"

Bang-bang-bang.

Lincoln pulled out his Glock 17 and unloaded three bullets into the dumpster that had failed to protect his money. A trio of bullet holes sprawled up the front of the plastic, and smoked into the night sky.

Lincoln turned his gun on Howard and signaled to him to cut the call.

"I'll, uh, call you back, James," Howard said.

"What?"

"Lincoln's not taken this too well. I'll call you back."

Lincoln took a step forward and threatened to blow Howard's head off. "Motherfucker, you best start speaking."

"Lincoln, I swear, every one of us is getting fucked, here. I already told you. Please, stop pointing that thing at me."

Despite his fury, everything Howard said made sense. Lincoln lowered his gun, but reserved the right to use it if he didn't like whatever Howard was going to say next.

"Your white ass gon' end up like this motherfucker dumpster for real less you tell me where my goddamn paper's at. You hear me, Howard?"

"Yes, I hear you."

"I *ain't* playing, man. Before the night is up, shit's gonna go down, and I'mma have my fuckin' money back in my hands."

"I feel the same way."

Howard closed his eyes and tried to think on his feet. After a few seconds of pure silence, a streak of common sense entered his mind.

"You're right."

"What?" Lincoln asked.

Howard took out his cell phone and swiped the screen. "Where's your car?"

"Out front, why?"

"Get dressed and tell Barbara we're going out for a few minutes," he said as he marched away from the dumpster at speed. "I wanna go check on my stash. We'll have to take your car."

Beep-beep-beep.

Lincoln clutched the end of his robe as he traipsed through a murky puddle. "Who are you calling?"

Howard glanced at his screen and saw the call cut off. "My Dad."

"Why are you calling him?" Lincoln asked, just in time to witness a wave of sheer horror creep across Howard's face.

"Shit, he's not answering," Howard snapped as he fumbled for the redial button.

"Your pops ain't answering?"

"No, I'm trying again. Oh, *Christ.*"

Howard stormed past his friend and pointed at the house. "Quick, go in and get dressed. Make your excuses, and I'll meet you round front."

Lincoln wasted no time. He rushed through the yard gate, and ran up the garden path to the house, leaving a nervous Howard close to losing his mind with worry.

"C'mon, Dad. Pick up. *Pick up.*"

The call went dead, unanswered, pushing the fear of God deep inside Howard's chest.

"Shit."

He scanned each end of the back alley with worry and felt his tongue turn to sand. Quick-thinking, he returned to his phone and made another call, this time to Ben.

"C'mon, Benjy, you useless prick. Answer."

Howard squeezed his cell phone with such strength that it nearly popped out of his palm.

"Answer your goddamn phone, you—."

Click.

Ben's voice blew out of the speakers on the phone. *"Yeah, Howard?"*

"Thank God. It's me, listen, where are you right now?"

"We've just got to Freeway Five."

"Okay, tell James that me and Lincoln are going to see if my stash is safe."

"Where's that?"

Howard splashed through the same mud-strewn puddle that Lincoln had stepped in, and turned the corner into the side alley leading to the boulevard road.

"Doesn't matter. Both of you keep your phones on. Ben, you hear me?"

"Yeah, hold on," came the response. *"James wants to speak with you."*

"Put him on."

Howard stepped onto the main road and scanned the sidewalk for a white Ford Escort. The road was eerily quiet now that nightfall had blanketed much of the boulevard in darkness.

Just then, he spotted Lincoln's car at the bend in the road.

"Bingo."

Lincoln shut the front door to his house behind him. Now dressed in jeans and a *Public Enemy* hooded sweatshirt, he nodded at Howard and unlocked the Ford Escort.

"Let's go."

A few seconds later, James took the call as Howard crossed the road.

"Howard?"

"Yeah, look, we're going to where I've stashed my bag. Keep your phone on—"

"—Why are you going there?"

"The fuck do you think?" Howard snapped. "I just called my dad to see if everything was cool, and—"

"—You kept your stash at your Dad's house?"

Howard reached the car and slipped into the passenger seat. "Ugh. Yeah. It's safe there. Or, at least I thought it was. God, I hope it is, and everything's okay."

"Why? Isn't he answering?"

Steeped with concern, Howard began to stammer as he talked. "N-No. Oh, shit. I hope n-nothing's happened. Fuck."

Lincoln pulled into the road and hit the gas. "Don't worry, Howard, man. It'll be cool."

Far from convinced, Howard wiped a tear from his cheek and sniffed. "James?"

"Yeah?"

"Gimme a call when you find out what's up at Danny and Knocktoe's. I'll call you when I get to my Dad's. Just, you know, keep your phones at the ready."

"Okay. We've just parked up, and we're in the fifth tower, now…"

Danny and "Knocktoe" Joe's Apartment
—#1776 Freeway Five, Tower Five—

The elevator area in the building had seen better days. Ben took a deep breath as they waited for the single elevator to arrive on the first floor, and felt like dry-heaving.

"Ugh, it stinks in here," he said.

Howard's instruction came as James pressed his index finger to his mouth. "Ben, hush. I'm trying to listen—"

"—*I'll call you when I get to my dad's house. Just, you know, keep your phones at the ready.*"

James listened out for the slow, grinding, whirring of the elevator thunder down the walls. "Okay. We've just parked up, and we're in the fifth tower now."

"*Oh, Christ. This is all my damn fault.*"

"Howard, seriously. I think it's better you come here to Freeway Five."

"*No. I need to go check he's okay, and my bag is still there. Shit.*"

Ben slammed the elevator panel with the butt of his palm. "C'mon, hurry the hell up. Damn it, I hate this piece of shit estate."

Ping.

The elevator doors opened up to introduce a pool of urine on the cracked floor, and a flickering light which illuminated the interior like an epileptic disco ball.

"Howard, the elevator's here. We're going up."

Ben jumped into the elevator with his Glock 17 in both hands. "Come on, let's go."

As soon as James walked in, Ben hit the button for the seventeenth floor.

"We're in the elevator, Howard."

"*Okay. Be careful up there.*"

James watched the buttons light up for the second, third, and fourth floor. "We dunno what we're gonna find when we get to their apartment."

"*No. If they've been fucked-over as well, then we're okay. If they're the ones who fucked us over, do you really think they'd be in their apartment waiting for a visit?*"

James shrugged and gripped his Glock 17 in his jacket pocket. "They might."

"Just check and keep your phones on. I'll speak to you—"

"Howard? Howard, are you there? Hello?"

James scanned his phone to find the call had been cut off.

"Goddamn elevator. What's it made of? Fucking *Kryptonite*?"

Ben gripped his gun in both hands and readied himself for the doors to open. "Never mind that, now. Get ready."

"Yeah."

Ping.

Ben hopped out of the elevator cage and sprinted across the seventh floor landing. James followed behind, ready to fire his gun.

"Which apartment?"

"Lincoln said seventeen seventy-six," Ben whispered. "Over here."

The opened window on the far wall at the end of the landing offered a superb view of the Chrome Valley cityscape. Various buildings of all shapes and sizes provided a healthy glow against the night sky.

A gust of air rolled through the window and hit James' in the face as he approached the door to apartment 1776.

"Here."

The first thing he noticed was that the door had been left ajar.

"Huh? Door's open."

James pulled out his Glock 17 and prepared to enter the dwelling. "You ready?"

Ben slipped his finger around the trigger on his firearm. "I'm ready."

"At least the fucking cops aren't here."

"We don't know that, yet," Ben said. "Be careful. I got your back."

James pressed the tip of his right sneaker against the door and pushed it in.

Creeaaaak.

The door swung in slowly, and allowed James through.

"Danny? Knocktoe?" he said, stepping forward with great trepidation. The rush of air from the landing window rolled over Ben's shoulders as he caught up to James.

"Hello? Anyone there?"

James leaned into the front room to discover bottles of alcohol and weed paraphernalia scattered across the glass table in the middle of the room.

The television was still on, and had been left on mute.

A news report showed the aftermath of the Chrome Valley Federal Bank heist, with several covered bodies being stretchered off-screen by paramedics.

Ben paused to point his gun at James in the front room. "Anything?"

"What? No—*Hey*, don't point that fucking thing at me, you dumb ass."

"Sorry."

"Go and check the first bedroom on the left," James snapped, before lowering his tone to an intense insistence. "I'll check the other one."

"Okay."

Ben glanced at the kitchen on his way to the master bedroom. The stove was still on, as was the radio sitting on the window ledge.

"—I mean, it comes to something, doesn't it? When five armed robbers wearing dumb animal masks can get away with something like this," the radio DJ asked.

"Ah. Shut the fuck up," Ben said. "You don't know shit."

He didn't notice James sprint across the corridor behind him, and turn into the bedroom to the right.

Ben spun around, exited the kitchen, and moved to the first, smaller bedroom.

He kept his eyes on the worn, cream-colored carpet as he moved forward, one foot in front of another.

Just then, Ben noticed a patch of red dampness by the door to the bedroom. "What the fuck?"

When he lifted his head, he saw a splatter of blood just above the door handle.

"Oh, shit."

James moved out of the second bedroom and shut the door behind him. "Okay, the master bedroom is empty."

"James, *look*."

"What?"

Ben pointed to the door handle and nearly soiled himself. "There's blood everywhere, man."

James pushed Ben aside and went to elbow the door. "Shit."

Whump.

The door sprung open, and both Ben and James' tongues fell out of their mouths in horror.

"Ohhh, *holy shit*."

Ben gasped at the grizzly sight. "My G-God," he stammered. "Danny?"

James frowned with disgust and pulled Ben away from the bed. "No, don't go near him."

"Danny?"

Ben wrenched his arm away from his friend's clutches and walked up to the bed.

"Oh, Jesus."

Danny's corpse lay on the bed in a deep ocean of his own blood with his limbs twisted in all directions.

The ends of his t-shirt were torn as if he'd been in a fight.

A cauterized, oblong cavity hung between the man's eyes.

"S-Someone shot h-him in the head," Ben muttered. "Right between the eyes. Jesus, look at the state of him."

"Not a suicide, then?" James said.

A huge splash of blood from where Danny had been shot dried on the wall, with long ropes of thick brain matter caked onto the bed sheets.

"Fucking Knocktoe did this," James said. "I fucking knew it."

"He's not here?"

James flew into a gigantic rage. "Of course he's not *fucking here*. He's the one who did this. He shot Danny and took off with his money, and our money, and—*shit*, he's probably halfway to Rio by now with all the money, the back-stabbing, shit-stabbing fucking crippled *fuck*."

Ben crouched by the bed and looked at a spent, charcoaled bullet that had singed the carpet. He pinched it in his fingers and examined it.

"PDX1s. The same bullets we used."

Both men looked down at their guns, thought about what the revelation might have meant, and then quickly pocketed them.

Ben pulled the ends of his jacket down and cleared his throat. "I don't get it. One shot? Right between the eyes."

"Yeah, whatever. We can't stay here."

"Why would Knocktoe shoot his lover between the eyes and take off with his money?"

"Oh, yeah, that's right," James fumed through his intense sarcasm. "You've not been married long, have you, Benjy?"

"No, but I mean—"

"—Yeah, just wait till you get fucking divorced, man."

"What?"

"Doesn't matter. We can't stay here. Let's go."

"You're right."

James pulled out his phone and raced out of the bedroom. "Come on."

"Where?"

James ran back into the hallway. "I'm calling Howard. Let him know that our crippled dead man is probably waddling to Terminal 2 at Waddling Gate Airport with all our money."

"That's why Joe isn't answering his phone?" Ben spat. "That club-footed asshole. I *knew* we couldn't trust him."

James nodded, relieved that, at the very least, they now had their culprit. "Yeah, I never liked him either. I kept on telling all you guys, but no fucker would listen to me."

Ben raced in front of James and shut the door to the apartment behind them.

Whump.

Ben slammed the door shut a second, third, and fourth time to a vicious slap of perplexity. "Huh?"

"What is it?"

"The door. It won't shut properly."

James tucked his ringing cell phone under his chin as he hit the elevator panel. "Of course it won't shut. Knocktoe probably broke it."

"Eh? Why would he do that?"

Lincoln answered the call. *"Yeah, Gilmour? Speak."*

"To make it look like a fucking break in—Oh, hey, Howard? I got some news—"

"—No, it's me. Lincoln, Howard's a bit uh—"

James waved Ben over to the elevator panel. "C'mon. Leave the door alone. Yeah, Lincoln. I got some news."

"Uh, James? Yeah. So do we."

James focused on the lights rifling up the floors on the elevator panel. "It's Knocktoe. He shot Danny in the head, took his cash, and ours, and he's taken off. We gotta get to the airport. Turn around, and drive there—"

"—James, just shut up for a second and listen, man. You and Ben need to get your asses here right fuckin' now."

James felt his knees turn to jello just as quick as his hands began to shake. "What? Why?"

"No time to explain, man. Get your asses to Howard's dad's pad. Thackeray Road. I mean, like, right fuckin' now."

Worried, James checked his phone to find he had been cut off. "Uh, what? You're not my boss."

"What did Howard say?" Ben asked.

James felt his mouth turn to stone and threw his friend a look of concern. "It was Lincoln. They want us to go to Howard's dad's house."

"What? Why?"

James took a lungful of air and shrugged his shoulders. "Dunno. But it didn't sound good."

Chapter 17

Thackeray Road was even emptier at this time of night than it was earlier in the day.

An apprehensive Howard scanned the dash on Lincoln's white Ford Escort, and took a moment to survey his father's house. It was close to 10 pm by now, and the bedroom light in the house was on, which went some way to alleviate his concerns.

Lincoln raced around the car and joined Howard, who trained his eyes on the filthy underpass a few feet away from the house.

"Howard, man. I'm sure everything's gonna be okay?"

"Yeah. I just need to go check.

"I'm sure everything is cool, man," came the reassuring response. "C'mon, let's go and check on your pops, man."

As Howard walked up the path in the front yard, he looked over his shoulder and immediately saw the same blocky, red graffiti on the wall across the road.

The block "Capitalism Sucks" text lit up under the streetlamp. "Amen to that," Howard said, as he faced forward and raced up the three steps on the porch.

Lincoln followed behind him and felt his index finger get itchy. "I got my piece if you need it."

Howard pulled out the door key and inserted it into the lock. Before he turned it around, he paused and took a deep breath. "Nah, that's not necessary. At least, it'd better not be."

"I hear you."

Clunk.

Howard pushed the door in with his right elbow and raced in, just past the staircase. "Dad? Dad, are you here? It's me, Howard, I just wanna check—"

Lincoln watched his friend stop at the entrance to the kitchen.

"Oh, no."

He moved in and saw that the kitchen window had been broken. A dirty, oil-infused rag had been used to gain entry, and draped over the jagged shards of glass.

"Shit."

Howard pushed Lincoln out of his way, and raced over to the front room. "Fuck. *Fuck.*"

"Hey, Howard, wait. It might be—"

"—He's not here," Howard yelped as he scanned the sofa and dining table. "Dad?"

There was no sign of a struggle to be found anywhere.

"Check upstairs," Lincoln said.

"Yeah."

Howard grabbed the handrail and jumped up the steps, two at a time. "Dad? Please, Dad? Where are you?"

Lincoln checked the front room and tutted. A picture frame containing Miranda, Howard, his father and mother, and a six year old Bonnie, greeted him from the cabinet in the corner wall.

"Very nice."

Once again, no sign of a struggle, which offered Lincoln a few seconds of respite. "Thank God—"

Crash.

Lincoln looked up at the ceiling in terror. "Eh?"

An ear-piercing shriek of pure venom thundered down the stairs.

"Aww, no. *Noooo.*"

"Howard? Fuck."

340

Lincoln bolted out of the front room to a cacophonous sound of stomps and thuds coming from upstairs.

Howard's grief blasted down the walls as Lincoln reached the top of the stairs.

"Motherfuckers."

"Howard, man? What is it?"

Lincoln raced up the steps and followed the sound of enraged turmoil to the largest of the three bedrooms.

"Howard, what are you—oh, *oh, sh-shiiit.*"

Howard kicked the bedside table with incredible fury and burst into tears. "I swear to fucking *Christ*, I'm gonna—"

Lincoln swallowed hard at the sight of Howard's dad's corpse on its knees, and bent over the side of the bed with its face down in the pillow.

"Oh, no."

The white sheets were drenched with fresh blood. Someone had executed Howard's father, and left the old man in a praying position with his knees buried into the carpet.

"Howard, man, listen—"

"—Don't *fucking* speak to me, Mumford, I swear, I'm gonna murder some—oh, Dad. *Dad.*"

In a state of unfiltered apoplexy, Howard fell to his knees, dropped his cell phone by Lincoln's foot, and scrambled under the bed. "Shit, shit—"

"—What are you doing now?"

Howard shuffled under the bed with his behind poking next to his Dad's legs.

"Awww, *fuck.*"

In his haste to stand back up, Howard banged the back of his head on the springs underneath the mattress.

"Oof."

"What?"

Howard rolled out from under the bed and scrambled to his feet. "They've taken my fucking money."

"Under the bed?"

"How the *fuck* did they know it was there?" Howard choked, seriously failing to comprehend what had gone wrong.

"Gone?"

Howard paced around the room for a few seconds, and immediately jumped into accusatory mode with his friend. "How did you know that?"

"Uh, you just looked under there?" Lincoln said, matter-of-factly. "You just told me?"

Howard gulped and took another look at his father. A gunshot wound to the back of the head had killed him, and explained the soaking wet blood splatter on the bed sheets.

Howard burst into tears and fell into Lincoln's arms. "My dad, Lincoln. Look at him. Those fuckers killed my dad."

Lincoln struggled to console the screaming, crying animal in his arms. "Hey, man. It's cool."

Howard bawled into his friend's chest and thumped his back. "I swear, I'm gonna kill that motherfucker."

Lincoln couldn't help but stare at the dead body hunched over the side of the bed. With red mist now in his eyes, he gripped Howard's arms and hugged him back.

"Yeah, you and me both, man. We'll get 'em."

Howard moved his tear-strewn face in front of the sympathetic Lincoln's, and stared him dead in the eyes.

"You know who did this, right? You know. You *know*."

"No, man—"

"—You f-fucking know—shit, uh, m-my Dad, man. I only l-left him for a f-few hours, h-how—?" Howard squealed as Lincoln pulled him forward for some comfort.

"Please, man, calm down."

"You *know* something," Howard screamed. "You *must* know something."

"I swear I don't."

Lincoln took pity on the bereaved, pathetic man crying before him. Howard wiped his eye on his sleeve and brushed it against his collar.

"I'm sorry, man."

Before long, Howard's turmoil subsided, only to be replaced with a desire for revenge.

"We made a big, big mistake today," Howard said. "This wasn't worth it. None of it was worth it. *Sorry* doesn't cut it. Too many people have suffered. All those innocent people, you know. You know?"

"Yeah, man. I know."

"I wish I could turn back the clock and stop it."

Howard teared up once again at the sucker-punch of helplessness and regret. "I mean, I mean—"

"—I know what you mean, man. None of this was worth it."

Howard cleared his throat and forced what little remained of his dignity to the fore. "I need a minute alone. I need some air."

"Yeah, cool."

Stuffed to the brim with internal regret, Howard moved past Lincoln and slowly traipsed down the staircase. He needed a few minutes to himself, and before Lincoln had a chance to take a closer look at the corpse, the carpet seemed to spring to life next to his right foot.

Bzzzz.

"Huh?"

Howard's cell phone bounced around the carpet demanding to be answered. Lincoln scooped it off the floor and checked the screen

Someone named *James* was calling.

Lincoln swiped the green button up and placed the phone to his ear.

"Yeah, James?"

"Oh, hey, Howard? I got some news."

"No, it's me. Lincoln. Howard's a bit, uh—"

"—Yeah, Lincoln? I got some news."

Lincoln focused on the corpse laying face-down in a pool of its own blood. "Uh, James? So do we."

'It's Knocktoe, man. He shot Danny in the head, took his cash, and ours, and fucked off.'

Lincoln gasped at the revelation. Suddenly, everything made sense.

He bolted out of the bedroom and ran down the stairs to see Howard sitting on the porch and sobbing his eyes out.

"James, shut up for a second and listen, man. You and Ben need to get your asses to Howard's dad's house."

All the missing pieces of the jigsaw formed in the man's mind as he gave his instructions. If Knocktoe Joe had stabbed everyone in the back, then he couldn't have gotten far on one, scraggly, crippled foot, and needed hunting down immediately.

"No time to explain, man. Get your asses here right now. Thackeray Road. I mean, like, right fuckin' now."

Lincoln swiped the call dead, and approached the door, mindful of not scaring the hell out of his friend from behind as he entered the porch.

"Ugh," he sniffled. "This is bullshit."

Lincoln stepped to Howard's side, and sat next to him on the cold hard step at the front of the door.

"Hey, you okay?"

"No, I'm *not* fucking okay. I'm very fucking far from okay, okay?"

"Okay."

Lincoln passed Howard's phone over to him. "You left this on the floor."

He snatched it out of the man's hand and immediately scrolled through the recent call list. First among the entries was James, who had called just two minutes ago. "Gilmour called?"

"Uh, yeah."

"What did he say?"

"Danny's dead. Knocktoe's missing."

"What?"

"So, now we know who we're looking for, at least."

Howard wiped a tear from his eye and slipped his phone into his jacket pocket. "Ugh."

"What?"

He pulled out a bunch of old receipts he'd collected from the Jeep's foot well and released them next to his knee. "My life is messed up. My family is messed up. Even my clothes and pockets are messed up."

"Yeah, really," Lincoln snorted. "You think you got it bad?"

"At least your better half knows you lost your job. Miranda still doesn't know."

"You never told her?"

Howard absentmindedly flicked a lone piece of paper with his finger, and read the black imprint on the front.

"How could I, Lincoln? I tried, you know, but she's always beating me to it. Always hogging the conversation, telling me how bad her day was. She never listens. Which is fair enough, I guess."

Howard scanned the ticket in his hand, and then looked at his watch. It was 10:45 pm, and life seemed in very short supply.

"She's gonna find out sooner or later, Howie. She should find out from you, you know. Not by some dumb news report."

"I know, I know."

The will to live slithered down Howard's spine and looked for a way out of his body. He stared at a ticket stub in his hand and lowered his voice.

"What's become of us, Lincoln?"

"How do you mean?"

Howard spoke, but took more interest in the ticket stub in his hand.

"A week ago we were just like everyone else. Family men, most of us, with a career. Quietly getting on with our lives. And then we got greedy. We became animals."

"Yeah. Really."

"Trigger-happy, gun-wielding psychopaths. When the going went rough, we shot anything that got in our way."

"Hey, man, stop speaking that nonsense. We robbed a Federal bank, man. The guns were a backup. We all knew if someone got in our way we'd do whatever it took to make sure they got out of our path. All we wanted was the money, man."

Howard sighed and wiped his eyes. "Nobody was meant to get hurt."

"I dunno about you, Howie, but for me? If it was a choice between going to jail because someone didn't do what we told them to do, then they'd got shot. I ain't going down the road Driscoll went. Survival, man. Like regular animals. Nothing personal. We did what we needed to do. So don't grow a conscience on me, now, man. Ain't none of this your fault."

Howard's attention waned as he focused on the text on the paper on his hand.

"Howard? Did you hear me? What? You'd rather read some *Store-N-Go* stub than listen to me? Pfft. No wonder you're all fucked-up in the head and Miranda's fed up with your ass, man."

Howard scrunched his face and looked up at the graffiti on the brick wall on the opposite side of the road.

"Capitalism sucks," he read aloud in a hazy stupor.

"Yeah. Ain't that the fuckin' truth."

Howard climbed to his feet as the front tires of a Jeep rolled in front of the graffiti, and blocked the last 's' of the text.

Suspicious, Lincoln looked up the length of Howard's back. "What are you doing, man?"

"Get up."

Lincoln shifted off his ass and stood up straight. "What?"

Howard pointed at the Jeep just as the headlamps dipped down. "James and Ben are here. I, uh—Go and get them and come meet me in the underpass."

"The underpass?"

Howard's behavior changed in a heartbeat as he stepped away from the porch. "Just around the corner. My father's house isn't any place to have a discussion on what we do next. Just do it—oh, wait. You have your Glock on you?"

"Yeah."

"Give it to me."

Impatient, Howard clicked his fingers as his buddy reached into his pocket. "What's this all about, Howard?"

"Just give me it."

"Okay?"

Lincoln pushed the grip into Howard's palm, and turned to the Jeep to see James and Ben arguing behind the wheel.

"Howard? You're acting weird, man, what's up?"

"Bring them to the underpass. I'll see you there."

Howard jumped over the white picket fence and raced down the ramp at the side of the house, leaving Lincoln to cross the road and catch Ben's attention.

"Yo, Cherry."

Ben kicked the Jeep's passenger door open in a furious fit of rage. "Goddamn it, we should never have have trusted that fucking crippled prick. This is *your* fault, Lincoln."

"My fault?"

"Yeah, you introduced us to Knocktoe and Danny."

"Man, you best shut your fuckin' crazy ass up chatting shit about me."

James slammed the door shut and barged past the two feuding men. "Hey. Stop acting like a pair of fucking homos. Where's Ross?"

Lincoln waved James and Ben across the road as he headed for the underpass. "Come with me. Someone broke in and murdered his fuckin' pops, man. Took his money."

"What happened to him?" Ben asked.

"Come on, we're reconvening at the underpass. We'll get this sorted."

***

Howard seethed with quiet rage as he leaned against the water-logged brickwork in the underpass. He felt around his jacket pocket and prodded the grip on Lincoln's Glock 17.

A flurry of argumentative echoes accompanied the splashes through puddles as three men made their way to meet Howard.

A trio of elongated shadows stretched up the wet concrete, formed from the powerful street light at the top of the road.

Howard looked to his right and sneered at the three men on their approach, arguing and shouting amongst themselves.

"I dunno," Lincoln snapped. "Fuck. We need to find Knocktoe, then, if he's the one who did it."

James nodded at Howard, only to be met with a vicious look of evil. "Hey, man. I heard about your dad. I'm sorry."

Howard clenched his fist. "Yeah. I heard about Knocktoe."

"Yeah. Fuckin' disabled prick. I *knew* it was him."

"Yeah, me too," Ben said. "I never liked that guy. Did he say where he was going, back at the rendezvous? He must have mentioned his plans, and where he was going?"

Lincoln didn't have anything to add to the conversation, in particular due to the spit of venom drooling from Howard's mouth. The man barely acknowledged him, or Ben, and instead concentrated his eyes on James' frustrated face.

"Howard? Why are you looking at me like that? You wanna kiss me?"

Howard's top lip vibrated, indicating a desire for blood and pain.

James chuckled and wiped his mouth. "Look, we need to find out where fucking Knocktoe is—"

"—It *wasn't* Knocktoe," Howard said.

"What?" James spat. "What the fuck are you talking about, you crazy bastard? He's fucked us all over, and halfway to the airport by now—"

"—And it wasn't Danny. Or Benjy, or Lincoln, or me," Howard finished and opened out his right hand. "So, that leaves just one murdering, back-stabbing prick, doesn't it?"

Everyone's eyes turned to the ticket stub in Howard's fingers.

"What the fuck are you talking about, anyway?" James snapped.

"You gave Knocktoe and Danny a ride home after the count, right?" Howard asked.

"Yeah, but—"

"—So you took care of them first, then took Lincoln's and Ben's money, and then paid a visit to my dad's house."

The more James protested, the weaker his defiance became. "Huh? I dunno what the fuck you're talking about?"

Howard folded his arms and took on the role of prosecution council.

"That little ginger girl with the ponytail outside Ben's place said she saw you before."

"So?"

"Is that because you turned the trash over, hopped the gate, and broke into his garage using the crowbar in your trunk?"

"Motherfucker—" Lincoln snapped, and punched his hands together, leaving Ben to watch out for any sign of untruth from James.

"Is that true?"

"What—No!" James croaked, his voice starting to tremble. "Howie, man. I dunno what Knocktoe did to throw you off track, but we gotta find that asshole—"

"—Your Jeep was parked by the brick wall when I left my bag at my dad's, earlier."

"So?"

"You followed me," Howard snapped. "That's how you knew where my stash was."

"Have you been smoking Ben's weed? Okay, *now* you're really fucked in the head if you think—"

"—You know, you nearly had me, there," Howard said as he shoved the receipt into James' chest. "Store-N-Go. Today's date, October seventh. 7 pm."

Ben and Lincoln had no idea what Howard was referring to.

But it sure seemed as if James did.

"What?"

"What time did you turn up at my place?" Howard asked. "Around seven-thirty, right?"

James stood his ground, failing miserably to conceal the quaking muscles in his now-reddened face. "Yeah?"

"Someone broke into your house, beat you up, and stole your cash? While you were at *Store-N-Go*?"

The corner of James' mouth began to rock with fear. His bottom lip opened half an inch and revealed his tongue.

"You fell asleep on your sofa? Woke up to find you were getting robbed? Did you go to *Store-N-Go* after they beat your sorry ass, or before?"

James' eyelids fluttered, and his jaw of speechlessness lowered, fully unequipped to provide a satisfactory answer.

"Answer me, James, because I'm *this* close to putting a bullet in your fucking head."

Ben and Lincoln connected the dots and turned to James for an answer. "*Fucking answer him.*"

Fraught with anxiety, James kept his eyes on Howard's, hoping to God that he was kidding.

But Howard wasn't kidding.

James had just one course of action left to take. He reached into his pocket, pulled out his gun, and aimed it at the three men. "*Shut it.*"

Howard sneered and put his hands in the air. "I fucking *knew* it."

James walked backwards and wiped his brow on his sleeve. "Fuckin' *stay there*. You stay. Get your hands up."

"You're gonna kill the three of us now, are you?" Howard snapped, caring little for his own wellbeing.

"Fuckin' stay there, Ross. Benjy, be a good doggy and keep your hands up. You too, Mumford. Get your goddamn hands up and stay right where you are."

Howard shouted after James, who continued to walk back, and entertain every intention of running to the far end of the underpass and out of their lives for good.

"You think you can get away with this, do you? Fuck off with our money?"

"Actually, yeah," James barked as he kept his gun point at the men.

"Where are you gonna go, James?"

"Fuck you."

James' walk turned to a sprint as he turned around and ran across the wet concrete.

Howard whipped out his Glock 17, along with Ben, and chased after him. "Get him."

Ben pointed at James' back as it shrank in the distance. "You bet your ass we're gonna get him."

Ben pulled out his gun and blasted James in the back of his right leg just as he turned around to run.

"Gah."

James' heels skidded across a puddle as he fell to his knees and grazed the butt of his palms across the ground.

"Ahh, *fuck*."

Howard picked up the pace and kept his gun aimed at the thieving murderer, who squealed in pain as he clutched his bloody leg.

"M-My l-leg, man."

Lincoln picked James' gun off the floor and wiped the dirt off on his shirt. "I'll have this, thank you very much."

Ben pulled the hammer back on his gun and threatened to shoot James in the face. "You want me to kill this piece of shit?"

A swift boot to James' stomach was the response. It forced the pained man to puke his guts all over his ankles. "Wugh."

"You fucking murderer."

Lincoln and Ben joined in with Howard and kicked him in the face, chest, and stomach with such a ferocious frequency that it pushed the man against the brick wall.

"Wugh—" James coughed up several ropes of blood down his front and clutched his stomach. "P-Please, st-stop—"

Howard crouched to his knees and punched the man in the face. By now, James' battered, bloodied face was barely recognizable. The skin had torn from his jaw and right cheek, and coughed blood up down his chin and onto his white shirt collar.

"Whu—uh, ugh, ugh."

James tried to talk, but the beating he'd received was so severe that it threatened to snap his vocal cords if he tried to beg for mercy.

"Okay, he's had enough," Howard said. "Stop it."

Ben delivered a final kick to James' groin. "Aww, but I wanna fuckin' kill him."

"Stop it, Benjy," Howard said. "I think Gilmour owes us an explanation."

James could barely breathe, let alone speak. He pressed the back of his head against the brick wall, blinked the blood from his eyes, and licked around the missing teeth in his mouth.

"Why'd you do it?" Howard asked.

"I n-needed the money."

"Yeah, asshole, we *all* needed the fucking money," Lincoln snapped. "Where'd you get the brass balls to pull off this shit, anyhow?"

"Yeah. Like kill Danny?" Ben asked. "And Howard's dad?"

James groaned in sheer agony as he squeezed the mucky detritus from his eyes. "Nggg. I d-didn't w-wanna kill 'em, I swear. I only w-wanted to get in and take their b-bags."

Howard flinched at the explanation. "Why'd you do it?"

"I d-dunno, I freaked out when we s-saw how much we g-got when we c-counted the money. It w-wasn't enough."

"Enough?" Ben asked. "Enough for what?"

"Ugh. I, uh—ugh," James struggled through his turmoil. "Eighteenth gate Rollers, man. I owe 'em. Promised to pay 'em off tonight, otherwise Oxide was g-gonna kill me. He still w-will when he hunts me d-down and sees I haven't g-got most of his cash."

Howard could barely prevent himself from blowing a hole in the man's head.

"You're telling me that Danny and my father are dead because you owe some dread-locked hood rat back-pay for your coke and gambling habit?"

"Y-yuh. They're g-gonna kill me, man."

Lincoln turned his head away and considered executing the man right there and then. "That's ironic."

"Yeah, w-well," James spluttered. "You did a good job on Danny and Knocktoe, didn't ya, Mumford?"

"What the fuck did you just say, Gilmour? You stank-ass, lying piece of shit?"

Ben turned to Lincoln who, in turn, grabbed his gun and aimed it at James' forehead. "The fuck you talking about, asshole?"

James tried for a wink and cackled through the blood collecting in his mouth. "I never thought you'd go through with it."

Howard threw Lincoln a stern eye. "Is this true?"

"Of course it ain't true," Lincoln protested at speed. "This dead-ass piece of shit is lying through his fucking broken teeth."

James clutched his ribs and tried to laugh through his pain. "Y-Yeah, I'm only k-kidding. You're a good lad, ain'tcha, Lincoln?"

James puked down his shirt as Lincoln kicked him in the stomach once again. "I'mma fuckin' *murder* your ass right here."

"Whoa, whoa," Howard said. "Hold up for a second, there, Mumford. James?"

"Y-yeah?"

"Where's Knocktoe?"

James licked the blood away from his mouth. "In his bed, back at the Freeway Five. Where I left him."

Perplexed, Ben pressed the man further. "What? No, we checked their apartment. Danny, and Knocktoe. We checked their rooms."

James struggled to breathe as he spoke. "You checked D-Danny's room, and I looked in the other one. The one with Knocktoe in."

"He's dead?" Ben asked.

"Y-Yeah."

Howard closed his eyes and let the echo of the man's last sentence drift into his ears. The only sound in the underpass was of a constant drip of water falling from the bridge, and the distant pitter-patter of scurrying rats looking for food.

"Ugh."

Howard tightened his grip on his Glock 17 and prepared to ask the inevitable. Before he did, he turned to Lincoln and Ben and shooed them away. "Get in the car."

"What?" both men asked in tandem.

"I said get in the fucking car."

"Whose?"

"The *fucking fourteen year old Escort*, what do you think?" Howard snapped. "*Go.*"

Just then, Lincoln realized what Howard meant by *get in the car.*

"*Oh.* Get in the car."

He grabbed Benjy's arm and pulled him back.

"Yeah, yeah, c'mon, Benjy, man. Let's go. Leave Howard to talk to James for a while."

Howard turned to Ben and screamed. "Stop standing there, looking like a dough-eyed puppy bitch, Ben, and go with Lincoln to the car."

"Okay."

Ben kept his eyes on James as he sprinted out of the underpass and headed for the main road. "See ya, Gilmour. I'm sorry."

James tried his best to speak as he doubled over onto his side in a sea of his own blood. "Y-Yeah, Benji. Lincoln. Thanks. See ya l-later."

Howard inspected his Glock 17 and crouched before James. Repulsed by the man's actions, it was all Howard could do to stop himself from stomping on the man's face and killing him stone dead.

Every subtle movement of his arms and legs caused James to screech in pain. "Umma, um, my—ugh, I c-can't f-feel my l-legs. I th-think my nose is b-broke."

"I don't give a goddamn shit how much pain you're in, Gilmour," Howard seethed. "Try asking Danny, and

Knocktoe, and my Dad how they feel about your sob stories—"

"—It was an accident."

Howard screamed into the man's face. "Try telling that to them. They're not even around anymore to argue with you."

Clitch.

James knew the metallic snapping sound all-too well; it came from a Glock 17's safety catch sliding free in Howard's hands.

"P-Please, Howie, I n-never—"

"—Don't call me *Howie*. Only two sets of people in my life get to call me that, now. My family, and my friends. And you're neither—"

"—I'm sorry," James shrieked at the top of his lungs, one of which sounded like it might have burst.

"You killed my fucking father, you fuck."

James shifted around and yelped in pain. "Ngggg. *F-Fuck*. Howard, man, I s-swear, I didn't m-mean to kill him. I just w-wanted your bag—"

"—You shot him in the head."

"I h-had to."

"What happened? Tell me."

"I f-followed y-you. Parked up by the wall, waited f-for you t-to leave, and broke in," James said as his nostrils snored down to his throat. "He—he p-put up a h-helluva fight, your dad. Caught me r-right in the f-fucking eye. By then, he'd seen my face, so I h-had to—ugh, I never meant to shoot him, I s-swear to *God*."

James' chest expanded faster and faster, forcing his lungs to wheeze and chuck more blood over his tongue.

"Aww, look at me m-man. I'mma f-fuckin' m-mess."

Howard's heart filled with scorn as quickly as James' throat filled with his own blood. He watched on as the man started to fade away before his very eyes.

"H-Howard?"

"What."

"I n-need an ambulance, or s-something," James muttered. "I'm f-fucked, l-look at me."

"No. You're not getting an ambulance, Gilmour."

"P-Please, Howard?"

"There must be a dozen *Store-N-Gos* in the valley. Which one is the money at? The one by *The Y*?"

Unable to speak, James shook his head. "Nuh."

"The one by the Kaleidoscope?" Howard asked.

James shook his head once again, "N-Nuh—"

"—Oh, *shit*. It's not the one right around the corner from the goddamn bank, right?"

James nodded quickly and tried to speak, but couldn't. He coughed up a wad of bloodied phlegm and spat it on his legs.

"Y-Yeah."

"Madhoff Avenue?"

"Yeah, m-man."

Howard rose to his feet and pointed the Glock 17 at his forehead. "Which locker?"

"If I t-tell you, you p-promise not t-to shoot m-me?"

Howard stared down at the puny man's pathetic face without mercy. "Which locker number is it?"

"P-Promise not t-to shoot m-me?"

Howard thrust the gun three inches away from the man's head. "No. It's just a risk you're gonna have to take."

"Whu-whu—"

"—But you have a chance, now, to make good on the shit you just pulled on us, you backstabbing piece of shit," Howard spat. "Now, tell me the locker number."

"Ngggggggg—"

"—Stop squealing like a fucking *goat* and tell me the locker number."

"Okay, okay," James grunted, finally accepting his fate. "Seven, zero, six."

"Seven-oh-six?" Howard repeated, suspiciously.

"Yeah, it's all there. All the b-bags, all the c-cash."

Howard lowered his gun, somewhat satisfied. "You're not lying to me, are you?"

Relieved, James thumped his chest to dilute the pain from his body. "No, I s-swear."

Howard relaxed his grip on the gun and believed what the dying man had said.

"Thanks, H-Howard, man. I'm s-sorry about what happened. B-But, you go there. Take Benjy and Lincoln and get them their m-money. It's yours."

"You're goddamn right it's fucking *ours*," Howard chuckled, poisonously. "I'll make sure I get what's mine, and that Cherry and Mumford get their cut, too. And I'm gonna take a slice out of your take and make sure Amos' family gets some, as well. Seven-oh-six, right?"

"Y-Yuh, yeah."

Howard paused for a second, and then whipped his gun at his father's murderer's face a final time.

Shocked, James held his right hand over his face and screamed. "Huh?"

"When you get to where you're going, tell my father you're sorry, asshole."

"What?" James gasped and squealed for his life. "No, Howard, p-please—"

Howard pulled the trigger and blew the traitor's brains out all over the brick wall. The spent bullet ricocheted off the walls and splashed into a puddle as Howard emptied five more bullets into James' chest and abdomen.

James' corpse slumped onto its side, leaving Howard to assess his work, and move away from where he'd been standing.

His work was done.

He felt nothing as he watched the nostrils on James' face blow dark red bubbles into the murky puddle.

There was little in the way of conversation between Lincoln and Ben as they waited in the white Ford Escort.

A dark figure moved out from the underpass and caught Ben's attention. "Here he comes."

Howard hadn't bothered to conceal his Glock 17. He traipsed forward in a daze, steadying his path toward the car.

Lincoln checked his rear view mirror as he started the engine. "He killed James, right? He definitely shot him dead."

Ben covered his face with his right hand, obfuscating any view Howard might have. "Yeah. I dunno. He looks like he's just seen a ghost. Put your seatbelt on."

Clunk-click.

Lincoln leaned forward seconds after fastening his belt and checked his side mirror. "You said James said someone was following you, back in the Jeep?"

"Yeah. He was getting paranoid. Now we know why."

Ben was on the verge of freaking out.

The dark street kept both he and Lincoln ill at ease as Howard opened the back door and climbed into the car.

Whump.

Howard pulled the door shut and examined his Glock 17. He had just a few bullets left in the magazine.

Ben dared to look up at the bereaved man in the back seat. "Sorry about your Dad, man."

Howard inspected his Glock 17 and bounced it in his palm. "Yeah. So am I."

Lincoln offered a pathetic and contrite smile, and allowed the tension to dilute for a moment.

"Gilmour stashed our cash at the *Secure-N-Go* on Madhoff," Howard said, struggling to come to terms with the cyclical irony of it all. "Right next to the goddamn bank, of all places."

"Seriously?" Lincoln asked.

"Yup. Locker number seven-oh-six. Talk about returning to the scene of the fucking crime."

"Hey, Howard?"

"Yeah?"

"Are you suggesting we go there *now?*"

Howard palmed the magazine shut and slipped it into his jacket pocket. "That's exactly what I'm suggesting, Mumford."

Ben bit his lip and had second thoughts. "I dunno, you know. I really dunno about this—"

"—Shut the fuck up, Cherry," Howard said. "First Amos, then Danny and Knocktoe. Then my father, and now Gilmour. No more dead bodies. I'm not going back home, there's no point."

Lincoln eyed the rear view mirror for a closer look at Howard's face. Seconds after his eyes landed on Howard's, he noticed a pair of headlights spring to life through the back window.

"Listen, Howard, man. I'm with you on this. But if the score is holed up at the storage place, then it's safe. Maybe we should chill out for a few days till the heat's off?"

"Mumford?"

"Yeah?"

"If the police find out who did this, where do you think they're gonna start raiding? After a pile-up of bodies and the Federal Bank's cash is gone, how far back do you think they're gonna retrace everyone's steps?"

Howard nodded at Jame's Jeep parked at the far end of the street.

"A corpse in the underpass? Tire tracks everywhere? This isn't the nineteen-seventies, the whole of the valley is under constant surveillance, twenty-four seven. That money is as good as gone if we don't get to Madhoff Avenue and take it right now."

Ben grimaced and closed his eyes. "He's right. It's now or never."

Howard leaned back, happy with his decision. "We just roll up at *Secure-N-Go*, take what's ours, split everything three ways, and run."

Lincoln struggled to come to terms with their predicament. "What? We split six hundred grand between us?"

"No, it's more like two-eighty divided between the three of us. More than half of the take was tied up in those negotiable bonds Knocktoe was gonna give to Jimmy the Fence. They're as good as gone."

"Shit."

"So, at two-eighty, it's just under one hundred grand each." Howard said. "Not ideal, and not exactly what we signed-up for, but it's better than nothing. And I don't give a shit. It's enough, at least, to get outta this godforsaken valley and start afresh."

Ben looked over his shoulder around, finally, to face the man with the master plan directly. "Leave Chrome Valley?"

"Uh-huh."

"Howard, I have a wife who's about to give birth, if you hadn't noticed. Lincoln has a family, and so do you."

"It's either go back home with four times our annual salary strapped to our backs, or not. Which would you rather?"

It was a hell of a dilemma to consider. Ben turned to Lincoln to find his attention drawn to the side mirror once again.

"For Christ's sake, Lincoln, what the hell are you looking at that's so interesting?"

"I ain't too sure. I think it's a middle-aged man and a woman. Unmarked car. Been there for fuckin' ages, you know."

"Huh?"

Howard turned to the back window and spotted the headlights blaring up the glass from a car parked further down the road. "What, *that* car?"

"Yeah. Beige Crown Victoria. Right up our asses, man."

Howard muttered angrily as he unfastened his seatbelt. "Right."

Lincoln waved his hand at the man as he booted the door open. "What? Howard, no, where are you going—?"

Howard stepped out of the car, elbowed the door shut, slipped his hand into his jacket pocket, and marched up the road with blood on his mind.

Ben sank into his seat as he watched Howard approach the vehicle. "The man's lost his fucking mind."

"I dunno if we wanna stay around for this," Lincoln said. "He's about to get our asses busted."

Howard slowed his pace as he made eye contact with the balding overweight man in his fifties wedged behind the steering wheel.

A brunette woman in a white shirt sat next to him. She looked away from Howard, and took an interest in the sidewalk.

Howard reached the driver's side window and knocked it with his knuckles.

Knock-knock-knock.

"Roll the window down."

The driver raised his eyebrows and shook his head.

Howard raised his voice and knocked again, making damn sure the driver could see his hand buried in his jacket pocket.

The pudgy man behind the wheel turned to the woman, who refused to look back.

"No. Don't look at her, you fat fuck. Roll the window down."

After a few seconds, the driver caved in, scrambled for the window button and pressed it down.

Click—whiiirrrr.

"Uh, yeah?" the man asked.

Howard kept his hand in his jacket and leaned in through the window. "Why are you following us?"

"What?"

Howard lost his temper and raised his voice. "I asked why are you following us?"

"Uh, w-we're not?"

The woman kept her focus on the sidewalk, and her head turned away.

"Hey, you. Lady," Howard said. "Look at me."

With great reluctance and concern, the woman turned to Howard. "What?"

"Why are you following us?"

"We're n-not following you," the driver said. "I swear."

"You're not one of 'em, are you?" Howard asked. "You're not a filthy pair of pigs waiting to pounce?"

"Ha," the man chuckled with fear. "Do we look like policemen?"

Howard grinned, evilly. "No," he said as he brushed the flap of his jacket enough to reveal his Glock 17 for the pair to see.

Both the woman and the driver gulped and tried to fend off their forthcoming heart attacks.

"So, if I see either of you pricks again, I'll blow your arms off. Okay?"

The pair nodded, somewhat relieved that the madman hadn't killed them. "O-Okay."

"Good. Now, pull off, and *fuck off*. You two lovebirds have a lovely evening."

Howard tapped the roof of the car, rolled his shoulders, and walked back to Lincoln's car, happy with a job well done.

The Crown Victoria pulled away from the side of the road and drove past Howard as he climbed back into Lincoln's car.

"Jeez, Howard," Ben heaved. "Have you lost your goddamn mind?"

The blood-red glare from the taillights on the Crown Victoria drifted across Howard's eyeballs as he watched it disappear up the road.

"That's a dangerous question to ask me right now, Benjy."

Lincoln breathed a sigh of relief. "They weren't cops?"

Howard squeezed his eyes shut as he spoke. "No. Well, they said they weren't, anyway."

"I hope to God you're right."

Howard fastened his seatbelt and punched his hands together. "It doesn't matter if they were, anyhow. If they're really following us, then they're waiting for us to take them to the money. And we're not gonna disappoint them. And if they're not filthy, squealing pigs, then we're in the clear."

"For now, at least," Ben added.

Lincoln thumped the steering wheel in a fit of bewildered exasperation. "Shit, man, if they *was* following us—"

"—*Were* following us," Howard interrupted. "Not *was*. Get your subjunctives right."

"—Now ain't the time to be correctin' my goddamn fuckin' English, Howie," Lincoln yelped in a haze of helplessness. "Man, if they *were* cops, then they were following James' Jeep, and thanks to your *Dirty Harry* shit back there, they're probably onto *my* ride, now."

Ben shifted in his seat and tutted. "You want us to go get our money now? Howard?"

"That's right, Benjy," came the cool-as-a-cucumber response from the back seat.

"Really? After everything that's gone down? I dunno about this, Howard. I really don't know."

Howard lost his patience and kicked the back of Ben's seat. "Benjy, we're fucked if the cops are watching us. So, we have three options left to choose from. One, we get arrested. Two, we get our money, and then get arrested."

"And the third?"

"Three, we go get our money and *don't* get arrested because the cops weren't following us."

The two men up front considered their options and felt like bursting into tears.

"Fuck it," Lincoln said. "Option three, man. Let's go get our paper."

Now outvoted two-to-one, Ben hung his head down and regretted the day he was born. "Aww, *fuck*."

"Atta boy, Benjy," Howard grinned and patted the pair on their shoulders. "Good doggy. C'mon, gentlemen. Let's *fetch* what's rightfully ours and finish this."

Chapter 18

Store-N-Go Storage Facility
— Lombardy Street / Madhoff Avenue —
<u>Chrome Valley Financial District</u>

To Howard, tonight felt as if it was all going to end where it had started.

The fire hydrant on the sidewalk reminded Ben of where they'd parked at eleven-thirty this morning, right before they entered the bank.

It was now 11:15 pm, according to the dashboard clock; almost twelve hours since they'd robbed the bank across the street.

"Ha," Howard chuckled. "What a difference a day makes, eh?"

"Shut up, you madman," Ben snapped. "Just stop speaking."

Lincoln caught the *Ammo Domini* gun shop in the corner of his eye, which provided a none-too-subtle reminder that they were close to their destination.

The whole financial district had been secured and cleaned. Now, it resembled a derelict ghost town, consigned to the history books of having hosted one of Chrome Valley's most deadliest heists.

"We just passed the gun shop. Man, look at this place. It's as if nothing ever happened," Lincoln whispered. "It's a little *too* quiet, you know."

He was right.

There was nobody around.

No vehicles to be seen.

And nobody was following them, which provided some comfort to the three men about to turn off Lombardy Street, and into a parking lot a few meters up Madhoff Avenue.

The brightly-lit and imposing *Store-N-Go* building loomed at the far end of the parking lot. Its walls were made of glass, revealing three levels of what looked to be hundreds of lockers.

A huge, red neon sign *Store-N-Go* sign illuminated the covered entrance several feet below.

The Ford Escort was the only car in the lot as it circled around and parked in a disabled bay, three spots away from the glass-covered entrance.

Lincoln hit the brakes, and switched off the ignition.

"You got your pieces on you?" Howard said.

"Yeah," Ben replied. "Hey, shouldn't we mask up?"

Howard scoffed and chuckled, evilly. "With what, Cherry? Your socks? Your stupid *Space Invaders* socks?"

"Hey, that's not funny."

"The masks and balaclavas were trashed back at the rendezvous."

Ben stammered at the thought of having to walk into the place. "No, you know, I mean—uh, *shit.* I dunno what I mean, anymore."

"Relax," Howard said. "We can't go in there all masked-up and demand to get in, and risk causing more trouble than we're already in."

"Yeah, man," Lincoln said. "Five-oh's itchy-trigger-fingered enough looking for the bastards who emptied the bank."

"Exactly," Howard said. "So, we walk in, make up some shit about forgetting our ID, or whatever. They let us in, we grab our stuff, and we go. If they don't, we go brute force with our pieces."

Ben closed his eyes and cursed to himself. "Christ, not *again*."

"Benjy, if we play this right then we won't even need to *persuade* them, okay?"

Lincoln nodded. "Yeah, straightforward. In and out."

"A bit of the ol' *in-and-out*," Howard sniggered as he performed his best Droog impression. "No? *A Clockwork Orange*?"

Neither of his two accomplices found the joke very funny, and so kept quiet, concentrating more on the second robbery they were about to pull off.

"Fucking philistines. Ah, whatever. C'mon, let's go."

***

A chirpy muzak rendition of Elvis Presley's *Jailhouse Rock* played through the wall speakers in the *Store-N-Go* reception area.

A young man named Bernie, as evidenced by his bright, red name badge, sat behind the reception desk busying himself on the main computer terminal.

To his left, a security guard named Peter guarded the door that led to the hundreds of lockers on all three levels.

Bored out of his mind, Peter felt around his hip to ensure his firearm was in place, and then folded his arms. "Ugh, I hate this damn song."

"That's a shame," Bernie said without looking up from his computer.

"Hey, Bernie?"

"What is it, Peter? Can't you see I'm busy?"

"You hear about the heist at the Federal, this morning?"

Bernie kept on working, offering his colleague approximately five percent of his attention. "*Yeeees*, Peter."

"Turned into a bloodbath. People got shot and killed."

"Mmmmm."

"Yeah, they were dressed animals, I heard. A rabbit, dog, goat, *chicken*—I think one of 'em was a gerbil, but I can't remember."

Bernie sniggered to himself. "A gerbil? What a pain in the ass that must've been."

Peter nodded, failing to get the crude reference. "Yeah. Oh, plus, there's a rumor going around that it was an inside job."

Bernie couldn't have been less enthusiastic if he'd tried. "Is there really?"

"Yeah," Peter said. "They must be halfway outta the country by now, whoever did it."

"Well, they'd be fools if they hung around," Bernie said. "Chrome Valley is the safest place in the world right now with the pigs on high alert. Only a fool would stick around and try to cause more trouble, tonight."

Beep-boop.

Bernie looked from his monitor and saw three men walk through the double doors. "Ah. Welcome to *Store-N-Go*. How may I help you?"

Howard kept his friendly grin on his face as he arrived at the counter. "Hi. I was wondering if you could help us?"

Ben and Lincoln followed behind Howard, and immediately caught Peter's attention. The pair seemed to be more staid and apprehensive than their friend who spoke to the receptionist.

"Certainly, sir. How can I help?"

Howard's award-worthy performance seemed to be working a treat on the man behind the counter.

"Yeah, the thing is, I do actually have an account, but I've forgotten my details, and I've left my card at home."

"Oh, that's no problem, sir," Bernie said. "Do you have the Store-N-Go app? You can download it and use it to gain entry."

Howard rapped his knuckles on the desk and sighed. "Oh, uh—no. No, I'm not very good with phones and apps and all that stuff. Could you just let me in? I'll only be a few seconds."

Lincoln raced over to the giant transparent wall that overlooked the parking lot. A wave of relief swept across his face when he saw that the lot was still empty.

"Can I help you, sir?" Peter asked Lincoln, who turned back to him with a pained expression on his face.

"Oh, uh, no. Sorry, I was just checking my car."

"Okay."

A hassled Howard pointed to the computer behind the desk. "Is it possible you could look up my details on the system?"

"Sure, let's go old school, shall we?"

"Okay, yes. Good."

"Your name?"

"It's, uh, James Gilmour. With a *u*," Howard said as he watched Bernie type the name on his keyboard. "My, uh parents were Irish."

"Ah, yes," Bernie said. "We have you on the system. Can I have the first line of your address and date of birth, please, Mr. Gilmour?"

Howard's breathing quickened.

He hadn't the first idea of the answer to either of those questions.

Ben's ears pricked up at Bernie's question, prompting him to slip his hand into his jacket. "Shit."

Peter stepped forward with his arms folded and cast a stern eye in Ben's direction. "Are you feeling okay, sir? You look a little pensive?"

Ben gulped and lifted his hand away from his pocket. "Oh, no. I just need the bathroom. We, uh, had tacos for dinner. You know how it is."

Peter took Ben's rickety explanation badly. "Yeah. I know."

"Uh-huh."

Bernie waved at the catatonic-looking Howard for a response. "Mr. Gilmour?"

"Uh, yeah?"

"First line of your address and date of birth, please?"

Howard feigned a chuckle and began to sweat as he realized his plan wasn't going to work. "Oh, yes. It's—uh, oh. I've just moved," he stammered like a babbling moron trying to snatch his luck out of thin air. "Sorry. It's one-ten, uh, King... *Street?*"

"King Street, you say?"

Bernie typed the address on the keyboard and hit the return key. "Hmm, no. Sorry. We don't appear to have—"

"—Y-Yes, as I said," Howard said. "I just moved house, so, uh—."

"—There isn't a King Street in Chrome Valley, sir," Bernie said, before launching into a characteristically sarcastic quip. "Why don't we try your date of birth? You haven't changed that, too, have you?"

"Oh, ha. No, no, I haven't."

"Well?"

Howard felt his heart climb into his throat as he racked his brains for anything James may have revealed in the past. "Uh, June... *first?* Nineteen-eighty—"

Ben's eyes nearly popped out of their sockets when he saw Howard getting the year of James' birth completely wrong. "Oh, shit—" he mouthed at Lincoln, as he reached into his pocket.

"Huh?"

"No, no—" Ben snapped as Bernie read the result on the screen. "Umm."

Lincoln reached into his pocket just as quick as Ben had done and stormed over to Peter.

"Fuck's sake, man."

Bernie scrunched his face, knowing something was rotten with Howard. "I'm sorry, sir. Are you seriously expecting me to believe you don't know you're own date of—"

Howard whipped his Glock 17 out of his jacket and aimed it at the Bernie's face. "*Shut it.*"

"Oh, shit."

"Open the door, asshole. *Now.* Or your mother's gonna need a closed casket funeral."

Bernie soiled his pants and lifted his arms. "P-Please, Mr. Gilmour. Don't shoot—"

"—Aww, no, I never told you to put your hands up, you fucking idiot," Howard yelped. " Just open the damn door to the fucking lockers. Do it."

Ben pointed his Glock at Peter, who was nanoseconds away from clutching his firearm. "I wouldn't do that if I were you, asshole. Get your hands up."

Peter did as instructed and put his hands in the air.

Ben shooed the guard away from the door, and pointed his gun at the floor. "On your knees. *Do it.*"

Bzzzz.

Bernie pressed the button for the locker entry door, which unbolted and swayed out.

"Yes!" Howard screamed, and then aimed his gun at Bernie. "Stand up, you little shit. Get over here."

Peter slowly fell to his knees with his hands behind his head.

Lincoln raced up to him and retrieved the firearm from the man's holster. "Got it," he said, before turning to Howard and *almost* calling him by his real name. "Uh, *Rabbit?*"

Howard instinctively turned to the entrance to the lockers and smiled at Lincoln. "Yeah, *Squirrel?*

Peter heard the unusual names and put two-and-two together in his mind. "Oh, *wow.*"

Howard shoved Bernie onto the floor, next to Peter, and yelled at Ben. "Dog?"

"Yeah, Rabbit?"

"Keep an eye on our two girlfriends, here. We're gonna go do our *thing.*"

A rush of pure adrenaline shot through Ben's veins, forcing his face to heat up with excitement as he aimed his gun aimed at his two terrified hostages.

"*Stay*. Good boys."

Lincoln held his Glock 17 in his right hand as he led the charge along the first floor corridor; a seemingly endless white wall containing scores of opened red doors to each of the lockers.

Howard as he caught up to him in the hasty search for their locker. "Hey, wait."

He turned left and faced his reflection on the glass wall. The huge lamps in each corner of the parking lot illuminated Lincoln's Ford Escort, and every empty bay stacking up to the entrance gate.

"C'mon," Lincoln said. "Seven-oh-six, right?"

"Right."

"Check the numbers."

Locker 120… 130… 140…

The doors on the unoccupied lockers on the first level were all slightly ajar.

"Shit, seven-oh-six must be on the upper levels, or something," Lincoln barked. "Over there. Staircase."

Howard raced past Lincoln and clutched his left arm. "Ugh, this sucks."

"What?"

"Nothing, I'll be okay. I can feel it seeping through again."

"Feel what seeping through?"

"My arm," Howard said. "It's killing me. But never mind that, let's just find this damn locker and get going."

Both men reached the end of the corridor, pushed past the fire escape door, and up the staircase…

Back in reception, Ben kept an eye on Bernie and Peter. An intermittent sheen of red light folded across both men's heads.

"Where's that coming from?"

A lone security light had come to life a few feet above the door. The bulb inside spun around and around, the source of the red light that blasted along the walls.

"What the hell is that?"

"It's the warning light," Bernie said. "If the door's been opened without a registered user, it sets off the alarm."

Ben gasped and turned his gun to Bernie's face. "Make it stop."

"I can't stop it," came the muted response. "It's automatic."

Ben pushed his gun further into the man's face. "It better not alert the fucking police, though."

"No," Bernie lied. "It's just a precaution. It's to alert security in the building."

Ben wasn't so sure. He slipped his free hand into his jeans pocket and pulled out his cell phone. "You better not be lying to me, asshole."

"I swear. He ain't lying," Peter said. "It's cool."

Unsure, Ben held his phone to his face as the call was answered. "Hey, Howar—uh, *Rabbit*?"

"Yeah?"

"Some alarm has gone off, man," Ben snapped. "No police, but it kicked off when you got in."

"I know, I can hear it. How are our two friends back there?"

"They're cool. Did you find the locker yet?"

"No, we're on the second floor, now. There must be a thousand doors, here. But we'll find it. Stay on the line."

Ben scowled at the two men and cleared his throat. "Okay."

The second floor looked just like the first; miles and miles of bright white wall with at least ten feet between each red door.

754… 752… 750…

"Okay, we're in the sevens, now," Lincoln said as he counted each one on his way past. "These ones are smaller."

"Who the hell designed this place? Stevie fucking Wonder?" Howard snapped as he raced along the series of red doors. "It's all ass-backwards."

Lincoln called the numbers on the doors out as he jogged past them. "Seven-sixteen, seven-fourteen—"

"—Stay on the line, Dog," Howard said into his phone as he walked up the corridor. "Hey, Lincoln, how are we gonna get inside it when we find it?"

"I dunno."

Ben's concerned-sounding voice came out of Howard's phone and into his ear.

"Uh, Rabbit?"

"Ben, wait, we're almost there. Hold on."

Lincoln arrived at Locker #706 and chuckled. The metal door was locked, and showed no signs of an easy entry without the key card.

"Got it. It's here."

"Good," Howard said, and returned to his phone. "Okay, Dog. We've found it."

"Okay, but—"

"—It's locked, and we don't have the key card. Get that speccy little shit with the stupid face to open seven-oh-six. If he gives you any shit, put a bullet in his brain."

Back in reception, Howard's instruction fell on deaf ears. Ben was more preoccupied with the view of the parking lot, and a beige Ford Crown Victoria driving past the entrance gate. "Uh, Howard?"

"What?"

Ben raced over to the reception desk and took cover behind Bernie's swivel chair.

"Shit. Shit. Do you see that? In the parking lot."

"What are you talking about?"

"Shit. Someone's coming."

Howard glanced at his phone, and then turned to the window overlooking the lot. Sure enough, the same beige Crown Victoria that had been following them for the night made its way across the disabled bays, and up to Lincoln's Ford Escort.

Howard pointed at the window and bopped on Lincoln's back. "Fuck. *Fuck.*"

"What?"

"Down there. Look."

Lincoln raced over to the window and gasped. "Oh, shit."

Without pausing to think, he took out his Glock 17 and pointed it at the handle on locker #706. "No time for that four-eyed prick downstairs to open it for us, stand back."

"Lincoln, what are you doing?"

"Stand back."

"No, Lincoln," Howard said. "You'll set off the damn alarm if you shoot—"

"—Rabbit, man, some guy and a girl just got out of that car. They're coming—"

"—Ben," Howard yelped into his phone. "Get out of there."

Lincoln turned away as he fired two shots at the locker.

Bang-bang-spatch.

The handle busted off the door, producing a cloud of smoke, orange sparks… and a vicious-sounding alarm.

Drrrriiiiiiinnng.

Howard screamed and covered his ears as Lincoln ran forward and drop-kicked the door.

Boot.

The door flung inwards and crashed against the inside wall. "We're in, come on."

"What's that noise? What's going on?"

Howard ran into the locker and screamed over the ear-screeching alarm. "Ben, get up here. Now."

Ben jumped out from behind the reception desk and raced over to the locker corridor. He tucked his cell phone under his cheek as he threatened the two men with his gun.

"Stay where you are."

Howard's hurried voice blasted out of Ben's cell phone. *We're on the second floor. Get up here, now.*

"I'm coming, Rabbit," Ben spat. "I'm coming."

"*Rabbit?*" Peter asked. "All these animal names. Oh, shit! *You're* the guys who ripped the bank off?"

Ben's heels skidded across the floor as he stopped to answer the man. "What? No."

"Fuck yeah, it *is* you. Rabbit? Squirrel? And you're the Dog?"

Ben scanned the entrance to the building, and saw the same woman and man that had been following them from earlier. Both drew their firearms as they made their way across the parking lot.

"No I am not."

Peter could barely contain his excitement. "Aww, dude. You guys are fuckin' *awesome*, man. Sticking it to the *man*, man. Hell, yeah, fuck the corporate bank bloodsuckers, man."

"Shut the hell up," Ben snapped. "You don't know shit. It wasn't us."

Bernie whispered through his closed lips and prayed his colleague would shut up. "Be quiet. You're gonna get us shot."

Peter winked at Ben, knowingly. "Hey, dude. It's cool. Your secret's safe with me, man."

"I said shut up."

"Yeah, you guys are fucking *heroes* to us nine-to-fivers, man. "

Ben couldn't help but smirk at the revelation that he and his friends may have gained cult status without them realizing it.

"What, *really*?"

"Yeah, dude. You guys are *the shit*."

Ben booted Peter in the stomach in an attempt to back out of any undue attention.

"Oww."

"Well it wasn't us. So, stop talking, dickhead. I mean it."

Before Peter could get back up, Ben had disappeared into the corridor, just as the woman and overweight man entered the building.

Lincoln and James ran into Locker #706.

Much like the corridor, the interior walls of the locker were a light beige and utterly without feature.

"There they are," Lincoln said. "Bingo."

Five *ProState* sports bags stuffed with cash lay in the middle of the room, just waiting to be taken.

"Fuckin' James Gilmour. Useless, back-stabbing prick."

Lincoln shifted forward on his knees as he tossed two of the sports bags over his shoulder.

"Howard, he brought all the bags here. There's, like, a bunch of money in one bag, and a bunch in another."

Howard's eyes grew as he witnessed Lincoln reach into the first bag and pull out James' shotgun. "Well, well, well, he even kept his pump-action."

Howard dropped to his knees, bit down on his gun, and grabbed the heaviest of the five bags. "Gummon, engtie guh vag."

"Huh?"

Furious, Howard spat his gun onto his knees and shouted over the alarm. "Come on. Empty the bag. Three equally, and let's get the hell outta this shit hole."

"Oh! Yeah, I know that."

"Put all the cash in this one."

Lincoln unzipped the second bag, lifted it up, and tipped it upside down.

Stacks and stacks of bills wrapped in rubber bands plummeted down and spread about within the bag in Howard's hands. "Is that all of it?"

"Yeah."

"Good. Come on, we need to run."

"I'm going as fast as I can, man."

"*Go faster.*"

Lincoln emptied the second and third bag into Howard's. The latter reached over and pulled the zipper along the two flaps and sealed it shut.

"Okay, that's three bags."

Lincoln strapped his bag across his chest and rose to his feet. "Yeah. I got mine, you got yours and Ben's. Let's go."

Howard grabbed the first bag's strap and wound it over his head, and across his chest. He reached for the second bag, and grabbed it in his left hand.

Lincoln jumped out of the locker and pressed his hands against the huge window overlooking the parking lot. "Ohhhh, *shit.*"

Howard raced up behind him and nearly puked when he saw what Lincoln had seen. "What the—Ohh, *shiiit.*"

Dozens of police vehicles bolted through the gates and dispersed in all directions. A powerful beam from a helicopter crashed through the crowd below, banked across the police vehicles, and across the giant, windowed Store-N-Go front.

Lincoln pushed Howard against the white wall. "Fuck, get back."

Ben raced along the corridor with his Glock 17 in both hands. "Hey, guys."

"Ben, get down," Lincoln yelled. "Goddamn five-oh all over this goddamn place."

Howard clutched his left arm. Fortunately for him, the sports bag on his back cushioned the impact when he was thrown against the wall.

"Quick," he snapped. "The fire escape."

He threw the second sports bag into Ben's chest. "This is yours, I believe."

Ben caught it and produced a brief grin of victory. "Thanks, man."

Just then, a swarm of armed officers snaked around the cars fifty feet below. The helicopter lowered and blasted its lights across the second level of the building, lighting the three men up like a startled Christmas tree.

"This is the Chrome Valley Police Department. Drop your weapons, and get on your knees, carefully, with your hands behind your heads."

Lincoln used one hand to pump his shotgun. "Aww. *Fuck you.*"

Just as he was about to take aim, a bullet rocketed across the length of the corridor and struck Ben in his left knee.

"Gah," he shrieked as he tumbled back and fell to the ground in agony. "M-My l-leg—"

"—Lincoln," Howard screamed. "Get down."

"What?"

He turned to the far end of the corridor to see an overweight plain-clothed officer firing at him. The young woman with him hid behind the corner of the main staircase with her gun drawn.

Effectively trapped, Ben and Howard froze still, and watched as Lincoln swung his gun at the man firing at him. "Eat lead, you fat fuck."

Blam—blam—spatch.

The first shot crashed into the wall behind the man's head.

The second hit him in his over-sized belly.

Lincoln ejected the spent bullet, pumped the shotgun, and chambered a fresh round. "Hey, lady?"

"Yeah?" came a stern but concerned voice from behind the corner.

"I killed your chubby buddy, just there. Shot him in the gut. You wanna join him?"

"Drop your weapon and get on the floor," she said. "Don't make me come out there."

Lincoln backed up to Howard with his shotgun aimed at the corner. "I got a better idea, lady. Why don't *you* haul your white ass out here and drop *your* gun?"

"The whole building is surrounded," she said. "There's no way out. We know who you are. All of you. Just give up now before you make things even worse for yourselves."

Ben screamed for dear life as he rolled across his own blood splattered up the floor. "Ugh, ugh, my l-leg. H-He hit me in the f-fuckin' l-leg, man."

"Come out, you stupid bitch," Lincoln yelled. "Show your face."

The woman made the mistake of peering around the corner for a glimpse at the monster she was dealing with. The instant Lincoln saw the bangs on her forehead, he pulled on the trigger and blasted her in the face.

The back of her head exploded and vomited the contents of her skull against the wall.

"Ha. *Gotcha.*"

She dropped her gun as her body somersaulted on the spot and crashed to the ground, dead.

"Goddamn fuckin', stinkin'-ass racist motherfuckers, man. I swear, they need killing. And my black ass is only *too fuckin' happy* to oblige."

Howard draped Ben's left arm around his neck and helped him to his feet. "Ben, you're gonna be fine. Lincoln?"

"Just call me Mister fucking *Cop Killer*," Lincoln growled as he slotted a fresh round into the chamber of his shotgun. "When I woke up this morning, I was a nobody. Now, I got at least five fuckin' murders under my belt, and a hundred fuckin' thousand bills strapped on my back. Not a bad day's work."

"Lincoln? Fire exit."

Howard went to turn around and carry Ben to freedom, but stopped in his tracks when he heard the sound of a pump action shotgun belonging to the angry man who'd just reloaded.

"Fellas?"

Howard exhaled and closed his eyes, and turned to face Lincoln, who threatened him and Ben with his gun.

"Gimme your bags, gentlemen."

"What?"

"I said give me your fucking bags, you pair of cracker-ass faggots. Do it."

Howard's soul evaporated into his feet at the bare-faced deception. "You bastard."

"Yeah, and don't ever forget it," Lincoln snorted. "Gimme your bags."

Ben squealed like a petulant child, half in pain, and half in utter disappointment. "Lincoln? Y-You f-fuckin' prick."

Howard wanted to raise his right hand and blast Lincoln in the face, but knew if he tried that he'd got shot and killed. Besides, he thought, none of this was worth it anymore.

Furious, Howard unfastened the strap, pulled the bag away from his back, and chucked it at Lincoln. "Back-stabbing prick."

"Nah, this ain't nothing but free market economics," Lincoln said. "Yours, too, Benjy-boy."

"Take it."

Ben threw his bag at the man, who caught it and wound the straps on both to his left hand. With his own take strapped to his back, and two more in his hand, all Lincoln Mumford had to do was head for the fire escape and escape to freedom.

"Get in the fucking locker."

The lights from the helicopter drifted across the window.

"I repeat, this is the Chrome Valley Police Department. Drop your weapons, and get on the floor with your hands behind your head."

Lincoln barged past Howard and Ben and made for the far end of the corridor.

"Well, *shit*, boys. This is where I say goodbye. Sorry it had to come to this, but, you know, what good are we when we fail to take the opportunities presented to us. Ain't that right, Ross?"

"No, *Mumford*," Howard snapped, desperate for blood. "It *ain't* right. At all."

Lincoln saluted the men as he walked backwards. "Nice idea about the fire escape, Ross. I think I'll take you up on it—"

Bang—Splatt.

Ben's chest exploded, having been hit by a bullet coming from the main staircase at the far end of the corridor.

"Gaaoooww," he screamed and slumped into Howard's arms.

"G-Guuuh, H-Howard-d-d."

Lincoln lifted his shotgun and blasted the armed officer who'd shot Ben as he entered the walkway.

"For fuck's sake, won't these white pigs ever learn?"

The first armed officer's neck burst open as the bullet sliced through it and hit the back wall. The man fell face-first to the ground, creating a blockade for the swarm of officers racing up behind his corpse.

Lincoln pumped his shotgun and fired over and over again. "Goddamn fuckin' filthy pigs, yo' can suck my *dick*."

Howard had no choice but to pull the screaming Ben's back against his chest and use him as a bullet shield.

"Walk with me, quick."

Ben vomited a fountain of blood down his chest as he staggered back with Howard. "Nuh-nuh—I c-can't b-breathe—"

Bam—bam—bam.

Most of the return fire from the armed police caught Ben in the chest, puncturing through his chest, torso and stomach. The flesh on his right leg burst through the skin as Howard dragged him back.

"Guh—guh," Ben struggled. "G-Go without m-me."

"No, I'm not going without you—"

"—Take c-care of B-Brianna f-for—"

"—Shut the fuck up, Benjy, you can take care of her yourself."

Howard hoisted the man up and took cover as he turned to Lincoln, who pumped his shotgun and kept firing.

"This is all *your* fault."

"Shut the fuck up and help me take these motherfuckers down, you stank-ass piece of shit banker."

Howard kept Ben in front of him with his left arm and squealed as he opened fire with his Glock 17 in his right hand. "Nyaarrggghh."

Ben's weight pulled at Howard's bullet wound as he and Lincoln stepped back and kept shooting.

Three bullets whizzed past Howard's head from the end of the corridor. He wrenched Ben up just in time for one of them to hit the young man in the forehead.

Ben slumped in Howard's arms, dead.

"Aww, nooo," Howard said through his suffering. "No, no more, I c-can't—"

"—Shut the fuck up and kill these pigs, man."

A rancid stench of death and asphalt lifted into Howard's nostrils and tugged at his brain. The struggle to keep Ben's corpse upright for use as a bullet shield proved to be near-impossible.

Ben's corpse absorbed the onslaught of bullets and threatened to break apart in Howard's arms.

Then, Howard turned to Lincoln, and spotted his opportunity.

Instead of firing back at the police, Howard raised his Glock 17 at Lincoln, who was too busy reloading his shotgun to notice.

The sight at the end of the Glock 17 gun slid from right to left in Howard's right eye, before landing on Lincoln's temple.

He pulled on the trigger and yelped.

Blam—schplat.

The side of Lincoln's head burst open, sending fragments of brain and skull splashing against the walled glass.

"Gotcha, you back-stabbing fuck."

Lincoln took three steps back, confused, and fired a shot at the officers at the far end of the corridor. It would prove to be the final, most useful thing he'd done all day for Howard.

"Gah!"

A pile of dead bodies blocked the staircase at the far end of the second level. Howard dropped Ben's corpse to the ground and clutched his left arm in agony.

"Ngggg, goddamn it."

Lincoln blinked hard and wondered where he was.

Clang.

He dropped the shotgun to the floor, stumbled back, and threw Howard a shit-eating grin as he felt around the smoking cavity in his head with his fingers. "You sh-shot me—" he said as his eyes rolled up into the back of what little remained of his head.

"Uh, yeah."

"N-Nice sh-shot, Howard, m-m-m-maaaa-aaan."

Whump.

Lincoln staggered back and fell to the ground, dead, in a puddle of his own blood.

The gunfire had stopped - for now.

Howard dropped to his knees and scrambled over to Lincoln's legs. He grabbed the two bags from the corpse's still-warm hand and tugged at the third bag strapped to his chest.

"Ah, shit, shit, *shit*. Come on."

Rumble-rumble.

The sound of hurried, murderous footsteps rumbled along the walls, forcing the floor to shake around.

The police were seconds away.

Howard exhaled and released his grip on the third bag strapped to Lincoln's body.

He faced a peculiar dilemma; make a run for the exit, or risk sticking around to remove the third bag and having the approaching officers catch him.

"Fuck it."

He chose the first option, shoved Lincoln's body aside, and stumbled to his feet.

"Freeze, asshole."

Howard screamed as he ran as fast as his feet could carry him.

Bang-bang-bang.

It was a miracle that none of the bullets caught him in the back as he ran towards the fire exit door.

The big, red exit to freedom grew larger and larger the faster he ran. The two, heavy sports bags in his left hand slowed him down, but he kept on running for dear life.

The helicopter banked to the right, and opened fire across the window as Howard ran for his life.

Thraaaa-aaaa-aaaaaat.

Two concurrent canons unleashed a dual stream of thousands of bullets that smashed through the glass and sprayed the locker walls from right to left, chasing Howard as he ran.

Thraa-a-tat-a-smaaashh.

Howard squeezed his Glock 17 and screamed as the bullet storm from the helicopter thrashed inches behind him as he ran across the corridor.

"Yaarrgghhhhhh—"

Howard smashed his left elbow into the fire exit door, pushed through, and slammed it shut behind him, sealing him from the bullet riddled second floor.

Howard's banshee scream of anguish from the impact on his wound crashed around the cold, dark staircase.

"*Goddamn* it. *Fuck*."

Howard caught his breath, shook his head, and jumped down the stairs two-at-a-time.

"Uh, uh, uh."

Tears of pain blew across his face as he jumped the last few steps and arrived at the first floor.

Rumble—rumble.

More footsteps and sound of heavy artillery pounded at the stone walls surrounding him within the humid throat of the fire escape.

Just then, Howard felt his lungs heave, and an impending bout of hyperventilation. He burst into tears and went to descend the final set of stairs.

Something made his hand reached into his pocket and take out his cell phone. He climbed onto the first step and swiped the screen.

He hit the call button just as an array of muffled voices from what felt like heaven itself encouraged the scores of officers to tear the place apart.

"Multiple officers hit. Advance all levels. Go, go, go."

Howard licked the dryness away from his lips as he carried the two sports bags down the first series of steps.

Then, Miranda's voice erupted from his palm. "Howard?"

He burst into tears as he made his way down each step in pain. "Y-Yeah, it's m-me—"

"—My God, where are you? What the Hell is going on?"

"Listen, I—"

"—Are you in a tunnel? Christ, have you seen the news? The bank. It got robbed earlier this—"

"—Y-Yuh, I know," Howard cried. "M-Miranda?"

Her voice changed to that of immediate sympathy and concern. "Howie, what the hell is happening? Where are you? Christ, say something, Howie."

"Are y-you at your mom's?"

Her voice drifted into a knowing reaction of horror. "Yeah, and Bonnie knows to go there when she's home. Howie?"

"Nggggg, f-fuck," he struggled as he hit the bottom step amid the God-like thunder of hell erupting around him. "M-Miranda?"

The call went silent as she waited for him to speak. Howard knew that she knew something truly terrible was happening, and that this could be their last phone call.

Her voice broke as she attempted to fend off the inevitable explanation.

"No, Howie," she said. "No, d-don't you dare, okay? Don't you *dare*—"

"—I'm s-so sorry."

His plea echoed up the endless series of stairs, bounced off the walls, and melded into the dull instruction seeping through the walls of his new tomb.

"Fire escape, all units. Go, go, go."

"What's that noise, Howard? Just tell me everything is okay, okay?"

He coughed away into a temporary streak of confidence and dignity. "Tell Bunni I love her, okay? I, uh, and—umm, tell her I'm sorry. God, I'm so sorry."

Miranda didn't have the nerve to say anything. Utterly traumatized, Howard glanced at the fire exit door and coughed into his hand.

"I did it for y-you, and for her, and I've f-fucked up so bad," he said, before crying up a storm. "But I g-got the money, Miranda. I got the money. *I fucking got the money.*"

He went to grab the bar across the door and chucked the first of the two bags by his foot.

Spatch.

When the underside of the bag hit the floor, the flaps opened and sneezed an ocean of red dye up his shirt, neck and face.

"Ugh."

Even the side of his phone and right hand caught most of the pack of paint.

"Awwwww, n-nooooo—"

Miranda made no sound as Howard felt the lifeblood in his heart drain away.

Now in a state of pure delirium, Howard pressed the phone to his cheek and continued crying. "M-Miranda? Miranda, I only got *half* the money, but it's okay. I g-got the rest. I love you. I love you so much—"

Boop-boop-boop.

The call went dead.

He looked at his phone to find that Miranda had missed much of what he'd said, due to the confines of the staircase.

With his face, and heart, and dignity, now covered in red dye, he stopped crying and accepted his fate.

He tossed his phone over his shoulder, tightened his grip on the last remaining sports bag, and held his Glock 17 in his right hand.

All he had to do was kick the door open and *pray* that the path ahead was empty.

Whump.

The fire exit door slammed open, and Howard walked into the fresh, night air, and a blanket of brilliant white lights.

It almost felt like heaven, despite the cacophony of heavy artillery preparing to open fire on him.

"Freeze, asshole."

An angry voice blasted in his face from behind the blinding white lights of Heaven.

"Drop the fucking weapon."

The sound of a thousand guns preparing to fire rocketed across the concrete and waded around his sneakers.

"Not gonna ask again. Drop your weapon, and get on the floor with your hands up."

Howard enjoyed the cool night air on his painted face and licked his lips. He obliged the men by lifting his right hand in the air.

"No, put the weapon down," came the order.

Howard half-chuckled as he processed his own misfortune. He kept his Glock 17 on show as he dropped the bag to the ground

"Gun!"

Bang—bang—bang.

Howard chucked the gun on the ground as the bullets burst around his feet on the concrete.

Two bullets hit the sports bag.

It exploded and puked white stuffing, hundreds of coins, and a flurry of bills, into the air, which then rained down around Howard like confetti.

"That's right, asshole. Get on the floor."

Howard dropped to his knees and placed his hands behind his back. As soon as he did, the white lights dimmed to reveal scores of armed officers and dozens of police vehicles before him.

The helicopter that had nearly shot Howard dead as he ran to the fire escape circled above and flashed its two beams across his shoulders.

"Shit."

A blackened silhouette peeled through the bright light, and formed into the shape of a plain-clothed officer.

Howard squinted at the man's black suit, and then spotted the MP5 in his right hand. His face seemed familiar, but he recognized the voice straight away.

The man's face focused into Howard's eyes.

A man by the name of Lieutenant Vincent Fox, who looked down at the defeated criminal with an inordinate amount of glee.

Six armed officers rushed either side of Fox and moved in behind Howard.

"Well, well, well," Fox said. "Rabbit?"

Howard sneered and looked anywhere other than in his foe's direction.

The man offered Howard his hand. "Lieutenant Vincent Fox. Chrome Valley Police Department."

Howard glanced at the nicotine-stained fingers and scoffed. "Fuck you."

"Oh, yeah, I forgot. You can't shake my hand, can you?"

Clunk-click.

The first officer cuffed Howard's wrists together behind his back. "Okay, buddy. Get up."

The police assisted Howard to his feet, which enabled both he and Fox to stare each other in the eyes. The latter sized up his prey, and averted his eyes to the red splattered on the man's neck and shirt collar.

"I hate to say it, *Rabbit*, but I told you I'd catch you."

Howard sneered and licked his top lip. "Fuck you."

"Ha," Fox smirked. "So. It seems the Fox finally caught the Rabbit, huh?"

Howard's left nostril pinched, barely concealing the contempt for the man who'd beaten him.

Fox enjoyed his little victory a little too much.

"Well, I *say* Rabbit. Maybe I *should* say Howard J. Ross, former Head of Lending at Chrome Valley Federal. Am I right, or am I right? Am I right?"

Howard turned away and held his gaze at the beautiful array of bright stars in the night sky.

"From nine-to-five to twenty-five-to-life. *At least.*"

Still no response. Howard would rather have died than accept the man's statement.

"You're not talking now, huh?" Fox chuckled, and threw a cheeky wink to his arresting team. "Fair enough. You don't have to say anything, you know. But anything you *do* say will be taken down and used against you in a court of law. It seems like you're enacting your right to remain silent, which is probably for the best until we hook you up with some useless pro bono twelve year old lawyer we dig up from the slums to represent you, you murdering, thieving asshole."

One of the two officers grabbed Howard's collar and pulled him forward. "C'mon, buddy. Move it."

Fox walked alongside Howard as they entered the parking lot, and a whole lot of bloodied carnage splattered against the third floor window above them.

"Howard?" Lt. Fox asked. "Do you understand these rights as I have just recited them?"

Howard focused on the ground and refused to answer as the officers bundled him into the back of the nearest van.

"I'll take that as a *yes*, then."

The sirens blasted atop the van as it pulled away, leaving the forensics team to arrive on the scene.

Fox folded his arms and surveyed the carnage that had taken place. The helicopter banked away from the building and rocketed into the horizon.

Several members of the clean-up team had already entered the building, and began attending to the corpses that littered the corridors.

Fox could see it all through the bullet-riddled walls of the *Store-N-Go* building.

He shook his head with despair, and made his way through the crime scene and back to his car, all the while taking pity on the valley he was meant to serve and protect.

"Ugh," he said. "What a *shitty* day for a heist."

— THE END —

Author Notes

Dear reader,

Well, that was quite a ride, wasn't it?

Red Collar turned into something of an epic while I was writing it. My original intention was to write the heist, and have the five robbers drive away, and kill everyone except Howard. One of my first visions while I was concocting the story was the image of Howard surrendering on the freeway, on his knees, with bank notes flying around his head as the police aimed their guns at him.

Then, as I was writing, the last third (the whole *whoddunit* thing) came to my mind. I had planned for about sixty thousand words (around 300 pages) at that point, but then the idea that the robbers got even greedier came to my mind. It added about another 35% to the length of the book, but also gave it more weight. The good guys turn bad, rob their bank, and then try to rob each other when things get desperate. They're no better, no different, to the people they despise, after all.

That's *Capitalism* for you.

I'm a big fan of heist/crime movies and novels, but there's usually a component that spoils it for me. I'm sure many of you were imagining something along the lines of Al Pacino and Robert De Niro facing-off in Michael Mann's 1995 movie *Heat*. Maybe Red Collar evokes memories of *Reservoir Dogs* for you? Or *Dog Day Afternoon*? These are three of many, many more films I revisited as I was putting the story together. I decided soon after that I'd just do *everything*, and wrap a satire of the corporate western world into it. It's a none-too-subtle study, in my view, of a capitalist society at work.

At the time of writing, a well-known airline company has announced they are cutting 12,000 jobs due to the Coronavirus pandemic hitting their business. Imagine that? There are some employees who have given their lives to that company, only to be laid off. By *email*, of all forums. The same has happened this week at a *very well-known* bank. Red Collar is nothing if not timely.

What interested me most about this story was Howard's reaction to being fired. He's angry, and comes up with a plan to rob the bank out of frustration. Nobody in their right, sane mind would ever carry out the plan. But once he's mentioned it, and everyone climbs aboard, it's difficult to go back on it. In a sense, he convinces himself to go through with it out of a sense of pride. If you think back to the very beginning of the story, Howard Ross and his colleagues are all mild-mannered and wouldn't hurt a fly. By the end of it, and after a series of errors, they've been forced into the various positions throughout the day. Their thought process is perfectly logical, until it builds up the body count and they can't go back on what they've done.

I write in many genres (horror, satire, thriller etc) and it never fails to strike me that the genre of a story is actually secondary, maybe even tertiary, to the central conceit; the story. The genre merely dictates the tone. If Red Collar had been a horror, then you'd have had a lot more deaths in explicit, gory detail. But, because it's a thriller, you get more of the suspense and consequences that drive the plot forward. I'm sure you've read many books, or seen enough movies, where it feels as if the characters are making decision simply to drive the story forwards. To me, that's inauthentic. It must be the other way around.

Some of you, my hardcore fans, might know that I have a specific way I that write my books.

I usually start with the first chapter to get a *feel* for the story, and then hop right to the end and write the last few chapters. Doing it this way enables me to keep my word count under control, and go back to the second chapter and build towards the end. Because I know the end, I can drop all the little foreshadowing moments (e.g. Ben's Space Invaders Socks, Mark's gold teeth) throughout, knowing that they will be important in the future.)

With Red Collar, I wrote it all over the place. I wrote all the alternate-chaptered heist sequences first, and then the last third of the book (the closing "Whodunit?" third act) and *then* went and wrote all the individual character's back stories. It was the first time I'd pieced together a book in this way, but it was necessary. I'm sure reading the book must have seemed like navigating a bit of a minefield, so imagine having to write it! I'm glad I did though, because I think Red Collar is certainly one of my better books

Also, for the first time in a long time, I had to cut down a lot of what you've read due to my editor's remarks. I discarded the first chapter entirely, which had Howard, Ben, James, and Lincoln, sitting around a coffee table at *Bean There, Done That*, talking about being laid off and getting angry. I tore it out and binned it, deciding that the best way to open the book was with three animals storming the bank. I think I made the right decision (with thanks to my editor Ashley Rose Miller's advice.)

Also, Mark's chapter had a last-minute rewrite to feature the gun practice with Knocktoe Joe. During the edit, I felt as if something was missing, and I couldn't quite put my finger on it. When I got the edit notes back, I finally figured it out. Knocktoe Joe (and by me as an author, vicariously) can't promise an arms training sequence at the weekend and never actually show it. I was glad to be able to explain why Mark accidentally shot Victor in the face at the vault.

I may, if readers ask nicely, send them the discarded first chapter to see what I removed. Email me if you're interested.

Incidentally, did you notice that the very last words spoken by Lt. Fox are the very *first* words spoken by Howard at the beginning of the book, with one minor word change? Ooooh, I *love, love, love*, cyclical endings like that. Without laboring the point that tells me that both the bad guy and the good guy feel the same way about *something* - in this case, Chrome Valley itself. I mean, what a helluva horrid place it's turning out to be, don't you think?

If you enjoyed the book, please let me know, and leave a review.

Okay, I have another thriller to write. It's a high concept, real-time suspense thriller called The Choice - and if you loved Red Collar, I think you'll really like this next one!

Happy reading, and I hope to hear from you!

Andrew Mackay,
Hampshire, UK
(August 6th, 2020)

Acknowledgments

For K
Also to:
My immediate family
The members and admins of 20BooksTo50K
Jennifer Long, Adele Embrey,
Stan Hutchings, and Eeyore
All the CVB Gang Members and
my Advance Reading Group Members

<u>Welcome to Chrome Valley Thrillers.</u>

Four thrilling tales that will rock your mind.

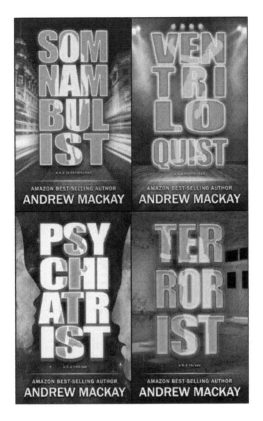

Start your paperback collection today!

mybook.to/somnambulist

Get Your FREE ebook

Subscribe to the
Chrome Valley Books mailing list!

Isolationist - the prequel to the
Chrome Valley Thrillers series.

*Just type the link below
in your internet browser.*

bit.ly/CVBThriller

About the author

Andrew Mackay is an author, screenwriter and film critic.

A former teacher, Andrew writes in multiple genres: satire, crime, horror, romantic thrillers and sci-fi.

His passions include daydreaming, storytelling, smoking, caffeine, and writing about himself in the third person.

A word from the author

I hope you enjoyed this book. Please check out my other books at Amazon and remember to follow me there.

If you enjoyed the book, please leave a review online at Amazon US, UK and Goodreads. Reviews are integral for authors and I would dearly appreciate it.

I love to engage directly with my readers. Please get in touch with me - I look forward to hearing from you. ***Happy reading!***

Email: *andrew@chromevalleybooks.com*